EXECUTIVE MALICE

A Tale of Corporate Deceit

R. L. Hann

The Good Manager Online

Fairhaven, Washington

Copyright © 2019 by R. L. Hann
Registration Number: TXu 2-156-538 July 2019

All rights reserved. No part of this publication may be reproduced, distributed, or transmitted in any form or by any means, without prior written permission.

R. L. Hann, The Good Manager Online
www.thegoodmanageronline.com
Published in Partnership with Village Books
Fairhaven, WA

Publisher's Note: Although inspired by work experiences in corporate environments of the 1990's, this is a work of fiction. Any resemblance to actual people, living or dead, or to businesses, companies, events, institutions, or locales is completely coincidental.

Cover Design: Audrey V. Steffan

Book Layout © 2017 BookDesignTemplates.com

Executive Malice by R. L. Hann. -- 1st ed.
ISBN: 978-0-578-53504-3
LCCN: 2020914308

Author's Note

The premise for Executive Malice originated in 1993 inside a windowless conference room in a large building of a major aerospace corporation in Southern California. Three coworkers finishing a training project were bemoaning senior management's latest strategic misstep: another failed improvement effort ending in chaos, workforce reductions, and deleterious cost-cutting. One of the coworkers observed that it did not seem possible for a multi-billion dollar corporation to be so mismanaged, due solely to incompetence or unfortunate circumstance. "It must be intentional," she said. "Someone at the top is trying to put our company out of business on purpose." When the third coworker responded, "Hey, that would make a good novel," Executive Malice was conceived.

Twenty-five years have passed, but the story's heartbeat remains best suited to the business environment of the 1990's, and thus the story is set in 1994.

The technology of business in 1994 was markedly different from today's online/wireless/remote business world. Cell phones were big boxy things referred to as "cellular," and only made phone calls. There was no texting. Most corporate employees wore Skytel pagers and had to find a phone (public pay phones were ubiquitous in strip-malls and gas stations) to call the person who paged them. On occasion, the page-sender would include "911" following the phone number, signifying the urgent need for a return call.

Although technological enhancements have certainly proven beneficial, other aspects of the 1990's corporate workplace remain unfortunate, evidenced by the need for the "Me Too" and "Time's Up" movements. The story is fictional, but several workplace incidents described in Executive Malice were inspired by actual events, and may seem eerily familiar to those of you working to survive in the "Corporate Jungle" of today.

"It will only take a few brave individuals who are willing to stand up and say it's time for the truth to come out."

–KENNETH LAY, THE ENRON CORPORATION

Dedicated to my big brother, Stu, who spent his life and career as a warrior for truth, integrity, and safety, in the design and production of commercial aircraft.

PROLOGUE

Friday, October 7, 1994, 9:32 p.m.

His Lexus hit seventy-eight, flying down a straight stretch of Highway 133, as Rich Richmond sped toward his sister's house in Laguna Beach. He was putting distance between himself and a Chrysler that had been annoying him on the freeway. When he'd noticed the Chrysler taking the same exit, he decided to leave it behind. There was no traffic—one of the few benefits of working late.

Rich navigated a tight curve, leaning naturally with the car winding into the turn. But the power of the 4.0-liter engine pressing him against the seat didn't evoke his usual smile.

Wow, I missed the line through that turn. What's wrong with me?

He'd raced the Lexus through this canyon countless times, totally at one with the road and the night. But on this night he was off. Could he blame it on his day at work? Bad, yes, but not much different from the string of troubling days for the past several months.

A flash drew his eyes to the rearview. Headlights. The car seemed to be gaining on him.

Is that the Chrysler again?

His thoughts snapped back to his preoccupation since leaving work: that Herrera report he'd been trying to read before his boss, Arthur O'Donnell, the Executive VP, had caught him. O'Donnell and the other VPs at McNeil-Everett appeared to be managing the company straight into the ground, and it seemed to Rich that he was the only one who could see it happening.

Teri will be here Monday. I'll tell her about the report...she'll believe me.

He glanced sideways at the electrical connector he'd retrieved from salvage. He'd put the plug in his coat pocket, but it had fallen out onto the passenger seat. It almost seemed to be staring at him; the nape of his neck tingled.

It's so familiar. Why can't I place it? And if it's obsolete, what was it doing on a list in a confidential eyes-only report?

"What the...dammit!"

The Chrysler's misaligned headlight, now shining directly in his rearview mirror, momentarily blinded him.

What is this guy's problem? He's been following me since I left work. I know I never cut him off. I wasn't anywhere near him.

Rich switched off the radio. He'd been singing to Steppenwolf—*Born to Be Wild*—when he'd entered the canyon, but now he needed to concentrate. The Chrysler was riding his bumper.

An unexpected wave of panic washed over him, accompanied by an urgent desire to get through the canyon to Laguna, civilization, and maybe even a police officer. For the first time on this road, he wished for more traffic, any traffic.

Rich headed down a hill into a sweeping left-hand curve. He glanced at the speedometer: *sixty-two.* He kept his foot on the throttle. He knew he was pushing it, but whoever was driving the Chrysler was either crazy or…

Wait a minute…This can't be about that damn report and this stupid plug, can it? This is McNev—We build airplanes for chrissake! This isn't the CIA!

In his sideview mirror, he spotted the Chrysler moving left across the centerline, followed instantly by a light-blue blur registering in his peripheral vision. He realized the Chrysler had pulled abreast of him—on the *inside* of the turn.

Oh, my God—I'm not gonna make it!

* * *

Sheila Richmond set her mug on the well-traveled steamer trunk that served as her coffee table, deciding to take a break before heading upstairs to her computer. She glanced at her watch.

Great. Ten o'clock. Lisa's gonna be grumpy tomorrow. I love my brother, but it'd sure be nice if his daughter took priority over work. I know I'll get another "thanks for being the best aunt in the world" when he gets home, but this is getting old.

She picked up the remote, tuned to the *"News At Ten,"* retrieved her coffee, and settled in on the loveseat as the anchor opened with breaking news.

"We take you live to Bill Mitchell in Newscopter Nine. You're above the scene of a pretty dramatic accident, right Bill?"

Sheila recognized the area glaring in the news chopper's spotlight. The reporter's voice vibrated in rhythm with the rotating blades.

"That's right, Gail. We're over Highway 133 in Laguna Canyon, and as you can see below, fire rescue is bringing up the victim on a stretcher. Judging by the skid marks, the driver must have missed that turn and ended up in the ravine."

Sheila shook her head, recalling how often she'd warned Rich about idiots driving that road too fast, which always elicited the same response. He'd say, "Sheila, I know little sisters are supposed to worry—but don't. I take the canyon road every night. I can drive those curves in my sleep."

She sipped her coffee, smiling at the thought of Rich still referring to her as *little sister* at thirty-seven, and deciding she'd play her role by using this newscast to bolster her argument when her brother got home.

The camera zoomed in for a tighter shot.

"The man on the stretcher looks unconscious but doesn't appear to be burned…His clothes seem mostly unscathed. It's really sort of a miracle, considering that his overturned car—could be a Lexus—is now completely engulfed in flames."

Sheila stared at the image of the man on the stretcher. He looked like a mannequin in a dress shirt and maroon tie. She leaped off the loveseat, spilling coffee all over herself.

1

Seven Hours Earlier

"It's about time, stewardess. I've had my light on for five minutes."

"I'm sorry, sir. It's a full flight, and other passengers also need my attention."

This was the fourth time the flight attendant visited row twenty-one in the last hour of the maxed-capacity flight from Dallas-Fort Worth to LAX. She turned off the call light above the heavy-set businessman in the aisle seat, keeping her tone level and swallowing her sarcastic comment. She settled on, "What did you need?"

"A pillow for my back. I've got to finish this before we land, and I need to be sitting up straighter. These seats are so broken down...and look at this."

He wiggled the tray table holding his Macintosh PowerBook 160.

"Do you know how expensive this is? This little tray is so flimsy, I can hardly type."

The flight attendant managed to resist her impulse for a less-than-professional comeback, opened the overhead bin, and pulled out a pillow.

"Here you are sir."

She made eye contact with the man sitting in the center seat, next to the complainer. His close-cut graying hair and rugged features complemented his well-proportioned build, evoking a sense of confidence, and his smile conveyed an empathetic understanding of her frustration. She acknowledged it in kind before turning back up the aisle.

Porter Bordon glanced to his right, regarding his aisle-side seatmate. The businessman leaned forward, irritably slipping the pillow behind himself, while his other hand held his laptop on the tray table.

You probably wouldn't be so uncomfortable if you weren't such a lard-ass.

The man turned toward him and said, "What're you looking at?"

"An asshole." Bordon's reply held no edge. He'd simply stated a fact.

"Excuse me?" the businessman said, with an attempt at bravado.

Bordon didn't reply. Instead, he maintained eye contact as he put his hands on both armrests, flexing his well-muscled biceps and forearms to lift himself an inch or two. He turned his head from left to right, popping his neck with a loud crack, and focused a well-practiced glower that crushed his seatmate's scornful look.

The businessman looked away and repositioned his expansive frame, reducing the encroachment on Porter's space. He returned to his PowerBook without further comment.

Bordon's relatively average five-foot-ten height belied his abilities and attitude, as it had throughout his youth. He'd discovered early on that power is as much about control as physical strength, and he'd been blessed with a natural aptitude for both. He turned them into an art form and had been gathering greenbacks with them ever since.

Watching the businessman busily typing on his laptop, Bordon sighed, reminded of how out of place he'd become in the business world of the 1990s. He hated computers and most people who used them. He remained mystified that his boss, Hugh McNeil, the Chairman of the Board of the third largest aerospace corporation in America, with a palatial office and two secretaries, enjoyed using a computer.

His irritation at the continued tapping of the keyboard was exacerbated by his center seat constriction. He longed for days gone by and the action that had earned him first-class privileges.

Shrugging off the depressing thoughts, he looked to his left, only to be faced with an unsatisfying glimpse of the LA basin through the tiny pane, obscured by the woman in the window seat. He inhaled sharply and focused on the vibrations of the aircraft's landing gear extending for final approach, granting deliverance through their imminent landing.

The plane taxied to the gate, and the *ding* of the seat-belt chime launched the well-established air travel ritual with the Pavlovian effect of a starter pistol. Passengers tugged carry-on items from overhead compartments, jostling each other to assert their superiority by being first off the plane.

Porter stood, slightly crouched, as his seatmate heaved himself into the aisle and reached up to open the overhead. When the businessman yanked his bag from the back of the bin, a hard case in front tumbled out with it. Porter snatched the case in mid-air, an instant before it smacked the head of a woman in the row in front of him.

The businessman pushed down the aisle, oblivious of the calamity he'd nearly caused, as Porter set the case down. The woman smiled at him. "Thank you. I think you might've saved my life—certainly my head."

In my younger days, I would've grabbed that prick's coat and smacked the case upside his head. He'd be on his knees, apologizing right now.

Instead, Porter simply smiled back and replied, "No problem, ma'am," then retrieved his own bag and headed down the aisle. He shook his head. *Maybe I am getting old.*

* * *

Knowing the vehicle might well be in less-than-perfect condition when he was finished tonight, Bordon had chosen the rental car company with an after-hours drop-off location in Orange County.

He was glad to see only two people ahead of him at the counter. Bordon hated lines, convinced they were an intentional strategy of large companies, conditioning customers to be overly grateful for any modicum of service afforded them.

The clerk was courteous and efficient, completing the process without adding to his annoyance. She handed Bordon the keys and paperwork.

"Okay Mr. Feldman, you're all set. Are you here on business or pleasure?"

With a demure smile, Bordon replied, "Well, young lady, I surely hope it'll be a bit of both," adding a hint of southern inflection to complement the false name on his bogus Arkansas driver's license.

Bordon drove the light-blue Chrysler LeBaron down Sepulveda Boulevard onto the new 105 Freeway, trying to engender a little excitement about this chance to use his driving skills. But when he transitioned onto the 405 South toward Orange County, the afternoon traffic came to a full stop.

His grip tightened, whitening his knuckles as he stared at the cars stacked in front of him like four infinite rows of dominos.

Damn LA traffic. Yeah, I know…I have control issues. But I really hate this shit.

He took a deep breath, then exhaled slowly.

What did my shrink say? Think about something I like…I'll think about how good the action's gonna be.

* * *

The wall-size picture window in the ninth-floor Board Room of the McNeil-Everett executive tower radiated vermillion in the late afternoon sun. The drapes were pulled back, as Bradley "Rich" Richmond finished his presentation to the Executive Council—twenty-two PowerPoint slides highlighting the current production issues of the ME-420 Widebody twin-aisle airliner. Sitting down, Rich turned to admire the sunlit view, appearing relaxed while concealing his inner anxiety.

He listened to the ten other VPs who comprised the Executive Council—commonly referred to as the ExCon—trying to gauge their reaction to the analysis charts he and Mac had created. Rich began to feel cautiously optimistic as he heard favorable comments on their proposal to form a root-cause analysis team.

Then Darren Duke, the Vice President of Manufacturing, shoved his chair back from the far end of the conference table. Known for his country-crass management style, Duke's Texas size, string ties, and the boots he wore with his suits, completed the package. True to his love of center stage and the sound of his own voice, Darren stood as his obstreperous twang took over the room.

"Fuck root-cause analysis and your teams, Richmond! You think we have all the time in the world to huddle around the table and analyze problems? I already know what the problem is—it's the goddamned incompetent assembly mechanics. All I need is a list of those problems by shift and assembly manager. Once I know who's responsible, believe me, I'll make the problems go away."

Laughter followed Duke's outburst, as the other VPs and Jackson Winton, McNeil-Everett's President, chimed in with comments like: "Go get 'em, cowboy!" and "Kick some ass."

Duke liked it. He thought he was John Wayne.

Finally, Arthur O'Donnell, the Executive VP spoke, silencing the room. "Okay, that's enough."

He looked at Winton and Duke, who were still chuckling.

"Jackson and Darren, are you finished?"

They looked up with expressions of unruly students being called out by the teacher.

"Jackson, I suggest that you, Darren, and I set up a time to discuss the proposal further."

They both nodded as O'Donnell turned to Rich.

"Thank you for your presentation, Brad." Then addressing the room, he added, "That'll be all, gentlemen."

Rich stood abruptly. He said nothing, but the manner in which he snapped his notebook closed, grabbed his papers, and bolted from the room left no doubt in anyone's mind about his disdain. He strode down the hallway, further inflamed by O'Donnell's penchant for calling him Brad, fully aware of how much Rich loathed his given first name.

He was only glad his colleague and close friend, Mac, wasn't there to witness the buffoonery of his peers that once again squelched his short-lived enthusiasm.

As he waited for the elevator, excess acid roiled his stomach. He looked down the corridor at the same glass wall, where the pleasant glow was now an ugly glare. He stepped into the elevator before anyone else appeared, taking out his frustration on the 5 button by mashing it repeatedly.

Looking at his reddened thumb, Rich reflected on how distressing work had become.

I used to love coming to work. How long has it been since that happened?

He recalled his pride in getting promoted to Vice President of Quality for Everett Aviation. Not only did his position rank at the senior executive level of a Fortune-500 company, but it was a crucial appointment for a commercial aircraft manufacturer.

The Quality VP is the primary liaison to the Federal Aviation Administration, the U.S. government agency responsible for issuing the Certificate of Airworthiness for every aircraft produced. This certification process ensures the integrity of safe design and manufacturing, a core responsibility of Rich's division.

Rich willingly embraced the accountability to the thousands of people who flew on his company's planes every day, entrusting him and his team with ensuring their aircraft's safety. He often used it as motivation when he faced the pressure of manufacturing delivery schedules. He'd look at himself in the mirror each morning after shaving and say out loud, "Rich, don't let the bastards wear you down. People are counting on you." That was when he'd loved his work.

Aviation captured Rich's imagination at an early age. He was drawn to the marvels of flying, inspiring him to follow his father's passion: the production of world-class airplanes. When McNeil Aerospace acquired Everett, forming the McNeil-Everett Corporation (coining the nickname McNev), Rich had been enthusiastic about the opportunity to reenergize Everett. Now he questioned the potential of the corporation to even survive.

The elevator opened on the fifth floor and Rich marched to his office, flinging open his door. Norton McKinley, known to everyone as Mac, was leaning against his desk, waiting for him.

"What are you doing here?"

Rich regretted his surly tone as soon as he saw Mac's expression. Fortunately, Mac's reaction was tempered by understanding the strong likelihood that the meeting had left Rich seething.

"Well, seeing as how I'm a Director in Final Assembly, and worked my ass off with you putting together the damn presentation, plus being your friend—at least until a second ago—I figured I had a vested interest. Why are you being such a jerk?"

"Sorry…I lost my head. You can probably guess by the steam coming out of my ears how it went. It was Duke. The pompous ass went off, totally dismissing our efforts. I have no idea how you can stand reporting to him when you're ten times the manager he is."

"I just focus on his endearing qualities: stupidity, short-sightedness, and vulgarity, and then try to be the anti-him."

Rich smiled, admiring not only Mac's cynicism but also his ability to maintain perspective—one of the things Rich was still working on.

"I don't know, Mac," Rich began. "Everett had a reputation for fifty years of reliable aircraft, and we've been a solid part of that. But these past three years since the merger, I swear it seems like the executive team is trying to destroy everything we've worked for."

"Are you going to start again with that theory of yours? Some terrible secret that's causing your own peers to run this place into the ground?"

"Mock me if you want to, but sometimes I gotta believe it's true. How else do you explain the VPs of a billion-dollar corporation acting like a bunch of high-schoolers arguing over the band for the spring dance?"

Mac chuckled. "I'd say you nailed their decision-making style, not to mention their median age of maturity. But I'm starting to worry about you, man. You're letting this place get to you."

"What about the report I saw from Herrera? Why did it have a parts list with an obsolete connector?"

"I have no idea—and neither do you, by the way. Why don't you just ask O'Donnell?"

"Oh, yeah, and admit I was looking at a document addressed to him with an 'eyes-only' label?"

Rich walked to the window and looked down at the main boulevard. He was quiet for a minute before sighing loudly. He turned back to Mac.

"Did I tell you Art threatened to have me fired the other day?"

He called Arthur O'Donnell "Art," because Rich knew O'Donnell hated it as much as he hated being called "Brad."

"What? No way!" Mac stopped leaning on the desk and stood upright.

Rich said, "I think his exact words were 'Brad, consider this an official warning. It's time you became a team player, or I don't think I can stop Winton from taking action that could jeopardize your career.'"

Mac whistled, adding, "Wow."

Rich continued, "Yeah…and before that, he said he 'liked me because I was good at the airplane business,' and he'd 'gone to bat for me with Winton.' Hah—what a crock."

Mac nodded. "That's his way of trying to convince us Winton makes the decisions."

"Exactly! The only thing Winton and the rest of the VPs care about is collecting their damn bonuses…You and I both know O'Donnell runs things."

In a serious tone, Mac replied, "Yes, he does, so you'd best learn to deal with it," then caught the disgust in Rich's expression, recognizing his frustration. He'd been Rich's first supervisor when Rich started at Everett part-time, working his way through college. He remembered being amazed at Rich's knowledge of airplanes and his keen analysis skills, born of his inherent curiosity. He'd mentored Rich through the years, teaching him his own common-sense management style.

One of Mac's most gratifying moments was seeing Rich promoted to Vice President of Quality, surpassing his own director-level position. But he'd been worried about Rich's constant struggles since the merger, due primarily to the one thing Mac had never been able to help Rich learn: holding his temper. He tried some supportive perspective.

"Look, Rich. You should be proud that you were the one Everett VP remaining after the merger, on direct orders from McNeil, no less. And you said O'Donnell acknowledged you know what you're doing. But you can't keep throwing your fiery attitude at everyone. It makes you look like you're working against O'Donnell and the whole ExCon."

Rich blew out another breath, this time making a contemptuous sound.

"You know, I don't even think those idiots know how stupid their 'ExCon' moniker is. I swear, when McNeil put O'Donnell in charge of the merger, Art hand-picked a team of total morons—in particular, his best friend, Winton."

"There you go again, overdramatizing. You know McNeil hired Winton."

"Yeah, but ol' Art was behind it—sure as I'm standing here."

It was Mac's turn to sigh. "Rich, I don't know how to say it any plainer—you keep fighting everyone and you're gonna get kicked out of the game."

Rich's face reddened. "Dammit, Mac. I can't sit by while these guys keep making one bad decision after another. O'Donnell knows it and doesn't appear to give a shit, and meanwhile, McNeil sits in Texas thinking everything is golden with his 'mighty McNev.' He hasn't got the first damn clue what's really going on—It's not right!"

Mac moved to the window, next to Rich who was looking outside again. He had to reach up to put his hand on Rich's shoulder. He said softly, "Rich, you need to relax before you end up in the hospital. Remember, every business runs in natural cycles."

"Yes, I know…and you taught me that timing is everything, which I completely agree with." He turned to face his friend, adding, "But this feels different to me, Mac. Something just isn't right."

Mac smiled. "Well I know I'll never squash your conspiracy theory spirit, but in the meantime, let's focus on what we *can* do. Tell me about the meeting, if you can, without getting all worked up again. Sounds like your lucky maroon tie didn't work so well."

After a brief recap, forgoing his snarky commentary, Rich got to the bottom line. "Art tabled the decision. Hopefully, we'll have an opportunity to discuss our proposal in more detail with him, Winton, and Duke next week once Teri gets here."

Mac brightened. "Oh, that's right! Teri starts on Monday. The famous Miss Harlan returns after—what's it been, ten years?" Mac's smile broadened. "Maybe she can improve your attitude. I remember the two of you together were a force to be reckoned with, when you were newbie managers. Of course, that was before she abandoned you."

"She didn't abandon me...she moved to Seattle for that Director position with AeroSystems, the little show-off."

Rich returned Mac's grin as he remembered how proud she'd been.

"How in the world did you convince her to come back?" Mac asked.

"Appealed to her sense of pride, and the opportunity to help put quality back into McNev's aircraft production. And besides you, she's the only executive I know who still has any real integrity."

Mac gave Rich one of his *seriously?* looks.

"What?" Rich asked.

"That was nicely worded total bullshit. You begged, didn't you?"

Rich's smile turned sheepish. "Okay, yeah, I did. But it *was* a real accomplishment to convince Winton and O'Donnell we needed her as my Deputy VP."

"They don't know you're bringing in 'reinforcements'?"

Rich just grinned.

* * *

After discussing their strategy to follow-up with Teri once she was on board, Mac left Rich sitting at his desk, staring at the stack of paperwork he didn't feel like dealing with. It was times like these he regretted his decision to go all noble and forgo his administrative assistant as his contribution to reduce expenses. He leaned back and stretched, letting his mind drift.

I know Mac doesn't believe me, but there is something weird going on.

He returned to the recent incident he'd been mentally replaying, for the umpteenth time. It stuck with him because it reinforced the possibility that his conspiracy theory may be something more.

Four days ago, on Monday evening, he'd walked the employment contract for Teri up to the ninth floor, because O'Donnell had final approval on all executive-level hires.

He'd been standing outside O'Donnell's office, waiting for him to finish a phone call, making small talk with their Executive Administrator, Karolyn Babcock. Karolyn's distinctive voice, an irritating nasal whine with a saccharin chaser, made an immediate impression, although her other charms were more memorable for anyone with a Y chromosome.

Rich recalled the conversation that led to his discovery.

"Hey there, Rich. Arthur should be finished soon. I was just testing my new Mark IV Electronic Signature Pen. It automatically signs Arthur's name on any document. He bought it for me because he's too busy to sign everything. I swear, it signs his name better than he does."

Rich decided to take advantage of her new responsibility.

"Cool machine, Karolyn. Why don't you try it on this employment paperwork for Teresa Harlan, so I don't have to bother Art?"

"Sure, I'd be happy to."

Karolyn took the document, and as she began inserting it into the machine, Rich noticed a cover sheet on a report from Felix Herrera, President of the aircraft mechanics union, sitting on the credenza behind her desk.

The report was labeled *MCNEV SENSITIVE–ADDRESSEE EYES ONLY*. Rich was curious. He'd moved around Karolyn's desk to get a closer look, trying to be nonchalant. He'd just managed to scan the first pages and flip to what appeared to be a technical section when O'Donnell appeared out of nowhere.

"Brad! What's up?"

Noticing immediately what Rich was up to, O'Donnell moved between Rich, the credenza, and Karolyn. Rich was forced to back up, dropping the report which fell onto the credenza with an awkward *thwack*.

Rich wasn't small. He was just under six feet, but O'Donnell was two inches taller with a commanding presence. His eyes conveyed a dark intensity that caused instant intimidation in almost everyone. He'd stood inches from Rich's face, staring at him.

Rich recalled his lame reply. "Hi, Art. I was…uh…just letting Karolyn try out her new auto-pen machine on this hiring paperwork for Teri Harlan. It needed your signature, and I was trying not to bother you."

Each time Rich replayed this incident, the memory ended in the same humiliating scene: his flushing cheeks in reaction to O'Donnell's stare. He stood up from his desk, trying to shake it off, as an even more disconcerting thought popped into his head.

What if O'Donnell approved Teri's hire because he's planning to replace me?

He spoke sternly to himself, attempting to be his own voice of reason.

C'mon—stop with the paranoia. I've known Teri for years. We were best friends, and more. Teri will definitely be on my side.

* * *

Porter Bordon arrived at the McNev plant in Orange County late in the afternoon, relieved when the guard at the executive gate allowed him entry with his corporate ID. He'd escaped the constricting tumult of the 405 but found the excessively quiet parking garage beneath the McNev executive tower to be equally disagreeable, as he once again found himself stuck in wait-mode.

Although less constraining than sitting on the plane, the driver's seat in his Chrysler was no less uncomfortable. Bordon adjusted the lumbar support, attempting to relieve his stiff back, and lost himself in self-reflection.

Man, the world has changed. I sure miss the seventies, working for the union.

In those days, situations often called for Bordon's best-in-class repertoire of specialized skills. Whatever his organization needed, he could handle. Pride filled his memory as he thought of the nickname that reflected his reputation: *Porter the Board.*

But the Wild West days of union business were long gone, and executive bodyguards were no longer in vogue, now being found primarily in the music industry. Not a good fit for Porter.

He'd been little more than a babysitter since taking a contract position for Hugh McNeil, the CEO of McNeil-Everett. Bordon's title was Executive Staff Driver, but he also served as McNeil's discrete personal security. Some of his old colleagues thought he was lucky to have this job, because most of them were now past their prime, and either retired or unemployed.

But "Porter the Board" had kept his edge. In the early 1970s, he spent two years in Joliet prison outside Chicago, for an assault conviction resulting from a rough time between the Teamsters and some wildcat truckers crossing picket lines. Bordon took advantage of his time inside to learn the essentials of keeping his head straight and keeping it on—literally.

For the past twenty years he'd carried out the disciplined daily exercise regimen he'd perfected during his incarceration. Porter thrived on action, which he desperately missed.

He replayed yesterday's meeting at McNev Corporate HQ in Texas, when he'd been summoned by Will Crandall, McNeil's Administrative Director.

"Arthur O'Donnell needs you out in Southern California tomorrow for a special assignment that's right up your alley. There's a guy out there who's causing major union unrest, and he's become a big problem to McNev. We need you to make the problem go away. I convinced Arthur to use you, so you could have a chance to do something you enjoy for a change, like that car thing in Chicago you told me about. This guy, Bradley Richmond, has had lots of issues lately. Everyone knows about the booze and drugs. He's about done anyway, so go have some fun with it, Porter. Enjoy yourself."

Crandall…what a prick!

A vivid picture filled his mind of the superior look on Crandall's pretty-boy face, arousing the urge he'd had to deck him. Porter slowed his breathing, then shook his head and refocused on the employees exiting the tower elevator into the garage. He compared each face to the badge photo he held of Bradley Richmond.

2

The McNev ME-420, strutting its impressive wing span and giant GE engines, emerged into the cool night under tow by a giant tug. Like a star on the red carpet, it basked in the bright lights from the Final Assembly hangar as workers walked alongside, escorting the gleaming jet to the flight ramp. Arthur O'Donnell stood at the window of his office on the ninth floor of the executive tower, observing from on-high.

Look at them all...so excited.

It was well after 8 p.m., long past the workday for everyone not on swing shift. But Arthur's definition of *workday* was as divergent as everything about him. He knew his success was due as much to his personal drive as his exceptional abilities. He operated on another level.

Morons. Who cares about delivering another ME-420?

Arthur shook his head and turned back to his desk.

Let them play with their shiny planes, go home to the wife and kids, and watch TV. Spend two weeks a year in an RV on a quest to some overcrowded national park—No thanks.

Arthur had never once wavered from his goal of absolute wealth. Endowed with an obsessive focus, Arthur had dubbed himself a *Corporate Financial Artist,* building a successful career that now approached the pinnacle with the McNev Project.

Returning to his native Southern California three years ago, he was hired by Hugh McNeil, following the merger of Everett Aviation with McNeil Aerospace. He'd landed his largest project by guaranteeing McNeil a fast-track enhancement of McNev's bottom-line. Although he'd initially encountered some inflated egos, once he'd tied cost-cutting to substantial executive bonuses and properly focused Winton's talent for intimidation, the senior team fell into line.

He recalled McNeil's recent praise of his progress. "Arthur, based on the latest quarterly results, I'm starting to believe you're almost worth the exorbitant salary I'm paying you."

He thinks he's so witty...he hasn't got a clue.

This was Arthur's fifth corporate makeover, each increasing in complexity and personal rewards. All of his projects contained two sets of plans. One designed to satisfy those paying for his expertise and a second, private set, more directly related to his personal goal.

He called the second set *PEPs: Private Enterprise Privilege.* Arthur loved the name, as it embodied everything he valued. It was his privilege to have a private enterprise because he could never be paid what he was worth, despite his seven-figure compensation. His philosophy was simple: the needs of the one outweigh the needs of the many. The one being, of course, himself.

With superior skills in creative accounting, financial systems, and corporate turnarounds, he'd executed four PEPs across different industries, all of which he couldn't have cared less about.

The McNev project, however, was pushing the boundaries of his own extraordinary envelope. Arthur designed this PEP as the one to launch himself into financial independence at the age of forty-four, precisely as scheduled. And its unique nature meant there was no going back.

His masterpiece also presented a host of new challenges. The enormously complex operations involved in aircraft manufacturing were causing constant distractions. Moreover, the complicated financial infrastructure required a more sophisticated approach to achieving bottom-line results than any of his prior projects. Because of this, Arthur had enlisted the help of a software development specialist to design a custom financial system extension.

After an unfortunate false start, contracting with the ethically enslaved Sheila Richmond, he'd rectified that mistake. His next programmer had completed his brilliant personal design, creating an application that not only worked perfectly, but saved him a great deal of time.

Time was crucial in this PEP because of the substantial human component. Although Arthur had mastered the art of managing people at a distance through skillful manipulation, it came at a price. Time-consuming, meticulous research was required to identify proper motivation to ensure that people performed precisely to plan without knowing they were players in carefully orchestrated PEP scenarios.

Tonight, Arthur had been rethinking the assignment he'd recently approved to deal with Bradley Richmond, an even larger branch on the family tree of aggravation. Richmond's headstrong nature, fueled by a relentless proclivity for digging into problems, caused him to constantly stray off script, forcing Arthur to take a more direct approach.

Using an unknown like this Bordon character is risky...but I can't take chances at this late stage.

Arthur sighed and returned to his special interface application, accessing McNev's financial database to input the day's journal entry "adjustments." His fingers moved with confidence, revising figures that offered no resistance. His mood improved dramatically.

* * *

When Rich finally left his office, the fifth floor was deserted. He nodded to the janitor as he stepped past her yellow "Wet Floor" sign. She wore headphones and sang to herself. Rich tried to evoke the feeling of contentment she appeared to have, but it didn't come.

He rode the elevator down to the tower garage, studying his reflection in the chrome doors.

God, I look like hell. Maybe Mac's right. I'm taking this job too seriously.

Rich trudged through the garage to his burgundy Lexus like a zombie, lost in a fog of exhaustion, and slid behind the wheel. He failed to notice the muscular man with closely cropped graying hair who was sitting in the sedan parked near the elevators.

He headed south on the 405 Freeway, toward the solace of Sheila's house in Laguna. Rich and his daughter, Lisa, had been living with his sister for nearly three years. Rich had the feeling they'd overstayed their welcome but talking with his sister and playing with his precocious seven-year-old had kept him sane.

Traffic was light, so Rich set his cruise control at seventy-two and tried to relax, but he couldn't leave work behind. As his thoughts returned to the events of the week, he identified with the frog in the old adage, blissfully soaking in a pot of water, gradually being heated until the oblivious frog boiled to death.

Rather than inducing Rich to quell his resistance to the executive team, O'Donnell's warning had fueled his motivation to investigate what he'd found in the Herrera report.

He'd spent the last three days researching the bits of information he'd seen before O'Donnell had caught him. The report contained several names, one of which he'd recognized from Mac telling him about a problem employee—an assembly mechanic by the name of Vale. When Rich noticed the name *Vale* in the report, he thought it might somehow be linked to the problem employee Mac mentioned.

He'd also discussed what he'd found with Sheila, as he usually did. He not only shared wild stories like Winton's escapades, but he talked through technical problems with her. Sheila had worked at Everett with Rich and Teri in their early years and was often able to give him a fresh perspective.

Rich shared his belief that the report could potentially be related to the recent rash of problems in Final Assembly. His sister teased him about his conspiracy theories getting the best of him, but Rich had seen things in the report such as work orders and parts lists, that were too irregular to ignore.

Realizing it was most peculiar for a confidential report from a union leader to contain technical information and part numbers, after he'd escaped the humiliation of O'Donnell busting him, he'd written down a part number he remembered.

The next day, Rich searched the parts database and found no record, which meant the part had no active application. He finally found a listing in an obsolete parts book. <u>*E-1101:*</u> *8-pin, lock-tite electrical connector,* which was absolutely no help to him. Loving a good mystery, Rich was undeterred.

He decided to examine the part, hoping for additional insight. So he took the half-mile walk to the northwesternmost corner of the multi-acre plant to visit his old buddy, Stanley, in Salvage. If a part existed, Stanley could find it.

Stanley took Rich's paper with the E-1101 listing and disappeared into the maze of racks. In a few minutes, he reappeared like magic from behind towering stacks of sheet metal, holding two electrical connectors.

"These two are the last of 'em, Rich," Stanley said, handing the plugs to him. "The bin count said there should be four, but I only found two—better hang on to 'em. Maybe they're worth somethin'."

Rich laughed and thanked him.

The part was a round plug, with eight male-female pins in a screw-type socket—likely used to connect an electric motor or actuating mechanism. Although there was nothing that made it unique beyond being obsolete, it looked familiar to him.

He took one of the plugs home to show Sheila. In the old days, she was known as the "Parts-List Wizard," so he thought she might remember it. He recalled being puzzled when she'd sounded annoyed.

"No, I don't recognize it," Sheila had said, turning quickly and handing the plug to Lisa. She added, "Here Lisa, you can take this and put it with your collection of Daddy's airplane parts."

Lisa was in second grade and liked to pretend she was working with her father, so Rich occasionally brought home various parts for her to use in one of her favorite games: "Let's Build Airplanes." Rich figured it was in her genes.

Rich had also walked out to Final Assembly and shared with Mac what he'd seen in the report. He'd shown him the second connector, but unfortunately, he had no clue about its significance either.

However, Mac confirmed Vale was a first-level assembly mechanic, assigned to electrical and mechanical installations, and that Vale had been discharged last week on suspicion of causing intentional damage to electrical wiring assemblies. It was one more coincidence making Rich think his theory of a dark conspiracy hiding within McNev might just be valid.

At that point, Rich and Mac had determined that running an analysis of electrical production issues might reveal a common thread, shedding some light on the report. Their plan resulted in the proposal Rich had presented to the ExCon this afternoon, receiving such stellar support from Duke.

Rich took the off-ramp from the 405 into Laguna Canyon, noticing the Chrysler with the misaligned headlight that had been bothering him on the freeway, exited behind him. He swore.

Damn, just my luck. Oh, well. I'll be home soon...not worth getting irritated. I'll just drive faster.

* * *

Bordon followed the burgundy Lexus onto the canyon road.

I wonder if my headlight is annoying him...I hope so.

He shifted in his seat, trying to lessen his lower-back pain from hours of waiting for Richmond.

When Porter had spotted him, finally emerging from the executive tower elevator, Richmond had been walking like he was in a trance. He considered what Crandall had told him, but in his opinion, Richmond looked exhausted rather than drunk or high.

He thought about it as he followed Rich up the first hill.

He didn't look like the loser degenerate Crandall described, or a trouble-making union guy, either. Dammit, I shoulda paid more attention to what Crandall was saying and done my homework.

Bordon cursed in frustration, watching the Lexus pull away as he tried to chase it with his rented Chrysler.

He began speaking loudly to his empty car as if he were giving Crandall an earful about the dubious intel he'd been given.

"This guy won't be suspicious, huh? You told me to rent a cheap, ordinary car because I wouldn't have to do any chasing. You told me Richmond had no idea about anything and wouldn't even know anyone would be following him. Hah! Just wait till I get hold of you, Crandall. I'm gonna tear you a new one!"

The squealing tires underscored his mood. Porter tightened his grip and clenched his teeth as he flew up a hill after the Lexus.

With skills honed over many years, Porter continued pushing the Chrysler past its limit, and managed to close the gap on a longish downhill stretch. He saw his chance.

Hey, this could work out after all. As fast as he's headed into that turn, it'll be nice and easy...If I can get this piece of shit to catch him!

He jammed his foot on the gas pedal, trying to push it through the floorboard. The Chrysler seemed to sense the force of Porter's will, responding with a burst of acceleration. The straight stretch of road was about a quarter mile, ending in an extended curve to the left. Porter roared down the hill, cutting inside the Lexus, as Richmond braked for the curve.

Bordon sideswiped the Lexus, partnering with centrifugal force to keep it from completing the turn, while maintaining control of the Chrysler—mostly.

Clean and simple. Damn, I'm good.

The Lexus skidded off the right shoulder in a blur of burgundy, the scream of its engine echoing off the hills, followed by a loud *crash* as it landed in a shallow ravine. Porter battled the fishtailing Chrysler, using both sides of the road and most of the shoulder before bringing it to a stop in the next straight stretch.

He took a breath, then backed to the curve and pulled onto the shoulder. Porter looked for traffic and listened for any sign that someone had seen something. The night was still except for the dust wafting up from the ravine.

Leaving the headlights pointed at the curve, Porter examined the skid marks, satisfied that the inside set was barely visible. He unzipped his utility satchel and retrieved the long-handled heavy-duty Maglite, a constant companion because of its many uses beyond effective illumination. He walked to the edge, aiming the Maglite's 136 lumens into the ravine. Blinding white light from the cloud of settling dust reflected back at him. No engine noise; only silence.

Is he still alive?

He swayed from an unexpected wave of nausea, bending over to counter it.

What the hell?

Porter couldn't identify what he was feeling. Uncertainty? He put his hands on his knees to steady himself, when just as abruptly another unexpected sensation rocked him: an urge to help Richmond.

As Porter hesitated, trying to decide if he should act on the impulse, the ravine came alive with a loud *whump!*

The Lexus ignited, shattering the darkness in a blaze of semi-daylight. Porter slipped and fell back, landing with a thump as his butt hit the dirt. He waited for his daze to clear, watching the orange flames casting light and shadows on the hillside, then got to his feet and stepped back from the heat and smoke.

After using a handkerchief to dust off his hands, he carefully wiped the dirt from his new boots. He stared into the ravine, still puzzled by his bizarre reaction, only to be hit by thoughts of Crandall and the entirely miserable, oppressively long day. No answer came to him.

The hell with this. I'm outta here.

He spat, trotted back to the Chrysler, clambered in, and started the engine. Venting his anger on the accelerator, the tires spun, and gravel sprayed, as Porter executed a hard U-turn and sped back toward the freeway.

3

Saturday, 9:35 a.m.

Teri Harlan's hand reflexively brushed back her hair when the plane's descent roused her from a fitful nap. She gauged their altitude at about ten thousand feet and airspeed around two-hundred-fifty knots, as the 737 settled into the approach corridor toward LAX.

Thankful for her window seat, Teri rested her head against the cool glass, her eye focusing on the small breather hole found at the bottom of all aircraft windows to regulate pressure. Realizing how much she knew about such things caused a fleeting smile. She watched the LA basin expanding below without really seeing it, regretting her decision to eat the airline-issued sandwich now under protest by her stomach.

Last night's phone call from Sheila had derailed the idyllic scenario she'd imagined for returning to Southern California and working with Rich. When Sheila called, Teri had been engrossed in one of her legions of lists being used to plan the transition of her life back from Seattle. She'd already arranged to stay with Rich and Sheila for the first couple of weeks while she found an apartment.

As soon as she'd heard Sheila's voice, Teri knew something was wrong. The tenor of a person who always had her act together was absent.

"Teri," Sheila had begun, with the dead air of the phone line following for several seconds. "It's Rich…He was in an accident last night."

"Sheila—what happened? Is he…" Teri remembered how she'd clutched the table, instantly unsteady. Like a blown circuit breaker had suddenly shut down her balance. "Is he all right?"

"Well, he's not dead." She'd sensed Sheila was struggling to maintain her composure. "He apparently lost control driving home last night and landed upside down in a ditch. His car caught fire, and thank God, someone saw it and called *911*."

A frightful vision of Rich in a burn unit covered in bandages flashed through Teri's mind. Almost as if Sheila had read her thoughts, she continued, "Amazingly though, he didn't get burned. The airbag kept him from being crushed, and he was able to pull himself free. But he has a gash on the back of his head, and a concussion, maybe from a piece of debris…" Sheila's voice trailed off.

Teri asked, "He's going to be okay, isn't he?"

"Well, the doctor said he was in and out of consciousness when the paramedics transported him to Saddleback Medical Center. And he was still confused when I saw him for a few minutes last night...too soon to tell, I think...not sure how long he'll be there. Does this mean you're not coming?"

"No way. Of course, I'm coming. I'll see if I can get a flight for tomorrow."

Shaking off the recollection of the phone call, Teri shifted her seat to the upright position, and ran her fingers through her hair again. *This is not how I'd planned my homecoming.*

When Rich had reached out to her a few months ago about returning to join him at McNeil Everett, she'd been skeptical. But as their discussions continued, reflecting on their past success, she'd warmed to the idea.

She and Rich had risen quickly at Everett. They started around the same time, hired as aircraft assembly mechanics on second shift while finishing college. Teri stayed in Final Assembly Systems, and Rich moved into Quality Assurance. Though in different departments, they continued working closely as two of the youngest middle managers in Everett's career advancement program.

Nine years ago, Teri was offered a Director position in Seattle with AeroSystems, an Everett supplier of hydraulics systems.

She thought about how proud he'd been of her, as well as a bit envious, when AeroSystems recruited her for an executive opening. Rich was both her strongest motivation to stay and her biggest reason to leave. That was the year they became more than friends and coworkers, teetering on the precipice of a real relationship.

They knew getting more serious would mean sacrificing one of their careers, because at Everett, fraternizing was not permitted—especially between fast-tracked managers. She recalled their lunchtime discussions debating the merits and risks of their involvement as if they were solving a manufacturing problem. When they were about to cast all logic out the window, the offer had come from AeroSystems.

Teri decided to take it. Even with her management skills providing a certain immunity to intimidation in the workplace, she was still a woman playing in the macho-driven world of aerospace. The new job was her opportunity to make that quantum leap from manager to executive. It also took advantage of the MBA she'd sacrificed all her free time to earn, preparing herself for just such a position. And though it resolved the situation with Rich, it had not been an easy decision.

They'd stayed close for the first couple of years, calling each other weekly, sharing ideas and commiserating. Then Rich had gotten married, making their calls less frequent. Teri never met Rich's wife, and soon after, Lisa was born. Although she got an occasional note from Sheila, her contact with Rich stopped altogether.

Four years ago, Rich wrote to let her know that his wife had been killed in a head-on collision with a drunk driver. She still remembered her gut-wrenching reaction reading his letter, knowing instantly why Rich had chosen to write rather than call. She identified with his awkwardness of sharing painful emotions, the very thing that caused her to shy away from flying down to see him. Now it all seemed like a long time ago…

* * *

The vibration of the flaps deploying for landing broke Teri's reverie. She smiled, recalling the challenge of rigging the control surface cables inside the wings, and the pride she felt, being part of a team that thousands of airline passengers relied on to do their jobs right every day.

But by the time the plane reached the gate and the *fasten seat belt* sign blinked off, the warm memory was displaced by a churning stomach as she collected her carry-on and strode into the chaos of LAX, looking around for Sheila. Her mounting dread of this moment—seeing Sheila racked with tears, concerned she would do the same—evaporated the instant their eyes met; her anxiety vanished in the warmth of their connection.

They embraced, stepped back from each other, said in unison, "It's really good to see you," and then laughed at their synchronicity.

"How are you holding up?" Teri asked, noticing Sheila looked considerably more together than she'd sounded on the phone.

"I'm doing okay. Better now that you're here. Sorry I was such a mess last night. I really appreciate you coming in a day early."

"Hey, I wanted to be here." Teri responded easily, feeling their closeness returning.

Years back, when they'd worked at Everett, the two of them had grown tight, slogging through long nights together, testing hydraulic systems. Their success led to them becoming stand-outs among their male colleagues as well as turning the occasional head, and the decade since had seasoned their attractiveness.

Teri looked toward Sheila as they started walking. "I see you kept your hair long. I really like the highlights you added."

"Thanks…boyfriend's idea. A few weeks ago he said, 'You need to try this new balayage treatment. It'll set off those sapphire eyes and turn you into a classic California girl.'"

"Not sure what balayage is, but to me you've always been a California girl. What made him think you needed a makeover?"

"He was my hairdresser… now he's also an 'Ex.' I kept the highlights though."

Sheila's snarky humor was a lot like her brother's. It made Teri smile.

By the time they reached the concourse, her smile had faded as Sheila explained Rich's condition in more detail.

"So last night I got to learn what a Glasgow coma scale is."

Getting a quizzical look from Teri, she elaborated. "It's the way they evaluate brain trauma, using a five-point scale for awareness, speech, and movement. A score of three is completely comatose, and anything eight or under means severe damage...the scale goes to fifteen, which is fully functional."

Teri went straight to worried. "What was Rich's score?"

"Thirteen, according to the EMTs last night. He was conscious when I saw him, and knew who I was. But he was loopy—definitely not himself. Fortunately, Saddleback Medical in Laguna Hills had an on-call neurologist, a Dr. Meyer, who ran a CT scan and told me before I went home that it showed no swelling or bleeding...so that's good, right?"

Assuming it was, Teri nodded as Sheila continued. "Meyer's diagnosis was 'concussion with possible retrograde amnesia.' That's the one where you lose your memory of what happened before the injury. I don't know how severe that part is. I'm just praying he gets through this with nothing permanent."

Suddenly contemplating the unpleasant prospect of Rich being unable to return to work indefinitely, Teri felt her chest tighten. She shook it off, shoving open the terminal exit door.

* * *

Sheila drove her Nissan 300 ZX out of the airport parking structure into the sunshine, down Sepulveda, and up onto the new 105 Freeway. Rich's daughter, Lisa, was staying with her best friend who lived next door to Sheila, so they decided to go directly to visit Rich at the medical center in Laguna Hills. Sheila accelerated into the banked transition to the south 405, and Teri felt the turn as Sheila's Z hugged the road.

"This is quite a ride you've got."

Sheila grinned. "Yeah, I love it. Another boyfriend worked for Nissan, and he got me a deal." She paused, then added, "The car turned out to be way better than he was."

Noting her old friend was recently 0-for-2, Teri tried to relax in the Z's body-glove seat, letting the familiar surroundings of Orange County awaken memories of their friendship. "Hey, do you remember those nights on second shift when you and I and Rich went out for pizza?"

"Wow, girl, that's going back a few years! Yeah, I remember our conversations about who was gonna be first to make a million dollars and hire the other two."

Teri chuckled. "I guess we didn't quite make it, huh?"

"I'd say you've done pretty well making director. You were only what, thirty-one, when you got that job? And now you're gonna be Deputy VP of Quality. Not bad for just turning forty."

Smiling, Teri replied, "Thanks, but please don't remind me. Besides, you're the one with your own business. You've come a long way from the inventory computer geek, spending every waking hour obsessed with that damn parts system."

"Ha, ha, very funny. I did love that old IBM 370, though. And it led me back to school, into systems programming." Smiling, she added, "So now I'm a major-league computer geek."

Teri said, "Well, I'd say you made a helluva good choice. Rich told me you can charge your clients basically whatever...and by the way, you certainly don't look geeky any more."

"Aww, gee," Sheila grinned, affectionately slapping Teri's arm, reminding her of their friendship from those long-ago nights on the assembly floor.

After a pause, Teri said, "Seriously though, Rich said you're doing great. I'm happy for you."

"Thanks, but it's also due to good timing. Most companies these days are trying to move from legacy systems to enterprise software that typically doesn't communicate with anyone else's systems."

"So, you teach systems how to talk to each other?"

"Essentially, yeah. I design interface software to integrate existing stand-alone systems. And yes, it does pay well. But the best part is being able to work at home and set my own schedule. Plus, I can take care of Lisa when Rich is at work...which, lately, seems mostly all the time..."

Sheila drifted into silence, and after several minutes, Teri noticed her expression had darkened.

"Hey, are you okay?"

"Honestly, Ter, I don't know. Last night before this happened, I'd planned to have a serious talk with Rich. I love my brother and my niece, but I'm exhausted, and I'm feeling like he takes advantage of me. Now I'm just really scared. If Rich has some long-term damage, I don't know what I'll do about Lisa. When she lost her mom, Rich became her world. And she's so bright...I could tell she wasn't buying it for a minute this morning when I told her not to worry about her father."

Teri looked out the window, her own thoughts turning cloudy.

First Rich, now Sheila. And I'm starting work on Monday without him. What have I gotten myself into? Time for some positive thinking.

She turned to Sheila. "Well then, Rich will just have to get better. Let's hope he's awake when we get there."

Teri put her hand on Sheila's shoulder, giving it a reassuring squeeze. It was as much for herself as for her friend.

* * *

Running down the hallway. Have to get to the elevator. Guitar riffs of "Purple Haze" coming from everywhere.
Why are they playing Jimi Hendrix at work?
Hard to run. Cold. Hurry...don't know why...must go faster. Running in slow motion. Mist everywhere...
Something's not right. How can it be foggy in the hallways? I'm in that Dean Koontz book, where the kid stopped time, and they were running, and there was fog. That must be it. Wait—how could time be stopped? I'm at work.
Into the elevator...press 9. Have to warn her—elevator's still going! Thirtieth floor, fiftieth, hundredth! Ding!
Step out...so cold. Can't stop shaking.
There she is—Teri! God, she looks stunning...body-hugging white skirt...almost transparent...beautiful auburn hair shimmering against her white jacket...she's walking away—wait!
Teri!...no sound! She's going into the conference room. They're inside...leering, beckoning to her...Winton has his arm around her waist—that dickhead!
Gotta reach her...stop her. She's in danger! She doesn't know!
O'Donnell! Where did he come from? Get by him—save Teri!
He's shoving Teri into the room, slamming the door! No!
Grab O'Donnell—hurt him—Squeeze his throat...he burst into flames! White hot fire! Hurt all over...can't make it...so tired...
I'm on fire...but there's no pain. Falling...down, down, down...an angel gliding toward me. She's beautiful. So white...radiant.
She takes my hand...safe.

* * *

Teri sat watching Rich sleep. He looked in good shape, especially considering he was lying in a hospital bed. There was a bit more gray at his temples, giving him a mature executive look, and that strong chin still held the attraction she'd felt years ago. Rich began to twitch from what she guessed to be a disturbing dream, then squeezed her hand. In spite of his clammy touch, she smiled at him, doing her best not to look distressed.

"Hey, you're awake."

Rich rubbed his eyes as if trying to wipe away his confusion. "Teri? My God, I was just dreaming about..."

He looked at Sheila. "Where's Lisa?"

"She's at the Taylors. I'll bring her by later. Teri wanted to see how you were doing. Remember I told you last night?"

He turned back to Teri and smiled. "You came all the way down from Seattle to visit me in the hospital?"

"Well, I came a day early...But remember, I start work on Monday."

"You what? Where? Not at McNev?"

"You don't remember? You've spent the last three months recruiting me. I'm your new Deputy VP—You couldn't wait for me to start."

Several minutes of very confused conversation resulted in Rich's agitation and a visit from the nurse. Teri felt relieved when the nurse told them they needed to end their visit because Rich was scheduled for an MRI.

They walked out into the late afternoon, not speaking until they reached the car.

"Wow," Teri said.

Sheila nodded. "Yeah, I agree. I knew last night he didn't remember the accident, but I had no idea he didn't remember hiring you, either...damn."

"Did Dr. Meyer give you any idea how long the amnesia could last?"

"Oh, he was *really* helpful. He told me 'it depends'..."

"On?"

"The extent of the trauma, the pace of healing...different in every case."

Reacting to the look on Teri's face, Sheila changed the subject. "C'mon, let's get to my place. Meeting Lisa will make you feel better."

* * *

Thirty minutes later, Sheila pulled into her driveway. Her two-story beach bungalow, off Glenneyre Street in Laguna, was blue with white trim and built like a model in four-fifths scale. It sat in the center of a proportionally diminutive, manicured yard bordered by a white picket fence.

They unloaded Teri's luggage, and when Teri walked through the front door, it was obvious that the proportions inside mirrored the outside. The thirty-two inch Sony TV and rack of stereo components Rich had brought with him, consumed a good part of the living room, leaving just enough space for a loveseat, an overstuffed chair, and an antique steamer-trunk.

Sheila went into the kitchen, returning with two cold Steinlagers as Teri was slipping off her shoes and settling into the loveseat. Sheila set the beers on the steamer-trunk coffee table and sat on the floor, neatly folding her legs to the side.

Teri took a healthy swallow, then set her bottle down with a sigh. "You know, Rich's accident seems kind of strange. I've seen him handle a car like...as well as you do your Z!"

Sheila smiled faintly, but said nothing.

Teri continued. "Is it possible another car was involved? Did you ask the police?"

Sheila was looking at the floor, hesitating, when the front door opened. Appearing grateful for the interruption, she stood to greet Nancy Taylor from next door.

"Thanks so much for watching her, Nancy."

"Never a problem. I think Kara wants her to move in..."

Before Nancy finished her sentence, a whirlwind in the form of a seven-year-old girl with pigtails rushed past her into the living room, straight for Teri.

"Hi! You must be Teri! My aunt told me all about you. I'm Lisa! Auntie Sheila said you and her and Daddy worked on planes together and were really good friends a long time ago. Would you like to see our workshop where Daddy and I build airplanes? He's in the hospital so he can't right now...but he should be home soon because I miss him." All of this before taking a breath.

Teri dissolved into laughter, a welcome antidote to the past forty-eight hours.

4

Saturday, 4:20 p.m.

Arthur O'Donnell stood in his front yard with his hand on his white wrought iron fence, striking a well-practiced pose that combined sublime confidence with slightly pretentious boredom. His home on Balboa Island was on a preeminent south-west street coveted for its nighttime view of the Newport Peninsula across the bay.

He wore a smile of contentment reminiscent of a lord surveying his manor, even though his front yard was actually a small patio. It was, however, a paragon on a block of exceptional patio-yards. His exquisite design featured intricate Pennsylvania Bluestone flagstone, custom Westminster teakwood decking, and a small, ornate lavabo wall fountain.

Between the homes and the water ran a narrow ribbon of sidewalk trafficked by ultra-tan hard bodies on roller blades, whenever the weather was nice—which in Southern California was essentially always. This afternoon, Arthur allowed himself a few moments to relax in the late-day sun watching the scenery roll by, in particular, the girls in bikinis.

A bit over six feet, he reveled in hearing himself referred to as *tall, dark, and handsome*. His olive complexion turned an urbane bronze with time in the sun, and this afternoon it was shown off beautifully. Clad only in a pair of charcoal Lands' End swim shorts, Arthur was the star in a scene perfectly suited for a commercial.

He was drinking Glenmorangie eighteen-year-old scotch in a Glencairn glass he kept slightly chilled. He never used ice because it would be a travesty to dull the complex flavors of the world's preeminent scotch. Arthur added precisely four drops of spring water to spark a chemical reaction with the amino acids in the whiskey, releasing the esters.

His sips were deliberate, properly savoring the scotch while contemplating the status of his current endeavor. He'd dedicated three years to the intricate McNev Private Enterprise Privilege, his masterpiece. His passport to absolute wealth.

The unique business circumstance and elaborate nature demanded deeper involvement in *people scenarios*, which Arthur found distasteful because they lacked precision. The scenarios also required an extended set of associates, whom he'd been reenlisting from earlier in his career.

He'd just identified Vale, the perfect former associate to finalize his contingency plan for Richmond's survival, when the ringing phone interrupted his thoughts. He picked up the portable handset sitting on his Janco Signature cut-glass patio table, and pressed the "Talk" button.

"Arthur? It's Will. Listen, I've got a big problem with Bordon—he's been harassing me since he got back, and he just showed up at my house!"

The voice of Will Crandall ruined his afternoon repose, realizing too late that the 817 Texas area code showing on the display told Arthur he shouldn't have answered.

Crandall's willingness to do whatever he was told, aided by the absence of a moral compass, was a double-edged sword. The benefit of Will's compliance came with the substantial downside of having to tolerate a self-absorbed sociopath with an unquenchable appetite for outré amusement.

"What's wrong, Will? Is Bordon interrupting your strip-Scrabble game? Why don't you invite him to join you?"

"Oh, you're *so* humorous. Just because you think a fun night involves working up new scenarios for your brilliant PEPs."

Arthur recognized the escalating abrasiveness in Will's voice, indicating an imminent tirade. His jaw clenched. "I'm not your personal fixer, Will. I don't have the time or inclination to solve every little problem you think is a crisis."

"Need I remind you, you're the one who recruited *me?*" Will spat back. "I'm the one who works in Texas, with the access to inside information. I'm the one with the corporate authority to get all your self-proclaimed critical tasks done in final assembly out there, plus the *only* one with the aircraft know-how to do the design work. Not to mention, I'm the one who whispers in McNeil's ear for you!"

Arthur bit his lip, attempting to control his irritation. He focused on his end game, just a few weeks away, when he could be finished with Crandall and devise a satisfying retribution scenario.

Will continued in Arthur's silence. "You gave your word, you'd run interference whenever I needed you, and I've got Bordon here in my face, disrupting a very private dinner party!"

Knowing Will could go on indefinitely, Arthur realized his best approach was to cut to the chase. "Okay, Will, go get Bordon. I'll handle it."

As he waited, Arthur continued to weigh the Richmond situation. He hadn't wanted to use Bordon because avoiding direct action had always been key to the *private* element of his PEPs.

But Arthur recognized shortly after the merger that Richmond could be trouble. When Hugh McNeil gave Arthur the reins for the takeover, he'd personally instructed Arthur to retain Richmond, so there was no way Arthur could get rid of him without a solid reason—and he'd had one working until Richmond had stuck his nose in that damn Herrera report.

He smiled at the irony. *Richmond was so close to being removed safely.*

Using his sources, he'd learned there were rumors of possible former romance between Richmond and Teri Harlan, which was why he'd approved Richmond's request to rehire her. It would have been simple to create a compromising scenario for Richmond and Harlan that resulted in their joint termination. He shook his head.

After catching Richmond snooping, Arthur had him watched for a few days, on the off chance his verbal warning had an effect.

But when he'd been informed of Richmond's visit to the salvage department, and his collaboration with Mac McKinley—another person sadly stricken with an unnatural devotion to airplanes—he'd been forced to act.

In a phone call with Crandall the other night, Arthur expressed the need to sideline Richmond, and Will eagerly volunteered a solution. In retrospect, Arthur should have seen the red flag in Crandall's noxious eagerness, describing Bordon's talents in gory detail as he'd recommended a car-accident scenario.

However, that dollar had been spent, as Arthur liked to say, so he'd worked out a way to take advantage of the current situation, as he always did.

Now I just need to devise the best way to leverage Richmond's accident in order to control his troublemaking sister, who's been dragging her feet...definitely runs in the family.

His thoughts were interrupted by Crandall speaking loudly to Bordon on the other end of the phone. "I still don't know how you got through the gate, but showing up here just put your job on the line."

Arthur couldn't make out Bordon's response, other than profanity. Then he heard Will again. "Here—Arthur O'Donnell, the Executive VP from McNev in California—he'll confirm it."

"Mr. O'Donnell? Porter Bordon here. Listen, Crandall really screwed up this Richmond deal. I don't mind taking care of things, but I need to know what's going on, with the particulars of who, what, and why. I got back to Texas at three a.m., after flying both directions in coach for chrissake, and I hear a message on my machine from Crandall, screaming that Richmond survived and accusing me of failing."

Arthur shuddered but let Bordon finish.

"I tried all day to reach the little prick, but he refused to take my calls. So I found out his address, and drove out here to Westlake to ask him face-to-face what the hell is going on. I seriously would like to pound a few nails into his ass!"

Hearing this, Arthur understood that letting Crandall take the lead on managing Bordon was a serious misstep, giving into his own inclination to distance himself from distasteful actions. He also concluded it would be counterproductive to allow Crandall's volatility to continue mixing badly with Bordon's apparent short fuse. He decided to take control before it led to further turmoil.

Bordon obviously had no real knowledge of what he was doing for them, and Arthur had no intention of telling him. But he could defuse the situation by separating Bordon from Crandall and McNeil as soon as possible. Arthur chose the precise words and tone for a person of Bordon's ilk.

"Porter, just between you and me, Crandall's a complete asshole." Hearing the hesitation, he knew he'd caught Bordon off guard. He continued, "I used you for this specialized assignment because I wanted the best. I know there aren't many of your kind left."

"Well thank you, sir. That means something to me, Mr. O'Donnell."

He heard Bordon's edge abating, and added, "You can call me Arthur." Then he laid in a strategic compliment.

"Listen, you did fine with Richmond. He's on the sideline where he needs to be."

"Thank you, Art. As I tried to tell Crandall, I'm not in the 'murder for hire' business, I just take care of problems. So I'm glad it worked out."

He had Bordon exactly where he wanted him, but for one issue that demanded immediate remediation. Arthur switched instantly to glacial—"Call. Me. *Arthur*," then returned seamlessly to cordial and continued. "Porter, some critical issues for McNev are coming into play that could use your talents. Can you come out here and report directly to me for a couple of weeks?"

"Sure, Mr. O'Donnell...Arthur. I'd need to get Mr. McNeil's okay, though. My contract says I report to him. I don't think I'm supposed to be doing freelance work."

Arthur had agreed to Crandall's original ploy of telling Bordon that Richmond was an unscrupulous union official, because it seemed expedient at the time. Now that he was taking more control, obfuscation was called for.

He switched to sincere.

"You know Mr. McNeil could never openly approve certain tactics we might have to use occasionally with the union challenges and such out here. And even though you did McNev a real service by taking Richmond out of circulation, you can probably guess that Mr. McNeil wouldn't totally approve of our methods."

"Well Arthur, you know I worked on the union side for most of my career. Now that I'm playing for the other team, I agreed when Crandall asked for my help. People trying to hurt the company gotta be stopped. But Crandall implied this whole thing came with Mr. McNeil's stamp of approval."

Arthur smiled at how easy this was. Giving Bordon a plausible-sounding, circuitous explanation with a complex word at the center, should leave him puzzled enough to just let it go.

"Well, Porter, let's just say I'm here in the real world, trying to prevent our corporation from being devoured by a bunch of LA fast-lane employees. Mr. McNeil tries to be the magnanimous corporate leader, and sometimes he's too much 'one-of-the-folks' for his own good, if you get what I mean."

After a brief hesitation, Bordon answered, "Yes, sir. I read you four-by-four."

Arthur smiled once more. He figured Bordon probably wore cowboy boots with his suit, like that idiot, Duke.

"Okay, good. I'll take care of clearing this with old man McNeil, and I'll straighten out Crandall. You just let Will get back to his dinner party, and get your butt back out here to help me ASAP, and this time, I'll be sure you get booked first class…and Porter? Just a couple more things. Let's keep this between us, and be sure you erase that answering-machine message from Crandall. That's probably not a good thing for the company."

Again, Porter hesitated, making Arthur wonder if he was going to question things, until he heard, "Thank you, sir. I'm looking forward to working with someone who's got their act together."

Arthur sighed as he hung up, satisfied in regaining control, but already anticipating the challenges of adding one more pain-in-the-ass to his list.

At least Bordon appeared trainable. *He is calling me Arthur, and he might actually be better for some scenarios than my local contacts…What the hell was Crandall thinking, leaving a message like that on an answering machine?*

He went inside to put the phone back in its base unit, and when he returned to retrieve his empty glass, his stunningly blonde neighbor and her girlfriend came skating up the walkway.

"Hi, girls. Those are nice bikinis you're almost wearing."

He leaned casually into an arresting smile, slightly mischievous at the corners, which brought them to a stop at his gate. They giggled. He decided there was time for one more short diversion.

* * *

Teri was working at the dinette table in the kitchen, and looked up when Sheila came down the stairs.

"Lisa all tucked in for the night?"

"Yep, but you're on tap to read her a story tomorrow." With a smile, Sheila added, "Part of earning your keep."

"Seems fair. I appreciate you letting me use the make-down in your office."

"No problem. It was no biggie to move my computer into my bedroom."

As Teri put a paperclip on her new-hire paperwork, she quipped, "Yeah, and your commute's better too…two steps instead of all the way across the hall." After Sheila called her a smart aleck, Teri said, "I'm actually envious of you working at home. I'm a little nervous about tomorrow."

Sheila nodded. "I can imagine. I know it'd be easier if Rich was there, but at least you'll know your way around."

With a thoughtful expression, Teri asked, "Sheila, do you know much about the current executive team? I've been trying to anticipate what they'll be like to work with."

"I know a little—mostly from Rich. But I thought Rich said you'd met them when you flew down for your final interviews."

"Yes, but I didn't have much time with them. I remember Jackson Winton looking like someone on the cover of *Executive* magazine, but he only asked me one question, so I have no idea about him."

"Not trying to be negative, but Rich says he's a moron. He looks the part and has this commanding voice, but apparently he spends most of his time traveling with his administrative assistant, Karolyn Babcock. Rich says the other VPs have a running joke about how she 'measures Winton's performance.'"

"Wow, sounds like something out of the seventies. Rich didn't tell me anything about that."

Teri paused again before adding, "You know I got the impression Darren Duke, the Manufacturing VP, was also a bit sexist."

Sheila shook her head. "Duke…him, I've heard a lot about. Rich doesn't think much of him, either. Rich said Duke spent all this money remodeling his office into some sort of lounge, and he invites cute female assembly mechanics for 'special visits.'"

"God, don't tell me that! He's the one doing my orientation. I meet with him first thing tomorrow!"

"Sorry. But I don't think you have anything to worry about. You're a Deputy VP now…and remember, you and I grew up on the assembly floor. We know how to take it, and dish it right back."

Teri nodded. "You're right—and I know this crap still goes on everywhere. Just last month at AeroSystems, my coworker, Angie, was running a technical meeting with three executives from a hydraulics actuator vendor. Angie started to present her analysis of our slat control system when the VP from the visiting company stopped her and said, 'Sweetie, why don't you go get us some coffee, and leave the technical details to the men who know about these things.' She didn't take that bullshit, and I don't either...I was just hoping I wouldn't have to armor-up right off the bat."

Teri began organizing her folders as she continued, "So, just one more: Arthur O'Donnell. In my interview, I could tell he was not only in charge, but also the smartest, and seemed totally professional." She smiled, adding, "I know I shouldn't say this after what we just talked about, but he's also really good-looking. Do you know him?"

Teri noticed that Sheila stiffened as she answered, "I know he's become Rich's least favorite boss...Rich is constantly at odds with him..." Her voice trailed off.

Teri asked, "Anything else?"

"Oh, jeez, it's late. You should get some sleep, and I've got a ton of work."

Avoiding eye contact with Teri, Sheila hurried upstairs.

5

Monday, 5:45 a.m.

Teri chose to reacquaint herself with the Southern California coastline by taking the Pacific Coast Highway—PCH—to work on her first day. She got an early start, on the road before six a.m., enjoying the view as she headed north from Laguna toward Corona Del Mar. Below the cliffs to her left, the breaking waves of the Pacific with their white crests shimmering in the new day's sun, seemed to welcome her home.

Being behind the wheel of her new Jeep further enhanced her mood. When she'd moved to Seattle she invested in a Jeep Cherokee for the four-wheel drive, which served her well in Seattle's rainy climate. She'd had her eye on the new Grand Cherokees since their release two years ago and decided that with everything she'd been through to get here, she deserved to reward herself.

Teri rolled down the window and turned on the heater—her favorite driving mode for PCH. She had fond memories of her old MG Roadster, speeding along the coast highway after dark with the top down and the heater cranked up full—one of the few things on that car that actually worked.

Praising the miracle of technology, she flipped the toggle switch for the seat heater. Teri savored the early morning, taking deep breaths of salty fresh air that filled her with an almost magical quality of renewal. If Rich were with her, it would be a perfect start.

Last night she'd prepared as best she could. After talking with Sheila, she stayed up working on a plan to take advantage of her familiarity with Everett and dazzle her new team by getting up to speed faster than anyone would expect.

She turned east, driving into inland Orange County. The view of the ocean disappeared, along with her upbeat mood. The traffic grew thicker as she drove through streets bordered by an endless blur of homogenous strip malls and peppered with stoplights that seemed to turn red just for her.

* * *

When Teri arrived at the sprawling McNeil Everett complex, she drove to the main gate with a vehicle entrance near the executive tower. She gave her name to the Security officer who returned quickly with an in-plant vehicle permit, a tower-garage parking sticker, and an executive badge with her name on it.

"Yes, Miss Harlan, you're expected. Do you know where to go from here?" Teri replied that she knew her way around, and he raised the bright orange security arm, waving her through.

To her left was the executive tower with a pristine concrete driveway, edged in impeccable landscaping, curving down to the subterranean garage. Seeing the garage entrance triggered a flashback of the envy she used to have for the executives authorized to park there. She glanced at her new parking decal and smiled.

Teri looked to her right, noticing the Security building and Visitor Center looked unchanged. Driving onto the main access road to her meeting across the plant sparked a rush of memories. The parade of noisy, gas-powered Cushman utility carts, many towing trailers of aircraft parts past the city-block-sized hangars, was instantly familiar. Although the Everett aircraft she'd worked on had been superseded by the ME-420, the unchanged plant layout made her feel like she'd never left.

Her meeting with Darren Duke was scheduled for 7:30 a.m., and when she parked outside the Sub-Assembly Building B-1, her watch read 7:05. She had time to walk around the building on her way to his office.

Inset into the enormous seven-story hangar doors—that opened on tracks to remove completed fuselage sections—were two eight-foot steel "people" doors. She opened one, stepping carefully over the four-inch threshold, and felt immediately at home. She walked past the huge Drivematic machines producing gunshot-like percussions with each massive rivet they drove into sub-assembly structures. She was careful to stay within the white paint outline, as main aisles and offices were the only designated safe zones not requiring eye protection.

The same huge sign still hung above the aisle. *Safety Glasses Must Be Worn in All Work Areas.* She noticed several employees working on sub-assemblies with their safety glasses hanging loosely around their neck. She shook her head as she recalled her old supervisor saying, "They don't do you no good if you don't wear 'em."

Teri walked the back line where the initial structures, including tail, nose, and fuselage barrel sections were constructed. Once completed, the sub-assemblies were moved to Final Assembly located in larger buildings on the east side of the plant. She made a mental note that there were only two tail assemblies active on the back line, while three of the five assembly jigs sat empty.

Low line rate. Not good.

Each enormous manufacturing hangar contained hard-walled office areas. Roughly the size of mini-marts, these office units were haphazardly assembled with unpainted drywall. Electrical conduit stuck out, along with heating and air-conditioning units displaying their backsides. They were essentially four walls with ceilings, offering a bit of protection from noise and dirt, along with better lighting for office work. Teri remembered how thrilled she'd been years ago to get an office in one of these complexes. The unit she approached that housed Darren Duke's office looked as if it hadn't been touched since she'd left.

Inside were several smallish offices and a central area with a conference table. She walked to the far end and entered the only large door, beneath an overly ornate sign that read: *Darren Duke, Senior Vice President of Manufacturing*.

She stood in a small anteroom and introduced herself to an attractive administrative assistant with a nameplate on her desk: *Marla*. As Teri was asked to have a seat, she heard raised voices behind the closed door.

* * *

"I told you I don't want to hear about any more electrical problems on the final line! In the last ExCon meeting, Richmond presented a big list of issues—which he said you helped put together! Do you know how that made me look in front of Winton? What the hell do I pay you for anyway, McKinley?"

"I thought you paid me to build airplanes. And despite what you might think, the best way to solve problems is to identify them so we can fix them."

"I don't need to hear your bullshit management philosophy. What I expect from you is to keep me informed so I can manage the information that gets up to the ninth floor. *You* work for *me*—I run things around here. In case you forgot, I'm a goddamn Vice President. Do you think I got this position by being stupid?"

Mac forced himself to stay silent.

Openness and honesty had always been, in Mac's view, not only the best way to succeed, but the only way to build good airplanes. Mac had been around Everett, now McNeil Everett, longer than almost everyone. Starting in Final Assembly more than thirty years earlier, Mac had worked his way up to Line-Position Supervisor, then Position Manager. A year before the merger, he was promoted to one of the two Final Assembly Directors, reporting to the VP of Manufacturing.

When Darren Duke was brought in as the new Manufacturing VP during the merger with McNeil Aerospace, Mac made an earnest attempt to support him. He'd always been taught to respect the boss's position, but soon found he was challenged to find anything to respect about Duke.

Mac sat defiantly, staring at Duke's sizeable bulk squeezed into his throne-like, high-backed leather chair.

How in the hell did he get the nickname, "Cowboy"? If he's a cowboy, I'm Michael Jordan.

Mac was only five-foot-seven, but lean and muscular, and equipped with street smarts he'd relied on many times when dealing with aircraft mechanics in a high-stress production environment. His natural athleticism and compact frame got him his first job at Everett, working nights as a fuel-tank mechanic, while he was still in school. That job required slender, agile people with flexibility to crawl inside an aircraft wing and seal the tank's interior seams.

Over his first years, Mac became the top-rated fuel-tank mechanic at Everett. He'd taken pride in that position and each one since, as he worked his way into management, respected by most everyone at McNev who cared about building airplanes. If there was a problem in Final Assembly, Mac probably had the solution.

He was having trouble paying attention to Duke. While most manufacturing managers were terrified of Duke's verbal abuse and threats, Mac settled on two modes of interaction: challenge him directly or ignore him completely.

He chose ignoring mode at the moment, preoccupied with the news that Rich had been in a serious car accident. This led to replaying their conversation yesterday, and a realization that he was more aligned with Rich's assessment than he cared to admit. He looked up, gripping the arms of the chair to keep his thoughts to himself.

No one will ever be able to make you see how stupid you really are. And still you sit there spouting BS while the only competent VP on the entire team...

"Mac, are you listening to me? I want these problems solved, and I mean *right now*. You find the idiots screwing up my planes and get rid of them. Are we clear?"

"Yes, Darren, let's do be clear," Mac shot back, as he rejoined the conversation. "Problems like this can't be solved like shoot-outs at the O.K. Corral."

Mac added emphasis by turning to look at the wall-sized painting of John Wayne astride a horse, ambling through a frontier town. He thought about what John Wayne might say if he were looking down at his boss.

Well, sir, the name doesn't make the man. Unfortunately for you, it's the other way around.

Duke drew a long, slow breath and Mac recognized his tell for pausing the conversation while he considered how to reestablish control. Mac had worked with Duke long enough to know how much Darren wanted him gone, and he took pride in successfully overcoming each of the challenges Duke had given him, attempting to break him. He smiled at his current thought.

And I bet it pisses him off even more that I'm Black.

As Mac was predicting, Duke's next move was to walk out from behind the desk to leverage his intimidation by towering over him. He was interrupted by Marla opening his office door.

"Excuse me, Mr. Duke..."

"Goddamn it, Marla, I said I didn't want to be disturbed! What is it about that you can't understand?!"

Mac wondered how Marla stood working around him, eight to ten hours every day. Nothing seemed to get to her.

She waited for Duke to take a breath and continued. "You had a seven-thirty meeting with Miss Harlan, and she's out here waiting."

Duke's demeanor transformed instantly as he adopted his hospitality drawl.

"Well, don't make the poor girl wait out there, Marla. Bring her on in."

Mac followed Teri's gaze as she surveyed the interior of Duke's office. The massive mahogany credenza with carved front panels ran the length of one wall, behind Duke's enormous matching desk. Both the credenza and the desk sat on a six-inch dais, lighted by a recessed ceiling panel simulating a skylight. The high-backed executive chair completed the regal ensemble, along with the *pièce de résistance*: wall-to-wall burgundy plush carpet.

When Teri's eyes reached the wall opposite Duke's desk, and the enormous portrait of John Wayne, Mac had to cover his mouth to keep from laughing at her expression. As their eyes met, they shared the unspoken absurdity of Duke and his office, along with a connection that felt as strong as ever.

In a regal tone, Duke said, "Welcome to my humble abode, Miss Harlan! Glad to have you aboard! This here is…"

He stopped mid-sentence, standing with his mouth open, as Teri walked over to Mac and hugged him.

"Mac, it's great to see you! I was gonna look you up this week, but I get to see you first thing!" Teri turned to Duke and said, "Oh, sorry, Mr. Duke, Mac and I go way back."

* * *

Duke was barely able to hide his displeasure. He had no idea they knew each other, much less appeared to be good friends. He would have to size Teri up and figure out where she stood. He replaced his expression with another smile, evoked by his current thought of sizing her up, then realized his appraising gaze was a bit too obvious. He turned back to Mac as he moved between them.

"Mac and I were just finished up…Mac, we'll talk later. I need to spend some time with Miss Teri, here."

As he started to leave, Teri asked, "Mac, did you hear what happened to Rich Friday night?"

Before Mac could respond, Duke interjected, "Damn fool ran himself off the road on the way home. Probably drunk or something."

He caught the simultaneous glares from the two of them and changed tack. "Uh…It's a real shame. I mean he hasn't been himself lately. Glad he pulled through. Hope he gets back to his old self real soon."

Teri told Mac she'd be sure to go see him so they could catch up, as Duke ushered him out and shut the door. Turning back to Teri with an overly zealous smile he said, "Please sit down and make yourself comfortable."

I'm gonna enjoy this orientation duty. She's hotter than I remember in her interview…looks firm under that skirt, and I like that silk top. I should offer to hang up her suit coat.

Rather than return to his seat of power behind his desk, he pulled up a chair next to her, better positioned to appreciate her legs.

6

Monday, 3:45 p.m.

Sheila sat next to the bed, steeling herself against the astringent smells and disquietude inherent in hospital visits. Watching her brother sleep, she reflected on the many conversations they'd shared since he and Lisa moved in with her. Understanding that her brother's success was driven by passion for his work, she worried about his future if he was unable to continue.

She and Rich had always been close. Four years apart, they were competitive and willful, never shying away from arguments, but fiercely bonded by family strength grounded in mutual respect. Although Sheila's business acumen was solid, she never shared Rich's love for airplanes, passed down from their father. Nightly dinner conversations often led to evening discussions that found her escaping to her room. Still, she appreciated Rich's dedication and commitment fostered by their father's influence.

When Rich stirred, Sheila thought it might help reboot his memory if she got him talking about his favorite subject: work. "Hey, sleepyhead. How're you feeling today?"

"Hi…My head hurts, but overall I'm feeling better."

Following some chit-chat, Sheila decided to try her idea.

"I forgot to ask you the other night. Did you and Mac ever get things straightened out with the flight-ramp guys?"

She knew her brother well. Rich jumped in as if he'd just finished his day at work.

"Nope—they're still out of control because Duke is constantly on their asses about the million-dollar late-delivery penalties."

"I know Duke is a jerk, but that *is* a lot of money. Not sure I can blame him for being pissed about that."

She instantly regretted her comment.

"Of course, it's a lot of money! But Duke is too stupid to solve the real problems! Do you know what the flight-ramp guys do? They steal parts from other planes to avoid Duke's wrath! Just the other night they pulled another 'midnight raid' on Ship 910 in Final Assembly, and stole two servomotors. When Mac's first-shift guys show up and find them missing, they have to replace them. It can take days waiting on the idiots in Procurement, even with expediting…and then *Mac* takes the heat."

Rich took a breath and plowed on. "It ends up costing more money and creating more problems. What does Mac have to do? Post guards to stop the flight ramp guys from going commando? And I can't get anyone to see that the constant infighting is killing our company! The asshole clones O'Donnell and Winton have Duke and the senior team focused on one thing: meeting cost and layoff targets to get their precious bonuses!"

Seeing his anger escalate so quickly, Sheila realized her idea had backfired. She searched for the right words to temper the conversation, but Rich only got more agitated.

"And did I see Teri here the other day? What's going on? Did O'Donnell hire her to take over because I'm losing it or something?"

Sheila reached for his hand. "Shhh...Take it easy."

She redirected the conversation to Lisa, which proved to be soothing, but not before his raised voice prompted another visit from the nurse. The RN made a suggestion—really more of an order—for Sheila to cut her visit short so her brother could rest.

* * *

After offering a few comforting words as she said good-bye, Sheila decided to look for Rich's neurologist, and found Dr. Meyer at the nurse's station.

"Miss Richmond, good timing. I was told you were here this afternoon. I wanted to give you an update."

They walked to Meyer's small office, and he gestured to the chair in front of his desk.

"The night your brother was admitted, we ran an EEG and a CT scan, which I told you showed nothing significant. Over the weekend, we performed an MRI, which provides better detail, such as remnants of hemorrhaged blood that may have been missed by the CT."

The look on Sheila's face prompted a quick response.

"Not to worry, it was negative as well. Actually, his progress has been excellent. His Glasgow score has been fifteen for three days. The gash on the back of his head and his other contusions are healing nicely. I'm not sure where the rash came from...I'm guessing from something in the ravine, but it doesn't look too serious, either."

"That's all great news, doctor. But he still seems irritable, and not himself. So without major damage or bleeding, what about his amnesia?"

"Even if the physical head trauma appears minor, there can be neural dysfunction, especially with memory. His frustration is likely caused by short-term memory issues."

"Like when he asked me what day it was three times?"

The doctor nodded. "Yes, and you probably noticed today that his short-term memory is improving. The longer-term is trickier because of the retrograde amnesia I mentioned before. Retrograde is typically limited to the seconds or minutes preceding the trauma, but in his case, it seems to be more like weeks. I think you've confirmed that."

Sheila recalled Rich's inability to remember hiring Teri. "Yes, it seems that way."

"I believe this more significant memory loss was caused by trauma from the severe deceleration impact."

Using a model on his desk, Meyer illustrated brain movement inside the skull, and used his finger to point out anatomy as he continued. "Memory and recall can be disrupted by abnormalities in neural function in the temporal lobe and prefrontal cortex—here and here."

He launched into a discussion of episodic versus procedural memory, explaining that Rich may have forgotten specific events, but would know precisely how to do his job.

As Sheila listened, she mentally bottom-lined the situation: *Cognitive function impairment related to memory is difficult to diagnose and impossible to predict.*

Sheila guessed it was unlikely that Meyer would have an answer, but she asked anyway. "So, what's his prognosis?"

"Difficult to say. Memory can come back in bits and pieces, but there's research suggesting that certain significant objects or circumstances can spark memory return…being in familiar surroundings may help."

Dr. Meyer stood, indicating they were finished. "Overall, his physical recovery is good, so I'm going to release him tomorrow. You'll just need to be tolerant of his memory recovery."

* * *

Walking to her car, Sheila's modest optimism was tempered by speculation that Rich's turmoil at work exacerbated his memory problems. This added to her growing concern over Rich's short fuse with O'Donnell.

She was no stranger to O'Donnell's ruthless side, having experienced it up close and personal just after the merger. Sheila knew now that she should have told Rich about her situation back then. But at the time, she was not only struggling to free herself from O'Donnell's grip, she'd also been sworn to secrecy and ashamed of the mess she'd gotten into.

When she'd decided to withdraw from O'Donnell's special interface software project, he'd threatened her to remain silent about the work she'd done for him, which reinforced her rationalization that not telling Rich was for his own good. She'd chosen to believe it was all behind her when she hadn't heard from O'Donnell in over two years.

Then two weeks ago, O'Donnell had come back like a bad migraine. He'd called her, again demanding her programming services, to design a new database linked with McNev's enterprise systems. As before, he provided detailed system specs, buckets of money, and for extra persuasion, brought up everything he'd put her through with the first project. She'd reluctantly agreed to develop the application for him, believing she had no choice.

Sheila nearly ran into the medical center's exit doors as they slid open, thinking about the night Rich brought home that connector.

She regretted snapping at him when he'd told her about seeing some mysterious report in O'Donnell's office, but she sensed where it could lead. Between Rich once again sticking his nose where it didn't belong, and her reluctance toward O'Donnell's latest project, Friday night really rattled her. She desperately wanted to believe that Arthur wouldn't be reckless enough to go after her brother, but her gut told her his accident wasn't random.

And now with Teri in the picture, it was only a matter of time before she started down the same dangerous road.

I probably should've told Teri everything last Saturday, but there's really nothing to prove Arthur's involvement. And confiding in Rich or Teri will just put them in his sights. My only choice is to finish what he wants and keep quiet...I'm sorry I ever met the bastard.

She got into her Z and slammed the door. The rear tires screeched as she left the parking lot.

* * *

LJ Vale hit the mute button, silencing his three-hundred-watt stereo, and said, "Shit."

He reached across his bed, pressing *answer* on the speakerphone panel built into his headboard. "Hello? Hey, Mr. O'D...yeah, doin' okay."

Arthur knew better. He knew Lawrence Vale's son, who everyone called "LJ" for Lawrence Junior, had recently been discharged for cause from his assembly job at McNev.

He used his concerned tone. "I was sorry to hear about you losing your job, LJ. I'll see what I can do to help, okay?"

"Sure, whatever. Wanna speak to my pops?"

Arthur struggled to resist the urge to berate LJ for his insolent attitude, inarticulate speech, and calling him "Mr. OD." But what did he expect from a twenty-something, spoiled pot-head?

"Yes please, LJ, and you hang tight. I'll do my best to fix things."

"Okay, Mr. O'D. I'll get my old man."

LJ rolled off the bed, opened his bedroom door, and yelled down the stairs.

"Yo, Pops, it's for you!"

"Got it" came the answer from below.

LJ slammed the door, leapt back on his bed, and tapped the mute button, returning his stereo to concert volume.

* * *

Downstairs in the study, Dr. Lawrence Vale glared up at the ceiling. He shut the door, but it did little to quash the pulsating invasion from The Offspring's trademark guitar and drums of *Come Out and Play*.

He picked up the phone. "Lawrence Vale here."

"Larry, so sorry to interrupt your Monday Night Football."

Vale recognized the voice and knew Arthur O'Donnell didn't give a damn about interrupting anyone's night, football or otherwise.

"I was sorry to hear about LJ getting fired."

"Yes...I was too." Counting to himself, Vale made note of bullshit statement number two.

Vale regarded O'Donnell with equal parts loathing and dread. He'd known him since college, where he'd first witnessed Arthur perfecting his manipulation skills. Several years ago, Vale had gotten in over his head, trying to expand his practice and build his own medical facility. He'd found himself panicking as his financial overextension forced him toward a high-interest swing-loan. Then O'Donnell called out of the blue.

O'Donnell offered to help with a no-interest loan if Vale agreed to use his influence at the hospital to try a new line of biotech devices. At the time, it seemed to be a win-win situation; the loan saved him, and the new devices were effective. However, Arthur continued to call when he needed "favors," which usually pushed the boundaries of medical ethics, and sometimes the law.

Vale thought he was clear of Arthur until last year when LJ got into a serious jam with a drug arrest. Once again, Arthur called at just the right moment with an offer to help. In exchange for Vale accessing some medical records, O'Donnell pulled strings with the Orange County Sheriff's Office, and the case against LJ was dropped.

Then he got LJ a job at McNev, and for the past year, Larry began to have hope for his son's future.

He should have known better. When LJ bragged about getting a bonus for doing some "electrical surgery," as he'd called it, Larry knew Arthur was likely behind it. Vale had enough trouble with his son, and he was dreading the fresh misery about to come his way.

"Listen, Larry. I can get LJ reinstated. With back pay."

Vale thought he might avoid further trouble by declining his offer. "Thanks, Arthur, but you've done enough for him already. He doesn't need the money."

No luck. O'Donnell always used both carrot and stick. "Now Larry, I know you wouldn't want to see LJ prosecuted when that drug case suddenly gets reopened. Wouldn't you rather see him get his job back?"

Vale had to acquiesce. He knew LJ couldn't handle jail time, and Arthur had shared an extensive resume of the ruin he'd been forced to administer on those who'd refused his simple "requests."

"Okay, Arthur, what do you want?"

"Just a small favor. It's really quite simple."

Vale resigned himself to the inevitable. "I'm listening."

Arthur's tone was noticeably smoother. "Are you planning to be at Saddleback tomorrow for anything?"

Dr. Vale had been practicing Neurology at Saddleback until last year, when he'd moved his office to Hoag Hospital in Newport Beach. However, he was still known to see patients at Saddleback occasionally, and still knew some of the staff.

Vale sighed. "I wasn't planning to, but I have the feeling I will be."

Vale could picture O'Donnell smiling. "I need you to stop by tomorrow afternoon and see a patient. His name is Bradley Richmond. He's been at Saddleback since Friday night, with a concussion he sustained in a car crash. He's being released tomorrow afternoon."

Vale scratched his head. "Uh, Arthur, doesn't he have a treating physician?"

"Yes. A Dr. Meyer, do you know him?"

"I've heard the name, but never met him. He started at Saddleback after I'd left."

"Perfect. Dr. Meyer will be unavailable tomorrow afternoon. I need you to be at Saddleback at 2:00 p.m. Tell the staff you're covering for him, and you're there to discharge Richmond."

"And I don't want to know what's going to happen to Meyer, do I?"

Vale knew that response would get a reaction, and like clockwork, he heard Arthur's tone turn frosty.

"Nothing bad—but that's *not* your concern. I need you to prescribe Promethazine and Chlorpromazine. Be sure Richmond's given both upon release…And make the dosage a bit hefty."

Vale was tempted to ask O'Donnell when he'd taken up practicing medicine, but pissing Arthur off invariably resulted in added grief. He opted for a less personal gibe.

"Okay…Clearly, you want him out of it for a while. Has he had an allergic reaction, or is he suffering from motion sickness?"

"Don't be a smartass, Larry. I've done my homework. The Promethazine is being used as an antihistamine for a rash he got from the accident site, and the Chlorpromazine is for his concussion headaches. It's all very credible."

Vale never ceased to be amazed by how brilliant Arthur thought he was about everything.

"Arthur, I'm taking a big risk here. If another doctor reads the file and sees what I've prescribed, I'm not sure I…"

O'Donnell cut him off. "Damn it, Larry. No one is going to find out. I just need Richmond on hold for a couple of weeks. Write the prescriptions for fourteen days, with no refills, and it'll be fine. I'll be sure to have your name removed from his file...And you *don't* want to see LJ in prison, do you?"

Realizing he couldn't win, Vale said nothing and let Arthur finish. "His sister, Sheila, will be picking Richmond up. You need to be reassuring, but be firm with her that it's imperative her brother stay on the meds for the full two weeks. Just handle this for me, Larry, and I'll make sure nothing bad happens...and tell LJ to be in Darren Duke's office at the start of shift next Monday."

Vale had no trouble recognizing the implication behind *making sure nothing bad happens*. "Alright, I'll take care of it, Arthur."

After disconnecting, he set the phone on the desk and stared at it, trying to send bad vibes through the line to O'Donnell. He wondered who Richmond was, but really didn't want to know.

Vale leaned back in his chair, the conceited voice of Arthur in his head, bragging about the brilliant methods he'd employed over the years to manipulate people for his own success.

I seriously hope that someday, someone you screwed over, somehow takes you down...and I'd be first in line to lend a hand.

He got up to make himself another drink.

7

Tuesday, 6:55 a.m.

Porter sat in his beige Lumina, parked in the middle of an upscale neighborhood in northern Irvine. He'd arrived by 6:15, despite heavy freeway congestion, thanks to his practice of leaving early. He recalled the words of his first boss: "If you're early, you're on time. If you're on time, you're late."

As he waited, Bordon studied the large houses in the new tradition of California, featuring identical Spanish-style white stucco with red tile roofs. He was ruminating about the money people must spend to live in these long rows of homogeneous people-coops, when he spotted Dr. Meyer in his driveway, identifying him by the photo in the file provided by O'Donnell.

Meyer got into his silver Acura and drove off with Porter following at a discreet distance. As much as Arthur differed in demeanor from Crandall, the instructions he provided were equally vague. His assignment today was to "prevent Meyer from driving to work at Saddleback Medical Center in Laguna Hills," but O'Donnell told him the *how* was for him to figure out. Porter determined he would tail Meyer as he left home and play it by ear.

Meyer parked at a local coffee shop a couple of miles away, and Porter waited to see if the doctor was going to dine at the restaurant.

Once he saw Meyer sit down and order, Porter acted quickly. He opened Meyer's Acura with a Slim Jim, pulled the power and ignition wires from under the dash, and was touching stripped leads to jump the ignition interlock two minutes later. He relocated the car a few blocks away, in an industrial complex parking lot full of cars. Then he fast-walked back to the restaurant, breaking into a trot and cursing at himself for wearing boots.

His timing was perfect for the second time. He arrived as Meyer was standing in the coffee shop parking lot, looking bewildered and swearing. From that point, monitoring was all that was necessary.

Meyer called and waited for the police. The officer who arrived and completed the report also drove Meyer to the police station. Porter tailed them, keeping his distance, and the situation took care of itself. Meyer spent the better part of the day inside the station, until his vehicle was recovered by police late in the afternoon, after which he'd gone directly home.

The traffic on the return trip to Newport Beach gave Porter time to assess his day. Although he'd accomplished his assignment with commendable efficiency, his satisfaction gave way to a growing unease with the peculiar, ambiguous tasks.

* * *

Teri entered the conference room on the fourth floor of Building E3, for her last meeting at the end of a long day. She immediately noticed the mismatched dirty chairs and broken table, dismayed by the room's blatant state of disrepair since her Everett days.
Clearly, we're not overspending on facilities and maintenance.
She was joining a team of managers from Engineering and Manufacturing assigned to help oversee a new Employee Involvement program for reducing rework.

When Duke asked her to attend this meeting in his stead, she'd readily accepted, embracing the opportunity to meet some mid-level managers and gain operational insight. She arrived a few minutes early and introduced herself to a manager named Carl. While they were waiting for others to arrive, she asked Carl about an oddity she'd observed.

"I passed several large trash bins on wheels in the hallways. Are you in the middle of a housecleaning project to discard obsolete documents?"

Carl laughed. "No, ma'am. That's our latest cost-saving effort. They laid off the cleaning crews, so we empty our own trash cans."

Another manager arrived and joined their conversation. "Yeah, and if we want our bathrooms cleaned, we have to rotate by departments, for toilet duty and floor mopping. The only building that still has janitorial service is the 'palace' tower, because our VPs are *sooo special.*"

Carl blushed. "Uh, Dave, I'd like you to meet Teri Harlan. She's the new Deputy VP of Quality."

The red in Dave's cheeks was beginning to fade as the meeting started.

Carl, as chairperson, reported on the new program, called *kNOw Excuses*, being pilot-tested in an Assembly work team. The poorest performer for the week was required to stand in the center of a circle, surrounded by their coworkers—each of them telling him or her how they'd let the work team down.

Dave was about to review the results of the pilot test when Teri interjected, "Holy hell, guys. Are you kidding me?"

Everyone turned to her with varying looks of surprise.

Teri had expected to hear something similar to the Quality Circles concept that involved employees recommending improvements to their operation. She immediately regretted her hair-trigger reaction, but with all eyes on her she was committed to continuing.

"Are you seriously telling me your new improvement program is based on shaming employees for making mistakes? Does anyone even know the original concept of Quality Circles?"

Silence.

"Well, first of all, it has absolutely nothing to do with standing in a circle—especially this 'circle of shame' crap—that's ludicrous, and an insult to a valid concept."

The managers seemed genuinely interested as she explained QC details, agreeing that pursuing basic cost-benefit analysis could validate real improvements, such as replacement of drill bits and worn tooling.

The remainder of the discussion, however, left her concerned. Although they welcomed her ideas, the managers voted for this program to go ahead as designed. It had already been sanctioned by Felix Herrera, the union leader, and approved by Darren Duke.

As the session ended, Carl summarized, "Teri, you seem to have a fresh approach and great insight—especially for a VP..."

Everyone chuckled as another manager interjected, "Yeah, you even talk like a real person."

Carl finished his thought. "But I think I speak for all of us when I say, as much as we hope we're wrong, we don't think you have a snowball's chance in hell to change anything."

Walking back to the tower garage after the meeting, Teri was struck by the contrast between the Engineering buildings and the executive tower, recalling the manager's "palace" comment.

She'd had lunch today with the VP team in the tower's Executive Dining Room. Delicious fresh Red Snapper was prepared by the full-time chef, which the VPs seemed to take for granted, and after lunch, she was shown the adjoining executive gym. By comparison, the other buildings, including E3 where she was now, looked like impoverished countries.

As she walked across the third-floor bridge connecting E3 to E2, she stopped to look up at a burned fluorescent fixture with blackened ceiling panels and dangling, melted wires. A young engineer passing by paused when he saw her staring at it.

"Nice, huh? Yeah, the fixture caught fire, and Fire Services put it out, but I guess maintenance didn't get the memo to fix it. It's been like that for months."

* * *

Driving toward the 405, Teri tried to wrap her head around the management and culture changes she'd seen so far. The decline had been so disconcerting that she was losing focus on her plan for her first week accomplishments. The traffic congestion, however, gave her time to clear her mind, and when she reached the exit to Laguna Canyon Road, she turned her thoughts to the anticipation of seeing Rich.

Sheila told her on the phone he remained woozy and would likely need weeks to recover. But by the time she pulled into Sheila's driveway, Teri was visualizing a scene from a *Lifetime* movie, running to Rich, who embraced her and said soothingly, "I'm back, Teri. Everything is going to be fine."

A tiny portion of her fantasy turned out to be accurate. Rich was sitting on the couch, reading a book with Lisa, and he got up to give her a hug.

"Hi, Teri. Sheila told me you were staying with us. Sorry I don't remember much else, but it's good to see you."

Lisa was noticeably more enthusiastic.

"Aunt Teri!" Lisa shouted, as she wrapped her arms around Teri's legs. Lisa had started calling her "aunt," deciding it was a good thing to have two.

Over a dinner of pizza and salad, Teri and Sheila attempted to help Rich catch up. Teri told him about how hard he'd worked to coax her into returning for the new position as his deputy, and was considering sharing some of the issues she'd seen so far, when his quip brought her up short.

"Are you sure Art didn't plan this so you could take my job and he could fire me?"

He said it in jest, but with enough edge to be disconcerting, prompting her to think to herself, *Not much chance of him being helpful at this point.*

After dinner, Teri watched Rich drink a third beer after snapping at his sister for reminding him about the warning on his prescription to avoid alcohol. Teri was convinced Rich wasn't himself when he lit up a Camel Special Light. He'd told her that he quit three years ago, but now Rich was acting as if he'd always smoked.

Teri went for a walk after dinner, hoping the beachy vibe in downtown Laguna would assuage her disillusionment. But even though the bed in Sheila's spare room wasn't prohibitively uncomfortable, at 1:00 a.m. Teri's eyes were still wide open.

* * *

Bordon's introduction to the head of McNev Security, Antonio del Balso, made his Wednesday morning memorable. To account for Bordon's presence at McNev between tasks, O'Donnell had him assigned to the McNev Security Department.

Del Balso was two inches shorter than Porter, with thinning hair in contrast to copious eyebrows above a prominent nose. Porter got the impression that del Balso believed himself capable of emulating Joe Pesci in *Goodfellas*. He was fairly sure Mr. Pesci would disagree.

O'Donnell had instructed del Balso to set up an office for Porter in the Security building, under the guise that Bordon was a consultant from Corporate HQ, here to conduct a Security Audit. Porter guessed that hearing the word *corporate* associated with him somehow meant something to del Balso, because the first thing del Balso did was try to impress him.

"Hey, Bordon, wanna see the big time? My security team is major league. Come on, I'll show you."

Tony walked double-time out of the Security office toward the Control Center, requiring Bordon to jog slightly to keep up. He fell into step with del Balso's hyper-quick stride, as the Security Chief continued his speech, attempting to parrot O'Donnell's tone.

"First rule for all my people. Always walk like you got to be somewhere fast. If you hurry, people take you serious."

Porter just smiled.

They continued down a short flight of stairs, and del Balso opened a steel door, entering a small room with two officers seated at a console, surrounded by a bank of monitors. One officer was speaking into the microphone to another officer on patrol. The second officer flipped a switch on the screen in front of him, making Porter smile again as he saw a flash of a scantily clad woman disappear.

Tony said proudly, "Here's our Control Center—it's our brain trust!"

Porter was impressed by the technology: a state-of-the-art array, fed by cameras that covered office buildings, assembly areas, the flight ramp, and main access roads.

Glancing at his watch, Porter was trying to think of a way to excuse himself gracefully so he could go to lunch, when an urgent call came in.

"10-78 southwest exit—HR Building!"

Del Balso said, "10-78—that's a call for assistance—let's go! You can see how we kick ass!"

They jumped into Tony's Ford Explorer security vehicle parked outside the control room and roared off with full lights and siren. As they sped out of a south gate and across the parking lot, Tony excitedly briefed Porter—this time doing an admirable impression of *Alvin the Chipmunk* in a uniform.

"See, I assigned my guy, Jimmy, to stand outside the HR building at lunch time to nail these HR employees for using the public entrance. It's for retirees and spouses and we don't have no security officer. There's just this clerk who sits at a counter and buzzes people in. So, we told the HR employees a hundred times, don't use that entrance to leave for lunch—they gotta use a regular lobby. But nooo...they can't walk around two frickin' buildings. HR's so special, they keep using the shortcut. And today, Jimmy is out there writing them citations!"

"So these employees are just trying to save a few minutes getting to their cars to go for lunch?"

"Yep—and that, my friend, is a major security violation. And I betcha one of them tried to make a break for it!"

Porter tried to fathom how leaving for lunch could possibly be considered a "major violation," thinking this foolishness was not only an overreaction, but also potentially dangerous. He shook his head and flipped the toggle switch, shutting off the siren, then looked sideways at del Balso. Doing his best to remain respectful, Bordon said, "I don't think the siren's really necessary, Tony."

Tony stayed quiet but shot Porter a look as he raced the Explorer toward a young female employee in a green windbreaker who was hurrying to her car.

Using the mic for the loudspeaker, he shouted, "You in the green jacket! Stop right there!"

Del Balso screeched to a halt and jumped out as Jimmy came trotting across the lot from the HR building, gasping for breath. They confronted the employee like they were making an arrest. The terrified young woman backed against her car, shaking and on the verge of tears.

Porter exited the Explorer as well, trying to deescalate the situation. As he approached the three of them, he said, "Miss, it's okay." He turned to Tony. "Tony–Chief del Balso, why don't you let this poor girl be on her way? I believe she learned her lesson."

Del Balso was having none of it. "No way! She disregarded Jimmy."

Jimmy took a step toward her, attempting intimidation. "Yeah, she didn't stop when I told her—she's getting double citations."

Porter rolled his eyes as del Balso continued. "I'm sick of these entitled HR *inetto* employees, thinking they can disrespect our rules."

He turned to the employee to enlighten her.

"*Inetto*. It means useless. As in, your *inetto* butt is mine now, girlie. You're coming with us to the Security office. Jimmy, here, is gonna write you up and escort you to your supervisor."

Porter stepped in front of him to help the young woman, whose facial complexion mirrored a whiteboard, into the rear seat of the Explorer. As the four of them rode back to the Security Center, what bothered Porter more than the total nonsense of the situation was the look of smug satisfaction on del Balso's face.

Back at Security Administration, Porter accompanied the distraught employee as Jimmy escorted her into the office. Mary, the lead Security Administrator and the one genuinely decent person he'd met in the department, was sitting at her desk near the door, and looked up at the three of them with a questioning expression.

Porter said, "Mary, I think this young woman could use someone with a heart."

8

Wednesday, 4:40 p.m.

Set aglow by the spotlight of a setting sun, the haze layered against the San Joaquin Hills assumed a color suited perfectly to Orange County. The day shift had ended more than an hour ago, leaving the Final Assembly hangar too quiet and too dim for Mac McKinley's taste.

A small crew was working second shift, but not on the aircraft Mac was about to enter: Ship 916, an ME-420 Widebody, in the third position on the final line. There were no engines, but the wings were joined to the fuselage, and the interior installation was in progress.

Mac climbed the portable stairs used by assembly mechanics, and entered through the cargo door. The forward cargo compartment, directly below the passenger cabin, was about eighteen feet in length and ten feet across. A single work light provided the only illumination. There was just enough headroom for Mac to stand upright, but anyone over five-feet-nine would have to crouch to avoid cracking their head on the exposed structural beams in the passenger cabin floor, or "ceiling" of the cargo compartment.

He walked gingerly to avoid slipping on the rows of cargo rollers set into tracks on the floor. Halfway down the side, opposite the open hatch, was an unattached interior panel. He moved the panel to expose the aircraft frame. The frame was made up of curved metal "ribs," structural members to which the exterior skin panels were riveted during assembly, forming the fuselage barrel structure.

These ribs ran vertically, along the curvature of each fuselage section, evenly spaced approximately twenty-four inches apart. Unlike the passenger cabin where interior panels follow the fuselage curvature, in the cargo compartment these panels are perpendicular to the floor. This leaves a space known as a "tunnel" between the vertical panels and the curved fuselage, used for such things as running wire bundles and hydraulic lines. There were also insulation blankets against the fuselage, similar to fiberglass insulation between studs in house framing.

The unattached side panel happened to be for a tunnel section that was currently empty, and taking advantage of his compact size, Mac was able to squeeze in, pressing himself against the insulation blanket. He set the loose panel in front of him, covering himself for the most part.

It was far from comfortable. There was no room to move to his left or right, and he had to turn his feet sideways because there was almost no space where the panel met the bottom of the fuselage.

His reasons for doing this did not include loyalty to Duke. After an hour of verbal abuse earlier today, Duke's bottom-line message was: *Eliminate the latest string of electrical problems, or you're out.* Although Mac knew Duke couldn't really fire him, this was the most direct threat he'd made.

As always, Duke blamed the problems on incompetent mechanics "screwing up his airplanes." Mac had been tempted to ask Duke if he actually owned all these ME-420s, as he invariably referred to them with possessive pronouns.

In Mac's considerable experience, problems were more likely attributed to factors such as worn tooling, broken equipment, or lack of proper training, rather than the workmanship of assembly mechanics. These were the real-work details Duke neither understood, nor had any interest in.

But what made Mac so angry he could spit rivets was that in this situation, Duke actually appeared to be right—at least, about a few of the latest problems.

LJ Vale had recently been terminated after being caught in an ME-420 electrical power center with a pair of bolt cutters, a tool with no conceivable use in aircraft assembly. In addition, two days ago, an assembly mechanic reported overhearing coworkers discussing plans to clip wire bundles running through the cargo compartment tunnels. Mac called a meeting with his supervisor staff to discuss the best way to stop the apparently well-planned sabotage.

Direct action wasn't his first choice, especially being older, but contacting McNev Security was not a viable option. After the merger, O'Donnell brought del Balso in from his former company and appointed him Director of Security. Mac had watched most of the competent security officers get replaced by del Balso's cronies. It was a safe bet that involving del Balso's Security team would result in a swarm of armed goons keeping potential perpetrators from showing themselves, while significantly increasing the odds that someone could be shot.

Agreeing that intentional damage would most likely be attempted on second shift, Mac and his three supervisors had been rotating stakeouts of the planes in final positions, in the quiet period after shift change. Mac hadn't looked forward to his turn tonight, and now his discomfort level was rapidly catching up to his annoyance.

Before Mac had time to ponder further, he heard footsteps coming up the stairs into the compartment. With his right eye, he looked through the gap along the side of the unattached panel, and recognized Reiss and Davis, two of Vale's co-mechanics in a second-shift work crew.

Cursing his luck for drawing this rotation, Mac steeled himself, struggling to regulate his breathing as his pulse answered the jolt of adrenaline. Davis and Reiss began using electric screwdrivers to remove a panel across from where Mac was hiding. Davis pulled a set of heavy-duty wire cutters from his coveralls and reached for the wire bundle behind the panel. They had their backs to Mac, focused on the task at hand.

Mac burst from his hiding place with a loud *crash*, as the panel hit the floor, and yelled, "All right you two morons, you're busted!"

Echoing off the compartment wall panels, his shouting caused the two mechanics to spin around, dropping their tools. Davis drew a work knife from another coverall pocket. It had a ten-inch, razor-sharp, curved blade, looking like a miniature samurai sword in the low light. This was something Mac hadn't anticipated.

Davis was north of six feet, and although slender, he looked intimidating as he stalked toward Mac, waving the knife. Mac's back was against the wall, and the two men were between him and the door. His mind raced, thinking up his next move. He looked Davis in the eye, trying to sound empathetic. "C'mon, Davis, don't be stupid. Put the knife away."

When Davis hesitated, Mac took advantage. He lunged forward, and just as he'd hoped, Davis reacted by lurching upright to dodge him. His head made a sickening *thud* as he smacked it on the exposed beam directly above him. He fell to the floor, dropping the knife, and lay there, groaning.

Mac shook his head. *Tall guys never learn.*

Reiss turned and bolted for the door, figuring Mac couldn't get past the now-prone Davis fast enough to stop him. As many times as they'd talked in safety meetings about exercising care in cargo compartments, Reiss apparently never listened. His feet flew out from under him as he slipped on the floor rollers, resulting in a perfect face-plant.

Despite the blood running from Reiss's nose, he scrambled up, reached the exit, and ran smack into Al Greer, a supervisor who worked for Mac. At six-four and pushing three hundred pounds, Al wasn't someone you slipped past.

"Why don't you sit down for a minute, Reiss?"

Al shoved him back inside onto the floor rollers, and this time Reiss stayed there.

Al looked at Mac. "You all right, old man?"

"Don't be a wise-ass, Greer. Go call Security."

"I already did."

Still chuckling, Al helped Mac get the two mechanics on their feet. A small second-shift crowd gathered as security officers arrived, driving their vehicle into the hangar with lights flashing in a typical display of excess.

As the officers escorted Reiss and Davis to their vehicle, Greer turned to the crowd. "Forgot to wear their safety glasses…Now, let's get back to work." He and Mac smiled as a couple of mechanics clapped.

* * *

Porter found himself stuck in hold-mode again, this time in the east parking lot past the Final Assembly hangar. As he waited in his beige Chevy Lumina rental car, Bordon mulled over the earlier incident, wondering what had happened to the young employee when Jimmy escorted her to her supervisor.

Loyalty had always been a core value for Porter. Accepting the McNev contract came with the serious responsibility of protecting both McNeil and the company. But since accepting O'Donnell's assignment, he'd started to be concerned about McNev's operations here in Orange County.

As he considered the idea of looking into things on his own, a compact, athletic-looking black man walked slowly to a Chevy Blazer parked in the next aisle. He was wearing a white shirt with a large tear, open at the collar, and carrying his tie. Porter looked at the badge photo he was holding of Norton McKinley. *Yep, that's him. Damn, looks like he's had a hard day.*

Porter followed the Blazer out of the parking lot, down the main boulevard, and onto the 405 freeway.

Back on the damn 405 again. Hope it's less crowded this time.

* * *

Just past Wilmington, traffic on the northbound 405 came to halt.

"Dammit," Mac swore out loud. "Not tonight. Not after the day I've had."

He switched on his radio in time to catch the traffic update, reporting an overturned big-rig at Hawthorne, about eight miles ahead. After ten minutes gained him less than half a mile, Mac eased over into the only moving lane, the transition to the 110 North. He didn't notice a beige sedan behind him, making the same move.

Mac hadn't taken this route home in more than a year. He lived in a quiet section of Inglewood near Westchester. In the last couple of years, he hadn't used the 110 because his exit off that freeway took him west through the devastation left from the riots.

He'd been at work, over forty miles south of Inglewood, the day the Rodney King trial verdicts were announced, and riots broke out. That day topped his list of worst days ever. He'd spent more than seven hours getting home to his wife, all the while terrified of what he might find. Fortunately, his wife and his home were safe. But he'd never forget the night sky filled with flames and smoke of nearly one-thousand burning buildings just miles away. It felt like a cataclysm.

He exited the 110 Freeway now, heading west. Passing vacant lots and boarded-up buildings brought a heaviness to his chest. Soon he was staring straight ahead, lost in thoughts inflamed by his anguish from two years ago.

About halfway through the ten-mile stretch of four-lane boulevard to Inglewood, Mac stopped at a red light. The smallish cross street was relatively quiet. Next to him was a lowered '64 Impala convertible with a gray primer finish, highlighted by touches of poorly applied yellow paint.

Four twenty-somethings were slunk low in the seats, listening to Dr. Dre's "Nuthin' But a 'G' Thang"—shared with the population of South Los Angeles via a two-hundred-watt car stereo. Mac's window was down, enabling a clear view of the occupants.

All four young men turned to stare at him. Mac returned their glares with an impassive expression, keeping his thoughts to himself. *I'm really glad my grandson is still young enough I can forbid him to listen to rap music.*

He looked ahead as the light turned green, but the car ahead of him didn't move. The convertible remained alongside him, even as the car in front of it drove away. He glanced quickly in his rearview mirror, to see a third car nearly touching his rear bumper. The four young men exited the Chevy, hopping over the sides in a sort of synchronized vault. Mac's gut assimilated the situation a split second before his head.

The driver walked around the front of his convertible toward Mac's truck and slid back his jacket to reveal a revolver, complete with taped grip, tucked into his waistband. The occupants of the cars both ahead of and behind Mac stayed inside their vehicles. The kid with the weapon looked to be in his early twenties, and the oldest of the four. He stood next to Mac's open window and addressed him with contrived bravado.

"Hey man, nice truck. How 'bout you get the fuck out of it."

Mac met his eyes and replied with genuine sincerity, "Son, I've had a real bad day. Why don't you all just get back in your car, be on your way, and leave me alone?"

"Look, you fuckin' old Uncle Tom, you wanna do this the easy way or the hard way?"

Mac wasn't sure which of those adjectives made him angrier, but feeling old wasn't as troublesome as realizing his tire iron was no longer within reach. He'd kept it under his front seat for several months after the riots, but he'd changed a tire about a week ago and returned it to the back of his truck.

The three younger boys joined in, flaunting their extensive vocabulary of epithets, and banging the side of his Blazer. The leader reached for Mac's door handle. Mac hadn't yet figured out what he was going to do, but he knew he'd run out of time to consider options.

His thoughts were derailed by two loud *cracks* from behind, instantly commanding everyone's attention. The four teens turned in unison and stared, frozen in silence.

About three car-lengths back, in the middle of the street, sat a beige Chevy Lumina. Next to it stood a man of medium height, powerfully built, with short-cropped gray hair, dressed in a business suit with gray boots. He was holding a Glock 21 .45 ACP with both hands, pointed skyward, the retort of the shots still echoing.

He spoke loudly, in a professional *you better believe I mean what I say* voice.

"Hey! Dickheads! Yeah, you four! Are you gonna get away from that truck, or do you wanna try me?"

The man stood with his feet apart, saying nothing more, but watching them intently. Assuming a two-handed shooting stance, he brought the handgun down, aiming at the apparent leader next to Mac's door. He moved deliberately, training the Glock on each of the other three in turn, and then at the car behind Mac.

All four underwent an immediate transformation, suddenly appearing several years younger.

Although they shared a collective expression reminiscent of deer in headlights, they did not remain frozen. They jumped into their Chevy, and the car screamed forward through the intersection, in an urban portrayal of escaping into the woods.

The car ahead of Mac did likewise, its tires squealing. The third car pulled around his Blazer and over the sidewalk, accelerating around the corner, out of sight.

Mac rose from the prone position he'd assumed on the front seat when he'd seen the man pointing a gun in his direction. He was not about to stick around to see what was going to happen next. He stomped on the gas pedal, and his truck charged from the right lane across to the left lane, where he turned left at the intersection in a reprise of squealing tires.

Mac caught a glimpse of the man still standing in the street, lowering the Glock, and shaking his head. He looked vaguely familiar.

Mac drove several blocks south before he became aware that he had no idea where he was headed. The adrenaline diminished slightly, but he hadn't calmed down. He pulled over for a moment to gather himself, taking several deep breaths and trying to stop shaking.

Don't know what I would've done if that guy hadn't come along.

Slightly more composed, he turned around and drove back to the intersection. There was no sign of anything that had just happened. He visualized himself lying there while his truck was being joy-ridden, and cursed to himself.

Maybe I should be more like that guy in the street...Who was he? I know I've seen him somewhere.

9

Friday, 5:50 a.m.

Porter headed to the plant with remarkable energy, considering his troublesome Thursday had been compounded by an essentially sleepless night. Yesterday had begun at a low point, being summoned to the ninth floor by O'Donnell to report on McKinley. O'Donnell had been contentious from the start, challenging Porter's decision to save Mac from impending disaster.

"Why? Why in the world would you do that? If you hadn't stepped in, the McKinley problem would have solved itself!"

Porter left O'Donnell's office with those words echoing in his head, generating a mix of fury, confusion, and doubt. He'd spent the rest of yesterday morning questioning why he'd silently submitted to O'Donnell's reprimand, why he'd even agreed to work for him, and why the final stretch of his chosen career path appeared to be leading directly into a pit of quicksand.

His stress level diminished slightly when he had lunch with Mary. They shared war stories and Mary's refreshing up-front honesty put him at ease, surprising him by how quickly he'd felt a rapport with her. He learned that Mary had also worked closely with Hugh McNeil a few years back, performing undercover investigations at McNeil Aerospace. Her exceptional skills led to exposing a managerial crime ring in electrical assembly that was reselling stolen high-tech components.

The fallout included the firing of a security manager involved in the cover-up, and unfortunately led to a hostile work environment. She'd told Porter how grateful she'd been to Hugh for transferring her out west when her son had gotten accepted at UCI.

Although Porter didn't disclose his time spent inside Joliet prison, or the Chicago assignment, he'd felt comfortable enough to share a couple of memorable moments, like June of '74 when he'd escaped capture after being "sidelined by anti-union consultants." And because his morning was still gnawing at his insides, he'd chosen to confide his apprehension with his assignment from O'Donnell to sideline McKinley. He'd explained his intervention—"I couldn't stand by and watch a felony carjacking, especially against one of our employees, problem or not"—expecting her to be supportive of his actions. But her reaction caught him off guard.

Not only had she looked upset, but her reply had stung. "Oh, I see. An enforcer with ethics."

Porter's initial reaction had been defensive anger, but before he'd said anything, she explained that McKinley was an outstanding Final Assembly Director, revered by his employees and loyal to a fault. As she continued, Porter felt his anger and frustration building not only toward O'Donnell but himself.

Going against his self-imposed edict of keeping his assignments private, his gut pushed him to ask her what she knew about Richmond. Hearing similar specifics of a competent, devoted executive, Porter's throat had tightened to the point of near panic.

He'd spent last night in deeper reflection than any he could remember. Porter suffered no illusions; he'd hurt people more than once. But he'd spent years convincing himself he was justified in what he'd done. And once again, when Crandall asked, he'd jumped at the chance for action, assuming he was on the right side and following orders. Only this time, his assumption and actions appeared to have been nearly dead wrong.

Somewhere past two a.m., he awoke from a fitful dream, sat bolt upright in a cold sweat, and threw off the covers. His brain fog gradually cleared as the vision of staring into the dust-filled ravine faded, leaving him with the same sick-to-his-stomach sensation.

Listening to Mary had been a powerful eye-opener. He hadn't even known that McKinley went by Mac instead of Norton, or that everyone called Bradley Richmond, "Rich." He realized he hadn't known anything at all. And yet he'd nearly killed someone. It was time to throw away his rose-colored glasses and take responsibility for his actions.

Before he showered this morning, he'd said a prayer of thanks that Richmond had pulled through. By the time he'd finished dressing and had coffee, his real assignment became clear: He had to help set things right for McNeil, McNev, and for Rich Richmond.

* * *

Friday-light morning traffic moved quickly, matching Porter's approach to his new agenda. During their conversation yesterday, Mary had mentioned her friend, Al Greer in Final Assembly, one of McKinley's supervisors who thought the world of him. He remembered Mary's words, "Al's definitely my kinda guy—straight shooter, no bullshit."

He decided a conversation with Greer would be a good way to begin his own investigation; Greer sounded like someone he could relate to.

Porter arrived outside Final Assembly in time to catch a group of mechanics entering the hangar at the start of the first shift. Several of them knew Greer, directing him to the wallboard, shack-like office structure in the middle of the Final Assembly floor. He found Al's tiny office and knocked, greeted by a loud, "What's up?"

He opened the door to find Al, who barely fit behind his desk, motioning for him to come in. Although built like an NFL lineman, Al's smile put Porter at ease.

Bordon introduced himself, sticking with O'Donnell's premise that he was from HQ conducting a security audit of the McNev production facility, without mentioning him by name. Porter embellished a bit, adding that McNeil had requested he get the "real lowdown" from McNev's workforce, as an entrée to garner hopefully useful information.

Al was quiet for a moment, appearing to be sizing Porter up, then offered an unsolicited critique of McNeil.

"He leads the entire corporation, but he's been a total ghost out here. Our employees would love to see Mr. Hugh 'High-Horse' take some interest in the troops, now that his almighty corporation took over."

Porter's response was authentic, having spent significant time observing the Chairman.

"Honestly, Al, I'd have to say McNeil's a decent enough guy. Yeah, he's definitely focused on the bottom line, but I believe he really does care about employees. I haven't seen him operate like typical asshat executives, and believe me, I seen more than my share of those!"

Porter couldn't resist throwing in a comment about his pet peeve.

"The one thing that really bugs me about McNeil though, is how much he loves his computer. I see him in his office doing I-don't-know-what on that damn thing. I just don't get it."

Al turned, pointing at the Compaq Pentium Deskpro sitting on a table behind his desk. It was completely covered in a mountain of paperwork. He grinned. "Don't have much use for computers myself. Spend most of my time out on the floor, getting my hands dirty."

Porter noticed Al's body language relax slightly, recognizing some common ground. Al suggested they walk the assembly floor while they talked. Stopping next to a sixty-foot-long wing, Al asked, "Ever wonder how they get the wings attached to the fuselage?"

Porter whistled in amazement, watching the massive structure being rolled into place on a motorized stand with vertical hydraulics to position the wing with the fuselage jigs, enabling inch-by-inch precision alignment for the join.

As they walked, Al opened up to Porter about cost-cutting and staff reductions since the merger creating the vicious cycle of problems and rework. He went on a rant about Duke.

"He manages the place like it's his kingdom, and the planes are his personal property. The prick spends most of his time zooming female assembly workers…inviting them to an after-shift 'meeting.' That sonofabitch spends truckloads of money turning his office into some kind of private club, while I can't get new drill bits for my crews. Meanwhile

Duke and the other genius VPs save money by cutting out maintenance. Our Marklifts, there, are the perfect example."

Al pointed to a work platform with a railing, sitting on a hydraulic scissor-lift mechanism. The entire apparatus was on wheels and motorized. They were driven into place to elevate assembly mechanics ten to thirty feet above the floor for working on the tail, horizontal stabilizers, or cargo doors.

He said, "Let me tell you about Sammy, one of my mechanics, getting an unexpected thrill ride. Sammy's working on the tail section, some twenty feet up on the lift, when all of a sudden, *bam!* With no goddamn warning, the hydraulic pressure gives out, and the thing drops fifteen feet! Sammy hits the floor of the platform, spread-eagle, holding on for dear life, as the lift bounces like a bungee cord before it finally stops. Scared the livin' shit outta him, I can tell you that!"

Al paused for dramatic emphasis. "Sammy wasn't hurt, thank God, but I been havin' one helluva time finding mechanics willing to work on a lift. What I'd love to see before I quit or die is dickless Duke up on one of these maintenance nightmares, and watch it drop *him*! Maybe he'd see more clearly what people who do *real* work around here have to put up with every day."

At a pause in their conversation, a position manager walked up, asking if Mac was here today. Al excused himself and turned to the manager.

"Nope, he's still out." Al hit the highlights of Mac's near miss car-jacking for the manager, ending with, "Yeah, I believe the old man may have gotten in a world of hurt if it hadn't been for some crazy dude that came along with a big-ass handgun…Called him his Rambo guardian angel."

Porter turned to watch the mechanics working on the wing join, pretending not to listen.

Before they parted ways, Porter asked Al if he knew of any trouble in Final Assembly he could share.

"Yeah, we caught two idiots a couple nights ago." He gave Porter a quick recap of the Reiss and Davis incident, adding, "If you want my opinion, it starts and ends with Herrera, the scum-sucking head of the mechanics union—His middle name is trouble."

Porter thanked Al, and walked back through the hangar, mulling over what he'd heard.

It was obvious that McNeil, sitting in his cozy corporate office in Texas, had no clue about the chaos in his plant out here.

Hearing from Mary about McKinley and Richmond, plus his conversation with Al, were more than enough to confirm that Crandall and O'Donnell lied to him. But he had no idea why they seemed to want capable, loyal executives put in harm's way.

EXECUTIVE MALICE 69

Don't have a clue what they're up to…except it smells bad, and I seem to be stepping in it.

* * *

Bordon reached the end of the hangar and was about to exit through the access door, when he heard voices coming from behind a fuselage jig in the corner. Recognizing an opportunity to attain candid information, Porter stepped quietly around the far side of a massive support stand where he could hear without being seen.

He spotted two men with their backs to him, talking quietly in what looked to him like a shady conversation. One was stocky, middle-aged, and used-car-salesman-slick, dressed in casual business attire not suited for working on planes. The other was in his early twenties, judging by his acne and slender build. He was dressed in raggedy jeans and a torn Metallica t-shirt, complemented by his stringy shoulder-length hair.

"It's all good now, Mr. Herrera. Tell him thanks for me."

"Yeah, LJ, I guess the boss thinks you're still worth something. Me, I'm not so convinced."

LJ said, "Whatever…see ya."

Herrera grabbed his arm.

"Hey—you don't walk away from me! You still gotta hold up your end…the special second-shift job? Here's the Change Order for Ship 913—the custom install for Tailia."

He shoved a multi-page document into LJ's hands.

"I signed you up with the usual crew. This is on direct orders from HQ—J.C. William from Corporate authorized it, so don't screw it up. Here's the door-lock failsafe assembly for the forward cargo door."

He handed LJ a small mechanical device with a motor and actuating arm, and continued talking as LJ looked bored and turned away.

"Hey, asswipe, don't forget! The existing electrical connector won't work in the circuit with this new mechanism. You need to use one of those E-1101 plugs I gave you. I could only swipe two of them from salvage without that old fart, Stanley, noticing, so don't lose 'em…you still got 'em in your locker?"

"Dude, chill. I got 'em," LJ mumbled as he tried to walk away again. Herrera stopped him once more.

"Damn it, LJ, this is important! Do this right and there's a huge paycheck in it for you, but fuck it up, and you're history for sure—got it?"

"Okay, okay…jeez." LJ pulled away from Herrera and disappeared down the aisle.

10

Friday, 4:50 p.m.

"Don't start with your bullshit again! I don't care how much you're paying me...how do I know this is for McNev, and not more backdoor crap for your personal schemes?"

Sheila stared at the National Park calendar on her kitchen wall without seeing it, seething as she listened to the voice on the other end of the line. She continued, acrimony driving her words. "I already explained that! He's still dazed. He doesn't remember anything about it...no, I don't think he'll be safer this way!"

She took a breath, trying to control herself.

"You were behind his accident, weren't you? You sonofabitch...how can I think that? How about what happened to Beth four years ago? Yes, I'll finish your damn interface program. And then we're done. All over—forever!"

Sheila slammed down the receiver, wishing it were O'Donnell's head. At the same moment, she heard Teri's voice as she came in the front door.

"Sheila? You home?"

"Hi, Teri. You're home early."

"Yep, I finished my last meeting at three-thirty, and told myself, 'Hey, it's Friday, I'm leaving.'"

Teri took off her blazer and heels, about to sit on the loveseat.

Sheila turned back toward the kitchen and spoke over her shoulder. "I'm gonna make myself an Absolut and cranberry juice. You want one?"

"*Absolutely*," Teri replied, following Sheila into the kitchen.

Teri noticed Sheila's grim expression, and the lack of response to her smart remark. Attempting to sound upbeat, she asked, "So, is Rich any better today?"

"Not really," Sheila sighed. "He seems edgier. He's out back in the workshop, playing with Lisa."

They sat at the kitchen table. Teri nodded her thanks as she took her drink and tried sounding reassuring. "Well, didn't his doctor say this might happen?"

Sheila took a large swallow before replying, "Yeah, but that doesn't mean I'm not worried sick about him."

Her brusque response told Teri to keep her thoughts to herself. *Like you're the only one who's concerned? This hasn't exactly been a fun week around here for any of us...*

In addition to worrying about Rich, she'd been struggling to get up to speed at McNev. The tension in Sheila's cute little house had been as thick as the nightly fog rolling in.

For the past few evenings around this same table, Teri had talked about her day, hoping for Rich's counsel, but getting only a distracted, disturbing version of him. Rather than the challenges facing their company, Rich recounted the VPs' antics, focused predominately on their sexual escapades.

Among other unhelpful things, he'd told her, "I know Darren Duke—he's got one thing in that tiny brain of his…getting under your skirt. You'd better watch yourself around him." As if she hadn't been able to figure that out on her first day.

He was treating Teri like a different person, acting as if she'd taken the job at McNev to replace him as VP, using flirtation and sexual innuendo.

When she'd told him the executive team expressed their concern for him, Rich had replied with a mock cough. "Yeah, right, sure they did. That's why Art hasn't called me."

The following night, when Teri shared Arthur's compliments about her first week's contributions, instead of being pleased, Rich appeared unimpressed. And hearing the news that O'Donnell and Winton planned to announce her as Acting Quality VP until his return elicited such a look of devastation that Teri experienced guilt rather than pride.

But when she'd mentioned her invitation to join them on Winton's boat this Saturday, his unexpected and tasteless reaction made her want to slink under the table.

Rich had jumped up, shouting, "Teri, they just want to screw you! Can't you see that? They're sucking you into their game! And you like it, don't you? I'll bet you can't wait to get out on his boat and enjoy the ride!"

Fortunately, Lisa had been in her room and hadn't heard his outburst. While Teri and Sheila stared at Rich, dumbstruck, he'd sat down just as suddenly, looking ashamed of himself, putting his head in his hands and apologizing profusely. "I…I don't even know where that came from."

But his apology hadn't helped much, and last night, Teri ended up crying herself to sleep.

Replaying the week of misery as she stared at the ice in her Absolut cranberry cocktail, Teri sighed and slowly shook her head, catching a tear just short of escaping. She was looking at Sheila but paying little attention, consumed by her own thoughts.

Rich knows I'd never take his job, and he must know I would never…with Jackson or Arthur. Now suddenly he thinks I'm some sort of career whore?

Sitting across the table, Sheila was mirroring Teri, staring past her, oblivious to Teri's glistening eyes. Sheila suddenly broke their silence, blurting out, "Maybe it's those pills he's taking for that rash on his neck...You think that could be it?"

Without waiting for an answer, Sheila continued her monologue.

"Remember? That new doctor—what's-his-name—Dr. Vale...he took over Rich's discharge. He said he needed to treat the allergic reaction, as well as help him recover. What is that stuff he's taking?"

Sheila hardly paused for breath. "I think it's called Prometh-a-something. Maybe it's reacting with the Chlorpro-mo—whatever the other shit is for the concussion. What do you think, Teri?"

"I don't know, you're the one who spoke to him."

Teri was only half-listening. *Where are the Sheila and Rich I used to love working with?*

Sheila had shown no interest in Teri's job and said nothing of her own project that seemed to keep her up all hours of the night. When Teri was at the house, Sheila kept herself unavailable, working or using Lisa as an excuse.

Teri tried more than once to ask questions about Rich's car accident, still pondering the potential for something nefarious. But each time she'd broached the subject, Sheila got agitated and found something urgent she had to do. Naturally, this added to Teri's suspicions. She'd gone to look up Mac yesterday to talk things over with him but found he'd taken the rest of the week off.

Teri looked at Sheila, trying to reconcile the current mess with her memories of her two long-time friends, putting their heads together and talking everything out. Her smoldering frustration erupted.

"Sheila! What the hell is going on? What's *wrong* with you?"

Caught off guard, Sheila met Teri's eyes for the first time in several days. Teri watched her expression change, struggling to hold in her emotions. Just as Sheila seemed on the verge of letting go, a loud *crash!* followed by the sound of breaking glass startled them. They jumped up simultaneously, running out of the kitchen door through the tiny yard to the garage.

* * *

In the back of the pre-war, single-car garage was a room not much larger than an oversized closet, that Rich had converted into a workshop. He'd constructed a workbench, scaled to fit the tiny space, and a pegboard wall to hang tools he'd brought with him when he and Lisa moved in. Lisa and Rich spent Sunday mornings there puttering and playing at building airplanes, sometimes using models and other times just playing with parts he'd brought home.

When Teri and Sheila burst into the workshop, Lisa was standing in the middle of the floor, crying. Rich was standing next to her with a blank look on his face. There were small tools, parts, and hardware scattered across the floor, along with shards of glass jars, shattered from Rich sweeping everything off the workbench in an apparent temper tantrum.

"She's fine," Rich snapped.

Sheila scooped Lisa up and took her out to the backyard, as Lisa clung to her aunt and sobbed. Rich turned to face Teri. His pain was as evident in his voice as on his face.

"I can't remember anything, Ter. I'm losing it. I don't feel like I'll ever be able to go back to work. I'm really *scared*. I can't even play with my own daughter anymore—What's happening to me?"

Teri walked to Rich and put her arms around him, and they stood there in the tiny workshop for a moment, in silence. Teri felt their closeness from long ago, but when their embrace started to become something more, she felt awkward. She stepped back and Rich turned away, appearing flushed. He grabbed the broom and began sweeping while she started picking up parts.

He broke their silence. "I'm really afraid something terrible is gonna happen to you."

"What, Rich? Why would anything happen to me?"

"Dammit, that's the problem. I can't remember! But I have this feeling I'm involved too…and whatever it is, it's my fault."

Teri said, "It's going to be all right," the very words she'd desperately wanted to hear from him. As she picked up a pair of pliers to hang them on a hook, she sensed Rich becoming more like his old self, recognizing a sincerity she'd not seen since their time at Everett years ago.

When he spoke, his words were soft and deliberate. "I'm sorry for the way I've acted lately. It's like I'm somebody else, looking at myself from outside. I hear me saying things I don't recognize, even detest. I can't seem to focus, and when I try to remember the past few weeks, I hit a fog bank. I'm tired all the time, and when I sleep, I have horrible dreams."

"Can you share one? Maybe it could shed some light on things."

"I see Karolyn and O'Donnell in some kind of clandestine meeting. I see Winton chasing you, and I'm trying to save you, but it's like I'm running in quicksand."

"Karolyn Babcock? I barely met her, but she seems harmless. And Arthur and Jackson have been perfect gentlemen…I promise."

He said, "I know it sounds nuts."

Teri smiled at him. "Maybe not. Sometimes dreams are signs of something your subconscious is trying to figure out."

"If I tell you the one from last night, you'll really think I'm crazy."

"Try me."

"You and I were lying in the bottom of the cargo compartment of an ME-420. Sheila was standing in the cabin with O'Donnell, looking down at us through the access door. He was pointing a gun at us while she cried hysterically."

Teri gave him a contemplative look, choosing not to share her thoughts. *He's right...that's pretty out there. Maybe his subconscious picked up on Sheila's weird behavior.*

She let her breath out slowly, and tried to be supportive. "Let's not forget that you're recovering from head trauma. You need to give yourself a chance to heal...and you can rest assured, I haven't seen any indication of some deep, dark secret at McNev." After pausing, she added, "But it's definitely screwed up—you were right about that."

Rich smiled. "Well, hopefully I'll be able to come back soon and help."

Teri almost let herself feel optimistic as Rich took her hand and led her back through the yard into the kitchen. Sheila had calmed Lisa down, and Rich took his daughter into the living room for a few quiet moments as Sheila and Teri started dinner.

* * *

Rich sat on the loveseat with Lisa in his lap, talking to her and quietly apologizing. "I'm sorry, Ladybug. I haven't been feeling very well since my car accident. But I love you more than anything in the whole world, and nothing will ever change that."

He held her close for another moment and then gently flipped his finger on her nose, making her giggle. They held hands and walked to the kitchen to join Teri and Sheila.

Lisa returned to her bouncy self when Sheila asked for her help making her favorite dinner: tacos. Lisa was in charge of stirring the ground beef. As they worked together on the final touches of lettuce and cheese, the cloud of tension seemed to have dissipated.

In her first enjoyable dinner with them, Teri noticed Rich wasn't smoking, appearing the closest to normal since his accident. When they finished, Rich took Lisa to start her bath, and Teri heard them laugh as Rich tickled his daughter going up the stairs.

When he returned to the kitchen after tucking Lisa in, Rich and Teri had their first meaningful conversation about the state of McNev. Rich also apologized to his sister, but chose not to mention his dream of her holding them at gunpoint.

Teri said, "Sheila, I really enjoyed dinner tonight...I've missed being able to talk like this."

Rich rapped his knuckles on the table in a sudden insight. "You know, I just realized I got so involved this afternoon in the workshop with Lisa, I forgot to take my meds, and I'm actually feeling better! I wonder if the dosage could be too high. Maybe I should back off and see what happens."

Energized, Teri jumped into problem-solving mode. "Do you think missing your meds led to your outburst? Or maybe releasing your frustration cleared your head."

Before they got any further, Sheila interjected. "Well, I'm glad you're doing better, but Dr. Vale said you should stay on both meds through next week. I'll be happy to call him tomorrow, but let's not jump into any rash decisions, okay?" She abruptly pushed her chair back from the table and stood up. "I've got to get back to work. This miserable project is driving me crazy." Her voice died away as she headed upstairs to her workstation.

Appearing taken aback by his sister's brusque exit, Rich said, "Rash decisions—good pun...not like her to miss it."

He looked concerned as they both shook their heads.

When Teri excused herself to go for a walk, Rich decided to turn in. As he walked up the stairs, something flickered in his fractured memory. *That name, Vale, sounds so familiar.*

* * *

Bordon's information gathering had confirmed that most everything O'Donnell had been telling him, along with Crandall's original briefing, was total BS. But he was still no closer to understanding what they were up to, or why.

He'd returned to the Security office late in the day and asked Mary if she could give him O'Donnell's home address so he could perform a security check. He'd smiled at the look Mary gave him, letting him know she was able to recognize a tissue-thin pretext when she heard one.

After dinner, Porter looked up Arthur's address in the *Thomas Guide* street map book he'd purchased. Arthur, most likely inadvertently, had made things easy. The corporate apartment in Newport Beach that Arthur arranged for him was less than two miles from O'Donnell's own place on Balboa Island.

Porter changed into sweatpants and a sweatshirt, directing his evening run across the Balboa Bridge past the main drag to O'Donnell's house. If detected, he could feign coincidence of an innocent evening jog. On the other hand, with a little luck, he might turn up something useful.

He slowed when he reached Arthur's street, and shook his head at the multi-million-dollar homes with yards the size of postage stamps and all the privacy of a multi-block college dormitory.

Surveilling O'Donnell turned out to be a piece of cake for Porter. Although the patio entryway of his narrow house fronted the sidewalk that ran along the waterfront, with no place for anyone to stand without being seen, the back of the house and garage faced a relatively quiet street.

On the second story was O'Donnell's bedroom, with a full-wall sliding glass door opening to a large balcony above the garage and driveway.

Porter stood in the shadow of a mulberry tree across the street, with a perfect view of Arthur in his bedroom, which conveniently doubled as his office. The whole scene was easily visible, thanks to bright interior lighting. This not only made it effortless for Porter to observe O'Donnell, it also made it nearly impossible for O'Donnell to detect anything outside.

After an hour of watching O'Donnell working, Porter hadn't found anything useful. He was about to jog back to his apartment when he saw the most beautiful blonde woman walk out through the sliding glass door onto the balcony.

He found her attractiveness magnetic; sultry and athletic, blended to perfection. She stretched sensuously, looking up at the night sky. Porter stayed a while longer, transfixed.

She must be Charlie's fourth angel.

11

Saturday, 2:00 p.m.

The pneumatic closer on the door of the women's restroom in the Newport Marina emitted a soft *hiss* as it shut behind her. Inside, Teri chuckled to herself, reflecting on the month-end Excon financial review.

Rich's comments over the past week had gotten to her. When she'd walked into the McNev Board Room this morning, she'd half-expected to see VPs in masks and black robes, getting ready to tie her to the conference table and perform a sacrificial ritual.

The meeting, however, turned out to be uneventfully normal. The VP team welcomed her, expressing dismay over Rich's accident, and thanking her for stepping into his role under difficult circumstances.

O'Donnell began the session with a review of the monthly performance results, followed by Winton's speech on the need to continue cost cutting. Although it was a bit crude, she did enjoy Jackson taking Darren Duke to task for committing to cost reductions he hadn't made.

She was astonished, even considering the source, when Duke put his boots up on the conference table, appearing totally unconcerned. Then she smiled at O'Donnell's pointedly sharp humor when he told Darren he'd have to cover the next executive bonuses with his own money if he didn't get back on track.

The meeting finished with an update on the status of a sale to Tailia Air, the airline owned by TaiChin Industrial, a Far-East consortium that could potentially purchase twenty aircraft. This was an important customer, and Winton was personally involved.

Stepping into a changing stall, Teri pulled off her turtleneck sweater and unzipped the long skirt she'd worn to the meeting. She'd dressed ultra-conservatively for her first executive meeting, perhaps overly influenced by Rich's remarks.

Now the sun was out, and the day was turning beautifully into a classic Southern California afternoon. She slipped into shorts and a tank top, regretting her lack of a bathing suit and cover-up, but when she emerged from the restroom, Teri couldn't stop smiling. The marina shining regally under the Pacific Coast sun was a definite mood enhancer.

Walking down the cement path leading to the boat docks made her feel better about her return, soaking in the lifestyle of the Newport privileged.

The marina seemed to be making a statement that the local economy hadn't gone completely south. There was an exhibitionist feel of affluence, as beautiful people prepped their boats to enjoy the October Saturday afternoon.

I do love Southern California.

Her musings were interrupted by a loud wolf-whistle as she reached the ramp for Slip 18, where Winton's boat was docked. She was surprised to find it was coming from Winton, standing on the swim deck, waving at her.

* * *

Jackson E. Winton was on his third rum and tonic and feeling frisky. Winton liked to tell people his boat brought out the best in everyone, and then he would laugh, and say that was because every girl he brought out on his boat was the best he ever had...until the next one.

Winton knew he was born with a natural gift of humor. Everyone laughed at his jokes, except women. But he understood that, because a man can't expect women to grasp manly humor, and Winton was his own epitome of masculinity.

People who'd remarked that his "tall, dark, and handsome" physique was similar to O'Donnell had sometimes asked if he and Arthur were related. He wasn't quite as tall as Arthur, but he'd also been blessed with strong features, plus the added benefit of a high forehead and a rather dashing widow's peak, well-suited to the commanding look of a corporate leader. Even though he'd developed a small executive paunch, Winton knew he could have any woman he wanted, because privilege came with the power of his birthright, a born executive.

He and Arthur made a great team. O'Donnell lacked the qualities necessary to be in the number one spot, preferring to operate behind the scenes and appearing not to revel in the power of putting others into action. So Jackson let Arthur manage the boring numbers and interminable minutia, knowing Arthur relied on him to use his talent for authority to run things.

Winton had confidence in his second in command, because Arthur provided the know-how to keep him above the fray and save him time. His time was valuable. He need only look at his paycheck to know that.

Sailing held no interest for Winton. Learning the terminology and the myriad techniques was not an effective use of an executive's time. In addition, his Sea Ray 550 Sedan Bridge, with its five-hundred-fifty horsepower twin diesels, manifested virility, especially compared to a boat with canvas sails, which he regarded as borderline effeminate.

His Sea Ray got him maximum benefit with minimum effort, and he was now looking at something he'd just determined would be of great benefit to him this afternoon.

Earlier this morning, he'd had zero interest in Teri Harlan. She'd not only spoken like a technical expert, but her appearance had been all-business as well, with her hair pulled back and her body concealed by a sweater and long skirt. A body he was now able to appreciate.

Her hair was down, flowing in auburn waves that looked stunning against her navy-blue tank top, and her white linen shorts revealed long legs that could easily belong to a model.

The satiny sheen of the polyester top, highlighting her form, immediately seized Winton's attention. Staring as she walked closer, he conjured an image of Teri beneath it, and was caught off guard by the distention in his suddenly too-tight swim trunks. He realized he might be tiring of Karolyn, who'd been his executive perk going on two years.

Karolyn had certainly lived up to his high standards. Her abundant, naturally blonde hair, which fell past her shoulders, had a definite wild appeal. His attraction to Karolyn was reinforced by most of the senior executive team lusting after her.

Winton found it hilarious each time one of them would tell her she looked like Pamela Anderson. Karolyn never took that well, and he enjoyed watching her make it clear. Jackson chose to tell her she reminded him of Sharon Stone, which he'd found to have a consistently advantageous reaction.

He loved having Karolyn whenever he wanted, knowing the rest of his executive team could only fantasize. But today he decided he deserved a new executive privilege.

* * *

"Hi, Teri," Winton said too loudly, as he took her hand to help her onto the swim deck. "Where've you been? You're already two drinks behind…you've got some catching up to do."

As she stepped aboard, Teri experienced a flash of déjà vu from Duke's office. Winton's boat bore all the signs of too much money spent with too little taste.

She followed Jackson through the sliding glass door into the salon. Karolyn was sitting on a stool at the bar counter that separated the galley, and Arthur was working at the dinette table.

Looking over a planning document, O'Donnell was clad only in a nice-fitting pair of white Lands' End shorts. She noticed his tan chest was adorned with just the right amount of hair, and his stomach was as well-toned and muscular as his biceps.

Karolyn's tan and body were equally impressive, shown off by her bright orange bikini under her semi-sheer cover-up. Teri had met Karolyn only briefly, earlier in the week, and remembered her voice: alarmingly nasal, with an exaggerated drawl. But when Karolyn said, "Jackson, why don't you get the lady a drink?" Teri heard no sign of either.

Teri asked for a beer, not only because she could drink beer all day with little effect, but also to see his reaction.

Winton said, "Well, I just love a woman who drinks a man's drink! Lowenbrau okay?"

Teri took pride in her knowledge of beers, and since Lowenbrau had been taken over by a U.S. bottler with an Americanized recipe, it had fallen off her list of favorites. She decided, however, that this wasn't the time to impress them with her lager and ale expertise. "That would be fine, thanks."

Arthur seemed to catch her lukewarm reaction, smiling as he made eye contact with her over his half-moon reading glasses. Winton refreshed his own drink as well as Karolyn's and handed Teri the bottle of Lowenbrau.

"Teri, do you need to use the head?" Winton asked. "It's below, along with two fully equipped staterooms. I'm especially fond of my custom-made round bed. Very comfy."

He gestured down the companionway. "Would you like the tour?"

Teri caught the tiniest headshake from Karolyn, and replied, "I'm fine for now, thank you."

Arthur glared at Winton.

"What? I thought she might like to see below…"

Arthur shook his head.

Winton shrugged. "So, are you-all ready to get underway? Why don't we go topside and enjoy the sunshine?"

Arthur said he had work to finish. Karolyn said there was nothing she wanted to see until they were outside the breakwater, so she preferred to stay in and keep Arthur company.

* * *

Jackson took Teri out the sliding door and followed her closely, up the molded-step companionway to the enclosed flybridge, counting his good fortune that Karolyn decided to stay below.

He bellowed, "Yo, I'm leaving!"

Two dock-boys appeared out of nowhere, ran down the ramp, cast the front and rear lines off the cleats, and were back up the ramp and gone, in under three minutes.

He smiled at Teri. "I like efficiency."

The flybridge had full amenities, including a wet bar and seating for eight. Jackson climbed into the large captain's seat and motioned for Teri to sit next to him in the companion helm seat.

"I'd like to stand for a while, thanks. I can see better."

"Suit yourself," he said, with a tone of mild annoyance in response to her non-compliance.

He took the wheel, looking over the extensive array of helm gauges with a master-of-the-universe air, and then fired up the twin Detroit Diesel engines.

"Ah, feel those babies? That's power."

As Winton maneuvered the Sea Ray out of the marina, paying little heed to the five-mph speed limit, Teri asked him about the current condition of McNev, breaking his reverie.

He looked up. "What do you mean exactly?"

Teri explained, "Well, based on the month-end figures we saw this morning, our cash position is certainly tight. And even with the low line rate, the continuing layoffs not only appear to be causing a lot of expensive overtime, but from my initial research, it looks like rejections on the final line are up significantly from last year."

She took a breath and continued. "We have only six aircraft bookings for the fourth quarter, which puts us approximately two hundred million behind the revenue forecast by year's end. I don't see how all the cost-cutting in the world will make up for that."

Jackson stared at the breakwater for a moment, and then smiled as the appropriate answer came to him. "Teri, my dear, you're an executive now. You have to learn to rise above the trees and look at the whole forest."

He caught her challenging look, countering with an expression to indicate he was stating the obvious.

"To be a successful executive, you need to stay above the fray. We have middle managers under us, and we pay them to manage the details. You should focus on being a cooperative player on your new team, and don't waste your time getting bogged down with problems, like your friend Rich—Look where it got him."

Momentarily thrown by her unanticipated glare, he quickly adjusted.

"Don't get me wrong, I didn't mean Rich brought it on himself. He just worked too hard—it's tough up here at the top. We have to make sure our people know we're in charge, so they'll manage the daily work."

As they cleared the breakwater into bluer ocean, Winton surveyed the extensive collection of catamarans, powerboats, and sailboats, secure in the knowledge that none were in the class of his Sea Ray.

Giving Teri his best executive smile, he asked with a magnanimous wave toward the bow, "And why are you asking all these work questions on a beautiful afternoon like this?"

But instead of returning his smile, she continued her analysis, observing that the company appeared too under-capitalized to develop a derivative aircraft, and asking, "Where do you see McNev headed in the next three to five years?"

Jackson sighed in annoyance. He couldn't fathom Teri's lack of proper deference to being aboard the best boat in the water in the company of a corporate president. Rather than talking shop, they should be much more pleasantly engaged. Besides, he needed O'Donnell if she was going to persist in this constant questioning.

It was time to leverage his position. Lowering his voice for emphasis, he said, "Teri, there are some pretty exciting things in store for us at McNev—big plans. Unfortunately, as I'm sure you'll respect, I'm not at liberty to discuss anything specific with you just yet. But I promise you: stick with me, and you'll be well taken care of for as long as you want a career here." He chuckled, adding, "Hell, you're in your prime. If you make permanent VP—and I can see to that—you may end up as McNev's President someday."

Jackson smiled broadly at his stellar executive IQ, using just the right words without saying anything. As if he really believed a woman, even one this good-looking, could actually lead a major aerospace company.

He put an end to the course of her conversation by changing the subject. "So, tell me. What do you think of my little boat?"

* * *

In the week Teri had been there, she'd realized the company was facing tough challenges. But so far, she thought the VP team, with the exception of Duke, was up to the task. Winton seemed credible at first glance, especially in his element. But what she saw now was different. It was as if she were on a movie set, where the buildings looked real until getting close enough to see they were nothing but facades.

Teri felt the urge to step backward as she answered. "It's very nice," she acknowledged, silently questioning how the company could afford the compensation package Winton must be getting.

The traffic dissipated, leaving them alone in open water, cruising north, paralleling the shoreline. Making better than twenty knots kept Jackson occupied, and Teri was enjoying herself as the Sea Ray crested the swells.

After a relaxing few minutes, Jackson backed the throttle down to high idle and got up from his captain's seat. Teri bent over to adjust her sandal and felt her shorts slip down slightly, suddenly aware of Jackson behind her, staring intently.

She stood up and turned to face him; he was too close. He raised his hands above his head and brought them down dramatically to rest on his red swim shorts, as he said, "See anything else you think is 'very nice'?"

Taking in Jackson's unsubtle pose and attempted sexy baritone, a couple of thoughts came to mind. *Damn, Rich might have been right*, and *this is too depressing for my first week.*

But these two thoughts were overwhelmed by a third: *Is he serious?*

Teri couldn't help herself. She burst out laughing, nearly choking on a swallow of beer. Regretting her reaction when she saw the mixture of confusion and disbelief in Jackson's expression, she stepped aft, uneasily.

Jackson followed swiftly, corralling her against the back of the bench seat next to the wet bar. He put his arms around her and slid his thigh between her legs, catching Teri off guard. Finding herself suddenly encircled, she resisted, but Winton tightened his embrace and she could feel his erection pressing against her.

His tone was urgent—heated. "Teri, you're part of my team now. You take care of me, and I'll take care of you. I guarantee you won't regret it."

Keeping her snug with one arm, Winton began kissing her neck and slid his other hand beneath the front of her tank top.

Whether she'd underestimated his belief in her compliance or his level of intoxication, she realized this had gone too far.

"Jackson, please! Don't be ridiculous!"

She was about to ram her knee into the prominent bulge of his swimsuit when O'Donnell, with Karolyn right behind him, reached the top of the companionway, suddenly standing next to the entangled pair.

"Jack—What the hell? Are you trying to scare Teri back to Seattle?"

"Hey, Arthur," Jackson mumbled, letting go of Teri. He lurched awkwardly to the captain's seat, and sat down to hide his excitement.

He took hold of the wheel and throttled up, spluttering, "Teri and I were…uh…just getting to know each other."

"Uh, huh." Arthur's response bristled with sarcasm. "I can see that."

With Jackson at the helm, staring straight ahead, Teri, Karolyn, and Arthur looked at each other as the flybridge became uncomfortably close.

Arthur broke the silence. "Jackson, why don't you come below with me? There're some figures I need to show you." Nodding to Karolyn, he added, "The helm's yours, KB."

Arthur turned to Teri, meeting her eyes with a look that conveyed, *I apologize for this idiot. I know you're out of his league.*

As Winton slipped past Teri, his hands covering his still-noticeable embarrassment, Arthur asked her if she wanted him to bring her another beer. She nodded, attempting to smile as she composed herself.

* * *

Inside the salon with the sliding door closed, Arthur shoved Winton into one of the captain's chairs and stood over him. "For chrissake, Jack, what the hell were you thinking?"

Jackson gave Arthur a sullen look and got up to pour himself another rum and tonic. "What? You want her for yourself?"

"Do you ever think with any part of your anatomy other than your dick? Did you forget what a pain-in-the-ass Richmond has been? Did you think I told you to make her acting VP, so she'd be appreciative and screw you?"

When Winton's expression turned sulky as he gulped his drink, Arthur backed his tone down slightly.

"Look, Jack, Teri's a professional. She's smart and capable, and you agreed with my idea of replacing Richmond with a much more amenable team member. But you can't treat her like that. She's about to be a VP on your team, for God's sake—She's not Karolyn."

* * *

The Sea Ray was moving fast, pounding on the choppy water as Karolyn slid into the captain's seat. She looked at ease and competent at the helm, adjusting the trim tabs to lower the bow and cleave the waves.

"I swear, Jackson can't even trim his own boat properly."

Teri noticed how much smoother the ride got, mentally castigating herself for being surprised, and sat down in the companion helm seat next to Karolyn.

Karolyn continued looking ahead as she spoke. "Teri, he didn't mean any harm. He tends to get extra...*friendly* when he drinks a lot."

Not exactly sure what to say, Teri asked, "What's it like to work with him?"

"Truth be told, it's mostly a pain in the ass. But fortunately, I work for Arthur, not Jackson." She paused before continuing.

"Jackson's like that with me almost every time we're alone, so I just let him screw me and get it over with...It makes him feel like a man, and a more effective leader."

Karolyn turned her head and smiled at Teri. "Actually, he finishes so quickly, it's really no more than a minor inconvenience."

Teri was even less sure how to respond. "How does Arthur feel about all this?"

"Arthur not only knows about it, he wrote it in as part of my job description." She turned to Teri, a wry smile crossing her face. "Although I certainly don't prefer it this way, Arthur assigned me to keep Jackson out of trouble. As you probably already gathered, Jackson's not much on social graces, and has an uncontrolled tendency to stick his foot in his mouth. He needs a constant companion and Arthur can't always be with Jackson, especially when he travels...so I'm elected."

Teri struggled to reevaluate her opinion of Karolyn, wondering just how ludicrous things could get as she discovered the reality of McNev. They sat in silence with Teri trying to assimilate this latest revelation.

"Sorry for hesitating Karolyn, but I have to admit, I've never heard of anything like this. You obviously have brains and insight. Why do things this way? And what's with the voice and affected manner at work?"

Karolyn's change in body language amplified her resigned tone. "I'm not like you, Teri. I don't have a chance at the kind of career you've got. I wasn't even raised working class—I was raised alley cat. My talent for survival was based primarily on two working skills: lying on my back and landing on my feet…and I always got by."

Karolyn sighed and fell silent. Then after a moment, she continued, "Arthur gave me a real opportunity to do more than just get by. I've learned so much from him. And I have a chance here to make enough money to do things I never allowed myself to dream about. As for the act at work, all the VPs and most of the employees at McNev think I'm simply Jackson's executive whore first, and executive administrator, second."

"Doesn't that bother you?"

Karolyn reached under the control panel and pulled out a pack of Kool Ultra Lites. She took one out, lit it, and took a long drag. "Arthur doesn't like me to smoke—thinks I quit."

She exhaled away from Teri, resuming her explanation. "VPs, customers, employees all need to see a strong leader at the top. That's what Arthur says it takes to make things work. Jackson looks and talks like a leader, at least from a distance. So Arthur taught me about business and assigned me to stay…"undercover"—she made air quotes with her fingers—as Jackson's ace-in-the-hole, to keep him out of trouble. Left on his own, Jackson could easily alienate people so much they'd refuse to follow him. But Arthur knows that if he stays on track, he's good at getting people to follow orders."

Karolyn winked. "Believe me, that's really all he *is* good at!"

After a pause, she added, "You're the only one besides Arthur who knows this. If you tell anyone, I'll have to kill you."

They both laughed, and then Karolyn's tone got somber. "Seriously though, I need to know you won't say a word. Not even to Arthur." She stuck out her hand. "Deal?"

"Deal."

Teri shook Karolyn's hand, and in spite of everything, felt better. "At least I made one friend at McNev so far."

Karolyn smiled. "Absolutely. And believe me, I could use a friend around here."

She maneuvered around a small sailboat with one hand, jettisoning her cigarette overboard as she heard footsteps.

Arthur reappeared, giving Karolyn a disdainful look as he caught the lingering wisps of smoke. He said, "Jack wants you below. I'll take over."

Karolyn said nothing, but her slumping shoulders spoke volumes as she disappeared down the companionway.

* * *

Arthur handed Teri a bottle of Anchor Steam and took over the helm. She took a sip and held the bottle up, smiling gratefully.

"Thanks...how did you know?"

Arthur smiled back. "I noticed your expression earlier when Jackson handed you the Lowenbrau. I figured you might like this better."

After a moment, he asked, "So what did you and Jackson talk about?"

"First we discussed the company's outlook...then we moved on to 'avoiding relationships in the workplace.'" A sardonic smile formed on her lips.

Arthur mirrored her expression. "Ah, yes...Teri, please don't take his inappropriateness too seriously. He just needs to sleep it off."

He paused for a second before adding, "You may find this tough to take at the moment, but we're both impressed by your competence."

Teri nodded. "Thank you. Your excellent timing prevented me from having to quite personally offend Jackson."

"Of which, I have no doubt he was fully deserving."

Continuing to smile, he added, "I also wanted to say how glad we are to have you here. I've been worried about Rich..." He paused again, acknowledging her concerned expression. "I didn't mean to alarm you. I just appreciate you stepping in."

"You're welcome...But I'm rooting for Rich to make an amazing recovery."

Behind his disarming smile was a dark intensity in his eyes that made her feel he was peering into her thoughts.

He said, "Yes, I know you're close to him...And not to bring up an uncomfortable subject, but I've heard rumors around the plant that you two used to have a thing."

Before Teri could react, he took one hand off the wheel and held it up in a reassuring manner. "Don't worry, I'm not saying there was—or is—anything to it. But people's perceptions, unjustified though they may be, are still important. Given your history, and his condition, I think the sooner you move out of his sister's place in Laguna, the better."

Teri tried to avoid looking stunned. *He knows where I'm staying?*

Arthur continued, "McNev's got a beach house in Newport, near the water. We use it for out-of-town guests, and sometimes off-site meetings. It's actually just a small condo, but you're welcome to stay there until you find something permanent. As a matter of fact, it's only a couple of miles from my place. Are you a jogger?"

Seeing her reaction, he added, "Whoa, don't look at me like I'm Jackson. I was just talking about jogging."

He flashed another beguiling smile. "Don't answer now. Just think about what I'm saying, okay?" He glanced at his Rolex Sea Dweller.

"Wow, it's almost four, and we've managed to get pretty far up the coast. We better head in."

He came about smoothly, back toward Newport. They fell into a comfortable silence, enjoying the simple perfection of the ocean wind and sea spray. Teri appreciated the quiet time. She had a lot to ponder.

At the marina, saying good-bye to Karolyn and Arthur, Teri heard Jackson snoring through the closed salon door. She had no inclination to wake him up in order to thank him.

As she walked up the ramp, Teri looked back over her shoulder and noticed the name of Winton's boat. *Executive Privilege* was painted in bright red letters on the stern. She just shook her head.

12

Saturday, 9:35 p.m.

Porter was back, standing in the shadows across from O'Donnell's house, staring at the balcony and hoping to see her again.

Although he was there to surveil O'Donnell, his mystery woman was the main focus of his attention. Staying longer than necessary last night to determine that O'Donnell was doing nothing more than working on his computer, he'd returned to his apartment preoccupied with discovering her identity.

Early this morning, Porter had driven to the plant to ask Mary for help in finding out who she was—although he didn't know if she was even an employee.

Unfortunately, Mary wasn't at work on Saturday, and the Security office was essentially deserted. There was one administrator, chewing gum and flirting with a security officer who was leaning on the front counter.

The nameplate on her desk said *Gina* and Porter thought she looked about nineteen.

He'd introduced himself, and Gina replied without looking at him. "Yeah, I know who you are. Tony told me. Somethin' I can do for you?"

It was obvious she was more interested in doing something for the young officer than helping Porter. He had no intention of telling her anything about his investigation, or the woman. However, as long as he was here, he'd decided to play a hunch.

"Can you pull up everyone who reports directly to Arthur O'Donnell?"

Holding up one finger to the officer, her body language indicated that Porter was merely a temporary interruption. She accessed the badging database org-chart function.

"Here ya go." She turned her monitor toward Porter.

The screen displayed a list of VPs and staff, with titles and employee numbers: all male names, except two. Gina's expression clearly conveyed her expectation that Porter should thank her and leave, or just leave.

"So, you want me to print this, or what?"

What Porter wanted was to slap the attitude out of her, but figured it would have little effect. "Can you open this one—Teri Harlan?"

When she'd selected the name and hit *enter*, displaying Teri's badge photo and information, he'd seen an attractive redhead who was obviously not the woman he saw last night.

Gina had grown even more impatient.

"So, print it?"

"No. Try this one." He pointed to the other name: Karolyn Babcock.

Gina sighed, moving the cursor, and opening the file.

There she was. Radiant blonde hair, cornflower blue eyes, beautiful even in a badge photo.

"Thanks. Print this one for me."

Porter was as happy to leave as Gina was to be rid of him, but his trip this morning paid off. Now he knew her name: Karolyn. He loved both the sound and the spelling. She was listed as O'Donnell's Executive Administrator, supervising two assistants who comprised the administration team for O'Donnell and Winton. Porter realized he must have walked by her desk when he'd gone to O'Donnell's office.

He'd spent the afternoon re-reading the brief file and staring at her photo. He went to a neighborhood bar for dinner and started a conversation with the pleasant, nice-looking server. Normally, that would have kept him engaged for the evening, but instead he'd returned to his apartment alone and tried watching TV. It took him all of ten minutes to accept where he really wanted to be.

After jogging over, Porter watched O'Donnell in his brightly lit bedroom like he was on stage, wondering why he never drew the blinds. O'Donnell sat at a huge corner desk, alternately typing on his PC's keyboard, and using a palm-sized electronic gadget. Porter sighed and stretched, unsure if this was worth his time, acknowledging his real reason for being there had little to do with O'Donnell.

As if on cue, Karolyn walked out through the sliding glass door, wearing dark, form-fitting slacks, and a white top that shimmered in the moonlight. She stopped near the balcony railing and stretched luxuriously with her hands above her head, arching her back.

Porter beamed. "Yes! I'm in luck," he said under his breath. He took a step back to be sure she wouldn't see him, but she was staring skyward.

He watched her, entranced, when his elation suddenly gave way to a sobering thought. *Karolyn is there for a second night in a row, and on a Saturday too.*

* * *

Arthur sat at his hand-carved mahogany worktable built into the corner of his bedroom, working on his HP Palmtop. The fax machine next to him came to life with a *ding*, whirring as it discharged a report. He reached for the paper without looking at the machine, putting it in front of him in one smooth motion. It was the second shift activity log confirming the installation of the special-order lock mechanism for the forward cargo door on Ship 913 for Tailia Air.

I've got to hand it to Crandall. Using Herrera and his crew worked perfectly. He even slipped it past inspection...excellent.

Arthur smiled, continuing his silent self-congratulations.

That makes two wins for me today. Getting Teri away from Asshole and his sister—right into the condo...so smooth.

But when he returned his attention to finalizing the TaiChin Hong Kong scenario, his smile faded.

* * *

Karolyn loved star-gazing, even though there were few to be seen most nights above Southern California, thanks to the multi-million-candlepower luminance of the LA-Orange County basin. She dreamed of returning to Idyllwild, where she'd grown up savoring a night sky filled with stars that went on forever.

Someday... She sighed and went inside. Karolyn walked up behind Arthur and began massaging his shoulders. "You want me to stay tonight?"

He didn't answer.

She put her arms around his neck in a gentle hug. "You do realize that even McNeil doesn't expect you to spend all your waking hours trying to turn that place around."

When he continued to ignore her, she sighed again, retrieved her book, and flopped on his bed to continue her reading.

After fifteen minutes and only two pages of Brigham's *Intermediate Corporate Finance*, she realized her mind was too restless to concentrate. It was nights like this, feeling like a piece of furniture in Arthur's presence, that made her question their relationship.

Startled, she realized Arthur was speaking to her. "KB, is everything in place for the trip to Hong Kong with Jackson and Will?"

Since overhearing Arthur's phone conversation with Will Crandall earlier that evening, she'd been wanting to say something. So rather than answer his question she voiced her concern.

"I don't understand what you're planning with that awful Crandall. It almost sounded like you two are intentionally trying to push Jackson into a situation where he could offend TaiChin and risk damaging the partnership."

Arthur still had his back to her, focused on a document. When he said nothing, she took a breath and continued. "It makes no sense for you to jeopardize what you and McNeil have been working toward for the past year..."

Karolyn froze mid-sentence. She knew by his reaction that she'd crossed the line.

Arthur spun in his high-back leather chair, and lifted himself out of it. He stalked toward the bed, instant rage flickering in his expression.

"Goddammit, Karolyn! Why do you insist on questioning things you don't know shit about? Asian culture negotiations are extraordinarily complex, and you aren't smart enough for me to invest the time it would take to explain it to you!"

Karolyn scooched herself against the headboard as her pulse jumped. It had been nearly a year since Arthur had taken on that violent countenance, yet her recollection was still clear: the night her innocent teasing remark on one of his plans pushed him over the edge. The memory flooded in, so vivid she could almost feel herself gasping for air as his fingers had closed around her throat.

She drifted away for a moment, seeing herself trapped in his unrelenting grip, having no choice but to surrender and hope for mercy. As the vision faded, she became aware of an uncharted feeling, as if some internal switch ignited a spark of determination. It surprised her to find she was glaring back at Arthur, which immediately provoked his intimidation posture.

"Just do what I tell you! Is everything ready for the trip?"

"Yes. It's set." Karolyn heard herself sliding back into her familiar inclination to placate him as she watched his expression soften.

"Good." Arthur's tone turned silky. "And I'm counting on you to be there for Jack too."

That was it—her own line just got crossed. Her compliance vanished, replaced by a festering anger. Arthur's manipulation was suddenly, painfully clear.

I'm not doing this anymore.

Karolyn had always adored Arthur, forever grateful for the opportunity he'd given her, but she was tired of being his remote control to manage Winton, and sick of being treated as a second-class assistant—or worse.

Talking with Teri today, watching the way she handles herself...I may not be on her level, but I can stand up for myself—starting now.

She slid off the bed and stood face-to-face with him.

"Arthur, I'm calling bullshit here. You've told me more than once how much smarter I am than Jackson. I'm tired of propping him up to be seen as the competent executive while playing the role of his arm candy and performing like a slut. After everything you've taught me, and all the times I've come through for you, I've reached the point where I should be your partner."

"You call bullshit? I'll tell you what's bullshit—you thinking you can be my partner! Just follow my script and do your job with Jackson! You're getting a truckload of money for making him credible and the minor inconvenience of sharpening his pencil a few times. You should be grateful! You should be on your *knees*—It's where you do your best work."

Karolyn snatched up her things and turned her back on him. As she reached his bedroom door to head downstairs, she turned and snarled over her shoulder. "And to think I actually believed you cared about me, you sonofabitch. Go to hell!"

After slamming his custom-made Milan door hard enough to rattle the hinges, she hurried downstairs smiling at the thought of Arthur staring after her with a disbelieving look, worrying about damage to his precious door.

* * *

Porter heard Karolyn yelling, but hadn't caught the conversation and was unsure of the situation. He watched her run out of the front door and jump into a red BMW 325i, reinforcing his growing assurance that he was falling in love.

He considered going to help her, but thought she might panic, seeing a strange man running toward her car. He heard O'Donnell's phone ringing.

That might be something useful, finally.

As much as Porter preferred to check on Karolyn, he knew it was smarter to move under the balcony where he could listen. He heard the sound of O'Donnell's footsteps walking above him, then Arthur's voice answering the call.

"Yeah, hi…Nope, not a problem. I was just working…Al Greer…Hmm, I'm not sure I know him. How long was their conversation?…That's good work, Tony—thanks."

So O'Donnell's got eyes on me…he's gotta be hiding something…and whatever it is, I'd better find out fast.

13

Monday, 7:15 a.m.

Teri stood in Rich's fifth-floor office staring out the window overlooking the main street that divided the two sections of the plant. A huge American flag waved in the breeze, reminding Teri of her Everett days when she'd attended meetings on this same floor and enjoyed watching the flag from an eye-level perspective.

This morning she looked past it, mulling over the discomfort of yesterday afternoon, when she'd packed up and left Sheila's house.

Giving serious import to Arthur's counsel Saturday on the boat, Teri rationalized that leaving could also help Rich recover faster and lessen Sheila's tension. Eventually, she admitted to herself that she really wanted to escape the chaos and focus on work, an inclination that was reinforced when Rich woke up yesterday doing an excellent impersonation of a zombie. Saturday night, he couldn't sleep and had taken a double dose of his meds. His resulting catatonic state lasting into Sunday afternoon confirmed her decision.

Leaving, however, hadn't been easy. When Teri came downstairs with her luggage, Lisa got teary-eyed. "Aunt Teri, can you still come back and read to me before I go to sleep?" Teri hadn't planned on the pang in her stomach when she'd knelt down to give Lisa a good-bye hug.

Sheila had also been upset, apologizing for the situation as if she were somehow responsible. She'd made a half-hearted appeal for Teri to stay, indicating there was something she still hadn't shared, and Teri made a mental note to continue her efforts to find out what it was.

Rich's behavior turned mystifying once again. As she was about to climb into her Jeep, he took both her hands in his and said, "Teri, watch out for Art," then let go and added a simple "Take care." She'd puzzled over his ominous tone all the way to Newport.

The McNev condo, off Pacific Coast Highway, wasn't far from the bridge to Balboa Island. It was a one-bedroom, located on the second floor at the end of an eight-unit complex. A sliding glass door led to a small balcony with, what was called in real estate jargon, a *peekaboo ocean view*.

The substantial living room was consumed almost entirely by a large conference table and chairs used for McNev executive off-sites. The only other furniture consisted of a pair of dated Danish Modern chairs, with an end table and lamp. To the right of the conference table was a bar counter, with a small kitchen behind it. A door at the far end of the living room led to the bedroom, where Teri found the only redeeming features: a walk-in closet, and spa tub in the bathroom.

As she began unpacking, she'd started to feel uneasy—as if someone were watching her. After a quick store run and an antipasto salad dinner, she'd spent the better part of a Berringer cabernet bottle attempting to convince herself of her sound judgment. But this morning, Teri still questioned herself.

Sighing, she turned from the window and sat down at Rich's desk, the top of which she'd managed to obscure entirely with stacks of reports. She plucked three of them from the top of one of the piles to focus on a project stemming from a phone conversation with Rich, prior to being hired. When she'd found Rich's notes and initial analysis of the subject in his office, she saw an opportunity to make a positive contribution before he returned.

The reports compared assembly rework statistics to associated tooling. She'd identified recurring problems in fuselage sub-assemblies correlating to requests from Sub-Assembly supervisors for new tools. However, when she examined the tooling log, she found no orders for replacing any of them.

Spotting the obvious anomaly, she'd requested budget/expenditure reports from Financial Accounting to see if the lack of tooling replacement was due to budget constraints. After more than an hour of flipping through page after page of endless numbers, she was still unable to decipher them.

She flipped the report closed and swore, running her fingers through her hair, and then twisting it in up in a knot, securing it by lancing it with her number two pencil. Developing this ritual over the years when reaching her boiling point, Teri found it often resulted in clearing her head. She paused for a moment, then grabbed the company phone directory and found the Manager of Financial Accounting: Vernon Ames. She called and asked him if he had time to come by.

* * *

In a matter of minutes, there was a soft knock on her door. It opened, and a bald head with glasses appeared.

"Miss Harlan? I'm Vernon Ames. You asked for me?"

"Yes, thanks for coming so quickly. Please come in."

She carried the massive computer printout she'd been studying to the small conference table, spread it out on the remaining uncluttered surface, and sat next to him.

"Can you explain this section, detailing the budget and expenditures associated with tooling?"

"Sure. I know this format can be a bit confusing…"

As they looked at the report, she glanced at Vernon, and though she avoided stereotyping, the thought popped into her head: *He belongs on the cover of* CPA Weekly.

He was in his sixties, slight in stature, with a smallish chevron mustache and thick glasses. The only things missing were the bow tie and green eyeshade. He seemed ill at ease, but she couldn't tell if it was due to sitting in a VP's office, her being twenty years his junior, or her gender.

She said, "Please call me Teri," trying to relax her body language, but it didn't seem to make a difference. He continued in a staccato-allegro manner.

"This column is McNev's cumulative actuals for tooling. You see, we're not only under budget, but we're doing very well here on our benchmarks against Boeing, McDonnell Douglas, and Airbus."

Teri recognized the technique as the current fad in Total Quality that most large corporations were adopting. Benchmarking was the practice of determining what your competitors were doing, as a way to see how your company measured against them.

In this case, the benchmarks were for comparable tooling expenses, however there was one aspect Teri found was usually missing: knowing what the information meant to your own operation.

She asked, "Why do you think this is a favorable comparison?"

"Well, Miss Harlan…uh, Teri…you can see our tooling expenditures are consistently below all three companies."

"Yes, I can see that," she said with a touch of annoyance. "I'm asking you why you think that's a good thing."

He lowered his glasses, peering over the top of the rims. "I'm afraid I don't follow you."

Teri explained, "On the surface, it may seem that our lower expenses are good. But what if our competitors are investing in tooling that will reduce rework, lowering their production costs in the long run?"

"I…uh…guess we never looked at it that way." Vern began tapping his pencil.

Teri grabbed her analysis and showed him the tooling correlated to rejections on the line, and the total lack of tool replacement.

"Doesn't it seem to you," she said, "we're patting ourselves on the back on paper but shooting ourselves in the foot with Sub-Assembly rework?"

"It wouldn't be my job to know that."

"Has Mr. Duke ever discussed this benchmark data with you?"

"No, ma'am, I would never presume to interfere with how Darren Duke runs manufacturing, but the ExCon has been very complimentary about our lower costs, bettering our competitors."

Teri thought about screaming *You're missing the point!* but figured he'd keep missing it. So she changed the subject and turned to another section of the expense report.

"What can you tell me about this indirect expense summary?" She turned to the pages she'd marked, pointing to the columns. "Right here. Indirect expenses for travel, marketing, and facilities don't add up—the total is higher than the subtotals. And when I looked up the details, I found this." She pointed to a page showing asterisks in the "Actuals" column where the dollar amounts should have been. "What is this?"

Her tone wasn't lost on Vern.

"Th-those are called 'Private Accounts.'"

Vern stood, appearing to consider making a break for the door. "Those p-private accounts are expenses associated with VPs. They're all controlled and approved personally by Mr. O'Donnell, and the actual amounts are never disclosed in any reports."

He inched toward the door.

"Wait a sec." Teri looked up at him, pointing again at the report. "Look at this. The difference in the totals for travel expenses alone is nearly fifty percent of the year-to-date figures, and you say these detail amounts are private? That's insane! How can you manage the expenses?"

Teri twisted the pencil in her hair, her tone no longer hiding the edge. "I'm an acting VP. Can I see the detail? Do any of the other VPs ask you for this detail?"

What little color Vern had in his cheeks abandoned them. His voice was as ashen as his face.

"No, ma'am. No other VP has ever said anything about it. As a matter of fact, no other VP ever asked me as many questions as you have in the past half hour."

He reached the door, putting his hand behind him on the knob as he turned to her. "I'm sorry, I have another meeting. But if I could offer you a piece of advice, Miss Harlan, off the record. It would be better not to ask. Being new here, you might not know, but the VPs have a thing about being team players. Asking questions like you are may get you off on the wrong foot."

He opened the door, adding as he backed out, "Hope I was of some help. Have a nice day."

After shutting it like he was escaping capture, she heard Vern hurrying down the hall, double-time.

Teri shook her head as she looked over at the picture in the wooden frame on the credenza. Rich stood next to Lisa who was holding a model airplane and smiling proudly.

She said softly, "Rich, what have you gotten me into?"

* * *

Returning after recovering from last week's action, Mac finished his Monday morning staff meeting with his Line Position Supervisors.

Al Greer reported on last Friday's visit from a member of HQ Corporate Executive Staff, Porter Bordon, conducting a security audit, and asking questions on behalf of McNeil. As the meeting broke, Mac asked Al to stay and tell him more about his discussion with Bordon.

Al filled him in, mentioning the unusual sense of trust he'd felt. Looking thoughtful, Mac asked, "What did he look like?"

Al gave Mac a quizzical look, and said with a shrug, "He wasn't real tall. I'd say around five-ten, gray hair—cut like a jarhead, and in good shape...looked like someone you wouldn't wanna mess with."

Mac felt a tingle; he needed to get to the security office. He made the fifteen-minute walk in ten, hurrying in and asking for Tony.

Del Balso emerged from his office, through the administration bay to the front counter. He reached over and shook Mac's hand.

"Hey, McKinley. Heard about them Kung Fu moves you used on Reiss and Davis the other night. Nice work. They're history, by the way, if that's why you're here."

"Thanks, Tony, but I'm here about something else. You know a guy named Bordon?"

"Uh, yeah, Porter Bordon. Why?"

"Can I see him?"

"Nope. Called to say he ain't comin' in. Don't know where he is."

"Can I look at his picture in the badging database?"

Tony hesitated as his brain attempted to shift out of neutral. *What the hell? Does he know something?*

"Mind if I ask why?"

"Because I want to tell my supervisors, so if this guy comes by Final Assembly again, they'll know who he is."

Like a computer with too little RAM, it took Tony's mind several seconds to access data. *Damn, that's a good reason.* He tried to recall the exact instructions he'd received. *Arthur said to keep McKinley and Bordon away from each other, and no one can know we're watching them, or my ass will be in sling...what should I do here?*

He tried evasion.

"Bordon ain't an employee...he's on a corporate contract."

"Yeah, but you still had to issue him a badge, didn't you?"

Oh, shit, he's got me there. If I say no, he's gonna be suspicious.

"Uh, yeah, I guess I can access that; c'mon back."

They walked over to Gina and asked her to pull up Bordon's badge photo.

This time the "oh shit" expression was on Mac's face.

* * *

Arthur paced around his office; several factors having conspired to cause his current unsettled state.

First, he'd been rehashing the call from del Balso reporting on Bordon's visit to the Final Assembly. He was irked at both the uncertainty of Bordon's independent actions, and the possibility, albeit tiny, he'd underestimated him.

Secondly, he'd gotten mired in a Tailia-TaiChin crisis. Although TaiChin was vital to his PEP, he had no time for irrelevant aircraft production issues.

Thirdly, the messy emotional residue left from Karolyn's outburst Saturday night could prove disastrous if he didn't get her back on track. He stopped mid-pace.

At least I can solve the easy one.

He hit his intercom button. "KB, can you come in for a minute?"

Karolyn opened his door, her usual attractiveness tempered by radiating enmity. He walked to her, taking her hands gently in his. She yanked her hands back.

"What is it you need?" Her tone rivaled the ice water on his table.

"The first thing I need is to apologize to you. I'm truly sorry about Saturday night. I acted like an ass…I'm more stressed than I realized, and there are so many details to manage, I feel like I'm drowning. I guess I'm not used to that feeling."

She'd never heard Arthur divulge the slightest hint of vulnerability. She waited to see if he continued.

"I do respect you, and I know you're a great deal more astute than Jack will ever be. KB, I need you. I can't do this without you."

Karolyn felt her determined indignation beginning to slip. "You *were* an ass," she said, unable to contain the tiny smile forming at the corners of her mouth.

"That's my girl." But instead of embracing her, he put out his hand. "Partners?"

Karolyn flashed back to Saturday on the boat, when she and Teri had shaken hands, and recalled her anger and mistrust toward Arthur later that night. She hesitated. *Do I believe him? But this is what I wanted….*

She returned his handshake.

"Partners." She felt herself warming again as he met her eyes with his irresistible smile.

He moved on. "We have that telcon in Jackson's conference room with the Tailia-TaiChin people at eleven. I think it would be a good idea to include Teri. Can you run down to Richmond's office and bring her up?"

Karolyn left to fetch Teri, and Arthur smiled as he walked back to his desk. *Did I detect hesitation? No matter. She's so in love with me, I own her.*

* * *

Karolyn stepped into Rich's office to find Teri sitting at the table, bent over in concentration, still twisting the pencil she'd used to put up her hair. The table was strewn with reports, and the surfaces of Rich's desk and credenza were similarly buried under stacks of computer printouts.

"Wow, girl, looks like someone's trying for a gold star."

Teri looked up and chuckled. "Hey, Karolyn. Yeah, I made quite a mess, huh? Rich would be very annoyed if he were here."

"I'm sure it's been tough on you so far. How's Rich doing, by the way? I hope he's okay. I miss his snarkiness."

Teri smiled briefly, but it faded as she thought about it. "You know, I'm not really sure. Physically he seems better, but mentally…"

"Well, give him time. He'll bounce back."

"I hope so." Teri tried to push away her anxiety, along with her chair, as she slid it back and stood up. "So, what's up? I'm thinking you didn't stop by just to say hello."

"Well, speaking of that, we should do lunch soon. But I'm here because Arthur wants me to bring you up for the TaiChin meeting that starts in a few minutes."

"TaiChin? Isn't that the consortium that owns Tailia?"

Karolyn whistled. "You *are* a quick study. Yes, TaiChin was started by executives in China and Taiwan to partner on aerospace ventures. Their official name is TaiChin Industrial."

"I'm familiar with Taiwan, but I'm afraid I haven't had a chance to learn much about TaiChin, so I'm not sure what Arthur expects from me."

"Not to worry…" Karolyn put her hand on Teri's shoulder. "He just wants you to sit in and listen. I'll sit next to you so I can slip you crib notes and help you get up to speed."

Teri was caught off-guard once again. *There's certainly a lot more to Karolyn than meets the eye.*

Looking down at the reports gave her a quick flash. "Hey, Karolyn, before we go, can you tell me about these indirect expense entries with asterisks where the dollar amounts should be?"

"Oh sure, that's Arthur's brain-child: Private Accounts."

She sounds like it's business as usual…this place is getting curiouser and curiouser. Wonder when I'll find the rabbit hole.

* * *

Teri and Karolyn walked into Winton's conference room, located in the Executive Suite between his office and O'Donnell's. Teri was seeing this room for the first time, as the prior ExCon meetings she'd attended were in the large Executive Board Room down the hall.

She and Karolyn sat down across the table from Winton and O'Donnell.

Arthur said, "Teri, glad you could join us on short notice," and turning to Karolyn, added, "Thanks for bringing her up, KB."

Jackson mumbled, "Morning, Teri," barely making eye contact.

Arthur gave Teri the same TaiChin and Tailia Air explanation she'd just heard from Karolyn, adding, "I wanted you to get an idea of what's going on with our most important customer. Based on what we discussed in ExCon last Saturday, I thought you might have some insight on the technical issues, okay?"

"Sure. Thanks for thinking of me." Teri hoped her smile conveyed her respect for him.

In total contrast to Duke's office, this room was furnished in understated elegance. There were eight chairs, richly upholstered in leather, with brass rivets detailing the arms. A hand-carved credenza adorned the paneled wall below a mirror with striking bezel edges framed by charred-iron wall sconces. The carpet was inlaid with a classic diamond pattern, not thick, but superbly crafted. The sound absorption was incredible; Teri could hear Winton breathing.

As impressive as it was, it still elicited Teri's cynicism. *I see where the money went for the replacement tooling.*

Arthur explained that two top executives of TaiChin's management team were meeting with Tailia Air operations managers in New York this week, discussing production delays on Tailia's first Aircraft: Ship 913.

Voices of several executives came through the speakerphone, and Karolyn began jotting notes on a pad of paper between her and Teri, describing the key players.

The Taiwanese exec—Philip Lin—smart, very Westernized—cool guy.

The Chinese exec—Zhou Quon—total prick. Don't forget the Chinese put their last name first. Don't be like Jackson and call him Mr. Quon.

The meeting dragged on for over an hour, and Teri had no trouble understanding that Tailia was infuriated by the delivery issues, with their displeasure reinforced by the horsepower of both TaiChin execs.

She noticed that O'Donnell supplied notes to Jackson, as did Karolyn a couple of times, regarding the airline's special requests and issues with McNev's suppliers. Teri was surprised at how well they played together.

Jackson did most of the talking, emphasizing each point with his resonant tone. When Teri made a relevant suggestion about dedicating a QC team to expedite Ship 913 production, Arthur smiled his encouragement, while Jackson scowled at her for interrupting.

When the meeting ended, Teri listened to the New York attendees leaving their conference room. Then she heard the two TaiChin executives, Lin, and Zhou, tell the other Tailia people they needed some time alone with the McNev people.

Teri figured Lin and Zhou were about to reiterate their outrage over the delivery delays when Jackson nodded in her direction and looked at Arthur with raised eyebrows.

"Well?" Winton asked O'Donnell.

"No. She stays."

Karolyn smiled in surprise, while Winton appeared livid.

Teri surveyed the three of them, bewildered.

Arthur said, "Okay, KB, patch McNeil in."

Karolyn hit a couple of buttons on the speakerphone, and it rang.

"McNeil here," came through the phone.

Arthur took over. "Good afternoon, Hugh. How're things in Texas?" Without waiting for an answer, O'Donnell continued. "We have Philip and Quon on the line from New York, and here in the office with me are Jackson, Karolyn—and I invited Teri Harlan, the acting VP of Quality I told you about."

"Hello, everyone. Thanks for getting this meeting together. Sorry it's not in person, but given the pace of things down the stretch, we thought it was better to seize the opportunity when we had it. Miss Harlan, I've heard a lot about you. Arthur speaks very highly of you, and the fact he invited you to be with us for this confirms his absolute confidence in you."

He addressed Lin and Zhou. "Philip and Quon, are you comfortable with Arthur inviting Miss Harlan today?"

Both Philip Lin and Zhou Quon said yes, they'd listened to her in the prior meeting with Tailia and they were pleased to have her on board.

Arthur spoke again. "Hugh, I see a puzzled look on Teri's face here. I haven't had a chance to discuss this with her; do you mind if I fill her in?"

McNeil replied affirmatively, and Arthur turned to Teri.

"We're working with the TaiChin Consortium toward forming a strategic partnership. We've been in good-faith contractual negotiations for several months. However, due to a number of factors, including the impact on stock prices, competitive advantage, and government red tape, our work thus far has been very discreet."

McNeil laughed as he jumped in. "Arthur, I do love your penchant for understatement. What he means, Teri, is this process is corporate-classified at the highest level, on a strict need-to-know basis. The people at both McNev and TaiChin, who've been providing analysis and data, are only being asked specific questions, with no knowledge of the context. As a matter of fact, the only other person here at HQ besides myself who has full knowledge of this is Will Crandall, who's working between Arthur and the legal team."

Karolyn wrote on the pad. *Lawyers—ugh. Will Crandall—2X ugh.*

As Teri glanced at it, slightly distracted, she heard McNeil's tone get serious.

"Teri, I need to know we can count on you to keep this unconditionally confidential. Can you do that?"

Teri affirmed her consent, and the discussion proceeded with recapping the first phase of the negotiation process: *Capability Assessment*.

The discourse got heated when they reviewed the current phase: *Due Diligence*, the critical final step leading to *Partnership Formation*. Due Diligence was an exhaustive verification of financial statements and accounting practices to ensure that financial and performance measures, such as income and expenses, assets and liabilities, ROI, and cash flow, were accurate and aboveboard.

For two hours, there was an animated exchange on how to move faster through the process, with Arthur supported by Karolyn, reviewing progress. Teri noticed Jackson contributed almost nothing, at times appearing bored—when he wasn't staring at her.

* * *

Not knowing how O'Donnell would react to the report of his conversation with Al Greer, Porter decided to avoid a miserable Monday by staying out of Arthur's range.

After a morning of extending his regular exercise routine with an additional run, he'd spent most of the afternoon wearing a path in the carpet by pacing around his apartment's cramped living room.

He'd replayed everything multiple times, from the original instructions Crandall had given him regarding Richmond, to O'Donnell on McKinley, and that weird business with Dr. Meyer. He contrasted it with his own observations and the information from Al Greer.

He'd agreed to work for Arthur, assuming he was supporting McNeil by protecting McNev. Now he felt convinced that this was no longer the case, and it appeared that finding out what Crandall and O'Donnell were up to would be the most valuable thing he could do for McNev as well as McNeil.

Unfortunately, he had no additional insight and no attractive options.

He could meet with O'Donnell and tell him he'd talked with Al Greer to gather intel on McKinley, but he knew he couldn't lie well enough.

He could confront O'Donnell, accuse him, and then punch him. He liked that idea. But accuse him of what, exactly?

He could meet McKinley to see if he knew anything, but O'Donnell would no doubt find out, and then he'd be in a worse fix.

He figured O'Donnell would most likely end his assignment and recommend to McNeil that his contract be terminated, no matter what he did next. But if he was going to have the rug pulled out from under him, he would at least have the satisfaction of telling his real boss about his suspicions.

He'd called HQ and asked to speak with McNeil, but of course, being the Chairman of the Board, he wasn't available. So Porter left an urgent message, giving McNeil's secretary the apartment phone number. It was now 4:00 p.m. in California, 6:00 p.m. in Texas, and Hugh McNeil hadn't called him.

Bordon was about to say, "Screw it" and go for another run when the phone on the little table started ringing. He had a sudden thought as he picked up. *What if O'Donnell has it tapped? Damn—why didn't I think of that sooner?*

Porter answered, "Mr. McNeil?"

"Hi, Porter, it's Will. You were expecting Hugh?"

Porter's stomach felt like he'd just hit the two-story drop on the *Texas Giant* rollercoaster. "Crandall? Why are you calling me? Where's Mr. McNeil?"

"Hugh had to catch a flight to DC. He'll be tied up in congressional hearings for the next several days."

Porter never felt comfortable calling McNeil by his first name. He detested Crandall acting as if Hugh McNeil was somehow a close personal friend.

"Hugh asked me to call you back to see if there was something you needed to tell him. I was in Hugh's office the other day when Arthur called and reported that you've been such a *big* help out there. Fortunately for you, Arthur didn't say a word about what you did to Richmond...Oh, by the way, it must have slipped my mind when I gave you the assignment, but Hugh is very fond of Richmond, and he was especially concerned to hear about his accident. Shall I tell Hugh what you did? I'm sure he'd be *pleased*."

If there were some way to telepathically shoot a laser through the phone line and melt Crandall's face, Porter would have done it.

14

Monday, 5:05 p.m.

Teri shielded her eyes, wincing at the setting sun reflecting off the tower windows. Once she entered the tunnel beneath the boulevard, she felt her headache ease a bit. A walk through Final Assembly always helped her think, plus she was hoping to catch Mac before he left.

Her mind was focused on analyzing the root-causes behind her tight shoulders and pounding head. Most obvious was the lack of sleep in a condo that gave her the willies. The tooling expense analysis and her meeting with Vernon Ames, listening to his accounting double-speak, hadn't helped either. Then the meeting this afternoon…

Teri, we want to let you in on a little something—we're forming a partnership with some consortium from Taiwan and China, and you can't tell anyone…God, no wonder my head hurts!

Teri thought she was coming back to work with Rich to help solve production problems, not walk into the chaos of a company on the verge of another major upheaval. Her thought this afternoon about calling her old boss to plead for her job back made her realize how much she'd been counting on Rich's support.

And why isn't Rich in on the partnership plans? I don't know if I can stick it out till he gets back…if he does. Maybe talking with Mac will help.

When she approached the wallboard structure in the center of Final Assembly, Teri could hear Al's booming voice in Mac's office.

"No shit? Are you sure?"

"Yep, it was him. You were talking to the same guy who saved my ass last week."

"Well, I'll be damned."

"What kind of trouble are you two getting into?" Teri asked as she walked in.

Teri knew Al almost as well as she knew Mac. After they exchanged grins and warm hello-hugs, without skipping a beat, Teri asked Mac, "So who saved your ass from what?"

Mac shared an abbreviated version of the averted carjacking, receiving multiple "Oh my Gods" from Teri, particularly when he got to the part with Bordon's Dirty Harry-esque handgun action. Al jumped in, summarizing his conversation with Bordon, and then added a back-handed compliment.

"So, I gotta hand it to the old man. He was just telling me he found out this Bordon character from Corporate was the dude who saved his ass!"

Teri shook her head. "Wow...so this corporate guy was following you?"

Mac shrugged, "Musta been, but I dunno why...If I ever see him again, I'll be sure to ask him."

"Well, I'm glad he was there, for whatever reason."

"Yeah, me too...say, you know anything about him?"

"Porter Bordon? Nope. But don't forget, I'm just the new girl."

Their laughter made Teri smile, reminding her of the good times they'd shared over years of working together.

Al ventured, "Well, my guess? McNeil sent him to put a stop to the sabotage."

"Are you saying there's been more than the two guys you caught?"

Mac told Teri about Vale's attempt with bolt cutters and his subsequent firing.

Al interrupted again. "You're gonna love this, Mac. I just heard that little shit, LJ, got his job back."

"How the hell did that happen? I don't understand what's going on around here."

"Apparently, Duke reinstated Vale on direct orders from O'Donnell."

"Well, let's be sure his supervisor keeps both eyes and a foot on him."

While Mac shook his head and swore, Al turned to Teri and asked how she liked working with Duke. Teri described her thoughts on Duke's office, along with her meeting on the new "kNOw Excuses" program, prompting a spirited discussion, including copious amounts of colorful language, on the state of McNev manufacturing.

After Al made them all laugh again by telling Teri she'd picked the perfect time to come back, he eased himself off the desk he'd been sitting on and said, "Teri, it's been a blast catchin' up, but I'm gonna head out."

* * *

Mac took Al's place, sitting on the desk, and asked how Rich was doing. Teri realized for the second time today that she really wasn't sure, responding with a sort of stream-of-consciousness summary.

"Well, he's been up and down—the crash really messed with his memory. The doctor told Sheila it should return at some point, but he doesn't even remember hiring me, which is totally bizarre. It's hard to tell if the meds he's taking are making him better or worse. Stating the obvious, it's been mostly a nightmare staying at Sheila's. So Arthur suggested I stay at that beach-house-condo McNev uses for offsites...I moved there yesterday. Figured it might help to give him some space...and frankly, I needed some too."

Mac whistled. "Wow, sorry…sounds like Rich is really struggling."

After a moment, Mac scrunched his forehead, adding, "Hmmm, I wonder…"

Teri raised her eyebrows.

Mac hesitated, choosing his words carefully. "Rich has been really…upset. It's more than frustration with the cutbacks and everything. Rich thinks there's some dark secret…something or someone trying to take down the company. He got a look at a report in O'Donnell's office that he wasn't supposed to see and told me about it. It had Herrera's name, and that asswipe Vale's name too, along with a bunch of others. There was also a work order list and some part numbers…weird."

Teri's skeptical look caused Mac to nod.

"Yeah, I know…and there's more. Rich found out one of the part numbers listed was an obsolete electrical connector. He even got a couple of them from salvage and showed me one. It didn't ring a bell, but we planned to do more investigation, hoping to find some connection. Then there was Rich's accident, and that Bordon dude showing up…"

Mac stood up to stretch and looked at Teri with growing concern. "You know, Rich hasn't had an easy time of it since you left. I know his marriage wasn't great, but then he lost his wife, and had Lisa to care for…then the merger. He's been getting more and more disheartened with O'Donnell and Winton. And this past week—I don't think I ever saw Rich so worked up. I'm wondering if the crash made his mind want to…maybe take a break."

"Wow, that's some theory. And I have to say, McNev appears to be in big trouble, from what I've seen so far. The part I don't understand is how the financial numbers can still look decent with the lack of orders and so many production issues."

Mac shook his head. "Could be O'Donnell's strategy is to maintain the bottom line with his ruthless cost-cutting, but…" His voice trailed off.

"So do you think Rich is right—Something suspicious is going on?"

"Honestly, Teri, I don't know. You know Rich—always looking for problems, and he can be sort of a conspiracy nut…but maybe this time he's right. Too bad we can't ask him to go through it with you."

Teri recalled her earlier meeting with TaiChin and wondered if it was related. So many unanswered questions. She got an idea. "Do you think it might help for you to talk to him? Maybe sharing what he told you would jump-start his memory."

"Yeah—might be worth a shot. Just let me know if you want to try it."

As she hugged Mac and thanked him, Teri had a final thought.

"Hey, Mac, do you know if that LJ Vale kid has a father who's a doctor?"

* * *

It was late, even for Arthur. He stood and arched his back, trying to fend off exhaustion, as he looked down at the lighted American flag outside his window. Then he looked at his watch, realizing he still hadn't called Crandall. He sighed, pushed the speakerphone button, and dialed the number.

"Hi, Will. Sorry to call so late."

They both knew he wasn't. Arthur began with a compliment as he'd been making note of the surprising usefulness they seemed to have to keep people on script. "Nice job with the install of that special cargo door-lock on 913."

"Thanks, Arthur. I do good work. And it'll be a snap to keep it under wraps through final assembly."

Hearing the overconfident attitude Will adopted whenever things went well always annoyed him. He switched to icy-caustic. "But you still need to stay on top of it—and on Herrera for the other work too. It's *your* job to keep them on task…got it?"

Arthur paused, knowing Will well enough to figure he was getting a middle finger on the other end of the phone. He waited for Crandall's usual passive-aggressive response.

"Got it…and oh by the way, our friend, Bordon, tried to contact McNeil today."

"Yes, I know," Arthur replied.

Del Balso had called O'Donnell earlier to report that McKinley coerced him into looking up Bordon's photo, and that Bordon hadn't come in today. So Arthur told Tony to bring him the day's recording of Bordon's apartment phone tap tonight, rather than wait until morning like usual.

Arthur listened to Will's predictable comeback. "Oh, of course you know. I forgot—you know *everything*." His first impulse was to match Crandall's sarcasm with another acerbic remark, but he decided to stick with his new approach.

"I was just going to tell you that was a nice move, calling him back."

He could tell immediately that he caught Will by surprise.

"Oh…well, thanks…Yeah, Porter was less than thrilled when I told him you'd complimented his work in your phone call with Hugh, and then I threatened to disclose what he'd done to Richmond—It worked like a charm."

Arthur's shoulders clenched at Will's constant self-congratulatory manner, but he had to admit that Crandall had been helpful.

"Agreed—good work."

Tired of both listening to Crandall and being cordial, he got to the point.

"I also need to confirm that things are on track for Hong Kong, while McNeil's distracted in Washington. Is Zhou ready? His role is crucial—his reaction has to look real when Winton starts the due-diligence review."

"Oh, he's looking forward to it, Arthur. He'll show genuine outrage, for sure. He can't wait to stick it to Winton. And he'll be all-in with me when we hook up in Hong Kong."

Arthur hung up feeling satisfied by the power of compliments as an effective manipulation tool, offset by the irritation of dealing with Crandall.

His thoughts turned to the other critical task needed to execute the Hong Kong scenario.

I still have to be sure my little headstrong programmer finishes the software.

Before contemplating additional steps that might be needed to compel Sheila's compliance, Arthur decided he deserved a short break.

He put his feet up on his credenza and leaned back in his *Optim-Balance Herman Miller* ergo chair, letting his thoughts drift to his new favorite subject: Teri Harlan.

* * *

Sheila's vision blurred slightly, staring at rows of numbers racing across the screen. She was sitting at the workstation in her bedroom that now doubled as her office, having chosen not to move everything back when Teri left. She'd decided having her computer five steps from her bed was a good thing.

Per O'Donnell's specification, modifying the existing database queries on the backend of three McNev systems made full use of the power CPU in her IBM AS/400. His design called for a simple *Execute* icon on the McNev Enterprise start screen to activate the software, which would redirect the three systems to the new databases. When she'd studied the specs and noticed the catchphrase, *must appear transparent to the user*, she'd shaken her head, recognizing Arthur's credo: Manipulate People for Success.

It was only nine-thirty, but Sheila was fading, having worked straight through last night to dodge Rich's persistent curiosity. She'd taken on this cursed project with all the enthusiasm of a vegetarian at a Texas barbeque, but per O'Donnell's forte, he'd backed her into a corner.

Pausing for a moment with a heavy sigh, she thought about the combination of defiance and guilt that had been fueling her resistance to this project. She was almost certain that her brother, in his penchant for digging into problems, had unintentionally stumbled into one of Arthur's secret plans. And she was no longer able to deny the likelihood that

O'Donnell was somehow involved in Rich's accident, even though he'd vehemently denied it.

Despite her misgivings, she still believed the best chance for her brother and Teri to stay safe was to finish O'Donnell's project and keep this whole mess to herself. Although tempted to confide in Teri, her experience told her it would end up putting both of them in Arthur's sights, once he discovered she'd talked.

He'd find out...He always finds out. Plus I'd really like to keep what little dignity I have left.

She jumped as the phone next to her rang.

"Hey, Teri...no problem, I'm still working. Sorry, Rich is already asleep...Yeah he was better today. He took Lisa to school and picked her up, and they walked over to the park...Yes, I called Dr. Vale twice, but he never returned my calls...No, I have no idea if he has a son. Why?"

Her train of thought continued as Teri talked.

I really hate evading her—I know she can tell. But I've got to stay quiet till I get this damn thing done.

"Hmm, a visit from Mac? Not sure he's quite up for that. Why don't you stop by and talk with him first...Tomorrow is fine. Want to come for dinner? Great—Lisa will be happy...yeah, me too."

Sheila hung up the phone and looked longingly at her bed.

Not tonight.

15

Tuesday, 5:05 a.m.

It was still dark outside when Arthur exited the elevator on the ninth floor and walked through the morgue-quiet executive suite. He unlocked his office door, continuing to reenergize himself via his self-taught affirmations.

Three hours of sleep is plenty...just one more reason why I'm better than everyone else.

He continued his "PEP talk," the name he'd given his affirmation process, immersing himself in thoughts of the opulent lifestyle soon to be his. He sat down at his desk and flipped open the lid of his HP 100LX Palmtop, accessing the folder labeled *Shangri-La*. He took a minute to admire the latest renderings of his oceanfront home in Barbados, specifically the sweeping arch of the entry's wishbone double staircase, his personal design.

Renewed by envisioning himself ensconced in the elegance and grace of his future home, Arthur turned his attention to crossing the finish line.

His palmtop, dubbed the *Cougar*, was the perfect electronic vault to safeguard his private information and PEP notes. No larger than a legal pad, it was the first computerized device that convinced Arthur to abandon his locking Montblanc executive notebooks. With 2MB of RAM, and the ability to run Lotus Notes, he could update his plans in real time and send email with the use of a pocket modem.

He opened the memo application and accessed *PEP007*, smiling at the perfect file number.

Today's first Action Item: *Sheila*. She was working on his top priority, unaware, of course, of its significance.

She's such a talented programmer. Too bad her misguided ethics hold her back...I did enjoy our liaison, though, even if it was short-lived.

A special memory of Sheila came to him: Her naturally-perfect body yielding to their fiery passion after watching his favorite movie. Slightly flushed from the unexpected intensity of the recollection, he shook his head to refocus.

The callous measures he'd used to control Sheila evoked a twinge of regret, but the culmination of this PEP, The Hong Kong Scenario, was riding on her software. He hoped she'd made sufficient progress so that he wouldn't have to resort to more draconian measures. He added a note to his schedule to call and check on her.

He scrolled down to Action Item Two: *Bordon—Sideline or terminate.*

Arthur leaned back, mulling it over. The annoying independent actions and attempt to contact McNeil clearly showed that Crandall's assessment of Bordon as "a moron who blindly follows orders," was inaccurate. It also validated his inclination to distrust Will's suggestions. He would not make that mistake again, but Bordon now required corrective action.

He decided that sending Bordon to Hong Kong was the most expedient and plausible way to keep him out of McNeil's earshot. In addition, he would change his approach to keep Bordon off balance and disarm any suspicions he might have formed.

He made a note to have del Balso fetch Bordon first thing.

Arthur set down his Palmtop, focusing on the doodle he'd made last night on his blotter pad: *Teri* in elaborate cursive inside a 3-D heart. He had to be careful. She kindled a desire that was not only distracting, but potentially derailing. His thoughts drifted to the TaiChin meeting yesterday, and he felt himself flush again.

Her physical appeal—chestnut hair complimenting her complexion, with those few tiny freckles creating symmetry on both sides of her nose. And her eyes—luminous green—totally disarming. But his attraction to Teri was something more. He'd never worked with anyone, male or female, who absorbed and comprehended complex business and technical information so effortlessly. He'd found himself enchanted by her aura of self-assured competence.

Perhaps I've finally met a woman who's in my league. A real PEP partner...maybe even a life partner.

He caught himself.

I know, I have to be certain.

He was optimistic that listening to the condo phone tap would confirm she was on track and staying clear of Richmond. Startled by the knock on his door, he closed the lid of his Palmtop and looked up as del Balso entered.

"Here's last night's tape, boss."

Arthur took the condo-phone recording cassette with a curt nod, and said, "Go find Bordon and send him up."

"Sure, boss." With a quick turn, del Balso was gone, and the door shut.

Arthur swiveled his chair to face his credenza and slipped the tape into his small portable cassette player. Hope and schoolboy excitement ran through him, very curious sensations. He focused, listening.

* * *

Teri jogged across the bridge to Balboa, a Southern California real estate marvel: fifteen-hundred homes jammed onto a man-made island with a perimeter of fewer than two miles, and a higher population density than San Francisco.

It was a quiet 5:30 a.m., with only a few people exercising and fewer still, leaving for work. The view of the water was spectacular, and combined with the exhilarating ocean air, it should have been a utopian running environment. But Teri found herself distracted.

The conversation with Mac late yesterday had pushed her into mental overdrive, and she found her thoughts in a hodgepodge, akin to the buildings on the island. *Is Rich onto something? Is it related to the partnership with TaiChin that no one's supposed to know about?*

Everything and everyone in this mess was a paragon of duplicity. Her two closest friends seemed like they were auditioning for *Invasion of the Body Snatchers*. Winton was obviously not what he appeared to be, and neither was Karolyn, albeit in a much better way.

Then there was Arthur O'Donnell, the biggest enigma of all.

Arthur was the one McNev executive she'd met who appeared to operate by her standards of professionalism, and by far the sharpest executive she'd worked with, perhaps including Rich. In addition, she couldn't deny the physical attraction, recalling their conversation on the boat and his magnetic smile.

But lurking somewhere below the surface, she'd sensed a private agenda. *Is he the key to leading McNev's future, or a master puppeteer pulling peoples' strings according to his script?*

She increased her pace, trying to outrun a sudden case of the jitters.

* * *

Porter arrived at McNeil-Everett, deciding it was time to face the music with Arthur. After his horrible luck yesterday, getting his call intercepted by Will, he saw no way of communicating his suspicions to his boss. He'd followed up with McNeil's secretary, verifying McNeil was unreachable for the rest of the week. Now that his best option had been eliminated, he guessed the same thing was about to happen to his contract.

Figuring he'd be summoned to the ninth floor to face his discharge as soon as Arthur knew he was on the premises, he arrived extra early to attempt one last investigative effort. He parked outside the Security Administration office, grateful to see del Balso's parking space empty and his friend, Mary, approaching the entrance. He hurried to open the door for her, as she had her hands full with her purse, tote bag, and coffee.

"Thanks, Porter, that was sweet of you…are you feeling better?"

Porter was so focused on taking advantage of the quiet office and del Balso's absence, her question escaped him.

He said, "Hey, Mary, I really need your help."

"Holy moly, give me a sec, will ya? Can I set my coffee down and put my stuff away? If you need something from the system, it has to boot up first, anyway. Oh, and good morning to you too."

"Sorry...I need some information, and I'd like to get it before Tony gets here."

Mary gave him an understanding smile.

Porter filled her in on his conversation with Al, and overhearing the two workers in the assembly hangar, followed by a quick recap of being cut off by Will Crandall when he'd tried to contact McNeil. He finished by summarizing the conclusion he'd reached this morning.

"If there's something dirty with O'Donnell and Crandall, and they're out to hurt the company, the best thing I can do is find out as much as I can. And seeing as how this is liable to be my last day, I thought I'd try to get some more information, in case I get the chance to tell Mr. McNeil."

He took a breath and smiled at her, adding, "That's assuming, you're still okay helping me."

"Hey, Hugh's a stand-up guy, and we go way back....I'd be glad to help. Besides, I'm certainly no fan of O'Donnell. I wondered what McNeil was thinking when he put that guy in charge, so it wouldn't shock me if O'Donnell has his own agenda. And I *can* confirm Crandall is a total dirtbag...so tell me what you need."

"I wrote down the names of the two guys I heard talking. Can you run me a couple of those Personnel Info Sheets?"

Porter handed her his scrap of paper.

"Ah, Herrera. Well, if you're on to something, it would figure he's involved. Talk about scumbags, I think he may have Crandall beat."

She printed Herrera's employee summary, including job information, clearance and approval levels, and employment history. She looked at Porter's scrap paper again. "That one was easy. What's this other name...LJ?"

"Sorry, that's all I got. He's a young assembly mechanic, probably first level, and he was just reinstated last week after being fired."

Mary started typing.

"Okay, I can look up assembly mechanics, and then cross-reference the termination and hiring databases. It'll take a couple minutes."

Porter looked out the window, fidgeting, hoping del Balso wouldn't show up and ask what he was doing.

After five minutes that seemed like twenty, Mary found the records.

"Here we go. There're three prior terms that were reinstated last week: Joni Timberland, Ralph Valenzuela, and Lawrence Vale. Don't see an 'LJ,' sorry."

Porter looked over her shoulder at the screen, and then back to the window. Tony pulled up and got out of his Explorer.

"Uh, can you print all three real quick? I'll sort it out later."

Mary hit the print button as she spotted Tony coming toward the door.

"Oh, I see why you're getting antsy." She tore the three summaries off the printer, handing them to Porter. "There you go, darlin'—you better run."

"Mary, you're a doll. Thanks!"

She watched Porter walk double-time out the back door, just as Tony came hurrying in.

"Mary, was that Bordon?"

"Yep, you just missed him."

Del Balso ran after Porter who was now walking rapidly between two large buildings, stuffing the employee reports into his jacket pocket, and trying to look inconspicuous.

"Porter, wait!"

Oh, man, how could he know? Did Mary tell him?

Tony caught up, a bit out of breath. "Hey, man, where you going so early?"

Porter tried to keep moving. "What? Just doing something for Arthur."

"Really? That's funny, Arthur just sent me to find you. He wants to see you in his office—right now."

"Yeah, I was just headed up there."

Tony gave him a dirty look, and then turned on his heel without another word.

Porter walked toward the executive tower, breathing a sigh of relief.

Shoulda known Mary wouldn't blab. She's good people.

* * *

Tony walked back into the Security office, directly to Mary's desk. "Show me what you were looking up for him."

Mary turned her monitor toward him. The screen was blank, with the cursor blinking on the *system ready* line. "Sorry sweet pea, the system refreshed. He had me looking up some name, but he didn't have it right so I couldn't find it."

Mary's stare bored into Tony's back as he walked away.

I wouldn't tell you a damn thing, you little turd. Porter is twice the man you'll ever be.

* * *

As usual, the rapid ascent unsettled Porter, along with the sudden stop and *ding* as the elevator reached the ninth floor. The familiar absence of ambient noise created by the plush carpet added to his unease. The floor was again vacant at this early hour—the only time of day he'd been here.

He walked past three empty desks and noticed the nameplate—*Karolyn Babcock*—on the largest one. He felt his heart skip.

Being sure the personnel sheets were tucked out of sight in his inner coat pocket, he steadied himself and knocked.

"Enter" came O'Donnell's voice.

Porter opened the door, expecting Arthur to be standing, poised for intimidation, but he was sitting at his desk.

What's up with him?

Arthur remained seated and pointed to the table. "Have a seat."

Porter's uneasiness increased with the absence of the aggressive attitude he'd been expecting. He pulled out a chair at Arthur's conference table, exhaling slowly as he sat down.

"Relax, Porter. I know we started off on the wrong foot, and I've asked you to do things that upset you. You're obviously a man of strong convictions, and I realize what side you think I'm on. Unfortunately, I can't tell you exactly what's happening, and why I've needed to put you in situations you didn't approve of. I *can* tell you I'm doing my best to save this place from itself."

Porter's brain swiveled, attempting to catch up with O'Donnell's latest one-hundred-eighty-degree turn.

Arthur continued. "I'm not going to send you back to Texas or tell McNeil to cancel your contract. I'm going to give you a straight-up assignment suited to your security qualifications. Once you finish it, things will be square between us, and assuming it goes well, I'll give McNeil a positive report on your work."

Taken aback not only by O'Donnell's apparent clairvoyance, but also by his collegial transformation, Porter had no idea what to say.

Arthur went on. "There's a critical meeting this week in Hong Kong with the Taiwanese and Chinese contingents of the TaiChin consortium…It's vital to McNeil and the whole corporation. Winton is leading it, taking Karolyn for support, and Crandall will be attending from HQ with corporate legal people.

"The TaiChin executives always have security with them, and given the sensitive nature of these things, I want you to be there for our team…Just to be sure nothing gets out of hand and everyone stays safe."

Arthur spent the next hour briefing Porter, describing Zhou, Lin, and the pre-existing tension between Taiwan and China. Arthur added his own concerns, including Winton's penchant for *faux pas* that could get crossways with the Asian culture.

"I won't bore you with the technical agenda of the meetings, but I want you to stay on top of the schedule and learn the hotel layout."

The schedule covered multiple days, with a break Saturday and Sunday, except for a formal dinner Saturday evening. Monday's closing session would finalize the Due Diligence Phase. He told Porter it was important for everything to run smoothly because McNeil was unable to be there, due to his Congressional hearings.

Next, Arthur gave him a file on the Hong Kong Sheraton in Kowloon, containing a brochure plus details of the banquet and meeting rooms.

Porter was having trouble paying attention. He'd abandoned any attempt to understand the reason behind O'Donnell's about-face, instead drifting into a daydream featuring Karolyn at a spectacular hotel in Hong Kong.

"Porter? Are you with me? I asked if you had your passport."

He reluctantly rejoined the conversation. "Yes, sir. I always keep it up to date and carry it with me in case Mr. McNeil needs me to travel."

"Good. Do you have any decent clothes?"

Porter hadn't packed anything fancy for his trip to California, bringing only one suit. Bracing for irritation when he told Arthur, he was surprised again when Arthur continued his accommodating manner.

"Not a problem. We'll get you a corporate card from Karolyn. I want you to take the rest of the day. Get some rest. Get yourself a couple respectable suits. And Porter…get some dress shoes and lose the boots."

* * *

Sheila managed to get herself awake enough to roll off her bed into a sort of half-stand. She rubbed her eyes and scooted her chair to her computer. After working through the night again, she'd executed her new program to load the test file Arthur sent her, and closed her eyes for a couple of hours. Now she was trying to focus on the data set she'd chosen for her test run, the latest Operating Performance Summary in the McNev financial system.

"Here goes." She entered the command to activate her program.

The format remained untouched, and the data transformed flawlessly, as if simply being refreshed. The new data was exactly what Arthur had given her to load last night, being read from the new databases.

"Holy shit! The damn thing actually works!"

* * *

Karolyn looked up to see Arthur walking out of his office with a nice-looking man who reminded her of an older Bruce Willis. They stopped at her desk.

"Karolyn Babcock meet Porter Bordon. Porter works personal security for Hugh, and he's been out here on special assignment. I decided it would be a good idea for him to join the Hong Kong trip as security for our team. I've just finished briefing him, so he's up to speed on the schedule and hotel. Can you please add Porter to the travel arrangements and issue him a corporate card?"

She motioned for Porter to sit in the chair next to her desk as Arthur returned to his office.

"So, Mr. Bordon, you get to come to Hong Kong with us. If you haven't stayed at the Kowloon Sheraton, you're gonna love it. You look familiar. Have we met?"

Porter was blushing and having trouble swallowing because his mouth had suddenly become a sand trap. He felt like a kid in high school talking to the best-looking girl around, trying to get up the nerve to ask for a date.

He managed, "No, ma'am, I don't think so…Please call me Porter."

Karolyn smiled. "Okay, deal, as long as you don't call me ma'am. Karolyn or KB works for me."

As they went through the arrangements, he found Karolyn so easy to talk to, he became as comfortable as if they'd been long-time friends. Perhaps it was her nature, or maybe his wishful thinking, but she appeared to be at ease with him as well.

Arthur came out of his office, and Karolyn looked up as he walked past them. He said over his shoulder, "Having lunch with Teri."

Karolyn glanced down at his schedule.

Noticing her puzzled look, Porter asked: "Problem?"

She shook her head and turned back to him. "Nope, it's fine. Do you have any questions for me?"

"Just one, Karolyn…why isn't Mr. O'Donnell coming with us?"

Her eyes widened and she leaned closer to him, speaking softly, in a conspiratorial tone. "He refuses to fly—hates it—scares him to death. But if you tell anyone, I'll have to kill you."

She winked at him.

16

Teri sat across from Arthur in the private alcove of the executive dining room, pleasantly surprised by the last-minute invitation. Within minutes, their lunch was being served on elegant white china, with the linen tablecloth graced by a rose in a crystal budvase, completing a picture-perfect table setting.

Arthur tried engaging Teri in amiable conversation, but her thoughts lingered on McNev's apparent chaos, the TaiChin partnership, and the absence of any logical reason for Rich being left out of the loop. Surely someone as intelligent and driven as Arthur would want to take advantage of Rich's talent when McNev's future was at stake.

Deciding this was the perfect opportunity to resolve her quandary, she met Arthur's eyes with an earnest expression.

"Arthur, may I ask you something?"

"Anything," he replied, with unexpected intimacy.

"Why isn't Rich in on the partnership negotiations?"

Teri thought she saw a tiny clench of his jaw as he answered. "I know you enjoyed working with him, Teri...maybe even had feelings for him."

When her expression tensed, his tone softened. "Don't get me wrong—I respect his aircraft production expertise. But he's made a career of digging up problems, and now he's seeing things that just aren't there. I couldn't risk it in the middle of a critical and delicate process...Doesn't that make sense?"

Teri paused in contemplation, cutting up a crostini-size crouton. She was about to explain why she didn't consider accomplished problem-solving to be a detriment, when he asked, "How is it?"

Caught off guard by the unexpected subject change, she turned her attention to her salad. "Excellent. The Caesar dressing is amazing, and grilled shrimp is my favorite."

Arthur beamed. "I'm so glad. I had Chef make it special for us." Teri began puzzling over how he knew she liked grilled shrimp when he switched topics again. "I was hoping you'd join me on the Peninsula tonight. There's this great restaurant, the Crab Cooker."

"Thanks. I love that place, but I'm busy tonight—sorry."

She recognized the same probing intensity in his eyes she'd seen on the boat as he asked abruptly, "Do you think it's a good idea to see Rich?"

Stifling the shiver from a chill skittering through her, she said, "Excuse me, but how did you know I'm meeting Rich, and why is it any of your business?"

He smiled again, and she felt her indignation melting in spite of herself. His reply was smooth and relaxed.

"Well, I know because you just told me, and it's my business because I care about you." His concerned smile somehow managed to further enhance his attractiveness. "Look, I'm not trying to creep you out here. You have such an amazing future in front of you, and...there's no easy way to say this, but Rich will only hold you back."

The cryptic remarks, compounded by the chemistry she couldn't shut off, caught her off balance again. "I...I'm not sure what you mean."

"Most people have no idea that I operate on a plane—forgive the pun—far above everyone else. People at this level share a unique combination of superior intellect, keen insight, and natural leadership, enabling them to attain the best of everything. They're exceedingly rare, and...I believe you are one of them."

Teri felt her pulse quicken, unsure if it was from his flattery or her uncertainty. "Thank you, that's nice to hear. But I have no idea where you're going with this."

"Special people like us need to stick together. In order to realize our potential, it's necessary to distance ourselves from those that hinder us..."

He paused. "I see that look." He reached across the table and gently touched her hand. "I know this is a lot to take in. Come to dinner with me tonight, and I'll explain everything to you."

"I'm not quite sure why you're being so mysterious, but if you're referring to Rich, I don't understand. He's certainly not a hindrance—he should recover soon."

Looking at his dubious expression, Teri felt a twinge of uneasiness, suddenly craving Rich's presence. "I worked alongside him for years. He's a smart, effective professional, and totally dedicated to this place."

Arthur sighed. "This is something I need to help you with—the biggest stumbling block for newcomers—misguided loyalty."

"Are you saying I shouldn't be loyal to McNev? To colleagues like Rich...and you?"

"I'm saying that fulfilling your future requires you to be loyal to *yourself* first...I can help you with that, but you'll have to trust me."

"And trusting you means joining you for dinner, rather than visiting Rich?"

"I think you'll find it's a much better use of your evening."

Although she found his obtuse manner to be off-putting, imagining herself at dinner with him and his alluring smile wasn't completely unappealing. Her expression brightened as an idea came to her.

"Arthur, how about this? I'll visit Rich tonight and see how he's doing...I've got some ideas that might spark his memory. You and I can have dinner one night later this week and discuss how he could help with the new partnership, once he returns."

She watched him hesitate. Though it was mere seconds, Teri sensed his thoughts extended far beyond her simple proposal. His reaction was something she never saw coming.

Arthur's demeanor transformed as instantly as if it were being injected with liquid nitrogen, and the degree of disappointed frustration in his tone felt just as chilling. "With all that's going on, I really don't think we'll have the chance—I've got to get back to work."

* * *

Karolyn knocked and opened Rich's office door, this time finding Teri seated at his desk staring at nothing that she could see.

"Hey—didn't mean to interrupt...we need to talk."

It took Teri a moment to respond. "Sorry...I just finished a rather bizarre lunch with Arthur."

"Yes, I know—he never takes lunch."

Teri shook her head. "That's not what I meant..."

Karolyn interrupted. "You mean the news he just gave me?"

Teri shot Karolyn a wide-eyed look. "What news?" A startling thought hit her. *My God, is he letting me go?*

"He didn't tell you at lunch? That *is* strange...He's sending you to Hong Kong with us—told me to add you to the travel arrangements."

Teri pictured her brain as the fried egg in the old anti-drug ads.

"He's sending me to Hong Kong?"

Karolyn cleared a space on the table and set down the reports she was carrying. Noticing the level of stress in her new friend's tone of voice, she said, "Relax, kiddo, come sit down. I'll go over everything with you...it'll be fine. The Kowloon Sheraton is really nice."

Over the next couple of hours, they reviewed the Due Diligence data Teri first saw in the meeting yesterday. The time flew by with her mind in warp-drive trying to absorb detailed financial analysis, providing a welcome distraction from her unsettling lunch conversation.

Karolyn stopped suddenly. "Oh, my God, I forgot to ask—is your passport current?"

"Yep, so are my hepatitis and yellow fever vaccinations. You know, I traveled to Taipei last year for AeroSystems."

Karolyn looked impressed. "Wow, that might be worth another 'A.'"

"Yeah, but I didn't meet Philip Lin in my travels...Does that mean I lose my extra credit?"

Smiling, Karolyn called her a smart-aleck, adding, "Seriously, Teri, I'm glad you're coming. I'll feel better having you there."

Realizing her comfort level with Karolyn had grown significantly, Teri decided to open up about her lingering concerns, gently touching Karolyn's arm.

"Feel free to tell me if it's none of my business, but can I ask you a couple of things?"

Karolyn nodded. "Shoot."

"I'm sure you know this, but your work here is way above your position title. You're more knowledgeable on the details of the partnership and financials than Winton…what's the deal?"

Karolyn sighed. "When I started working for Arthur, I was just his diversionary tool to help 'manage' Winton. Arthur picked him for his leadership presence, and quite frankly, because his ego is bigger than his brain. Arthur knew he needed someone up front to push things, while being okay with Arthur steering from behind."

Karolyn rubbed the back of her neck, continuing, "Unfortunately, it turned out Jackson was less…capable than Arthur anticipated, and I got more proficient, learning from him, and working my ass off. Together, we've made it work."

Teri's reply was unaccusatory. "Forgive me, but why keep up the act?"

Karolyn gave her a look that said *really?* "How do you think it would play if other VPs or TaiChin execs knew Winton couldn't find the White House if he was standing in the middle of Pennsylvania Avenue? I can be Arthur's voice guiding him, as well as Arthur's eyes and ears for whatever happens, while no one believes I'm anything more than Jackson's little travel buddy…And this is the home stretch, we're almost there."

Remembering their conversation on the boat, Teri didn't push the issue. Instead, she said, "But now I'll be with you, and it's pretty obvious what Winton thinks of me."

"Not to worry. As long as he looks like he's the boss in front of everyone…just follow my lead."

Teri arched one eyebrow.

"No, not that. I think he knows that ain't gonna happen…which is likely why he's giving you the pissy attitude."

Teri nodded. "Yeah, well, considering the alternative, I think I'll live with the attitude."

Karolyn looked pensive but said nothing, so Teri moved on to her final question. "Why in the world isn't Arthur coming with us to Hong Kong?"

Karolyn dissolved into laughter. "Have you met Porter Bordon?"

* * *

Teri headed out as soon as she and Karolyn finished, a little after three o'clock. She had too many things to do, and too little time to get them done, plus she needed space to process her lunch meeting as well as consider her strategy with Rich tonight.

She'd given her word she'd respect the confidentiality of the TaiChin partnership. Yet she was conflicted by her belief that Rich deserved to know, especially because it seemed to be a major piece of this whole crazy puzzle. And now it appeared that Arthur regarded Rich as an impediment, which baffled her completely.

She managed to run her errands, change, and leave for Laguna by a little after five. Driving away from the condo and turning south on Pacific Coast Highway, questions seemed to rush at her like oncoming traffic.

Is there something to Rich's theory? Or is he really losing it…becoming paranoid? Arthur seems to think so…Apparently, he also thinks I have some sort of special potential. But why does he seem so hell-bent on keeping me away from Rich?

* * *

Porter left the plant by mid-afternoon and used his corporate credit card in a diligent effort to be professionally outfitted for Hong Kong. He also focused on looking a little GQ for a more personal reason, especially pleased with his purchase of Dr. Martens dress shoes.

Instead of heading back to Texas to look for work, he was walking into the apartment with new clothes and luggage, courtesy of McNev, and marveling at his positive change in circumstance.

After stowing his purchases, Porter cleared off the coffee table to lay out the Personnel Summaries Mary had printed for him early that morning. He read Herrera's employment history, which included three different unions. He noted the one he knew well—It had a reputation for playing hardball and less-than-ethical tactics.

Next, he examined the summaries of the three reinstated employees. The mystery of *LJ* was solved immediately. Lawrence Vale's info sheet had *Jr.* in the suffix name field. Lawrence Vale Junior…Lawrence Junior…LJ. Vale's personnel sheet showed he'd received warnings for missing work and been through two grievance hearings, then terminated for cause, before being reinstated by Darren Duke.

Porter's hunch was that Herrera's conversation with Vale, directing some sort of covert installation on 913, could be connected to the wrongdoing he suspected of O'Donnell and Crandall. He should tell Greer or McKinley about what he overheard so they could look into it, except he was leaving for Hong Kong tomorrow.

For the moment, he put all his information into a folder, including his notes on the Herrera-LJ conversation.

* * *

Arthur drove up from the tower garage into the sunshine, and realized he couldn't remember the last time he'd left work in daylight. Although he'd been in high spirits this morning, embracing the possibility he'd finally met someone who deserved him, he'd been let down once again. When he'd listened to the condo phone-tap recording of Teri's prior night call to Sheila, he'd taken immediate corrective action.

Based on his intel from Teri's prior tenure at Everett, he'd had the chef prepare her favorite salad for a special lunch. He'd been tactful and persuasive, giving her the perfect opportunity to follow him on the correct path, and disassociate from Richmond.

He'd designed her scenario with just the right touch, certain she'd choose wisely. Unfortunately, her unwarranted loyalty and inability to see Richmond for what he was, eluded his control. His nails dug into the padded leather on the steering wheel of his BMW 740 as a nagging memory paid an unwanted visit.

The dreadful images were the same every time: a twelve-year-old boy sitting in the kitchen the night his father had come home and told his mother he'd been laid off, his father, shaken and devastated, and his mother in tears. Their fear and discouragement discussing their uncertain future left an indelible impression on Arthur. Their weakness sickened him still to this day.

It was then he'd first realized how much better he was. Arthur always knew he was different, but that night he knew why. *The best in life belongs only to that rare man who commands and controls—everything .*

He'd committed that same night to putting himself first, always, because his destiny was forged through that simple philosophy. Success depended on absolute mastery, which, in turn, required him to be smarter and work harder. He was fully aware that this approach to life would isolate him, but he'd let himself hope Teri was suitable to join him.

Sadly, by the time he'd returned to his office after cutting their lunch short, his only thought was to get her out of his sight, so he told Karolyn he was sending Teri to Hong Kong. Once he'd calmed down, Arthur allowed himself to acknowledge that her failure had been a major disappointment, provoking his angry reaction at her absurd decision to continue associating with that pathetic loser.

However, after considering things, he was applauding his wisdom, realizing, as always, his response was perfectly apropos. Dispatching Teri to Hong Kong would keep her separated from Richmond simply by eliminating her ability to choose otherwise. Plus it added credibility to the scenario.

By the time his garage door closed behind him, rational thinking was restoring his balance. It was better to have discovered her flawed nature sooner than later, giving him the advantage of not having to deal with feelings that could compromise decisions in the critical final stage.

Arthur removed his tie and walked out on his patio, anticipating being refreshed by the ocean breeze. But as he looked across the Newport Bay, an intractable sadness parked itself in the pit of his stomach.

I need a glass of Glenmorangie—perhaps two.

* * *

Teri pulled into Sheila's driveway, and before she shut off the engine, Lisa was bounding toward her car. Teri climbed out of her Jeep and knelt into the warmth of an embrace, admitting to herself that she found Lisa's hug surprisingly therapeutic. Lisa took her hand, leading her through the front door, and announcing, "Aunt Teri's here—Aunt Teri's here!"

Sheila was taking baked potatoes out of the oven and dishing up green beans. Teri noticed the color had returned to her cheeks; she looked relieved.

"Hey, good to see you—here." She gave Teri a smile and handed her a glass of Beringer Reserve Cabernet.

Teri held up the bottle, examining it with a melodramatic wide-eyed expression. "Wow—you broke out the good stuff, just for me?"

"If you must know, I'm celebrating finishing my project—and stop being such a smart-ass. Rich is out back barbecuing—go bother him."

Teri walked down the steps to the patio, her taste buds aroused by aroma of char-grilling steaks. Rich put down his spatula and hugged her like he meant it.

She said, "You look like you feel better."

His smile was reassuring. "Best I've felt since the accident. I backed off my meds, and then today, I didn't take them at all. I figured if I felt better at half, I might be better off without them…and so far, so good!"

Teri was about to tell him how great that was, and fill him in on her conversation with Mac, when Lisa and Sheila came out of the kitchen carrying the rest of dinner.

Sheila said, "Let's eat."

Although Halloween was fast approaching, the weather was still warm, and coupled with daylight savings time, they were able to eat at the patio table, enjoying a classic Southern California sunset.

After dinner, Lisa volunteered to help her Aunt Sheila clean up if her "Aunt" Teri would read her a story and tuck her in, later.

Sheila and Lisa took the dishes inside as Teri helped Rich pick up outside. After stowing the tablecloth and barbeque tools in a workshop cabinet, Teri asked if they could talk for a few minutes.

Seated on the workshop stools, she began with the highlights from Mac. She explained Vale, the report, and the connector, hoping to jog his memory. Rich listened intently, quiet for several moments before speaking.

"So you think the mechanic, this Vale kid, is the son of the Dr. Vale who discharged me from Saddleback? I'm not sure I see the connection."

"What if there was something that someone didn't want you looking into, and they used Vale's kid to pressure his father into prescribing meds to keep you doped up? Don't you think it's quite a coincidence that the doctor who took over your discharge is also named Vale?"

Rich concentrated. "Yeah, the report. Mac said I saw Vale's and Herrera's names in it? Well, I definitely remember Herrera's a complete asswipe, so that's something."

Teri smiled and kept prompting. "Can you remember anything else about the report…that obsolete connector?"

"Everything is just out of reach. Like when you're trying to remember the name of a movie, and it's on the tip of your tongue. It sounds intriguing, though, and you know I love mysteries."

Teri tried once more. "Mac said you showed it to him. An eight-pin lock-tite plug."

As Rich sat ruminating, they noticed Lisa, who'd come out to retrieve Teri for story time. She'd been standing quietly in the doorway, in her *Little Mermaid* nightshirt and bunny slippers.

Lisa moved between their stools and bent down underneath the workbench. She dug through a plastic bin at the back of a bottom shelf, retrieving a screw-socket plug.

Rich was about to scold her for crawling under the workbench in her clean nightshirt, when she held up the mystery connector and handed it to him.

"Is this the one Aunt Teri's talking about, Daddy?"

Rich took the connector and stared at it. Images flashed like a monitor powering up. He was in his Lexus, looking at the connector lying on the passenger seat. His mind began flipping through memories, doing an impression of the Main Street Arcade Kinetoscope.

Flashbacks: opening the report, getting caught by O'Donnell, talking with Mac, driving home—the crash!

He swayed, nearly falling off his stool, reflexively grabbing the back of his head with a loud, "Damn!"

Rich recovered his balance and gave his daughter a huge smile. "Lisa, you're amazing! You are definitely my favorite daughter."

He knelt down and held her in a long hug.

Lisa giggled, "You're silly, Daddy. I'm your *only* daughter."

Rich looked up at Teri, and she knew the instant she saw his eyes.

"Yes!" she shouted. "Welcome back!"

17

Tuesday, 10:15 p.m. Central Daylight Time

It was quiet in the Texas countryside neighborhood, save for the bush katydids singing louder than usual on a warm October evening. Will Crandall hoisted himself from his spa tub after a vigorous Jacuzzi massage. He stood naked before the full-length adjacent mirror, admiring himself before wrapping up in his over-sized Hydrocotton bath towel.

Will lived in Trophy Club, an affluent suburb thirty-minutes north of the Dallas-Fort Worth metroplex. Located inside a gated community, he purchased his custom home last year, declaring his *executive-suite-of-a-major-corporation* status.

Trophy Club's championship golf course provided an expedient platform for career advancement in a community of well-connected people who were just Will's sort. The sort of people with enough power to make them useful.

Will loved this house. Indulging his lavish taste, he spent excessively to create a master bedroom with what he'd christened his *"en-suite* bathing and rejuvenation facility," complete with pentagonal multi-head shower and mini-sauna, in addition to the circular Jacuzzi tub.

But the home's ultimate feature was its isolated cul-de-sac location, perfectly suited for privacy—something Will valued more than most. Privacy was key to Will's favorite hobby: personal pleasure, an avocation he pursued with abandon.

On most nights by this time, he'd be engrossed in a game of gratification with male or female playmates—sometimes both, depending on his mood. His crowning achievement in the master suite was the concealed closet behind his bookcase, which secured a spicy assortment of pleasure games, toys, and gadgets.

Tonight, however, he was pressed into solitude, focused on tomorrow's trip to Hong Kong, reviewing Arthur's scenario notes. On the positive side, the trip did include a rendezvous with Zhou Quon, a close partner in both business and pleasure.

Will grew up in Southern California, raised in the aerospace industry. Both his parents worked alternately between Northrop and Lockheed, at the whim of the hiring and layoff cycles. His upper-working-class family had been disdainfully ordinary in his eyes.

In 1969, while attending a local junior college, Will's mother got him a summer job at Lockheed in electrical assembly, leading him to discover his career goal. He'd never forget the day he got his first look at a senior executive who happened to visit the manufacturing floor. He was mesmerized by the way everyone kowtowed to the man in the suit, including his own supervisor, who he'd watched tremble when the VP stopped to talk to him.

That was the moment Will knew that one day he would be a senior executive, that special person, commanding deference from those around him.

He abhorred his monotone aerospace-worker parents, who'd expected him to follow their mundane careers, working as a nobody. He'd made a vow as a teenager: *I am not going to be my parents.* He wasn't ordinary. He was special.

Will had faced challenges with being special most of his life, particularly in school. Whether it was due to his slim stature and classic facial features bordering on delicate, or his proclivity for intimacy with both sexes, gym class became his personal hell. Being harassed during gym class was not especially noteworthy in the sixties, but the day Will ended up on the floor of the showers with a group of boys urinating on him, crystalized the need to fortify his emotional survival skills.

His answer: *privacy*.

To Will, privacy became more than a necessity. He turned it into an art, learning quickly that secrets create strong currency in trade for career growth. Developing his inventory of intimate experiences, he spent years honing his skill in leveraging the power of potential scandals. He put it fully into practice when he moved to Texas and joined McNeil Aerospace, under the command of Darren Duke.

Combining his obsession with pleasure and his mastery of coercion, Will climbed the corporate hierarchy, obtaining a position on Duke's executive staff. Some managers derided his position, staff assignments not being considered real management jobs, but Will knew their ridicule was born of jealousy.

He enjoyed his years at Duke's side for the most part. Not only did the position free him from the ranks of plebian assembly workers, it also gave him a taste of executive authority.

When Duke relocated to Southern California as part of the McNeil–Everett merger, he'd endorsed Will for Hugh McNeil's Administrative Director position. Will jumped at the chance to penetrate the executive inner sanctum, with access to the highest levels of management and confidential information, only to encounter an unanticipated and disheartening circumstance with McNeil. Not only did the Chairman have no interest in becoming a playmate, Will sensed McNeil had an aversion to him from the day he'd taken the position.

Working around McNeil's frosty rapport led Will to discover the perfect mentor. He cherished each lesson from Arthur O'Donnell, who he'd deemed the "Wizard of Machination." Arthur showed him another level of exploiting people for profit. His only reservation was Arthur appearing to be a bit of a stick-in-the-mud when it came to personal entertainment.

Will played with the cherry stem in his Maker's Mark Manhattan as he reviewed his Hong Kong notes one last time.

He'd confirmed the Saturday dinner arrangements that had Winton seated near Zhou and his team to give Winton's offensiveness maximum exposure. He reviewed the Due-Diligence legal material, satisfied it had the surface credibility to maintain the pretense.

His thoughts drifted to Bordon. He'd been told that he and Teri Harlan were now included, and really didn't care to deal with the potential confrontation by a still-angry Bordon while trying to handle the Hong Kong scenario.

Arthur was due to call any moment. He debated trying to talk Arthur out of sending Bordon, deciding it would depend on how much lingering irritation Arthur still held toward him for suggesting Porter in the first place.

How the hell was I supposed to know Bordon would go sticking his nose into things? He seemed like a one-trick pony, longing for the good old days, pushing people around. God knows he's got the body for it...

He smiled, and slid into a voyeur fantasy diversion, waiting for the phone to ring.

18

Tuesday, 9:00 p.m. Pacific Daylight Time

Teri descended the compact staircase wearing an accomplished smile. "She's all tucked in. I guess I did okay with story time, because I just got told I'm also a favorite aunt."

Sheila handed Teri a mug of fresh coffee and said, "Here you go—congrats on graduating to 'favorite' status."

Grinning as Teri gave her a friendly nudge, Sheila moved to her preferred over-stuffed chair, sitting down, and tucking her feet under her. Teri took a seat next to Rich on the loveseat, setting her coffee on the steamer trunk.

Just as Teri sat, Rich stood. Caught between elation at regaining his memory and disquiet from what he remembered, he spoke with energy that reminded Teri of working with him years ago.

"I didn't get a real good look at the car, but it was blue…pretty sure it was a Chrysler, and the left headlight needed adjusting. It kept shining in my mirrors. I guess it probably wouldn't do much good to file a police report at this point."

Teri said, "So there *was* another car, and he ran you off the road deliberately?"

"Damn right! I remember him sideswiping me in the turn."

Teri gave Sheila an "I-told-you-so" look. Sheila shrugged, responding with a slightly defensive tone. "I only said the police never mentioned anything about another car being involved."

Teri looked back to Rich. "Could it have been random road rage?"

"I don't think so…there was nothing to cause it. I know I sound like a conspiracy nut, but I remember the car following me for a long time on the freeway." He paused before adding, "I've never seen this level of crazy at McNev, Ter…It's seriously scary."

Teri thought back to her conversation from the night before. "Yeah, Mac and Al echoed your assessment…the unrest in production, and the attempts at intentional damage. Al seems to think it stems from Herrera."

Rich nodded as he drained his coffee. "If there was one person I'd believe to be capable of thug-tactic violence, it'd be Herrera."

Teri shifted into problem-solving mode. "And I also think there's something to the Vale connection. If his father took over your discharge, it might explain the prescriptions. Do you know if Herrera's tight with the Vale kid?"

Rich shook his head. "Don't know...Herrera's definitely slimy, though."

"But do you really think Herrera would hire someone to hurt you or try to kill you...that's just insane!" She stood emphatically, adding, "This whole thing is fucking nuts—maybe it *is* time to involve the police."

Rich was struck by Teri's intensity, using an expletive he seldom heard from her. "I don't disagree, Ter, but I don't know what we could tell them without more to go on. How about you and I get together with Mac tomorrow? The three of us could go through that electrical issues list. We might find a pattern."

Although Teri was happy to have Rich running on all cylinders, it was time for a reality check. "Slow down a minute, tiger. Before you and I go riding to the rescue on our white horses, you've got to get cleared by your doctor to return to work, and that might pose a problem, don't you think?"

Rich looked surprised. "How so? I feel great!"

Sheila, who'd been listening quietly to their spirited conversation, stepped in. "Well, there's a real possibility the good Dr. Vale may not be working in your best interests. He never returned my calls. Teri could be right about him."

Rich nodded. "Excellent point. If he is involved somehow, this isn't the time to confront him—not until we find out how the pieces fit. Why don't I call Dr. Meyer and make an appointment? If he doesn't want to do a return-to-work clearance for me, I'm sure he'd recommend someone. I could just tell him I'd prefer not to see Vale and leave it at that."

Rich stopped, looking thoughtful.

"What?" Teri asked.

"Something's still bothering me. That report I saw was addressed to O'Donnell. Herrera might be in on it, but this seems too big for him—he's not that smart. I've been getting a progressively sinister vibe from ol' Art the past several weeks. I trust him about as far as I can throw him...I think my gut has known for a while he's up to no good."

Teri's intuition alarm activated again. Recalling Arthur's smooth but less-than-subtle effort at lunch to build a wall between her and Rich, she tried to reconcile the contradictory perspectives.

Arthur is definitely being manipulative...But isn't he also leading the charge on a partnership to save this place? Damn, I wish I could talk about it with Rich.

Slipping into quiet contemplation, the two of them noticed Sheila becoming unnaturally still. She revealed an increasingly painful expression, which morphed into a grimace like a mold cracking, leading directly to uncontrollable crying. Sheila grabbed the pillow next to her and buried her face, while Rich and Teri looked at each other, totally bewildered.

* * *

Karolyn parallel parked, carefully negotiating the only space she could find after nine-thirty, two blocks from Arthur's house.

She'd changed out of her work clothes into her burgundy Russell Athletics sweat suit and sneakers before coming over, so she didn't mind the walk. She turned onto O'Donnell's street, and was a couple of houses away when she saw Arthur standing outside on his balcony, talking on his portable home phone.

Getting closer, she heard him say, "Will—how's the preparation coming?" so she lingered in front of the garage underneath the balcony.

"Yes, I already said I want Bordon there...No, I've just had a really ugly day...Good, sounds like that'll work for ramping up Winton...and don't forget the contract details need to sound real."

Karolyn froze, not breathing. Someone was behind her, holding her tightly with a hand clamped over her mouth. She focused on the self-defense moves she'd been practicing in class. She bent her knee, readying herself to kick her heel backward at her attacker when a voice whispered in her ear.

"Shhh, it's all right. It's Porter."

She relaxed enough to realize his hands didn't feel menacing. His grip was strong, yet somehow gentle.

He whispered, "I'm gonna take my hand away. I just didn't want you to make any noise. If you can stay quiet, nod your head."

Karolyn nodded and turned to face him as he let go.

Without saying a word, she took Porter by the hand and led him two houses away, into an alley, out of sight and earshot of Arthur's balcony.

"What the hell are you doing? You scared me shitless! I was just about to kick you..."

She could tell Porter's face was red, even in the dark. "I'm so sorry, Karolyn. I thought you might be startled if you saw me. And if you shouted or screamed, we'd both be in trouble."

"First of all, I don't scream. And second, what in hell are you doing here?"

"Well, to be honest, I've had questions about some of the things Arthur asked me to do, and I kinda lean toward being suspicious. So I've been spending a couple of evenings here to see if I could find out what he was up to."

He stepped back, looking like he expected her to slap the night air off his cheek. Instead, she smiled. "So, did you see me here the other night? Have you been watching me too?"

"Oh, no, not in that way. Not at *all*. I was worried when you ran out the other night, though. I thought you might be hurt."

Karolyn smiled again at the school-boy tone, coming from a man who'd just put her in a headlock. "Well, that's sweet of you."

She paused, and then added, "You know, I've been having the same feeling that Arthur could be up to something...Let's sneak back and find out what else we can hear."

* * *

While Rich sat down, still looking perplexed, Teri could see the dam Sheila created to hold everything back, just experienced catastrophic failure. Teri moved to the wide armrest of Sheila's chair, putting her arm around her friend, offering comfort that was gratefully accepted.

It took several minutes of crying into Teri's shoulder before Sheila's sobs subsided to sniffles. Rich retrieved a box of tissues from the kitchen, and after blowing her nose, Sheila collected herself to explain.

"I'm so sorry, you two. I didn't tell you any of this because...you're my family, and family is supposed to protect each other."

Rich and Teri regarded her with warm, concerned, and very confused expressions.

"I was afraid that telling you would put you in harm's way, but at this point it's probably more dangerous *not* to tell you. Besides, I can't take this evading shit any longer. I need to get it all out—so just let me talk.

"About three years ago, when I was getting started, Arthur became one of my first clients. Rich, I think you'd just met him, and I didn't know him at all. He called and said he'd heard from a business associate how talented I was. It was just after the McNev merger when McNeil hired him as Executive VP.

"He wanted me to develop some complex interface software. After our initial meetings, I was very attracted to him. He'd just given me my first big contract, and he was brilliant, great looking, and kind of mysterious. He told me I was gifted, in a rare class of people...I thought I was falling for him, and we...I slept with him."

Going directly from nonplussed to outraged, Rich got to his feet, ready to launch into a tirade. Sheila held up her hand, motioning for him to sit.

"I know—why do you think I never told you? Anyway, that's not the worst part."

Rich jumped up again. "Not the *worst* part?"

This time Teri reached up, taking Rich's hand, and pulled him back to sit with her on the loveseat. "Easy, Rich. We need to let your sister finish."

Sheila went on. "He said I was the key to helping him succeed with his turn-around of McNev. He had this whole scenario...how I was special, and together we'd have the best life had to offer. All I had to do was trust him and follow his plans."

Teri began to shift uncomfortably as Sheila continued.

"His concept for enhancing the new McNev Sybase System was really innovative, a cutting-edge remote interface to do direct database updates using an Advantage Database Server."

Teri got an *I'm lost* expression. "I hate to interrupt, but I'm not fluent in computer-ese."

"Sorry. The technical details aren't important. I was enthusiastic and thrived on his flattery. But then I figured out that the application I was building would provide unlimited power to change McNev production, procurement, or financial data, through a remote system totally undetected.

"As I learned more about enterprise systems security and accountability, I realized I was building the ultimate back door. It was completely unethical, and I told him I wouldn't finish it…that didn't sit well."

Sheila's voice began to crack. "Arthur took the express lane from Jekyll to Hyde. He broke off our relationship and told me he'd never really been interested in me. I'll never forget how much it stung when he called me a 'tiresome little nerd slut.'"

Rich couldn't sit any longer, bolting to his feet again as he swore between gritted teeth. "That no good sonofabitch. I'm gonna deck him!"

He paced, trying to control himself. After a moment, he apologized, asking his sister to finish.

Sheila's tone became softer and more pained. "It was a side of him I'd never seen. Icy…soulless. He found another programmer, Beth Quinn, to finish his system, and not long after she started working with him, she told me she was falling for him. Of course, I shared my experience, but she didn't believe me."

Teri handed Sheila a tissue. She dabbed her eyes as she kept talking.

"I didn't speak to Arthur again until several months later, shortly after you and Lisa moved in. Rich, you were a mess. I was trying to comfort you, help with Lisa, and keep my sanity. One afternoon, Arthur called, like he just wanted to say hello and catch up…and then he turned super-creepy.

"He asked if I'd talked to you, or anyone about him and me, or about the interface application. I told him no, and he said, 'Good—keep it that way. Remember, bad things can happen if people aren't careful.' That night on TV there was a news story about Beth—she was killed in a freak accident in the parking garage of her condo."

Rich blurted, "Holy shit," his angry expression turning to disbelief.

Teri chimed in with "Oh, my God!" Her head spun, trying to assimilate this side of Arthur.

Rich asked, "Why didn't you call the police?"

"And tell them what, exactly? I had no proof that it wasn't accidental. It's always that way with Arthur…"

Sheila looked up at her brother. "I was terrified to tell you anything. And you just kept going on about him. Then I got really anxious when you talked about finding some stupid report…"

She paused, continuing with a sad expression. "I knew you couldn't leave it alone, and sure enough, you couldn't!"

Rich stood still, looking down at the floor.

Sheila turned to Teri. "And since you arrived, I've been even more afraid…for both of you."

Sheila stood and joined her brother, pacing. Her shoulders straightened and her tone took on an edge. "*Then*, as if that wasn't bad enough, he calls and demands I develop *another* application! He used the same veiled threats he'd used about Beth, with *your* accident, Rich! He told me not to say a word to either of you…that it was the only way to keep you safe. That's why I've been acting so insane."

She took a breath. Her voice grew stronger. "Well, I finished his damn program last night, and it works. I'm gonna give it to him and be done. And I pray to God he leaves us all the hell alone."

Teri watched the two of them pacing, her mind overwhelmed and her stomach in knots. *Now I know why Arthur didn't want me staying here…and if I'd spent the evening with him tonight, I would never have known any of this.*

She visualized herself at dinner with Arthur weaving his web of charm and wielding his magic smile as he recruited her. Then she abruptly shook it off. *Special my ass—phony bastard. Sheila, me…and what about Karolyn?*

19

Wednesday, 11:15 a.m.

It was nearly 1:30 a.m. when Teri returned to the condo, exhausted, and upset by the conversation with Rich and Sheila, resulting in her struggling this morning from a woeful lack of sleep. Trying frantically to tidy Rich's office before heading to the airport, her escalating level of frustration was inversely proportional to the rate of her progress.

Teri took pride in her ability to multitask, and her flexible focus had often been key to her success as a manager. But at the moment, the capacity to concentrate escaped her. She was also distracted by unanswered questions, including Arthur's intentions for the new software—Sheila had told them last night that she had no idea of the program's purpose.

Although tempted, Teri hadn't divulged the partnership plans. Instead, she'd told Rich that the last-minute Hong Kong trip was to finalize the Tailia delivery schedule and discuss solutions for the remaining quality issues.

Rich had taken her explanation with a large measure of skepticism. Being familiar with Tailia's issues, he'd told her he found it "more than a little unusual" to require a meeting with TaiChin in Hong Kong, particularly involving Winton. His negative reaction capped off the stressful evening.

Teri was looking forward to the long flight, planning to unwind into some much-needed contemplation, relieved to be away from both Arthur and Rich for a few days. She was hoping that finalizing the TaiChin partnership would resolve whatever mystery might be lurking behind McNev operations, as well as the animosity between Arthur and Rich. But in the back of her mind was an ominous feeling that Rich's conspiracy theory could be legitimate.

She was currently focused on moving her things to her new office now that the painting was finished. Her goal was to clear out of Rich's office and be on her way before he arrived.

Rich had gotten a release from Dr. Meyer early that morning, and called to let her know he was on the way in, just needing to stop by McNev Medical Services to process his return-to-work forms. It was now late morning, and she figured he was likely to turn up any minute.

She put a file box of her reports under one arm, and grabbed a small box of personal items with her other hand. Lifting the lever with her elbow and pushing the door open, Teri found herself face-to-face with Arthur.

"Hi there—Can I help with that? Looks like you have your hands full."

Arthur took the banker's box from under her arm, leaving her to carry the smaller box. They walked two doors down the hall in silence, entering her freshly painted office and setting the boxes on the table.

"Did you need to see me?" Teri asked as she turned toward the door of her new office. "I've got to get the other boxes."

She didn't wait for his response. She hurried down the hallway, her speed increased by slacks and flat shoes, and back into Rich's office to retrieve the two boxes on his desk.

Finally catching up, Arthur said, "Hey, will you slow down a minute?"

Teri leaned against the desk, turning to face him. She blew the hair that had fallen across her face, and raised her eyebrows, hoping he'd recognize her haste and leave her alone. Not only was she pressed for time, but yesterday's lunch and last night's conversation had landed Arthur squarely atop her list of people she preferred not to see.

When he didn't take the hint, she tried flashing him an "I need to go now" smile, but Arthur simply returned it, emulating her lack of sincerity.

He said, "So I heard Rich is returning today. I guess meeting with him last night did the trick...you have some impressive healing powers."

She answered pointedly, "Actually, his recovery has been amazing since he stopped taking that medication. I just talked to him about work, and it was enough to jog his memory."

"I see...and what did he remember?"

Teri saw the wheels turning in Arthur's head and had no intention of being interrogated. She glanced at her watch and used his technique of switching topics.

"I'm sorry Arthur, I'm really pressed for time. Was there something specific you needed before I go?"

Arthur slid a chair out from the table. "You seem flustered—sit for a minute and catch your breath. I just wondered if you had any questions for me after your briefing yesterday from KB."

His words were friendly but all traces of the warmth he'd shown her were gone. She sensed the same frigid vibe she'd experienced ending their lunch, prompting her to ask the question Karolyn answered for her yesterday.

"Yes, one...Why aren't you coming with us? It would be so much better if you were there."

This time, Teri had no trouble catching that tiny jaw clench.

"I need to be here in order to run point on expediting any additional information..."

He was interrupted by the office door opening. Rich stood in the doorway, blinking. He ran a hand through his hair, and judging by his expression, was about to say something rude. But before he could, Arthur spoke.

"Rich! Perfect timing! I heard you were coming back today. I was just giving our lovely Teri a last-minute pep talk. I'm sure you must be so grateful to have her here. Especially so you don't have to make this brutal trip to Hong Kong."

Rich remained in his doorway, scanning his office as if he were hoping to find a Rosetta Stone. Arthur stood, walked to Rich, and shook his hand, then turned back to the table and slid another chair out. "Please, Rich—sit with us for a few minutes."

Not knowing what else to do, Rich sat down across the table from Teri. O'Donnell continued as if this were as natural for him as a regular staff meeting.

"I know you haven't had a chance to get settled yet, but I'd like to take a few minutes to bring you up to speed before Teri has to leave. I have important news to share with you on McNev's new direction and business strategy."

Arthur summarized the past several months of work with TaiChin on the imminent partnership, including the recent meeting Teri attended. As he talked, Rich's eyes were in constant contact with Teri's, conveying a frenetic mix of confusion, resentment, and disillusionment.

After ten minutes of Arthur's articulate briefing, seemingly without taking a breath, Rich's office door flew open again. Karolyn burst in, breathless.

"Teri, we have to go! We're gonna miss our flight if we don't get out of here right now. Is this your bag?" Karolyn gave Rich a quick "glad you're back" hug, and then grabbed the handle of Teri's carry-on.

Teri stood, her expression frosty, and thanks to Arthur, tinged with humiliation. She managed to say, "Okay, see you guys when we get back," then turned and followed Karolyn out of the office.

Arthur stood and shook Rich's hand again. "Well, Brad, I've taken up enough of your time. I'm sure you have a million things to do. We'll talk later."

As O'Donnell opened the door to leave, he turned, grinning. "And it's great to have you back—really."

* * *

Rich stared at his closed door, taking several cleansing breaths in an attempt to slow his pulse, currently pounding in his temples. He rose slowly from the table with a singular thought. *Damn, I'd* really *like to deck that asshole.*

He saw the two neatly packed boxes of reports sitting on his desk.
Most likely, Teri's stuff she didn't have time to move.

Rich sat at his desk and sighed. He missed Teri already.

Well, at least something is back to normal. Shithead called me Brad. What a way to come back...like catching a short-hop grounder in the nuts.

When O'Donnell was talking about *leveraging synergies*, Rich thought he might puke. He wasn't surprised Arthur hadn't told him about the partnership sooner, but what about McNeil? And why didn't Teri tell him last night?

I can't believe she's setting me up...more likely, Art is setting us both up. I wish I could talk to her. I'll page her. Maybe she can call me from the airport.

* * *

Arthur got off the elevator on the ninth floor, still grinning as he walked to his office. Julia, the assistant who took Karolyn's place when she traveled, looked up from her desk.

"You look happy, Mr. O'Donnell. Please let me know if there's anything I can do for you while Karolyn's in Hong Kong...and with Mr. Winton gone too, I'm all yours." Julia smiled.

Arthur ignored her. He didn't want to disrupt savoring his triumph.

A two-for-one slap in the face—perfect!

During his briefing, he'd paid close attention to Rich's expression, seeing clearly that Teri had kept the confidence about the partnership.

He felt vindicated by dispatching his irritation onto the two of them. It was obvious she'd played a role in Rich discontinuing his medications, leading not only to a fully functional memory but an early return to work.

But it doesn't matter now.

He sighed in satisfaction. His move to send Teri on the trip would keep them separated, and no amount of Rich's snooping could stop the Hong Kong scenario. He recalled his fervor for Teri from two days ago. But as he reflected on her latest betrayal, his thoughts turned dark.

Perhaps I should encourage Jackson to try his luck again in Hong Kong.

* * *

Porter boarded the plane and found his seat, appreciating being booked in first class, especially on a fifteen-hour flight. There were only two seats on each side of the aisle, and they were not only wide, with a console between them, but fully reclining.

Porter was making himself comfortable when he looked up to see Jackson Winton standing in the aisle. He thought Winton looked even more like the ideal executive in person than in the pictures he'd seen. He exuded a commanding presence, and Porter figured he'd own any room he entered. Winton stowed his carry-on in the overhead bin, above the aisle seat next to Porter.

Porter offered his hand. "Nice to meet you, Mr. Winton, I'm Porter Bordon. I've been assigned to accompany your team as your personal security on this trip."

Rather than returning Porter's handshake, Jackson put his hands on the seat arm and console, lowering himself into position.

"I know who the hell you are, and when we get to Hong Kong, Karolyn is going to be in deep shit for switching flights with you. Now shut up and don't talk to me."

He turned toward the aisle.

"Stewardess! Chivas—and make it a double!"

* * *

Teri and Karolyn slid into the rear seat of the company town car assigned to drive them to the airport. They sat for a moment in silence, catching their breath following their sprinting exit from the executive tower. Karolyn spoke first.

"You probably figured out I switched flights with Porter and sent him on the earlier one with Jackson."

"Yeah, I gathered. I'm glad you thought to come get me when you did. I spent the last thirty minutes trying to break free, thinking Porter was out here, about to leave without me..." Teri broke off and looked out the window.

Karolyn said, "So, it was good to see Rich back, even though I didn't have more than two seconds to give him a hug."

When Teri said nothing in return, Karolyn turned to look at her more closely. "Hey, are you all right? You seem frazzled."

"I guess I *must* be. You're the second person who's said that in the past hour."

"Hey, don't bite my head off. I was only asking."

"Sorry...I just finished the world's most uncomfortable meeting with Arthur and Rich."

"Arthur giving you grief?"

Teri hesitated a moment, deciding how much she should say. Surprisingly, Karolyn had not only become a friend but was the one person with whom she felt she could be completely open.

She turned to her and said, "Hold on a sec," holding the switch to raise the privacy glass behind their driver.

Karolyn said, "Wow, is it that serious?"

"I'll let you tell me when I'm finished." She launched into Rich's suspicions about the Herrera report and the possibility his car wreck wasn't an accident. Karolyn didn't comment, but her eyes widened.

Teri kept going, sharing her discussion with Mac, and detailing Sheila's tear-filled, unnerving confession. She finished with her complete indignation at Arthur gleefully disclosing the partnership to Rich in front of her, after he and McNeil adamantly demanded she keep it confidential. They were nearing the airport by the time Teri finished her rant.

Karolyn was silent for more than a minute before she exhaled through pursed lips. "Holy crap. I'm not sure what to say. I know Arthur pushes the envelope and manipulates people…but I've always thought it was just his way of getting things done."

Teri said, "I know this is hitting you cold, but I'm thinking there's more to this than trying to keep the partnership plans confidential. Let me tell you about my lunch."

Boarding the plane, Teri shared her puzzlement over Arthur's attitude toward Rich, which Karolyn took in thoughtfully as she stowed her carry-on. After a moment, she added her own concern.

"I've had the feeling lately that there's something big Arthur isn't telling me. And I think it involves Will Crandall. I don't know what Crandall's up to, but I've never gotten a good vibe from the man."

During a quasi-edible airline dinner, Karolyn opened up, confiding her angry outburst with Arthur at the disrespect he'd shown her the other night.

Teri stopped her with a question.

"If it's okay to ask, what exactly is your relationship with Arthur? I'm not trying to pry…just trying to understand. Believe me, I could see the attraction."

Karolyn reiterated her admiration for Arthur and her appreciation of the time he'd invested in teaching her business and financial management, adding a matter-of-fact description of their relationship's physical side—in a bit too much detail for Teri.

Teri noticed Karolyn struggling with her conflicted feelings, and when she ultimately revealed the night he'd nearly choked her to death, her voice caught. After clearing her throat, she continued. "Last Saturday was the first time I'd been honest with myself about this compulsion he has to be in control. It's like a shark swimming just below the surface. You never see it, and then, *wham!*"

Karolyn smacked the arm rest with her hand, making Teri jump.

She apologized, adding, "I see it clearly now, though, talking to you."

Teri looked at Karolyn and nodded with concern. "Scary…"

They were quiet for a moment before Karolyn spoke, shaking her head. "You know, I thought I was in love with Arthur. But hearing what happened with him and Rich's sister…it sounds too much like my own relationship with him. I don't even…" She paused, turning to face Teri. "Actually, I don't really feel anything, anymore."

Teri gave Karolyn's hand a supportive squeeze, as she said, "Can I ask one more thing? Did he ever call you 'special'?"

Karolyn looked at her curiously. "No, why?"

"Just wondering…" She paused, and then added, "Well, I think you are…And I'm glad to hear you say your feelings have changed. From what I see, Arthur doesn't deserve you."

Karolyn gave her an appreciative smile as they reclined their seats and dimmed the lights.

Teri closed her eyes, reflecting on Karolyn's and Sheila's descriptions of their experiences with Arthur's double-edged persona. She acknowledged falling victim to his charm and the flattery of being invited into his "special" class, but her animus grew as the narcissistic control-freak concealed in Arthur's core came into focus.

Her thoughts drifted from Arthur to working with Rich again.

Is my attraction to Rich the same as I started to have for Arthur? Am I like Karolyn? Surely, Rich is nothing like Arthur…

* * *

Walking into the Final Assembly hangar always improved Rich's mood. The sound of pneumatic drills and the hustle of assembly mechanics was to him, a sort of productivity ballet he found rejuvenating.

He especially liked the far end of the hangar where the planes were nearly complete. In these final positions, the engines were installed, interior installations were being finished, and systems were being function-tested. He saw Mac climbing down the portable stairs from the passenger door of Ship 914 and walked up to meet him.

They shook hands, and added a quick hug.

"Good to have you back, Rich."

Rich smiled. "That's the same thing O'Donnell told me earlier. Only I actually believe you."

They walked to Mac's office to catch up. Rich recapped the shock of regaining his memory, his suspicions about the accident, Teri's insight about Vale, and the ugly experiences Sheila shared last night.

Mac whistled. "Man, I thought you were over the top with your conspiracy theory, but someone running you off the road…and what your sister went through…sounds like our fearless leader could be a borderline psycho."

Rich leaned against Mac's table and spread his arms for emphasis. "So…*now* do you believe there's something to my theory?"

Mac paused before replying with a somber tone, "I'd have to say yes—especially when I tell you what's happened this past week."

Although Rich had heard some of it from Teri, Mac went into detail on the sabotage incidents and the carjacking. Rich nodded as he took it all in. "So Bordon being there to come to your rescue was no random coincidence."

"Yep, I'd say that's a for sure. Unfortunately, I don't know much more than that."

"Well, I'd bet my paycheck Bordon has something to do with O'Donnell's plan, whatever the hell it is…I did hear Karolyn mention his name this morning when she and Teri were leaving for the airport. She said he's going with them to Hong Kong as personal security."

Mac gave him a quizzical look. "Teri's going to Hong Kong? Is it some more BS with Tailia? Why do they need security?"

Rich stood up and pulled a chair out from the table. "You're gonna need to sit down for this…we're getting new partners."

* * *

It was dark outside, and the building was so quiet Arthur could hear the ticking of his Howard Miller brass wall clock.

His concentration was broken by a chirping sound: the annoying ringtone of the new phones. The recent phone system upgrade included a display of internal extensions. He'd been waiting for McNeil to call from Washington, which would show as *outside caller*. Instead, he saw the bright red numbers: 050. He pressed the hands-free button.

"Yes, Tony?"

Del Balso's voice came through the speaker. "How'd you know it's me, boss?"

"Recognized the extension."

"Damn, I oughta know that one. It's been a week ago now since we got these slick spy phones…My guy in Final Assembly seen Richmond a while ago, stopping by to talk with McKinley. They been in his office talkin' for at least an hour…Thought you'd wanna know."

Unable to decide if he was bothered more by the news of the two most annoying off-script players collaborating again, or Tony's inarticulate reporting, Arthur interrupted. His tone conveyed the full measure of his irritation.

"Are you saying they're in there now?"

"Oh no, it's late. I think they been gone a while."

Arthur leaned back in his chair, rubbing his temples. "You are correct, Tony. I did want to know…and what exactly do you think we should do about it?"

There was a long silence. "Um…you thinkin' we should bug McKinley's office, maybe?"

Arthur stood as he replied, letting sarcasm assuage his annoyance. "See, Tony? You *can* think when you try. Get it done tonight on third shift…and while you're at it, tap the phone in Harlan's new office."

He disconnected and decided to call it a night. As the tower elevator sped down to the garage level, he contemplated what Richmond and McKinley might be up to, and then shook his head.

It doesn't matter—I'm two moves ahead of them. With Teri in Hong Kong, there's no way those losers can figure out anything in time.

But the reflection in the chrome doors staring back at him didn't appear to agree.

20

Thursday, 9:35 p.m. Hong Kong Standard Time

Karolyn and Teri walked double-time through the elegant lobby of the Sheraton Hong Kong in Kowloon. Fortunately, the ride from the airport had been quick because they still needed to check-in and make a 10:00 p.m. meeting.

They were joining Winton and Crandall who'd arrived earlier, for a casual meet-and-greet with Philip Lin and Zhou Quon from TaiChin, prior to the first scheduled session tomorrow morning. As they approached the table in the Skybar, Philip and Quon stood.

Teri shook Philip's hand and said, *"Hěn gāoxìng jiàndào nǐ."*

Philip answered, "Nice to meet you too…you speak Mandarin?"

Teri admitted she'd only learned a couple of phrases, but Philip smiled warmly as Karolyn looked impressed and Winton glowered. She immediately felt comfortable with Philip, whose impeccable appearance complemented his graciousness. By contrast, Zhou's pretentious manner resulted in a comfort level more on par with Winton.

Then there was Will Crandall. With his perfect nose, Hugh Grant jaw line, and flawless complexion, Teri guessed most women would call his looks "to die for." But hiding below his model-quality exterior, she sensed a perverse undercurrent that for her, nullified any possible attraction.

Will appointed himself the facilitator in a misguided attempt at team building. His manner was smooth, but Teri noticed during a discussion of McNev's business goals, Will was subtly goading Winton's oversized ego toward the point of obnoxiousness. As the conversation continued, she also observed Crandall inching himself toward Zhou until his proximity appeared ill-suited. She found it interesting that Zhou either didn't notice or didn't mind.

Not having much to contribute, Teri entertained herself with considering the precise adjective to describe Crandall, until Karolyn mercifully suggested they call it a night. When they stood to leave, instead of a handshake, Will took Teri's hand and kissed the back of it with a flamboyant flourish accompanied by a beguiling smile.

Insidious.

* * *

Back in her room, Teri took a moment to admire the travel-poster view of Victoria Harbor and clear her head after meeting yet another member of the McNev executive team who was well outside the standard deviation. She glanced at her watch: 11:22 p.m. Jumping ahead fifteen hours into the next day felt like a time warp that had sapped what remained of her energy. Deciding on a quick review of her notes before a shower and bed, she sat at the desk and opened her briefcase. A soft knock on the door startled her.

Wondering who it could be at this hour, she looked through the peephole and recognized Karolyn's smile, despite the distortion of the fish-eye lens. As she relaxed and opened the door, Teri was caught off guard seeing a man standing next to her.

They stepped inside and Karolyn said, "Sorry for the late intrusion. I just thought I should introduce you to Porter Bordon. I wasn't sure when we might have a chance tomorrow, and I wanted to be sure you had a face to put with the name."

Smiling fleetingly, Teri thought of what Mac told her about Bordon and the carjacking, agreeing with his description of "someone you don't want to mess with."

"Pleasure to meet you, Miss Harlan," Porter said, extending his hand.

Deciding this wasn't the time to learn more about him, Teri simply nodded politely and shook it. His handshake was firm and professional. He said, "Please let me know if there's anything you need. I always keep my pager on." He handed her a card. "Here's the number."

"Thanks..." Something about his manner put her at ease, so she added, "And please call me Teri."

Suddenly remembering she'd stuck her own pager inside a pocket in her briefcase and completely forgot about it, she exclaimed, "Oh, that reminds me!"

They watched her with questioning expressions as Teri abruptly stepped to the table, retrieved the pager from her briefcase, and read the display. "Damn—Looks like Rich paged me a while ago. When was that? Yesterday? This stupid time change, I can't even tell."

Karolyn smiled and said, "Yeah, it's crazy. We're going back to the Skybar for a quick nightcap...might help you relax. Why don't you join us?"

She answered distractedly, "No, thanks. I better call Rich back. Nice to meet you, Porter."

Karolyn and Porter left Teri's room and walked to the elevator. As they waited, Porter asked, "When she said Rich, was that by chance the Bradley Richmond who goes by Rich?"

* * *

Will Crandall loved the view of Victoria Harbor from the Skybar. The towering high rises across the bay, with the glow of neon signage mirrored in the water, created a world-class panorama—worthy of senior executives.

Sitting in a booth in a dark corner of the bar, he looked up and beamed at Zhou Quon as he slid in next to him. They sat for a minute, enjoying the view, and Will placed his hand gently over Quon's.

He whispered, "I've missed you. I've been looking forward to this trip since last time."

Zhou turned to Crandall and replied equally softly, "I've missed you too. Is everything in place for Monday?"

Will nodded. "Yes, Arthur said the program is ready—I can't wait."

Will held Quon's hands beneath the table and spoke with enthusiastic hostility. "When Mr. Idiot-Winton accesses the McNev Due Diligence data in the meeting Monday, the look on his stupid face will be priceless. And now we get to watch the new wonder-girl, Harlan, have a melt-down as well."

Quon's eyes narrowed. "And I can stop pretending to cooperate with Lin. I will so enjoy my outrage, accusing Winton of fraud, and then watching that coward Lin take his annoying Taiwanese and back out."

Will chimed in as if they were practicing a duet. "We'll send a torpedo through the heart of this ludicrous partnership, and Arthur will lead McNeil straight to your sponsors...you will be a hero."

"Not until phase two is completed."

Zhou pulled his hands away and Will felt the cold edge of Quon's rancor. "The company *must* be in ruins, and...Lin *must* receive his surprise."

Will discreetly reached for Quon's hand again. "Yes, of course. Haven't I promised you? I'm taking care of it."

They were so wrapped up in themselves, they failed to notice the attractive blonde with the tough-looking gentleman sitting at a nearby table.

* * *

Rich was in his office Thursday morning, attempting to catch up, but his heart wasn't in it. He'd been reading the same paragraph for twenty minutes with no idea what it said.

His focus was compromised, speculating on the reason for Teri not returning his page, and fueled by lingering uncertainties from what he'd decided to call his *mental sabbatical* following the accident. As he moved on to vacillating about Teri's motives for not disclosing the TaiChin partnership, the weird ringtone from his new phone startled him. He looked at the caller ID: *outside caller.*

Thinking to himself how not-helpful the new phone system was, he answered, "Hello, this is Richmond."

Static hissed for multiple seconds, followed by Teri's voice. "Rich? Oh, my God, I'm so sorry."

Without waiting for Rich to reply, she spoke rapidly, as if the meter were going to expire before she could explain. "I put my pager in my briefcase before I left and forgot all about it. I didn't see your page until just now. I'm really sorry for that horrible meeting yesterday. I have to tell you, Arthur set me up. I was so angry—I wanted to slap that smug smile off his face."

After taking a breath, she added, "Anyway, I'm sorry and…I guess that's all…just, sorry. God, I don't even know what day it is here."

Perhaps it was the sincerity in her tone or the confirmation she was seeing Arthur's nature more clearly, or maybe he'd finally returned to his pre-sabbatical self. Whatever the reason, he felt connected to Teri despite her being halfway around the world. The same trust and adoration he'd felt nine years ago resonated in him as he said, "Hey, take it easy. It's gonna be okay."

* * *

Friday's session went as expected. Winton presented slides on market forecasts and engineering-production capabilities, packaged neatly into what appeared to be a sustainable business plan.

Although Teri could almost see ice crystals between Karolyn and Jackson, Karolyn had both the slides and Winton well prepared. Teri was surprised to find herself impressed with Winton's presentation skills, wielding his self-assured delivery with precision.

He opened with: "This meeting is to be an open book of McNev's Core Competencies, assuring we have our ducks in a row, so together McNev and TaiChin will be able to leverage our synergies."

Hearing that same "synergies" phrase from Arthur yesterday, Teri figured it came from Karolyn studying the book of "corporate-good-impression speak." Although she found a couple of opportunities to elaborate on production process improvements, overall, Teri didn't feel as vital to the meetings as O'Donnell apparently thought she'd be.

Winton's briefings were followed by TaiChin discussing their resources and the requirements to finalize agreements on Monday. Crandall facilitated the afternoon session with McNev and TaiChin attorneys, addressing contractual details. Teri noticed Winton paid little attention to the TaiChin briefing and no attention to the legal discussion. Instead, he divided his attention equally, staring between Karolyn and herself.

As the meeting broke, Jackson declared that the principals should have dinner at Morton's Steakhouse, near the hotel, so he could show Philip and Quon "what real American food was like."

Teri politely declined under the guise of fatigue and the need to finish a report. Truth be told, she wasn't up to keeping Jackson at arms' length for the evening, although she felt sorry for Karolyn having to deal with him on her own.

As they left the fourth-floor meeting room, she saw Porter and the two exceedingly large Chinese security men, also in suits, standing attentively by the elevator. No one else from the meeting acknowledged them, so she nodded to Porter, thinking to herself: *They look like those guys protecting the* oyabun *in* Black Rain.

* * *

Half an hour after Teri returned to her room, she was about to order room service when her phone rang. It was Karolyn, sounding giddy.

"Hey there. I managed to convince Jackson I had a migraine, and he got so angry, he told me off and went on to dinner without me! I'm so proud of myself! Now that I have to stay in our suite and pretend not to feel well, I was hoping you could join me, and we could order room service."

Teri arrived at Karolyn's suite and surveyed the large sitting room, complete with wet bar. "Wow, impressive digs...and separate bedrooms—good move. Just be sure you lock your door."

Her admonishment prompted a smile from Karolyn.

Their dinner arrived quickly, on a white-linen-covered rolling table: grilled seafood salad for Teri and the Chinese vegetables and noodles plate for Karolyn.

Karolyn said, "I really feel comfortable around Porter—safe...And he seems to like me for who I am, instead of what he'd like to do with me."

She finished a carrot and continued. "You know, spending time with him—and even more so with you—I'm starting to believe I have more to offer than just a good sense of business and a nice body."

Teri set down her fork and looked at Karolyn with a serious expression. "Karolyn, you don't have a good business sense. You have exceptional business *talent*. I watched you in the meeting today, and you were on top of every point. You have way more brains and competence than you give yourself credit for."

Teri smiled as she added, "And remember, your nice body is *yours*. The sexual favors for the boss BS isn't an executive privilege anymore...This is the nineties, for God's sake."

Karolyn nodded, and her expression indicated Teri's words had struck a chord. She changed the subject. "Oh, I haven't told you about last night."

Karolyn explained her enlightening nightcap in the Skybar.

"Porter confided to me that Arthur not only asked him to follow Mac, but he'd also been assigned to do other strange things, like detaining some doctor—I think his name was Meyer—who was supposed to be treating Rich. He also told me about overhearing a conversation in the Final Assembly hangar between some kid named LJ Vale and Herrera from the union."

Teri slid her chair back from the service table and walked to the window. She gazed out at the harbor. *Arthur must've needed Meyer out of the way because he used Vale's son to coerce his dad into prescribing those heavy-duty drugs for Rich—I was right!*

She turned back to Karolyn.

"This swamp is definitely getting deeper, KB. You add this to what I told you I heard from Rich and Mac, and..."

Karolyn interrupted. "I know! Remember on the plane I said Porter and I think Arthur may be up to something with Crandall? Well, guess who we saw in a dark corner of the bar? Crandall and Zhou! They were deep in whispered conversation, and I think they were holding hands."

"I *thought* those two seemed to be more than business acquaintances."

Like Rich, Teri shared a passion for problem-solving and getting to the bottom of things. Energized by a sudden conviction to discover Arthur's and/or Crandall's possible scheme, she strode back to her seat across from Karolyn.

"You know what? We need to get organized and team up. We're going to launch the 'McNev Internal Investigation Team.'"

"We are?"

"Yep. We're gonna find out what's really going on by putting our heads together. And we're gonna start by setting up a conference call with Rich and Mac and have them talk to Porter with us."

Teri continued. "If I go call Rich now, I should be able to catch him in his office...it'll be a little after 7:00 a.m. in California. And we have tomorrow free, so I'll ask him to get together with Mac for a phone call with us at noon our time—sound okay?"

"Sounds good. I'll tell Porter. We should come to your room though. Obviously, we need to stay clear of Jackson and Crandall."

As Teri was leaving, Karolyn said, "Hey—thanks. It feels better, you know?"

Teri stopped, turning to face her. "What?"

"Not being anyone's puppet. Not Jack's and not Arthur's. Arthur told me the other day I was his partner, but at this point I'm fairly sure it was just more bullshit."

As she opened the door and they hugged, Teri said, "And we're gonna find out just how deep his bullshit goes...partner."

21

Friday, 7:15 a.m. Pacific Daylight Time

"Hey, good to hear your voice again—the connection is better this time. Did you get some sleep? How'd your meetings go?"

"Yes, and fine, Rich—thanks. I've got something important to talk to you about."

"Yeah, me too. I didn't get the chance to tell you yesterday, but I asked Dr. Meyer about Dr. Vale. He'd heard of him but never met him. He told me his car was stolen the day I was discharged, and when he returned the following day, the staff informed him that my case had been referred…"

"Ah, that makes sense," Teri interrupted.

"I'm glad it makes sense to you…I thought it was weird."

Teri told him what she'd learned about Porter being assigned to delay Dr. Meyer, along with the rest of her conversation with Karolyn. She finished by sharing her idea for the "McNev Internal Investigation Team," starting with a conference call, and immediately received Rich's enthusiastic support.

When Rich hung up, he sprang from his office chair with renewed energy. Being right about Teri's ability to see connections that eluded most people gave him both a sense of validation and a rush of confidence. *God, I'm glad she's back!*

He decided to go see Mac and tell him everything in person. He found Mac still working on Ship 914, descending the stairs from the main cabin door. He shouted to Rich. "No farther without safety glasses, Richmond."

Mac grinned as he walked over to Rich and whispered under his breath, "I'm trying to get my guys to wear these damn things." Rather than talk in his office, Mac said he wanted to stretch his legs, so they decided to walk the floor while Rich recapped his conversation with Teri.

When Rich finished, he added, "So, noon tomorrow for them in Hong Kong means a nine p.m. phone call for us tonight. You up for that?"

Mac nodded. "Absolutely—if O'Donnell somehow got that Dr. Vale to keep you doped up, he's definitely playing dirty now…"

"I'm right there with you. But he's also hidden his schemes very well…even if we're able to discover what he's up to, we're gonna need to draw a damn flowchart for McNeil before he'll accept the truth about his boy wonder."

Mac chuckled. "Yeah, that sounds about right. But we could start by taking a close look at Herrera...You know that ridiculous 'kNOw Excuses' program Herrera proposed to Duke?"

"Yeah, Teri told me about the meeting she went to—pretty lame."

Mac nodded. "Definitely. But here's the thing. I heard that Herrera told a guy who ended up in the circle that he could get on an exemption list, *if* the mechanic would do some 'special project work' for him...we should look into that."

Rich looked thoughtful. "What if Herrera's organizing sabotage efforts as part of some scheme to destroy the company?"

"I don't know why anyone, even O'Donnell, would want to do that...but I'm glad Teri set up this call with Bordon. I'll be interested to hear from the guy."

Mac glanced up and then lowered his voice. "Remember what I said about O'Donnell playing dirty? Look at the guy over there by 913. Tony told me they hired new 'plain-clothes' officers to put a lid on potential sabotage. Except all they've done so far is follow me and Al around. And last night, one of my third-shift guys saw someone from Security nosing around my office."

They changed direction toward the back of the hangar and watched the man in the tacky leisure suit trying to be discreet as he turned and kept his eye on them.

Rich said, "Jeez, you're right. You know, we need to get off of Art's radar for our telcon. Why don't you come to Sheila's place and have dinner with us? She'd love to see you. Plus, I think it's a good idea for Sheila to join us on the call. She just finished some new software project for O'Donnell that could be related, and she hates his ass as much I do. She'd make a formidable ally."

They decided to walk a couple more laps around the building, just to piss off the man in the ugly suit.

* * *

"One of my weird assignments was to keep some doctor named Meyer from going to work at Saddleback Medical Center."

Porter stood across from Teri and Karolyn, who were sitting at the table in Teri's room for their noon telcon. Porter stared at the floor as he spoke, and Teri could tell he was uncomfortable.

Sheila's voice came through the speakerphone. "Ter, I owe you an apology too. I already told my brother I was sorry—I should have known something was off with Vale."

"Sheila, don't beat yourself up," Teri replied. "You've had a lot to deal with, and we just figured it out ourselves. This is a good example of what I said earlier—that we're stronger working together."

Teri nodded at Porter to continue.

"So when I decided to look into things on my own, Mary in Security suggested Al Greer. After talking with Al, I overheard that Vale kid in some covert discussion with Herrera—but I only had 'LJ,' so it took me a while to find out who he was. I also got Herrera's employment history and seen he'd worked for a union known to use dirty tactics…so maybe he should be watched."

Hearing this, Rich and Mac exchanged head nods.

Porter pulled out his notes and recapped their conversation, finishing with "I'm not sure what the small gizmo was that Herrera gave him, but he said something about a custom *failsafe vent*, and kept telling Vale to use some special connector."

Mac and Rich looked at each other and then exclaimed simultaneously, "E-1101!!"

Rich added, "You know when I went to salvage, Stanley mentioned the bin count was off."

Mac jumped in, "I'll bet Herrera swiped them for whatever the hell they're installing!"

Rich, Mac, and Teri had a quick side discussion, deciding the report Rich had seen likely contained more information.

Rich said, "The only way we can be sure is to get our hands on it. Karolyn, would you be able to do that?"

"I'll see what I can do when I get back, Rich." Teri noticed Karolyn's brow was furrowed and she was tapping her pen on the pad as she made a note.

At that point, Mac said he had a question. "Porter, do I have you to thank for saving my ass the day I almost got my truck jacked?"

After Porter reluctantly confirmed it and received a sincere *thank you* from Mac, a small voice came through the speaker, "Aunt Teri?"

Lisa had come downstairs, inadvertently joining the conversation and Teri took a moment to talk to her. Lisa was excited to say hello, especially when Teri promised to bring her something from Hong Kong.

Rich said, "Okay, Ladybug, tell everyone good-night," and after she melted Mac's heart by giving him a hug, Rich whisked her back upstairs.

As the Hong Kong trio waited for Rich to return, Porter looked lost in thought. Then, without a word, he turned and strode out, shutting the door behind him. Karolyn and Teri exchanged baffled looks.

When Rich returned, they explained to the California trio that Porter had left for reasons unknown. This caused a lull in the conversation, broken by Sheila.

"I'm not sure exactly how the new program I developed for Arthur fits into what you all are discussing, but I can try testing it and see if I can get a handle on what he's up to."

Teri said, "Thanks, Sheila, that could really help...I also wanted to mention this Private Accounts thing I found. I've never seen expenses posted without detailed figures, and my meeting with Vernon Ames was just bizarre."

After Teri relayed the highlights of her Ames meeting, Rich responded, "Wow—I never really thought about how strange those asterisks are. I shoulda paid more attention."

Karolyn added, "Don't feel bad, Rich. I've worked alongside Arthur for two years, and just accepted his explanation of the need to keep the VP expense accounting private."

Teri turned to Karolyn and said, "So why don't you and I follow up with Ames when we get back?" She laughed and added, "For the benefit of you in California, Karolyn nodded 'yes.'"

Karolyn nudged her, and mouthed, "*Smart ass.*"

Teri summarized. "Okay, I've got Sheila's testing, and our actions, so far. Rich and Mac, can you work with Al to see if you can find out more about what Herrera's up to, and that weird modification to the Tailia plane?"

Rich replied, "Yep, but if Karolyn can snag a copy of that report, I think that's the key."

Karolyn made a face at the phone, and Teri smiled again. "She'll try."

Rich had one last suggestion. "What if I speak with Hugh and get his take on the principals in this little scenario? It would help us to know what he thinks, especially about O'Donnell."

Again Teri noticed Karolyn's concerned expression as she replied. "Rich, I'm not so sure about that. McNeil not only trusts Arthur, he talks to him daily. If you decide to speak to Hugh, you need to tread very lightly, so nothing gets back to him. Because somehow Arthur always seems to find out everything."

* * *

Karolyn uncoiled her long legs, stretching out on the lounge chair alongside the Hong Kong Sheraton's rooftop pool. She lathered herself with coconut tanning oil, proud she'd moved up to SPF7 sun block. After all, she was getting older and had to make concessions. Having gotten Winton relaxed for his afternoon nap made her feel disgusted with herself for backsliding, so she decided some time in the sun would help her recover.

She closed her eyes and tried to relax, but her thoughts returned to Porter's abrupt exit in the middle of their conference call. Karolyn shifted positions, attempting to get more comfortable, when she felt a shadow cross her face.

"Hey Karolyn, I hope I didn't wake you," Porter said quietly, as he sat on the empty lounge chair next to hers.

He was dressed in swim trunks with a towel around his neck, momentarily distracting her with a vision of him in her suite, in place of Winton. She propped herself upright and smiled at him.

He said, "Thought I'd get in a swim...Sorry about bailing on your phone call earlier."

Karolyn caught sadness and a shadow of pain in his eyes. She instinctively reached for his hand as she spoke. "What's wrong?"

"I don't know...maybe I'm wrong about everything. Art apologized before sending me here...said he was trying to save McNev."

Karolyn smiled again. "And he told me I was his partner...I think we've established he's full of shit." She looked at him more closely. "That's not why you left today, though, is it?"

He turned toward her, hesitating in an obvious internal debate. Karolyn's smile became empathetic, waiting for him to continue.

"I'm not a good person, Karolyn. I've spent my life hurting people." He stopped again.

Karolyn sat up straighter and met his eyes. "Hey, I told you, I'm not one to judge...Whatever it is, you can tell me."

He lowered his head, continuing like he was in a confessional.

"I actually got my start as a kid in junior high. My best friend got beat up by these bullies for no real reason...It pissed me off, royally. I ended up choosing off their leader who was twice my size...took him out in about two seconds with an uppercut to the chin—lifted him clean off the ground. I was so mad, I saw red. That was when I knew I had certain talents I could use to make things right, you know? When I chose my career, I knew what it meant... never allowing myself to get close, or really care about anyone...but I was okay with it. I thought I was doing good, and I was particularly good at my work."

He shook his head and looked up. His tone softened. "I don't mean this to sound like a cheap come-on, but since I met you, everything's different. I care about you, and I can see you care about people like Teri."

"And this is bad, how?"

"Let me finish...I've been thinking about my life a lot lately. Something I've never really done much. When I looked back, I'm not proud of myself."

"I can relate."

"Not to this, you can't...I was working for a union in Chicago. There was this high-level manager, Walters, in a company we were trying to organize. Walters was a total slimeball and a bully, intimidating workers, not giving them a chance to vote their conscience. It was my job to get him out of the picture. I followed him from work one night through the city and sideswiped his car—pushed him into oncoming traffic—got him out of the way and into the hospital. I found out later he died from his injuries…He had a wife and young daughter.

"There was no evidence and no investigation. I kept telling myself he deserved it, and what I'd done saved a lot of guys' livelihoods. But I'm not sure I ever really believed it. Over the years, it ate at me, especially thinking about that little girl growing up without her dad. But when Crandall and O'Donnell gave me this assignment…I was so desperate to…"

His voice fell away as he looked down at the deck again before continuing.

"Then once I talked with Mary, I found out everything I'd thought was all wrong. I see how people like Mac and Rich, you, and Teri, really *are* doing the right thing, and I can tell the difference from what I've done. I always thought what I did was necessary, but now I see that's bullshit. I just followed orders, and hurt people…it's what I was good at.

"Spending time with you made me see I needed to be square with everyone. If I want to finish clean, I have to start with myself. I decided to tell everybody today, when we were with Teri on the phone…but then I heard Lisa and realized Rich had a young daughter. She sounded so sweet…it all came back to me, like a whack in the head with a sledgehammer."

He saw the confusion on her face.

"Don't you get it? I'm the one who ran Rich into that ravine."

22

Saturday, 8:15 p.m. Hong Kong Standard Time

Teri watched Karolyn enter the private dining room on the seventh floor of the Sheraton, stopping all conversation; she looked stunning. Winton wore her proudly on his arm next to his Rolex, as Zhou, Lin, and the others stood. He paraded Karolyn along the floor-to-ceiling windows around the far side of the long table, stopping to seat her between Teri and Philip Lin.

Unexpectedly, Winton smiled and winked at Teri as he slid the chair out for Karolyn, and then returned to take his seat opposite Will Crandall. He and Crandall sat to the left and right of the host, Zhou Quon, at the head of the table.

This was fine with Teri. She appreciated sitting as far away from Winton and Crandall as possible, and certainly preferred Philip Lin over his counterpart. Philip graduated from Harvard Business School with Anthony Leung, who became Hong Kong's Financial Secretary. His command of English was superior to most of the American executives Teri knew, and he conducted himself with an elegant formality, demonstrated when Karolyn took her seat.

"Miss Babcock, you look lovely this evening. Your dress is as dazzling as your smile, and it is my honor to have you at my end of the table...and you as well, Miss Harlan. I consider myself quite fortunate."

Teri had never been to a formal Asian dinner, and was glad Karolyn explained a little of the unique ceremony involved. Appetizers were served by Chinese women wearing traditional, body-hugging *cheongsam* uniforms. Each dish was garnished with food painstakingly crafted into art, such as the large Chinese carrots carved to look like parrots bordering beautifully arranged vegetables. The servers moved around the table with elegant efficiency, keeping everyone's glasses filled with Rémy Martin cognac to accompany the appetizers.

Philip talked easily to Karolyn, treating her as a knowledgeable and respected member of the team. Teri's mind drifted, puzzling over Porter's abrupt exit from their telcon, until raucous laughter returned her attention to the table. It was Jackson, howling at his own joke. She smiled at her good fortune, given the uneasy expressions worn by those within range of Winton's humor.

Despite feeling underdressed, she enjoyed herself until the main course: roasted pigeon, served with the same artistic achievement. The garnish on these serving platters, however, was a row of elegantly arranged pigeon heads.

Teri glanced sideways at Karolyn, who stood and excused herself to visit the ladies' room. Teri wasted no time in joining her.

Karolyn asked, "What do you think?"

Teri checked the stalls to be sure they were alone. "I think I'm glad I ate a lot of appetizers and soup."

They shared a laugh. But as they returned to the dining room, Karolyn turned serious and put her arm around Teri.

"There's something important I need to tell you about Porter."

* * *

Philip Lin left the restroom and continued past the door of the dining room, rolling his eyes at the sound of the Winton-precipitated guffaws. He walked through the foyer and out onto a small balcony.

He admired the harbor-lit night as he tried to work through his current conundrum. Philip had devoted five years getting to this point, and now he wasn't sure it was where he wanted to be.

Philip loved aviation. His precious-little free time growing up had been spent building a magnificent model airplane collection, and when his parents sent him to college in the U.S., he'd saved enough money to take flying lessons. It seemed he was fulfilling his destiny when one of the largest conglomerates in Taiwan asked him to spearhead their effort to get his country into the commercial aircraft business.

The first three years he was on top of the world, leading contingents of Taiwanese executives in exploratory meetings with Boeing, Everett Aviation, and McNeil Aerospace. But his work got more challenging when his country joined forces with China to obtain the financial resources to enter into serious negotiations on a partnership with a U.S. aircraft manufacturer.

McNev came to be the prime candidate because of their struggles with capital and market share since the merger. The initial meetings had gone well, based on his high regard for Hugh McNeil, who he'd met at a seminar on International Business.

Philip recalled his enthusiasm drafting the initial plan when he'd set a goal of being on board the delivery flight of the Tailia's first aircraft to Hong Kong. But tonight as he stood at the window, Philip reflected on how differently he felt now.

The partnership efforts had taken a wrong turn when the leader of the Chinese side of the consortium stepped down unexpectedly for undisclosed personal reasons, and Zhou was selected to replace him. Though Zhou was recommended by Arthur O'Donnell, and his own bosses had praised Zhou's negotiation skills, Philip never cared for him.

He tried his best to put aside his personal dislike of Zhou, whose insistence on limousines and bodyguards added to his grandiose self-appointment as "the protector of Asian culture against evil Western influence." But rather than displaying financial acumen, Philip watched Zhou repeatedly raise irrelevant concerns in the name of culture that created friction with his team.

His distrust of Zhou had grown to the point of speaking confidentially with others in the consortium as well as his senior management, thinking perhaps Quon had a hidden agenda. He also recognized that this was a risky course of action within Asian business culture. If his questioning came to light, the offense taken by the Chinese could destroy everything.

Although he'd found nothing specific to this point, Zhou's increasingly close relationship with Will Crandall had been adding to Philip's apprehension, and now the plan to finalize the agreement in a conference-call meeting on Monday filled him with a sense of impending disaster.

Philip was seriously considering a delay of the Monday finalization meeting to allow time to confirm Zhou's intentions. However, he'd not proposed it because he was unsure who he could confide in for support on the McNev side, other than McNeil himself, which could create other issues.

He considered the ray of hope that had appeared this past week in the person of Teri Harlan. She'd impressed him. Not only with her greeting in Mandarin, but by her conduct, both competent and principled.

She'd make a good ally. I'll broach the subject with her after dinner, and perhaps I can enlist her support...assuming she agrees there's a potential problem.

His mood lightened by a positive course of action, Philip returned to the dining room.

* * *

It was nearly ten o'clock when Zhou stood and thanked everyone, officially drawing the evening to a close. The majority of attendees had blood alcohol levels exceeding the legal limits of most states, with the exception of Teri, who'd switched to tea after the cognac made her light-headed, and Philip, who abstained.

Philip escorted Teri and Karolyn from the table to the foyer. They were standing amongst the congregants waiting for elevators when Winton staggered over to collect Karolyn. Teri had watched his offensiveness grow steadily as the night progressed.

Before Teri could sidestep him, Jackson embraced her. He held her tightly against his large frame with both hands firmly clasping her backside in an impertinent manner.

Jackson put his mouth to her ear and whispered, "I love your dress…especially the way your ass feels underneath it. I've decided to make you a peace offering. Being away from the prying eyes at the plant, it's the perfect chance to have some real fun. Come up to our suite—You, Karolyn, and me? I guarantee you a night that'd be *hard* to forget."

Anger flared inside her, but rather than slap him, she just smiled and spoke loudly enough to draw attention. "Thanks, Jackson! You have a lovely evening as well!"

Winton released her, because Porter and both Chinese security men appeared out of nowhere and were standing next to him, glaring.

Karolyn took Winton's arm, and looking at Teri, she mouthed, "*Sorry*" as she steered him to the elevator. Teri was considering following them out of concern for Karolyn when Philip touched her arm. "Might I have a word?"

As Teri turned toward Philip, Jackson and Karolyn walked to the elevator and disappeared inside.

Philip led Teri to the corner of the foyer away from the others and spoke quietly. "If you look over your shoulder, you'll see why I need to talk to you."

Teri turned slightly, seeing Crandall and Zhou joined at the hip in hushed conversation. Philip summarized his concern over the friction between the Taiwanese and the Chinese teams, adding that he'd been increasingly uncomfortable with the actions of his counterpart.

"Watching those two in our meetings, I believe there is a distinct possibility they could be planning something damaging to our partnership."

Teri nodded her agreement. Without going into detail about the informal team she'd assembled, she told Philip about Karolyn observing Crandall and Zhou in the Skybar the other night.

"So, yes, Karolyn and I share your concern. What do you think about meeting later to figure out how best to deal with the situation?"

"Yes, absolutely. And including Miss Babcock would be quite beneficial. She's insightful and well-positioned to be in the know."

Teri refrained from commenting on his unintentional double entendre, and said she'd contact Karolyn. They agreed to meet in an hour at the small café near the lobby, thinking it would be the least likely spot to encounter Crandall or Zhou.

* * *

It had been a long time since Rich had come in on a Saturday, but he was motivated by last night's conference call, and this was a good opportunity to catch up. After a couple of exceptionally productive hours without interruption, he leaned back and stretched.

He looked at his watch, trying to translate to Hong Kong time. He thought about Teri's evening spent at the formal dinner, dealing with Winton and Crandall without him, and found himself suddenly restless.

He decided to take a break and visit Mac, finding him in the Final Assembly Office conference room with Al. They were working at the large metal table, filled with scheduling charts and the overtime rotation wheel.

The wheel, actually a list of names, ensured that assembly mechanics were given the option to work overtime based on seniority. If they elected not to work, the supervisors moved down the list. If a more senior mechanic wasn't asked in the proper order, according to the union contract, that person had to be paid overtime—in addition to the mechanic actually working the shift. Scheduling exceptions were required for mechanics who were requested for specific assignments out of rotation.

Rich walked in, asking what they were up to, and Mac waved him over.

"Look at these. All of these exceptions have a pattern. See, there are eleven of them here in the past three weeks."

"That's not too unusual."

Al interjected. "Ah, but my friend, look at this. The same three names show up in all these crews requested on second shift. And whenever one is requested, they're *all* requested."

Rich flipped through the crew schedules and saw the names they'd highlighted: Vale, Reiss, and Davis.

Al smiled proudly at his detective work. "Yep, right up until Reiss and Davis were fired. And here's the best part. Because these were scheduling exceptions, they had to be approved by a director...and they're all signed by the same person: J. C. William."

Rich asked, "Didn't Porter hear that name when Vale and Herrera were talking?"

"Yeah, I think so," Mac answered.

"Great! So who is this J. C. William guy?"

Mac and Al answered in unison. "We have absolutely no idea."

* * *

The three security men sat at the table in Porter's room, looking more comfortable with their ties loosened and coats off.

Porter dealt the cards. Wang puffed on a cigar, and Li sipped cognac, both men barely fitting in their chairs.

"What game is this called, again?" Wang asked.

"Twenty-One. You like it?"

"Yes. Much fun."

"Yeah, especially when you keep getting tens and face cards, like you did the other night...so you mentioned you two have issues with Zhou?"

Neither Wang nor Li elaborated.

Porter said, "It's okay. I understand loyalty, believe me…until I had to work with Crandall."

Wang nodded, and said, "Stay," as he waved his hand over his cards. After a moment, he said, "Both bad…me and Li, heard…going to do bad things."

"Mr. Zhou and Crandall?"

Li banged his fist on the table, making the cards jump, then nodded. Wang spoke for him. "Li saw them…" He put his hands together.

Porter said, "Oh, got it. Yeah, they might also be…extra good friends."

He was about to suggest the possibility of teaming up when his pager started beeping. It was Teri's room extension, followed by 911.

* * *

Teri returned to her room following her conversation with Philip, and after changing into slacks and a casual top, she'd called Karolyn to tell her about their meeting with Philip. Karolyn hadn't answered. Teri downed half a bottle of water and paced. She thought Karolyn was out of her mind to share a suite with Winton, even if it had two bedrooms.

She called again. Still no answer. *Something's wrong. I can feel it.*

She'd paged Porter, 911, and he called her in under a minute. When she'd explained her concern for Karolyn, given Jackson's inebriated state, he said, "I'm on my way to their suite. Meet me there."

As Teri got off on the twelfth floor, the second elevator arrived with a *ding*. Teri and Porter stepped out, side by side, and heard muffled shouting coming from the direction of Winton's suite. Porter ran, with Teri keeping pace now that she was no longer in a dress and heels.

They reached the room and heard Karolyn's voice. "No, you sonofabitch! Get off me—I said no!"

Porter pounded on the door with such force Teri thought he might break it down.

The shouting stopped. *Silence.* Porter took a key card from his coat pocket and slipped it into the lock. It opened with an electronic *buzz-click*. Without hesitation, Porter burst into the room. Through the open door to the left bedroom, they could see Jackson and Karolyn on the bed.

Jackson was down to his boxers, and Karolyn's evening dress was around her ankles. Winton was on top of her, with one hand over her mouth, and his other on her bra.

Karolyn writhed ferociously, struggling to free herself, but Jackson had her pinned, thrusting himself on her. He stopped as he heard them come in. Lifting himself slightly on his elbows, Winton turned his head to look at Porter, who was crossing the living room at light speed. That gave Karolyn the opening she needed. She launched her knee into Jackson's crotch, causing him to scream assorted epithets and roll off her.

Karolyn leapt from the bed, getting nimbly to her feet, and kicking out of her ruined dress as Porter reached them. It was obvious he'd like nothing better than to beat Winton senseless and throw him out the non-opening window.

However, Jackson was in no condition to put up a fight. He lay on the bed, wincing, his swearing having given way to mumbling indignation. He looked up at Porter, trying to focus through half-mast eyes. His slurred speech was nearly impossible to understand. "Wha' the fuck are you doin' here?"

Before Porter could respond, Jackson fell back, out cold.

Karolyn stood unabashedly, straightening her Chantelle matching underwear, while she stared with fury in her eyes at the now unconscious Jackson. As challenging as it was for him, Porter politely looked away as Teri ushered Karolyn into the bathroom. He moved to the main room to wait for them.

When they emerged a few moments later, Karolyn looked remarkably composed in her Esprit designer warm-ups. She brushed back her hair with her hand, still simmering over putting herself in the position to need rescuing. Jackson was snoring loudly, and Teri suggested Karolyn grab what she needed and spend the night in her room.

* * *

As the three of them got off the elevator, Karolyn's resentment erupted. "I've had it with that fuck-stain. I am so not that person anymore. Arthur can fire me if he wants, but I'm done…just done."

"What did you call him?" Teri asked.

"A fuck-stain. Why? You prefer douche-waffle?"

Teri looked at Porter, who shrugged. The three of them burst into laughter.

When their laughing subsided, Karolyn said, "Thank you, by the way, both of you. You got me out of a mess. Ter, I owe you one."

She turned to Porter. "Teri told me she paged you. Thanks for responding so fast. But how'd you get in the room?"

"I stopped to visit with the hotel security manager yesterday, and he very nicely loaned me a master key. I like to be prepared."

He smiled, gently ushering her into Teri's room, as he continued. "I'm glad you're all right, and even happier to hear you say you're done. You're way too good for that…and for him."

After Porter bid them good-night, Teri closed the door behind him, and said, "He's right, you know."

Karolyn nodded, adding a fleeting smile. "Yeah, but my timing kinda sucks. I picked a hell of a time to stand up for myself."

"No, it was absolutely the right time, because it was the right thing to do, and you stepped up and did it. I'm proud of you…and you should be proud of yourself."

As she gave Karolyn a hug, Teri suddenly remembered their meeting.

"Oh, shit! I completely forgot. You and I are supposed to meet with Philip Lin in five minutes!"

* * *

Will stepped out of the elevator and turned right toward Zhou's room. He was numb from fatigue. The lawyers and staff associates he'd been seated with had turned dinner into an energy-draining chore, continually discussing the partnership contract.

Although his responses were merely pageantry in Arthur's play, Will was still required to act the part. Several times, his focus had drifted to the far end of the table, envying Philip in his proximity to Karolyn and Teri. He'd indulged in a fantasy to escape the bonds of his boring dinner colleagues, featuring himself with the two of them. His pleasure appetite with the fairer sex, having been whetted during his interlude, now had to be readjusted to focus on the business at hand.

As Zhou opened the door to let him in, Will glanced to his left. He saw Karolyn and Teri entering the elevator he'd just exited, which struck him as odd, given the late hour. Pondering what they were up to, Will was unable to stop himself from plunging into another sexual reverie.

* * *

Jackson admired his image in the mirror, displaying the casual elegance of the T. M. Lewin monogrammed white shirt, open at the collar, enhanced by sterling cufflinks. It was, of course, freshly pressed, one of the reasons elite execs like himself stayed in five-star hotels.

He felt especially accomplished at being able to look so magisterial, given the way his morning had begun. He'd awakened near nine, hours later than planned. He was alone, clad only in boxer shorts, with a pounding head and a stomach poised to jump overboard.

As his head cleared, Jackson vaguely remembered drinking too much and a horrible encounter with Karolyn, who for the first time apparently rejected him. He faintly recalled a strange dream, involving Bordon standing over him, and Teri staring at him in his underwear. He didn't know if there had been a good part.

He took a hot shower and was emerging from the bathroom, planning to call room service and order breakfast, when Karolyn walked in.

The rough start to his morning hadn't improved at that point. Karolyn was all business, informing him that she was moving to Teri's room. With her tone full of confidence, she told him as she was packing her carry-on, that their working relationship no longer included physical intimacy, and

EXECUTIVE MALICE 171

as long as he agreed to remain professional, she wouldn't bring charges of sexual harassment against him and the company.

Jackson had known there was something wrong with Karolyn from the start of this trip when she'd changed flights with Bordon. He replayed this morning's conversation with her, as he admired his powerful image in the mirror.

Shoulda fired her on the spot and sent her ass home on the next flight, unemployed.

He was hesitant to admit that he hadn't done it because he'd been so taken aback by the new Karolyn, he'd actually been slightly intimidated. He shook off that notion and came to his senses.

I'm the President, damn it. I deserve certain privileges, and she should be grateful to be in her position. How could she not want me, anyway? It's all Teri's fault, filling Karolyn's head with feminist nonsense.

As Karolyn left the room, she'd said, "Oh, one more thing. Philip Lin requested to speak with you…said it was urgent. I told him to be here at ten." Then as she wheeled her carry-on, she'd turned and added over her shoulder, "And oh, by the way, it's nine-forty now," and slammed the door behind her.

Living up to his executive capability, he'd recovered, now approving of his put-together look, just as he heard a knock. He glanced at his Panerai Luminor Marina timepiece: ten o'clock on the dot. As he walked to the door, Jackson wondered why Philip needed to see him.

Karolyn probably put him up to it just to annoy me.

* * *

He applied his well-practiced executive veneer and opened the door, inviting Philip in to sit down.

Philip described the tension he'd seen between the two sides of the TaiChin consortium, and shared his concern that the success of the partnership might be in jeopardy.

Jackson paid little attention. He'd already observed that Lin didn't demonstrate true executive capabilities, unlike Zhou, who closely mirrored his own. Accordingly, he had no interest in Lin's perceptions. Impatience grew to irritation as he felt his stomach rumble, and he was about to dismiss his annoying guest, when Philip delivered the preamble for his proposal.

Philip stood and bowed. "I have a very bold idea that I believe should be advanced, and it is my honor to seek the guidance of our leader."

Realizing that Lin knew how to conduct himself in the presence of superiors, Jackson decided to listen for another moment.

"I suggest that a change in venue for the Finalization Meeting might reduce the tension and bring our teams closer to ensure success."

Lin explained that instead of proceeding as planned, with the Monday conference call, relocating to the McNev plant in California to meet in person with Messrs. McNeil and O'Donnell would improve the team's relationship. It would also enable the TaiChin team to bond by returning together aboard the Delivery Flight of the first Tailia Aircraft: Ship 913.

Philip bowed again. "Mr. Winton, it is truly most gracious of you to hear me out this morning." He paused, then added, "I came to seek the wisdom of your executive counsel on the best way to advance this proposal without offending the delicate balance of cultures."

Lin's conduct caused Jackson to reevaluate. Philip was not only surprisingly bright but an excellent judge of character. He had no issue with the schedule or change of venue, but most importantly he saw an opportunity.

Arthur's been getting too big for his britches. Here's my chance to take command of this damn partnership. Plus, I can show Miss High-and-Mighty who's really in charge.

He needed to be smooth and assume the strategic advantage of Philip's suggestion.

"Philip, your proposal definitely has merit. But it would be significantly more effective if it came from me."

"Mr. Winton, I cannot express the depth of my appreciation for your insightful manner in which to carry this idea forward—Thank you!"

Philip left the suite, bowing once more.

Jackson called room service, and then Teri and Karolyn. He reveled in barking orders to arrange a mandatory emergency meeting of all McNev and TaiChin executives and key staff at three o'clock today, and told them, "I sure as hell better not hear any excuses for not getting this done!"

After his brunch, he changed into a suit and tie and slipped on his Rolex. He stood in front of the mirror once more, confirming his perfect image, ready to display his executive leadership for all to admire. On his way out, Jackson reflected on his presidential power.

I enjoyed giving Teri orders like she was a lowly assistant, same as Karolyn—two peas in a pod. And even better, by the time I tell Arthur and McNeil, it'll be a done deal...I'm in charge now.

* * *

Teri and Karolyn were upbeat as they dressed for the afternoon meeting. Karolyn had booked a meeting room last night, as soon as they'd finalized their strategy, and Philip called them this morning, just before Winton had, to relay how effective the game plan had been.

Zipping up her skirt, Karolyn said, "It was tough not to laugh when Jackson called, demanding to be put on speaker so he could yell his instructions at both of us. Philip played him like a Stradivarius."

Teri smiled. "I'm just glad it worked. Philip's relocation idea will not only derail whatever Crandall and Zhou may have planned for Monday, it'll give us more time to figure things out."

"Yep—and I have to say your approach for Philip to handle Jackson was masterful."

"Thanks, but Jackson is so easy, it's almost unfair."

Karolyn laughed. "Let's hope 'dear Jack' can actually pull this off."

They were both still chuckling as they walked out of Teri's room. On the way to the meeting, they practiced looking serious and surprised.

23

Sunday, 1:30 a.m. Pacific Daylight Time

Sheila stretched in her chair, accompanying a bone-deep yawn. Although she preferred sleep, she understood the importance of uncovering Arthur's intentions for the software. He'd been satisfied when she delivered the install file, even telling her "they were square" and he wouldn't bother her further. Being well beyond suffering more illusions, however, she jumped at the chance to join Teri's investigation team.

From the design, she knew that the program redirected the McNev Enterprise Systems to read from different databases. To understand the program's purpose, she needed to run operational data through the new software and analyze it against the original, so she developed a compare program. Now she was ready for data.

Unfortunately, the data Arthur provided was non-sensical test data, making any comparison meaningless. He'd also locked her out of the McNev system, apparently anticipating that she might do exactly what she was now trying to do. Without access to the actual data in McNev's enterprise system, she was going nowhere.

Absently raking the sand in the miniature Zen garden on her desk, Sheila thought about the power of the software she'd designed for Arthur three years ago.

If only I had that application…

In a flash, it hit her.

I wonder if Beth ever disabled the network connection to the test server when she finished Arthur's project.

The test server she and Beth used was inside the McNev network firewall because his project involved remote access. It had been set up to enable SSL connections to trusted IP addresses, and because she'd done the original work, her access might still be enabled. It was a long shot, but she decided to try it. She dug out her old notes and found the LAN IP address and host name of the test server. She entered it and waited for the server to respond.

* * *

When Zhou walked into Will Crandall's hotel room a little after 5:00 p.m. Hong Kong time, he was so agitated he rebuffed Will's embrace.

The two of them had been careful in Winton's emergency meeting. They sat apart and neither had shown their outrage as Winton announced his decision to move the partnership finalization meeting to McNev in

California, rescheduling it to Tuesday and Wednesday to allow travel time.

Zhou was pacing as he spoke. "Dammit! I cannot believe this. Our entire plan for Winton to take the fall has been shot to hell's bells! Do you think he knew?"

Will found Quon's butchering of English slang when he was upset to be amusing, but refrained from commenting. Instead, he tried being soothing. "No, Quon. I really don't think he knows anything about our plan. How could he?"

Zhou was shaking. "Winton is so full of himself. He's all things that make me despise Westerners! He made it sound like such a slice of executive genius, giving everyone a chance to visit California and return together on our ME-420."

Will replied gently, "Well, it does have credibility on the surface."

"How can you say that? Lin's surprise will be on that flight...and I have no interest in making it a suicide mission."

That remark made Will smile, but Quon was not in the mood.

"Damn it, Will! This is serious. You must do something!"

"Quon, calm yourself. It'll be okay. Arthur can adjust the scenarios to still meet both of your objectives."

Will was well aware of Quon's hair trigger hostility. He reached for Quon's hand, but was interrupted by the room phone ringing.

He was sorry he'd answered the instant he heard O'Donnell's fury blasting from the speakerphone.

"What in hell are you doing over there, Will? Winton just called me and Hugh, saying the finalization meeting has been moved out here! When were you planning to tell me?"

Will hadn't anticipated Winton calling California in what would be the middle of the night there, much less Arthur's immediate reaction to call him.

"Arthur...I...I just found out a few minutes ago myself. He didn't tell anyone he was doing this. Isn't it like two in the morning there?"

"Yes, you fucking idiot, it is! And Winton woke me up, going on about your 'too-close' relationship with Zhou upsetting the teams! What were you doing—putting your hand down Quon's pants in the meetings?"

Will looked at Quon and put his finger to his lips as Arthur continued.

"How could you let this happen? I sent you over there to manage things and set Winton up, but instead you let him screw us! We can't have this scenario go down with McNeil here, for chrissake! And even worse, he's giving Winton credit for his effort to save the partnership! If you were here now, I swear, I'd..."

As Arthur paused for a moment, Will made rude gestures at the phone. Quon started to laugh and put his hand over his mouth.

When Arthur resumed, the phone should have frosted over from the arctic chill in his voice. "I know goddamn well the moron didn't come up with this on his own. Who put him up to it?"

"My guess is Teri. She kept giving me dirty looks during the meetings."

"So then it was obvious—you and Quon?"

"No, Arthur. I swear, we were totally discreet. I don't think Teri likes me. She probably talked Winton into this just to dick with me."

"I'm extremely disappointed in you, Will. Karolyn could have done a better job. I should have made *her* my partner instead of you."

Karolyn, the little slut…thinks she's too good for me because she's doing Winton and Arthur. Hold on—I saw her with Teri last night. Maybe I can score some points.

"Arthur, here's something. I saw Karolyn and Teri together getting in the elevator late last night."

"Really? And what did you do?"

"Uh…nothing. I had to meet Quon. I actually figured they were sleeping together."

"Will, for chrissake! If you could stop being such a man-whore for two minutes, you might be able to use your other head for a change!"

Realizing this was a lost cause, Will fell back on servility to get himself off the hook. "Arthur, I'm sorry Winton's stupidity took us off course, but I have complete faith in you to come up with a brilliant solution. You always do, and I'll be there to support it, one hundred and ten percent."

More silence, and then "Go to hell!" followed by the sound of the phone being slammed. Will replied boldly to the dial tone. "Yeah, well, you first, Artie."

He hit the disconnect button and turned to Quon, grinning. "What say we make our plane reservations for late tomorrow. We deserve an extra day. How about a drink?"

* * *

"Here are the engines, Daddy. They go on the pylons under the wings."

"Exactly right."

Lisa was twisting plastic pieces off the molded frame in the Boeing 747 model airplane kit they'd just bought.

"Gently, Ladybug. We need to lay them all out on the tray before we start."

"I know, Dad—I got it."

Sheila appeared in the doorway of the workshop and handed him the portable phone. With a questioning expression, she whispered, "It's Hugh McNeil."

Rich took the phone and told Lisa he'd be right back, then stepped into the yard. "Well, hello, Hugh. Are you here in California enjoying this beautiful October Sunday?"

"Good morning, Rich. Yes...sorry to bother you on Sunday morning."

"Lisa and I were getting started on a new model we just bought. Unfortunately, there aren't any ME-420s out, so we had to settle for a 747."

Hugh chuckled. "Well, I'll let it slide, this once. I'll try to make this quick so you can get back to what's important. I'm at the office with Arthur. I'm going to put you on speaker, so we can both talk to you."

Rich was silently dithering over whether to ask Hugh about the key players, remembering Karolyn's note of caution.

He decided to chance it. "Sure, no problem. But before you put me on speaker, can I ask a favor? Can you please call me back in an hour or so, from someplace where you're alone, so you and I can speak privately?"

Hugh agreed, and then switched to the speakerphone. After a pause, Rich heard O'Donnell say, "Good morning," with a complete absence of sincerity.

Hugh explained that Winton informed them in the wee hours this morning of his decision to move the partnership finalization to California. Rich deduced from the bounce in McNeil's voice that he was pleased by Winton's initiative, while O'Donnell's sullen tone made it clear the decision had the opposite effect on him. Rich pictured O'Donnell sitting with his arms crossed in petulant silence as Hugh explained Winton's idea. He hoped Hugh's enthusiasm was compounding Arthur's irritation.

After a conversation on the logistics of the TaiChin meeting schedule for Tuesday, and the utmost priority of completing Ship 913 for delivery on Wednesday, Hugh and Arthur told Rich they needed to call Duke. Rich hung up, still grinning as he went back to airplane building with Lisa.

* * *

They left the finished 747 model on the workbench for the glue to set, and about an hour later, while Rich was watching Lisa construct a Lego airport on the living room floor, the phone rang. As soon as Rich answered, Hugh began, "Rich, you don't need to tell me. I understand you being upset, and I apologize. I should have listened to my gut and brought you in on the partnership from the beginning."

"Thanks, Hugh, and I'm fully committed to supporting it, but that's not why I asked you to call me."

"Oh, I just assumed..."

"I appreciate you apologizing, but I wanted to explain why my frustration level has been so high...are you alone?"

"Yes. I'm in a sixth-floor conference room. Is this something more than the partnership?"

Rich told Hugh about Arthur briefing him in front of Teri, ambushing him the moment he'd stepped foot in his office.

"Oh my God, Rich, I'm sorry. I don't understand why Arthur would play you and Teri against each other—That's totally out of line. I'll definitely speak to him about it."

"Actually, Hugh, I'd prefer you didn't say anything to Arthur—about that, or anything else we discuss."

"Okay...and why is that?"

"I'm gonna go out on a limb here...and I assure you my unconditional allegiance is to you and the success of McNev."

"Sounds serious."

"Yes, I'm afraid it is. I'm working with Teri and a few others to identify—and hopefully avert—some potential improprieties that you aren't aware of. I don't want to alarm you, and we'll explain everything as soon as we have all the facts. For now, I'm asking you to trust me on this."

"You know I trust you, Rich. I always have. It all sounds a bit mysterious, but I'm willing to help if I can."

"Yes, you can, sir. If you don't mind, sharing your perspective on some key players could help us figure things out."

"I'm not sure exactly what you mean, but shoot."

"To start, would you mind giving me your assessment of Winton?"

"Well, this needs to stay between us, but I'd have to say I've never had a lot of confidence in him. When Arthur convinced me to bring Jackson on board, he was open about needing a sort of 'figurehead,' so I never expected a strategic vision—that's up to Arthur. But on the positive side, I thought he showed a spark by deciding to move the final meetings here."

Having his own thoughts on Winton confirmed, albeit with a more courteous portrayal, he moved on. "Thank you, and I appreciate your honesty...How about Will Crandall?"

"Ah, yes, continuing to be candid. Will is good at details and getting things done, and Arthur certainly sings his praises. Plus he's fluent enough in contract legalese to manage the lawyers, which I hate. He's rather strange, though. I find myself wanting to keep my distance...He makes me uncomfortable."

Hugh paused. Rich figured he was thinking of an unpleasant "Crandall moment," which he'd had himself. When McNeil didn't mention anything related to Zhou, he decided not to probe further.

"Thanks, and I concur on the 'strange' part. My next question may seem a bit out in left field, but have you been keeping up with what Porter Bordon has been doing out here?"

"Only that Arthur said he's been helpful. But he didn't provide specifics...Oh, and Porter did try to get in touch with me before I left for DC. Crandall told me he took care of it, though, and then I guess Arthur sent him to Hong Kong for security. I can tell you, Porter's loyalty is absolute—to me and to the company. I'm sure of that."

Rich shook his head, realizing Hugh knew only what O'Donnell and Crandall wanted him to. Tempted to give Hugh an idea of what they'd discovered so far, Rich heard Karolyn's voice in his head telling him not to, so he moved on to his final question.

"Thanks so much, sir. I have just one more question. Do you have any idea who the hell J. C. William is?"

* * *

There were only three first-class tickets available for their hurriedly rescheduled flight home, so Porter volunteered to take a business class seat. Teri was grateful for this turn of events because she'd continued avoiding him since Saturday night when Karolyn told her about Porter confessing responsibility for Rich's accident.

Teri also appreciated Winton's seat being two rows forward of her and Karolyn because it eliminated having to endure his stares as she'd done for the past four days. Winton was in a surprisingly good mood as the four of them boarded the fight home, although he continued treating them as his lackeys.

When he'd told the flight attendant he was a magnanimous corporate president who allowed his "personal handmaidens" to fly with him in first class, Teri declined to comment out of pure exhaustion.

Finally arriving back at the McNev condo and climbing from the company town car, she attempted to reset. Having flown seven thousand miles in the last fourteen-plus hours, Teri was having trouble processing how she could be standing in Newport Beach while it was still Sunday, thirty minutes before the time she'd left Hong Kong.

She hoisted her carry-on onto the conference table in the living room, retrieving her bathroom essentials. After a shower, Teri donned the clean Seahawks t-shirt and cami shorts she'd left in her closet, deciding to check in with Rich and Sheila before getting some much-needed shuteye.

Rich answered, sounding upbeat. "Hey, I'm glad to hear from you. Sheila turned in early, so you'll have to settle for talking to me."

"No problem," Teri replied. "I'm just happy to be having a conversation without being on the other side of the world."

Rich recapped his early-morning call. "Sounds like Winton's decision to move the partnership meetings created quite a shit-storm. And Hugh's support seemed to render O'Donnell speechless. I don't know if Jackson deserves any credit, but he managed to piss off Arthur, big time. It was a sweet moment for me. By any chance did you have something to do with changing the plan?"

Despite her fatigue, Teri felt herself grin as she shared the impromptu meeting she and Karolyn had with Philip late Saturday night. She summarized their shared concern and their successful ploy to "guide" Winton to his decision, along with her confidence in Philip.

"He's not only committed to the success of the partnership but he's helping us get to the bottom of whatever our friend Arthur is up to."

Teri also shared how close she and Karolyn had become, and the inherent business talent she'd observed.

Rich said, "I've always thought there was more to Karolyn than Winton or O' Donnell gave her credit for. And I'm sure you've had a lot to do with helping her recognize it."

Teri was smiling again at how good it felt to be talking to the real Rich, when she heard Lisa's voice in the background.

Rich said, "Sorry, I've gotta go. I think she had a bad dream."

"No problem, we'll talk at work tomorrow. I think we're in meetings together, starting first thing. Go hug Lisa for me."

Teri hung up the phone and suddenly remembered the meeting she and Karolyn had said they would set up with Vernon Ames.

Ugh—not looking forward to seeing him again...but it'll be better with Karolyn there.

She collapsed into bed, filled with growing optimism. Her two friends were acting like themselves, and she'd made a new one. Working together with the help of Mac, Philip, and the others, they would unravel this mess, whatever it was, and set things right.

She was asleep before her head hit the pillow.

*　*　*

Rich navigated up the narrow staircase, thinking how glad he was to have Teri back, and suddenly remembered something.

Dammit, I didn't get to tell her that Sheila may have found a back door she can use to access the McNev system. Oh, well, we'll tag up tomorrow. Sheila will know more by then, anyway.

24

Monday, 7:00 a.m.

The mood in Arthur's office was as cold as the air-conditioning, which for reasons known only to the capricious maintenance department, was running full blast on a brisk October morning. When Karolyn handed him the document she'd finished, she knew it was going to be much worse than a typical Monday.

"Here's the agenda and schedule for the TaiChin sessions. Is there something else I can do to help get ready for their arrival?"

Arthur took the document.

"No, clear my schedule. I don't want to be disturbed unless it's McNeil. And Tony is bringing me something. Send him in as soon as he gets here."

He turned his back, signaling the end of their conversation. Karolyn took the hint and left him alone.

When Tony arrived a few minutes later and handed Arthur a cassette tape, he snatched it impatiently and swiveled around to his credenza without a word. Del Balso also recognized his cue to leave.

Arthur noticed his hand trembling when he slipped the cassette into the recorder and pressed *play*. So many people deserved retribution, he was unsure where to start. The anger clouding his mind escalated to fury as he listened to last night's recording from the condo phone of the call Teri made to Rich.

He popped open the tape door, yanked out the cassette, and hurled it across the room. It shattered against his office wall, punctuating his exclamation. "Goddammit!"

Karolyn heard the muffled epithet through the wall of her boss's office, triggering a surge of adrenaline.

Buzz!

Karolyn jumped. She had to put both hands on her chair arms to steady herself before reaching to answer her intercom.

"Yes?"

"In my office—*now*."

She opened his door slowly, predicting her unpleasant morning was about get more so. Arthur walked to his table and pulled out a chair. "Sit."

As she watched him lowering himself slowly into the chair across from her, Karolyn's mind raced to surmise what he knew about the impetus behind Winton moving the meetings. She'd worked with him long enough to sense he'd discovered their scheme. Somehow, Arthur always seemed to know.

Her internal alarm went off, spurring a moment of panic. But it passed quickly, replaced by a sense of calm. She knew the actions she, Teri, and Philip had taken were in the best interests of McNev. There was no need to be anything other than truthful.

* * *

Arthur scowled at Karolyn with probing intensity, barely able to contain himself. He knew releasing his wrath would be gratifying, an eruption engulfing her. She would cower and plead for forgiveness, and he'd take his time deciding if he wanted to give it.

A momentary fantasy captured his thoughts. He stood over Karolyn as she quivered, looking up at him with tears in her eyes. He unzipped his fly and told her to redeem herself. He knew she would. Sweet, yes, but only fleeting.

This PEP required his best, and that meant absolute control. He needed to know if Karolyn could still be used as he planned his next moves. Continuing to stare as he considered the optimum approach, he noticed her body language. The contrition was absent; she no longer looked like his devoted subject. Apparently, she'd forgotten her place.

With his smile annulled of charm, he asked, "Did you have anything to do with Winton's decision?" He knew she'd deny it. Catching her in the lie felt like cocking the hammer.

But instead, Karolyn explained her ongoing apprehension with Crandall and Zhou in a straightforward manner, reiterating that she'd tried to share it with him before the trip. She told him that she and Teri discussed it, and that Philip had confided his coinciding worry of potential harm to the partnership.

She finished by summarizing their strategy to persuade Winton, adding, "We believed moving things back here would give us more time to determine if there was really a problem, so we put our heads together and took a page out of your playbook."

Her unanticipated honesty and unexpected quip startled him enough that he actually had to concentrate to avoid reacting. Then, in the few seconds it took him to recalibrate how best to demean her, she crossed the line.

"*Is* there a problem brewing, Arthur? Are Crandall and Zhou in on it? Are *you* in on it?"

He slid his chair from the table and stood, noting with satisfaction that Karolyn braced herself. But rather than towering over her, he turned his back and walked to the window. The marine-layer overcast bathed a wave of employees in gray as they trudged in from the parking lot.

Here come the Troglodytes...now suddenly, my poseur assistant thinks she's no longer one of them just because she's teamed up with Teri...unacceptable.

Arthur stood in silence, his shoulders tightening at the outrage coursing through him. Turning to face her, he unmasked his contempt and let her feel the full effect. His cadence was deliberate—his tone vicious.

"So, my apprentice believes she's ready for the big leagues. After one elementary move with a couple of amateurs? You managed to manipulate a moron whose ego has long since eclipsed any capacity for rational thought—congratulations! Is there a *problem?* Hah! Even if you had an inkling, do you honestly think McNeil would believe you—an Executive Assistant?

"You and your new best friend Teri, searching for some big conspiracy...you don't know a goddamn thing! She's not good enough, and you're just a whore cloaked in corporate attire who managed to learn some business strategy at the knee of her master...when you weren't otherwise engaged in your primary skill."

He shook his head, adding, "This is how you repay me?" His words rang with a rhetorical acrimony that seemed to hang in the air.

He stalked toward her now. When Arthur saw her shudder, he knew he was back in control. His smile bordered on diabolical.

"Ah, fear...That's more like it. That's good—that's *smart*. You're astute...and you're one helluva lay. So let me tell you what's going to happen next, little girl. First, you go tell your new friends Teri and Rich to back off right now. Then you take a time-out and get that pretty head straight...Knock this shit off and get back on the right side, and I'll forget about everything."

He stopped behind her and squeezed her shoulders hard, sliding his hands toward her neck.

"Otherwise, all three of you won't live to regret it."

* * *

Rich and Teri sat next to each other in the Executive Board Room, sharing the unease of the 8 a.m. senior management meeting. Attendees included McNeil, Winton, and O'Donnell, along with Duke and other selected Vice Presidents. McNeil and O'Donnell decided to expand the circle of executives in the partnership process now that it was imminent and TaiChin would be on site. This briefing was to prepare for their arrival tomorrow.

Before all the chaos, Rich had envisioned their first meeting together in this room with a feeling of fulfillment, excited to be working with Teri.

But this morning, they faced an uncertain future with a new partnership threatening to be derailed, and no one seemed happy to be there.

Rich was at least able to elicit a small smile from her when he whispered, "There's enough tension in this room to defeat an entire army of massage therapists."

McNeil was annoyed about everything, particularly the absence of Will Crandall, who'd elected to take a later flight, not arriving until tomorrow. The sub-zero interaction between O'Donnell and Karolyn was obvious to everyone but Winton, who was reveling in acting presidential and arguing with Arthur about who should handle what on the TaiChin agenda.

Teri was taken aback by O'Donnell's petulance, even considering Rich's comments last night about Arthur's attitude. Arthur's persistent refusal to partner with Winton on presentations forced McNeil to end the argument by agreeing to co-present the Due Diligence data with Jackson in the final meeting, now scheduled for Wednesday morning.

The rest of their day consisted of staff and technical meetings, including a review of critical open items for Ship 913. These "squawks" were being worked across all three shifts to deliver Tailia's first ME-420 Wednesday afternoon. The new plan also included Lin, Zhou, and their respective staffs boarding the maiden flight to Hong Kong, following a special delivery ceremony.

* * *

Rich and Teri's last meeting of the day was a quiet tag-up with Karolyn in a conference room on the second floor.

They arrived before she did, and as they sat down to wait, Rich asked, "Could you believe Arthur in the briefing this morning?"

Teri shook her head. "He was certainly rude."

"Yeah, he made sure he's going to be nowhere near the spotlight when the Due Diligence data gets presented. Whatever his software does, I'm guessing it's not a good thing...speaking of which, I haven't even had a chance to tell you about Sheila."

"Did she find something?"

"She came up with a brainstorm over the weekend and managed to access her old test server. She thinks she might be able to use Beth's original prototype version of the remote access software to get into the back end of the McNev system. It could be the key to figuring out what Arthur's new program does."

Noting Rich's enthusiasm describing his sister's genius, Teri thought it was a good time to break the difficult news about Porter's responsibility for his accident. The words were almost out when Karolyn rushed in, shutting the door quickly behind her.

She sat at the table and slid a file folder across to Rich. "Here—take this damn thing."

Karolyn looked ashen, her voice strained. "I had to wait until I was sure Arthur was tied up with McNeil before I could grab the report and copy it for you. He's watching me like a hawk...Ter, he knows we worked with Lin to get Winton to move the meetings back here."

Teri's expression was wide-eyed. "What? How?"

"I'm beginning to think he's omniscient. Somehow the SOB just knows everything." Karolyn filled them in on her earlier sinister exchange in O'Donnell's office, prompting a second startled response from Teri.

"Oh, my God. You think he'll try to hurt you?"

Karolyn shook her head. She'd left out the part where Arthur simulated choking her, but it was on her mind as she replied, "I hadn't thought so, but now I'm not so sure. He seems...off. Honestly, we all need to be careful."

Teri reached across the table and put her hand on Karolyn's. "KB, do you think we should go to the police?"

Karolyn pushed out a breath of frustration through pursed lips. "Yes, and no, Ter. It's only my word against his, and knowing Arthur, he'd find a way to make *us* look suspect..."

"Or have us labeled whackos," Rich interjected. He shook his head adding, "And unfortunately, McNeil doesn't have an inkling either."

Karolyn said, "So you talked to him—You didn't tell him anything about what we're doing, did you?"

"Nope. I was tempted, but you're right. We can't risk Art finding out any more than he knows already...But I do have some good news."

Rich recapped Sheila's breakthrough, ending with, "Hopefully her test results will give us something solid to open McNeil's eyes."

Karolyn shoved her chair back, stood up, and began pacing around the table. "So it seems like we're at a crossroads, here. We either keep digging and meet with McNeil, hoping whatever we find, along with Sheila's information, is enough to take Arthur down...Or we let it go, back off like Arthur said to, and hope we stay safe."

She stopped short at the end of the conference table and leaned on it with both hands, looking at Rich and Teri.

"What do you two think?"

Teri and Rich looked at each other, then at Karolyn.

Rich said, "My gut tells me Art's flying our company straight into the side of a mountain...and he's got the only parachute." He added with a sober expression, "But it's your call, KB. You're the closest to him—and the most at risk."

Teri nodded her agreement.

Karolyn looked down, contemplating. Though she no longer had any compunction about seeing Arthur as their adversary, that didn't make him any less dangerous, and challenging him would only make him more so.

But she believed in Teri and Rich, and Philip Lin too. And with Rich and Mac able to research the Herrera report, along with Sheila's testing, they had a decent chance to find real evidence. Having Porter in their corner was also a major plus. And most importantly, she'd discovered a new ally: self-respect.

She looked back and forth between Teri and Rich. Then she straightened up and slammed her fist on the table.

"Fuck him."

* * *

After their meeting, Teri went back to her office and Karolyn left for the day to get as far away from O'Donnell as possible.

Rich looked over the copy of the Herrera report and called Mac immediately to say he was on his way. His pace was quick, making what seemed like his tenth trip in the past few days through the tunnel to the Final Assembly hangar. He noticed the increase in second-shift activity, crews working overtime on 913 and two other planes in final line positions, pushing to get all three to the flight ramp.

Mac was standing in his office with his coat on when Rich walked in.

"You just caught me. I came back to answer my phone. You said you got it?"

Rich held up the folder. "Yep."

It had been three weeks since Rich skimmed through a few pages outside O'Donnell's office. Now they had the entire report. Mac took off his coat and sat down at his table with Rich.

The report included a detailed schedule and a special second-shift crew, with OT exceptions, for "emergency" work in Final Assembly. They spotted the usual suspects, Vale, Reiss, and Davis, in the list of mechanics.

Mac said, "Buck a rivet—the sabotage wasn't random. Herrera drew up this crew and schedule. These codes are probably bogus, indicating where and what damage they were supposed to cause."

Rich nodded. "Yeah, the numbers are definitely *not* normal work codes. We need to have someone trace these right away. There could be damage that hasn't been discovered."

Mac wrote a note for Al to get on it first thing tomorrow, as Rich pointed to the section at the top of page five.

"Here's what I saw that started this mess. Look—here's the E-1101 connector. The work looks legit...It's the special request for the cargo door-lock on Ship 913 that Bordon heard Herrera and Vale talking about.

Unfortunately, there're no assembly instructions. Only, 'Details To Be Provided.'"

Mac took the document and flipped to the end, pointing to the bottom of the page. "Look who signed it."

Authorized: J. C. William, Director, Corporate HQ

"All roads seem to lead to Mr. William, whoever the hell he is."

Rich stood up. "Let's go."

Mac pushed out of his chair. "Where?"

"Duke's office. When I spoke with McNeil yesterday, I asked him if he knew of a director named J. C. William. Hugh told me he didn't remember the exact circumstance, but Duke talked about the guy in one of his famous anecdotes. He said it was a while ago though, before the merger." Rich chuckled. "Hugh admitted he wasn't really paying a lot of attention to Duke at the time."

Mac said, "This makes no sense. How can a director have full signature authority in the assembly work order system, and no one knows who he is?"

"Well, seeing as how this is the only lead we've got, let's try to find out."

They double-timed the half-mile walk, back through the tunnel and along the main road to the Sub-Assembly hangar, then down the main aisle to the complex that housed Duke's office.

Rich stopped suddenly and turned to Mac. "Did you see your Security buddy following us?"

"Nope. I think we caught a break, and he took off when he saw me getting ready to leave."

They found the outer office open. Marla was gone, and all was quiet. Mac walked behind Marla's desk and opened her center drawer, pulling out a key. He held it up.

"She let me into Duke's office once, to drop off a report. I happened to see where she put the key back. You sure you want to do this?"

Rich nodded. Mac slipped the key into the lock and opened the door. They shut it behind them as Mac switched on the light and looked at the huge picture. "I used to like John Wayne until I had to sit here, and watch Duke admire it like it was a self-portrait…So, what are we looking for?"

"Anything with the name J. C. William."

They were busily looking through stacks of papers and opening file drawers that weren't locked, when they heard the door to Marla's outer office open.

Before they had a chance to do anything other than look up from their search, Duke's office door flew open, with Darren Duke entirely filling the doorway.

"What the fuck do you two think you're doing?!"

25

The Newport neighborhood pizzeria wasn't crowded, as the lone smallish TV didn't attract the Monday Night Football crowd. The back room with its redwood paneling and low-level pendant lighting was mostly empty.

Porter slid a frosted mug of draft Pabst across the picnic-style table to Karolyn, hoping it would help lessen the anxiety he saw in her expression. His pulse jumped as she reached for his hand and said, "Thanks for meeting me."

He smiled. "Of course."

Karolyn returned his smile briefly, then it faded as she said, "I heard Jackson talking to Arthur today. I'm sorry they let you go."

Porter shrugged. "I knew it was coming. At the airport last night, I told Winton if he ever touched you again, or tried to have you fired, I'd cut off his balls and feed 'em to him. Guess he took exception…go figure."

Karolyn half-choked on a swallow of beer. "Oh my God! I wondered why he stayed so far away from me today. I wish I could've seen his face."

"He lost that high-and-mighty executive BS real fast…looked like he was gonna piss himself."

Their pizza arrived, and Porter continued talking about his day.

"So after I got my walking papers, I decided it was time for some real investigating—I looked in on the esteemed Dr. Vale. Hearing how you all figured out he'd doped Rich up, I thought I'd make an office call…he was real apologetic."

When Karolyn arched one eyebrow, he raised his hand reassuringly.

"Don't worry—the Doc didn't need any heavy persuading. Our introduction was a little awkward, but then he got downright chatty. Said he'd had his own strings pulled too many times…seemed like he'd just been waitin' for someone he could tell about all the scumbag tricks Art used over the years to get the drop on people. The most interesting was Art's fondness for phone taps everywhere he's worked. Told me Art had this long-time pal…A security goon with an Italian name—del-something. Ring any bells?"

Karolyn dropped her slice of mushroom and sausage pizza. "Holy shit! This morning, Arthur knew all about what we did in Hong Kong to manipulate Winton, and he got a visit from Tony right before he called me in!"

"Yep—Tony's up there a lot. And I noticed a small cassette player on Art's credenza. Whaddya think he's tapped?"

"The condo!" Karolyn put her hand on Porter's forearm. "That's gotta be it!"

"Bet he's listened to all her calls...Tell Teri not to use that damn condo phone anymore!"

She shook her head and reached for Porter's hand again. "I'm not sure I can handle this. It's like being caught in a bad imitation of a Bond movie. I felt pretty confident earlier with Rich and Teri, but the more I see who he really is…"

Karolyn went through her confrontation with O'Donnell in greater detail than she had with Rich and Teri, describing his ominous changes in behavior. "And on top of that, then he called me a whore."

When Porter squeezed her hand, she said, "I appreciate that it bothers you, but I've done a lot of shit I'm not proud of…just like you." After a healthy swallow of beer, she added, "And that wasn't the worst part."

Porter's eyebrows lifted.

She confided Arthur's chilling ultimatum to get her head straight and his offer to leave them alone if she agreed to return to the *right side*.

Porter set down his mug and held both her hands. "KB, you've been amazing, standing up to Winton, and now, Art. You and Teri and Rich—you're the ones on the right side…Don't give in."

"I don't want to, but the more I think about it…maybe I could just pretend…tell Rich and Teri." She took a long breath. "I'm scared. He made like he was going to choke me again…"

Karolyn haltingly revealed the incident last year when Arthur had choked her nearly to unconsciousness. The next moment she was sobbing, hiding her face with her hands. Porter moved around the table to sit on the bench next to her and put his arm around her shoulder. Pulling her closer, he said gently, "Hey, listen to me. It's gonna be all right. I'm not gonna let that psycho harm one hair on that beautiful head of yours."

He looked down at her. She sniffled and looked up. As he brushed some stray hairs away from her face, a hint of a smile began to appear. She said, "Okay, then I'm offering you a job, working as my bodyguard."

He gazed into those endlessly blue eyes and knew she would somehow be his salvation. He grinned. "Personal security, huh? That's my specialty."

* * *

Teri was about to leave her office when her phone rang, showing *outside caller* on the display. She wasn't going to answer but sensed it could be important.

"Teri Harlan. Can I help you?"

It was Rich, calling from a payphone. She heard the stress in his voice. "Thank God I caught you. You're not gonna believe this—I just got suspended."

She sat back down, slightly light-headed, and told Rich he was right; she didn't believe it.

Rich explained the information he and Mac discovered in the report, and how it led to them searching Duke's office for something to identify the mysterious J. C. William.

"Then all off a sudden, Duke appears out of nowhere with Tony del Balso. They escorted us directly to O'Donnell's office where Art invoked a three-day suspension, effective immediately.

"O'Donnell called HR to process the paperwork and Security walked us to the main gate. We had to surrender our badges and stand there like criminals while Tony's goons retrieved and searched our vehicles. It was a good thing we left the report locked in Mac's office."

Following a couple of epithets she'd found herself using too often lately, Teri asked how Duke had known what they were up to.

Rich explained del Balso's surveillance of Mac and Al, and guessed they must have missed someone who saw them going into Duke's office. Teri was stunned that her new employer seemed to be operating like a throwback to the McCarthy era.

"What can I do to help?" she asked.

"I'll be okay. If you can keep me posted, I'll do whatever I can from home." He paused. "But there is one thing...I hate to ask, but it would really help."

She could hear his apprehension as he continued.

"J. C. William may be the key to uncovering this whole mess...Would you be willing to stop by Duke's office, and if he's still there, try to find out if he knows who William is?"

She had no desire to be anywhere near Duke, especially with Arthur knowing she and Rich were working with Karolyn. Plus it was late, and she was wearing a skirt. The thought of Duke ogling her legs added to her lack of enthusiasm.

She stifled a shudder, trying to decide if she was up to it, as Rich added, "I'm only asking because we're running out of time. And he certainly likes you a whole lot better than Mac or me. You might be able to get something out of him."

Teri could feel her shoulders tighten. *Yes, it's obvious what Duke likes. Exactly what are you expecting me to do to "get something out of him"?*

She considered saying something, but gave Rich the benefit of the doubt. Teri knew he was right about learning the identity of J. C. William, and growing up in manufacturing, she'd dealt with more than one manager like Duke.

"Okay, I want to get to the bottom of this as much as you do. I'll see what I can do."

"Thanks...just keep your distance. And if he starts playing games you should get out of there, okay?"

She hung up and shook her head. *Gee, thanks for the sage advice.*

* * *

Once Sheila navigated her way past the packet filters in the server firewall, facilitated by being the one who'd originally set them up, she found an executable copy of Beth's prototype remote access program. Unfortunately, the execute file was protected with a five-character password she'd been unsuccessfully trying to break.

She hadn't known Beth well enough to try more than a few obvious combinations of personal information. But after those quickly proved unsuccessful, she began thinking like a programmer—what she might use herself. Based on her well-earned knowledge of Arthur's obsessions, Sheila focused her guesswork on special experiences he'd most likely repeated with Beth.

She recalled a memorable night with Arthur, lying in bed following passionate sex and watching the movie *Wall Street*. Movies were a waste of time, according to Arthur, but this one he'd committed to memory, even reciting lines to her. His favorite scene was the shareholders meeting of Teldar Paper where Gordon Gekko, whose character Arthur idolized, gave a speech proclaiming that greed was good.

Her memory drifted to the night he'd presented her with her first contract payment. When she'd protested it was too much, he'd kissed her, saying, "Remember what Gordon said? Greed is a good thing!"

She entered *greed*—the program opened!

Sheila worked quickly as Beth's application followed her own design, which made it relatively straightforward. She captured current month-end data from Production, Quality, and Finance Systems, saved the files, ran them with the new program, and executed her compare application.

She took a break and read Lisa a bedtime story, as the compare software and report writer generated the output. She'd just returned to her computer and opened the report file summary when she heard Rich walk in downstairs.

The comparison results showed a lower line rate with rejections and rework stats higher by nearly fifty percent. The ninety-day cash flow projection was nearly fifty percent less, and the debt-equity ratio increased from a healthy 0.5 to an alarmingly high 1.75.

The software redirecting McNev's systems to the new databases would replace current actual data with these detrimental figures. Sheila wasn't a business expert, but she knew enough to realize this would spell disaster for McNev's side of the partnership.

As Rich reached the top of the stairs, she said, "Hey, come in here, and look at this."

He walked over to her and looked at the monitor. "Ah, I see you got in. Were you able to find something?"

"Damn right I did."

He said, "Good. Let's nail his ass. The no-good SOB just suspended me."

* * *

Teri drove her Jeep west to the Sub-Assembly building. Unlike the all-hands-on-deck pace in Final Assembly, the absence of second shift activity left the cavernous hangar uncomfortably quiet. The echoes of Teri's heels added to her apprehension as she thought through her *Plan B* and emergency *Plan C*, hoping it wouldn't come to that.

When she reached his outer office, her reluctance suddenly escalated. She muttered, "Damn," when she saw his door open and the light on.

Darren stood behind his desk, closing his briefcase. He looked up when Teri knocked on his open door.

"Darren? Sorry to come by so late—Just had a quick question."

"Well, look who's here. My favorite executive on the whole team…and the best lookin', for sure. And she's come to visit lil' ol' Duke!"

God, I hate his third-person bullshit.

"Well, don't stand in the doorway, girl—Come in! I'll get the door."

Teri felt her shoulders tense, trying to make nice with the VP who got her vote for best portrayal of a Neanderthal. She took a breath and chose the chair farthest from his desk.

Not surprisingly, rather than sitting at his desk, Duke took the chair opposite her. He placed his hands in his lap with a dramatic flair, and without the slightest pretense of professionalism, focused his attention on her legs.

"Sorry we had to suspend your boyfriend tonight. You should tell him to keep his big nose outta my office…is that why you're here?"

"He's not my boyfriend."

Duke smiled broadly. Then he stood, stepped back to his desk, and reached underneath, flipping a switch. The overhead lights turned off, leaving a pinspot lighting his desk and soft indirect lighting around the perimeter of the ceiling. He sauntered back to sit across from her.

Gazing at Teri appraisingly, he spoke with a syrupy downhome drawl. "Well, in that case, what can I do you for, darlin'?"

Teri looked at the ceiling. "Seriously? Your office doubles as a lounge?"

"I find it relaxing...when I tend to things that keep me late."

"Well, I certainly don't want to keep you. I'll make this quick."

Trying to get comfortable in a chair better suited to a tavern, Teri crossed her legs, and the hem of her plaid pleated skirt slipped above her knee, showing the pink lace of her slip. She watched Duke, drawn like a bee to pollen, shift in his chair, trying to improve his vantage point.

She sighed, swallowed her sarcastic comment, and attempted a smile, hoping it didn't look too phony. She told him the story she'd devised on the way over.

"I need to ask your help with something. I've had the week from hell, and I'm stuck on this historical quality audit assignment from Arthur. I came across a name on some work orders that nobody knew: J. C. William. Vern in accounting said you've got a handle on everything in Manufacturing, and if anyone knew him, it would be you." Teri added a wide-eyed expression as she finished.

"Why in the world would you be asking about that name? I haven't thought of it in years. I'm sure we could find something more interesting to discuss."

He stood and removed his tie, opening his collar and another button. "Why don't you take off your coat, get comfy, and settle in a bit?"

She felt herself flush. He was behaving exactly as she'd predicted. She took her jacket off, folded it in her lap across her legs, and spoke with a bit of an edge in her tone.

"I really don't want to submit the report to Arthur without knowing who this guy is...so do you know him?"

Duke moved his gaze from her legs upward. "Well, yes and no."

He paused and held out his hand. "Here, let me have your coat and I'll hang it up."

She held it in her lap. "Do you know him or not?"

Darren laughed. "It's actually a pretty funny story, but I have to be in the mood to tell it...so how about you make a good impression on me."

He continued to stare, waiting expectantly.

Teri sighed again and stood up. *Time for Plan B.*

She began putting her jacket back on. "Look, Darren, I get it—you like my legs, and that's fine. If you need to have some sort of fantasy about me, I can't stop you. I tried being nice, and I really could use your help. But I guarantee nothing is going to happen, and frankly, I'm not interested in playing your stupid game."

Duke stood up to face her, his sleazy smile instantly replaced by open hostility.

"Oh, really? You think because you spend a few minutes playing nice and cross your legs, I'm supposed to trip all over myself and tell you what you want to know? Well, let me set you straight, honey—you're in *Duke's* kingdom out here—and I'm the fucking *king!* When people want something from Duke, they know there's a price…and everyone knows it's Duke who sets it.

"If Duke tells you to strip, your clothes come off. If Duke tells you to suck him off, you get on your fucking knees! And your price for information, Miss Teri, starts with seeing how you look in the pretty pink slip you're wearing. So unzip that little plaid skirt, and let's see it…or get the hell out of my office!"

Teri forced herself not to step back. *Time for Plan C.*

"Sorry, Darren, but this is 1994, and your little kingdom just got invaded." She pulled her small Olympus Pearlcorder from her purse and held it up, pressing rewind, and then *play.*

"…get on your fucking knees! And your price for information, Miss Teri, starts with seeing how you look in the pretty pink slip you're wearing. So unzip that little plaid skirt, and let's see it…or get the hell…"

"Sonofabitch!"

She was ready to bolt for the door, but his expression changed again, deescalating to a grudging acceptance.

"Okay, okay. Well played. I'll give you credit for creativity…you give me that tape, and I tell you what you want to know, right?"

"You tell me who this William character is and *then* I'll give you the tape—on my way out."

"Shit, you're one pushy broad, you know that?"

"Yeah, maybe so, but Marla seems to like me. I think I'll take her to lunch and see what she has to say about the way you run things."

"For chrissake, will you take it easy? You're like a damn wild filly that needs to be broke."

She didn't respond and didn't stop glaring.

"Okay, I'll tell you about J. C. William. It was so long ago, it doesn't matter, anyhow. Don't know why you'd even care."

Teri crossed her arms expectantly, and Duke finally assumed his storytelling mode.

"Well, it's gotta be more than three years ago, now. I was VP of Manufacturing at McNeil, of course, and Crandall was my assistant—I could tell you lots of funny shit about that…"

Catching her glower, he said, "Yeah, never mind," and continued. "So, there was a period where I traveled a lot and Crandall had to expedite these production work orders that needed my personal approval, only I wasn't around. See, Will didn't have my delegated authority for exceptions when I was gone, so he invented this director, 'J. C. William.' Will entered him into the manufacturing system and set up full signature authority for everything. Get it? William James Crandall; J. C. William—cute, huh?"

"Yeah, I got it." Teri forced a smile and asked, "So what did you do?"
Duke smiled back, seeming pleased that she'd asked him.

"Well, I'll tell you, Teri. I kicked the little prick's ass and told him that would be the end of that shit. When I told old man McNeil about it at a party that week, he laughed his ass off. Damn, it really was funny!"

Teri stepped toward his door, flipped open the lid on her recorder, popped out the microcassette, and handed it to him.

"Here's my part of the deal."

Darren grabbed the tape and eyed her, his grin turning cynical. "Wish I could say it was a pleasure doing business with you...if you want anything else from me, now you know the price."

She opened the door and turned back to him, smiling as alluringly as possible, given the circumstances. "What *you* should know, Darren, is that hell would freeze over before I'd pay it."

As she walked through the outer office, she added over her shoulder, "And by the way, your boy must have resurrected J. C. William. Apparently no one told you he's been actively using it right under your nose!"

Teri's pace walking back through the hangar was incredibly swift, in spite of her heels and shaking legs. But once she was behind the wheel, heading her Jeep out of the plant, she couldn't stop smiling at the thought of Duke's next conversation with Crandall.

* * *

Fortified by pizza and beer, Karolyn left the restaurant with Porter, determined to do what they could to help the rest of the team uncover O'Donnell's true intentions.

Because his Lumina was now familiar to del Balso's crew, Karolyn followed Porter to the car-rental agency to return it, and then drove him to a competitor to rent another vehicle. Next they dropped off Karolyn's car at her condo and drove Porter's newly rented Ford Focus over the bridge to Balboa Island. They parked around the block from O'Donnell's house just to be safe.

26

Monday, 9:05 p.m.

The evening breeze wafting through the open slider felt refreshing to Arthur as he sat at his custom mahogany worktable talking on his speakerphone to del Balso.

"See, Tony? The bug in McKinley's office really paid off."

"You were right on, boss, like always. It was a genius idea."

Arthur's boost from del Balso acknowledging his brilliance gave way to an unsettling thought.

My ranks of loyal followers appear to be thinning.

He sighed, picked up the Post-it Note stuck to his blotter, and dialed Zhou's pager.

* * *

Zhou Quon finished his shower and dismissed his security men, Wang, and Li, who'd been waiting in the small but elegant sitting room of his suite. When Winton announced the venue change, he'd proclaimed, "All my TaiChin guests will enjoy staying at the historic Hotel Laguna. It's well-known for its VIP guests, including Humphrey Bogart—and it's all on me!" Zhou remembered wondering who Humphrey Bogart was.

Lit softly by the final remnants of sunset, the waves of the Pacific, breaking just beyond the sliding glass door, held no interest for him. Quon sat with his back to their splendor, mentally replaying his limo ride through the north side of Laguna, which he'd spent staring at the devastation from last year's unprecedented wildfire. He was focused on the satisfaction he'd feel when Lin burned in just such an inferno.

Zhou grew up revering his heritage, certain of his superiority in all things: morals, religion, and the arts. The only aspect of his native culture he'd chosen not to embrace was Kung Fu, opting instead, for the power and destruction of gunpowder.

In the prime of his government economics career, Zhou was contacted unexpectedly by a group of clandestine power brokers known as the *Sponsors*. The group had a contract with Arthur O'Donnell to generate access to aerospace technology through a fast-track entrée into U.S. aviation. O'Donnell required an inside man for the project, and Zhou's single-minded focus on elevating his political position led to his immediate acceptance without question. Soon after, the Chinese head of TaiChin Industrial resigned and Zhou replaced him.

The project entailed destroying a proposed partnership, and entangling McNeil Everett in a scheme of fraudulent corporate performance. Creating a publicly ruinous scandal along with McNev's collapse into insolvency would compel McNeil to enlist the help of the group as the only alternative for his company to survive.

Even more important to Zhou than the extraordinary compensation was the favor of his well-connected benefactors, which he planned on leveraging to attain his rightful exalted position in the party hierarchy.

O'Donnell's original plan was well conceived to gut McNeil-Everett from the inside. However, Zhou found a kindred spirit in Arthur's rather eccentric partner, Will Crandall, and together they'd devised an addendum. Their added scheme would amplify McNev's devastation tenfold with a bonus of eliminating Lin, thereby fulfilling his duty to rid the world of a pro-Western hypocrite. Zhou visualized himself with Will, sharing the delight of the cataclysm when it transpired.

As his thoughts turned to the pretentious buffoon, Winton, blasting their well-planned scenarios into chaos, Zhou's animosity deepened. Even worse, Winton's revised plan called for him to fly home with Lin and the team on the Tailia plane, a decision that had been consuming him to the point of panic. And now he had to rely on O'Donnell to get their plans back on track.

Leaving this in the hands of our self-appointed master is too much uncertainty. He'd better have a solution, especially for the money he's demanding—the epitome of an arrogant westerner...

He jumped at the grating noise from his pager vibrating on the table.

* * *

Porter and Karolyn stood beneath the balcony, Karolyn silently mouthing, *Oh, shit!* when they heard Arthur praising del Balso for catching Rich and Mac in Duke's office.

She whispered in Porter's ear, "I wonder if Teri knows."

Porter whispered back, "Yeah, and how long has Mac's office been bugged? No wonder the asshole knows so much."

She pointed upward with her index finger, hearing Arthur walk out on the balcony, answering another call.

* * *

Arthur pressed the answer key on his portable handset, inhaling deeply. But even the ocean-fresh night-air couldn't offset his foul humor when Zhou's voice snapped in his ear. "I got your page. You'd better have good news to report."

Fresh out of cordialness, Arthur replied, "I'll get straight to the point. I need all my money up front."

As he predicted, Zhou protested with a nasty remark, informing Arthur that he would not be paid until afterwards. Arthur's increasing unpleasantness came naturally, amplified by days of escalating anger.

"Listen, *Mr. Zhou*, if you want this project completed, you'll make sure the full amount is wired to my numbered account no later than *eight o'clock Wednesday morning*. When Winton torpedoed the Hong Kong scenario, I had to completely re-orchestrate everything. My risk has increased substantially with the finale playing out here, and I've had to change my timing...Yes, it was that imperious bitch, Teri Harlan, joining forces with my slut assistant, who apparently thinks she's grown balls since Harlan became her new best friend. Oh, and your buddy, Lin, helped too."

Arthur switched the phone to his other ear. "Actually, you need to thank me. My revised scenario is *better* than Hong Kong—your requirements are being *exceeded*...Because I set up McNeil to present with Winton. Now he'll be directly implicated as well. Your sponsors may be able to take over McNev outright."

Smiling at his own genius, he expected to hear Zhou compliment him, but instead got an irrelevant question. Arthur began pacing irritably.

"No, for chrissake, Quon. I didn't forget your damn surprise. It's been confirmed. Talk to Will if you want—"

Arthur stopped abruptly in mid-sentence and pulled the phone away from his ear. The *beep-beep-beep* of a pager seemed to be coming from the street. He walked to the edge of the balcony and peered over, thinking he'd see the familiar red BMW.

"KB—is that you?"

When Arthur heard nothing, he pivoted and walked quickly back into his bedroom. He opened his bedroom door and looked downstairs, expecting her to walk in the front door. There was no one there.

His own Skytel was sitting quietly on his desk blotter.

That's strange...

Arthur's attention was drawn back to the phone by Zhou swearing loudly in Mandarin. He returned the handset to his ear.

"Quon—stop! I told you, my new scenario is perfect. What? No, it's not—it'll be a snap...and I want an extra ten percent because McNeil will be personally discredited."

Arthur had reached his limit with Zhou's attitude.

"Don't fuck with me, Quon. Remember, I'm the one who endorsed you for the TaiChin assignment, and I can land you on their shit-list just as easily—Now, get me my goddamn money!"

He mashed the disconnect button and walked back to the balcony railing, listening again. He heard only the sounds of the ocean.

I figured she'd have come to her senses by now.

* * *

Karolyn grabbed Porter's hand and they ran down the sidewalk, cutting into the alley in a reprise of the other week.

When they were once again out of sight and earshot, Karolyn apologized, catching her breath. "Damn, I'm sorry. I forgot to put my Skytel on vibrate—what an idiot!"

"Don't worry. I think we're okay—we got outta there fast."

"I hope so. I got distracted when he called me a slut."

Porter smiled. "He's wrong—and I'll be showing him just *how* wrong he is when we take the arrogant prick down…so, he was talking to Zhou, right?"

Karolyn nodded. "Yes, definitely. We have to tell the others, and we've *got* to get to McNeil tomorrow—he's walking into a trap."

Standing quietly for moment, Porter's thoughtful look prompted Karolyn to ask, "What?"

"You know, I hung out with Zhou's two body guards in Hong Kong—Wang and Li. They're actually really good guys, and they despise Zhou…mentioned being suspicious of him and Crandall…said they were doing their own private surveillance."

"How did you find that out? Do they even speak English?"

Porter smiled again. "Enough…in our business, you don't need a big vocabulary to understand each other. Maybe they've got something that can help us."

"It's certainly worth asking. They're all at the Hotel Laguna. I'll give you the address."

Porter said, "Good, I'll get over there tomorrow." Then he added, "I didn't catch the last part of the conversation, did you?"

"I heard something about some surprise for Lin and talking to Will about it…doesn't sound like anything good."

Karolyn frowned as her pager vibrated.

"It's Teri again, 911 this time—Bet she wants to tell me Rich and Mac got suspended."

27

Tuesday, 6:05 a.m.

Perched on a stool at one of the five bistro tables in the small "Starbucks-wannabe" coffee bar in a Newport Beach strip-mall, Teri felt conspicuous in her skirt and blouse. The only other customers, two early-rising locals, wore shorts and flipflops. She was taking a tentative sip of her latte, which tasted better than she anticipated, when Karolyn walked in with Porter.

Porter went to order, and Karolyn pulled up a stool next to Teri. "Good Morning. Sorry for making you get up extra early and meet here."

"So, did you hear Rich and Mac got suspended?"

Karolyn nodded. "Yes, but let me start at the beginning."

She summarized her dinner conversation, including Porter's decision to stay and help them. When she told Teri she'd gotten her page while she and Porter were standing under Arthur's balcony listening to his phone conversations, Teri looked nonplussed.

Karolyn chuckled. "Yeah, I'm becoming a halfway decent detective. Between your deductive skills and PB's surveillance knowhow, I may have a new career…probably a good thing, because we might not have jobs soon."

As Porter joined them and handed Karolyn her coffee, Teri said, "So, you're Karolyn's personal security now, huh?"

He grinned. "Yeah, I like it better than my old gig."

Teri caught the look he gave Karolyn. Although still unsettled by the knowledge of what he'd done, she felt better knowing Porter was watching her friend's back.

Porter's expression turned serious. "Our boy Artie is playing at another level here, Teri. I paid ol' Doc Vale a visit yesterday. He told me a lot about Art."

"You what? How did you get him to…"

Porter gently touched her arm. "Don't worry—No harm done. But I found out Art's into phone taps, bigtime. We're sure he's got one on the McNev condo phone, which means he's heard all the calls you've made from there. And Mac's office is bugged—that's how del Balso knew to call Duke and snag Rich and Mac last night."

Karolyn chimed in. "That's why I wanted to meet in person. No more using the condo phone. We need to warn Rich and Mac too."

"Holy hell—are you kidding me?"

Teri ran her hands through her hair as this latest revelation sank in, realizing Arthur overheard every one of her conversations. Her stomach reacted intensely enough that she slid off her stool to head for the restroom, but stopped short when standing up made her dizzy.

Karolyn stood and took Teri's arm. "Are you all right?"

With Karolyn's support, Teri sat back down unsteadily and shook her head. "Not really, no…God, I'm such an idiot. I told Rich how we managed Winton in Hong Kong…No wonder he wanted me staying at the McNev condo—that conniving SOB!"

Karolyn put her hand on Teri's shoulder. "Hey, kiddo. It's not you. Who even does this kind of shit?"

Porter added earnestly, "KB's right, Teri. Take it from me, neither of you are at fault here. Art seems to think he's some kind of real-life J. R. Ewing. Except he's more than just devious. In my opinion, he could even be a borderline psycho…and he's definitely dangerous."

Porter's concern and support seemed genuine, slightly reducing her stress. But as she listened to Karolyn's recap of O'Donnell's conversation with Zhou, she knew they were out of their depth. She had to admit she was grateful to have someone like Bordon on their side.

When Karolyn finished, Teri said, "So it also sounds like we're right about Zhou and Crandall."

"Yep—and last night we confirmed that Arthur is the wizard behind the curtain."

With a half-smile, Teri said, "Nice allusion, KB, but now it seems clear that the wizard at the end of *our* yellow-brick road has no chance of turning out to be a kindly man who helps us."

"Agreed," Karolyn replied, "So we've got to get to McNeil today, or he'll walk into the TaiChin meeting tomorrow and get blindsided."

Teri was quiet for a minute and then let her thoughts tumble out in no particular order. "You're right—and in order to let McNeil know what's about to go down, Sheila has to figure out what the hell Arthur's new program does…and what about Philip? Damn, I wish Rich was going to be at work today—Can you work on getting us a private moment with Hugh?"

The three of them formulated a plan as they finished their coffee and walked to their cars.

Porter was going to meet covertly with Wang and Li, steering clear of Zhou. Karolyn was to focus on how to connect with McNeil, working around the TaiChin agenda, without alerting Arthur. Teri said she'd call Rich, bring him up to speed, and check on Sheila's progress. And if this wasn't enough, they still had an 8 a.m. meeting with Vernon Ames.

As Karolyn got into her Bimmer, she yelled to Teri, "Be careful which phone you use. Maybe you should stop and call Rich from a pay phone!"

* * *

Looking around his office at the original John-Richard wall art, Bernhardt Design inlaid table, and his prized Christian Maas silver panther majestically gracing his credenza, Arthur exhaled wistfully.

I will miss you all.

Last night, he'd come to terms with reality. The nature of this PEP and the unmanageable dynamics of intractable players had combined to render the original closing scenario nonviable. But even a major dilemma can be redressed by a perfect solution. Case in point, "persuading" Zhou to move up his payment. Advancing the funds transfer to tomorrow morning was the key; his emergency exit plan was now fully enabled.

For the first time in several days, Arthur felt renewed, back in control of his way forward, soon to be free of this unexpected byzantine snare. Despite having to vacate the PEP before crossing the finish line, his standby plan creates the perfect alternate path to his ultimate goal.

As meticulous as everything he did, his contingency procedures had been anticipated, and could now be activated simply by accelerating preparations he'd already made for Caracas, Venezuela. First thing this morning, he'd verified LazerAir's delivery flight, confirming Ship 914 final production was on-schedule, departing midday tomorrow.

His emergency arrangements were perfect but for one inescapable drawback: *flying*. Unfortunately, the LazerAir flight was the only option to ensure he'd be on a cruise ship to Barbados, safely beyond the bounds of extradition, before anyone realized he was gone.

To steel himself, he focused on his stunning Barbados estate being constructed on a utopian ocean-front parcel in Christ Church. The two-year labor of love was the culmination of his personal design, featuring a commercial-grade kitchen, an indoor-outdoor pool and grotto, a full gym complete with Nautilus machines, and a library-chess salon with a hidden private reading /safe room.

After finalizing the details of the Caracas-to-Barbados getaway, Arthur spent the remaining wee hours of last night reviewing the latest turn of events and the resistance he'd encountered. The only logical conclusion was that this PEP's unique nature had incited unexpected opposition.

Three years ago, when Arthur's long-time Chinese associate approached him for a new project, he'd never considered that the objective of company destruction might become a matter of contention. Knowing the project request came from the *Sponsors*, with resources vast enough to shape future government and economic policies, Arthur's sole focus was on parlaying this unique opportunity into his PEP masterpiece.

Wealth, in sufficient measure to possess the best of everything, had always been Arthur's only value in life. The concept of worth inherent in a person's work, company, or colleagues, had never been within his frame of reference.

Completing his analysis last night, he'd admitted, albeit grudgingly, that he'd been caught off guard by these misguided fools. Not only did they seem to find significant value in both their work and in McNev, they'd apparently formed a team to protect it.

Although he was certain their recent success was a transitory fluke, when he'd calculated the odds of consummating this PEP as originally planned, without facing negative consequences, they were not good. As always, he made the correct decision: remove himself, forthwith.

Tomorrow, I'll be on my way, and they'll be stuck with the smoldering debris of a failed aircraft company...a lesson in worth they won't soon forget.

He jumped when his phone's annoying ring tone disrupted his morning contemplation, further irritated that Karolyn wasn't there to answer it.

"Yes? Oh, hi Vern. You're in awfully early this morning."

* * *

Vernon Ames entered Teri's office at precisely 8:00 a.m., more nervous than the last time she'd met with him.

"Good morning, Ms. Harlan. You're in a different office now. Last time you were two doors down."

Teri slid a chair out from her table motioning for him to have a seat. "Yes, I was using Rich Richmond's office then. Now I've moved into my own."

He said, "I like it better..." and turned to admire the Boston fern by the window, adding, "I like your plant."

Teri figured he was more comfortable with plants.

As they sat down, Karolyn rushed in. "Hi. Hope I'm not late."

Teri introduced her to Vern, explaining she'd invited Karolyn because of her familiarity with executive expense reporting.

When Karolyn took off her suit jacket and hung it over a chair, Teri noticed Vern glancing furtively at Karolyn's pink chiffon blouse, then turning away, fidgeting.

Their discussion was far easier than Teri anticipated. Expecting she'd need to pry information from Vern again, she was pleasantly surprised when he explained the details behind Private Accounts without prompting.

"When Mr. O'Donnell took over, he informed us that executive expenses should be kept confidential, prompting his decision to use a processing firm to manage them. In addition to his goal of privacy, he calculated the time saved by outsourcing tracking, managing, and posting of disbursements. We appreciated his innovative idea. Mr. O'Donnell understood how hard the accounting staff works."

Vern pointed to a credit entry in the cash account. "See this? We make one simple monthly payment to Executive Payment Management, and they take care of everything. They send us a monthly summary of all the bills they've paid."

Karolyn asked, "That means all the travel expense reports I get from the execs and turn in to accounting are just forwarded to this EPM company?"

"Correct—and not just travel. They take care of all executive-related expenses and reimbursements…saves us a lot of time."

Teri asked, "Why did Arthur insist on keeping executive expenses confidential? Isn't it important to track those expenses openly for accountability?"

"Oh, no. Mr. O'Donnell explained that privacy is crucial to executives being able to operate freely."

Teri tilted her head, trying to process Vern's inane reasoning, as Karolyn jumped in. "So, Vern, how do you know EPM isn't charging us more than they're paying in bills? Have you ever considered they could be paying fifty thousand dollars of expenses, charging us sixty thousand, and keeping the difference?"

Vern shook his head.

"That's not possible. Mr. O'Donnell hired EPM himself, and assured us of their stellar reputation. They seem very efficient, and they send us a monthly reconciliation report along with their reasonable fee."

"Does their monthly report include copies of receipts and supporting documents?" Teri asked.

Another shake of the head by Vern. "No, just the report."

Teri looked at Karolyn and then at Vern, arching one eyebrow. "So how does the approval process work?"

Vern hesitated. "It's quite straightforward. Mr. O'Donnell always reviews and approves them personally."

"Uh-huh, I see…and what if Mr. O'Donnell is on vacation?"

Vern smiled. "Well, I've never seen Mr. O'Donnell take a vacation, but he's made it clear that he's the only one with the approval authority for EPM monthly reports."

Teri looked back at Karolyn, who chimed in on cue. "Vern, who owns EPM?"

Vern's discomfort escalated dramatically. He looked up at Teri's wall clock. Then, in a reprise of his escape move, he stood, slid his chair beneath the table, and stepped toward the door. "Um…sorry, I just realized I'm late for another meeting."

Karolyn stood with him and stepped close. "Vern, please answer my question." His eyes flitted to her blouse as he reached behind himself to open the door. "I...I really don't know the answer, but someone in procurement could tell you—their database contains information on every vendor." As he backed out, he added, "Very nice meeting you, Miss Babcock. Please call me—anytime."

* * *

When Vern had called early this morning to report he'd been requested by "Ms. Harlan" to attend an eight o'clock meeting on Private Accounts, lesser minds would have seen this as a problem. Arthur saw opportunity. He'd told Vern to be completely forthcoming and cooperative. Although his directive caused Vern some consternation, Arthur had reassured him.

Smiling as he thought of Teri and Karolyn exercising their investigative skills on Ames, Arthur sat at his PC and opened his custom Remote Interface application, accessing the McNev Enterprise System. He located the Executive Payment Management vendor information file in the procurement database and changed the EPM ownership record, replacing his mother's maiden name with *J. C. William*.

Arthur could picture their potential triumph—Teri and Karolyn running to McNeil, proudly proclaiming they'd uncovered the culprit behind the Private Accounts. His smile widened.

Imagine Will's surprise if he's accused of fraud based on his alter ego owning a company he's never heard of!

Next, he opened the secret file on his Palmtop, checking the balance in his EPM account: $1,595,757. Arthur sighed in satisfaction at the reward for his two-plus years of work on his Private Accounts scheme.

Considering the minimum funds required for Will's malfeasance to appear credible, he decided to leave four-hundred thousand in the account. Should their investigation ever prove successful, they would believe they'd found the fraud, accuse Will, and look no further.

Finally, he called his personal banker at Pacific West Bank and requested a wire transfer of the remainder from the EPM account to a personal account he'd named "Epsilon." Using two-hundred-twenty-five thousand dollars from personal savings, he'd previously opened the Epsilon account with a PIN for electronic withdrawal, providing easy access to pocket money. He entered $1,195,757 and the confirmation number, updating his Epsilon account balance on the secure spreadsheet: *$1,420,757.*

With a contented smile, he closed his Palmtop and leaned back in his chair.

That should do it. I'll put Will in play tonight...The only remaining wild card is Sheila—certainly more talented than her loser brother. But even if Teri gets ol' Brad to convince her to help them, there's no way she can discover anything now that I revoked her access.

* * *

As the door shut behind Vern, Teri grinned at Karolyn. "I think you've got a fan, KB."

"Ha-ha, very funny...it was pretty obvious our questions made him uncomfortable, though. Shy little Vern's either unbelievably naïve, or he's hiding something."

"Yeah...and I'm gonna take a wild guess that Arthur's behind the curtain again...By the way, that was smart, asking about EPM ownership. Know anyone in Procurement?"

Karolyn shook her head. "No, sorry. I can make a call...but at this point, shouldn't we turn our attention to our number one priority—getting with McNeil?"

Teri nodded her agreement.

"Were you able to speak to Rich?" Karolyn asked.

"No, unfortunately. I stopped at a pay phone like you suggested, but I got Sheila's voicemail. And now I'm too paranoid to use this phone...How'd you do with McNeil?"

"Couldn't get near him, so far. Arthur stuck him in that guest office next to his, keeping everyone away to 'protect his privacy.' Arthur's even leaving his door open—which he never does—to keep his eye on me. When I told him I had a meeting with you, he said, 'You can go, but get back here the minute it's finished.' Plus, he rearranged today's agenda to have the TaiChin group spend most of the day with loveable Duke, doing tours."

"Damn, that reminds me. I need to tell Rich what I found out from Duke about *J. C. William*. I probably should've called him last night, but it was late, and I was thrashed."

Karolyn said, "You know, it was lucky you didn't. Whatever you found out, Arthur won't—" Karolyn brought herself up short. "Wait, did you say you got information from Darren last night? How'd you manage that? Did you take a gun?"

"Nope, didn't need one. We came to an understanding."

"Okay...is that a good thing or a bad thing?"

Teri shook her head. "I'll tell you sometime over a beer...maybe several." Refocusing on their current dilemma, she added, "So we also need to tag up with Philip. Heard anything from him?"

"No, and we forgot to give him our pager numbers—duh. He should be here by now, though. We could walk over to the Visitor Center and try to peel him away from Zhou and the others."

Teri took a thoughtful breath. "Maybe before we go look for Philip, we should call Rich and Sheila to check her progress, and I could tell Rich what I found out."

"Good idea. Hey, do you think Sheila could track down the EPM owner for us?"

"Great thought—Let's ask her."

Karolyn stood up slowly, coming to grips with their situation. "This really is falling on us now, isn't it?"

Teri nodded.

Karolyn took on a determined expression. "Well, we'd best get a move on, then. Let's use that small conference room on the second floor we were in yesterday. It's not booked, and it has a Polycom speakerphone."

Teri picked up her folders and purse as Karolyn looked at her watch.

"Arthur will probably call any minute to find out where I am. Somehow I don't think he trusts me anymore."

Teri shot her a wry grin. "Gee—go figure."

They left Teri's office, electing to take the stairs. As the door closed behind them, her phone chirped, showing *901* on the display.

* * *

Philip shook off a touch of claustrophobia from sitting in one of the guest offices in the McNev Visitor Center. Part of the Security complex located just inside the main gate, the center included a large Visitors' Conference Room, a lobby for visitor check-in, and four "guest offices"—tiny cubicles with desks and phones.

Moments ago, Philip slipped unnoticed out of the conference room where the TaiChin team, including Zhou, was dozing through the histories of McNeil Aerospace and Everett Aviation. A McNev Business Manager was slogging through more than one hundred PowerPoint slides, acting as highly effective sleep aids.

Philip needed to contact Teri and Karolyn, hoping they'd set up a confidential meeting with McNeil sometime today so he could share what he'd learned. He knew they worked in the tower and would have gone to find them, if not for his inability to leave the area unescorted. Visitors with badges labeled *Escort Required*, as his did, were restricted to the visitor center unless accompanied by a security officer or authorized McNev employee.

He looked at the yellowing half-peeled label stuck on the phone: *Visitor Center X601—internal calls only.* Next to the phone was a company directory with a dog-eared cover, and Philip wasn't surprised when he found no entry for Teri Harlan. He found Karolyn Babcock and dialed *902*, but it went directly to voicemail.

He swore to himself for not getting their pager numbers in Hong Kong. He'd asked himself why the onus to resolve this mess fell in his lap, but hadn't come up with an answer. Zhou and the others would likely miss him soon, and if he got stuck on the plant tour, he'd have no chance of contacting the only people he trusted.

He stood, as an idea came to him.

Rather than return to the conference room, he walked the other direction down a hallway and opened the door to the Security Administration area. A nice-looking woman with short hair and a trim, athletic appearance sat at the desk nearest the door.

He approached her desk. "Hello, my name is Philip Lin. I'm part of the visiting TaiChin team. I had the honor to meet with Mr. Winton, and several McNeil-Everett executives in Hong Kong last week." He paused, looking around the office. "I remember their security officer—a gentleman named Porter Bordon. I was wondering if you know where I might find him."

"Porter isn't here, but I know him well. My name is Mary, can I help you with anything?"

"I would be most grateful if you could provide me with pager numbers for Ms. Teri Harlan and Ms. Karolyn Babcock."

* * *

Arthur swiveled his chair around to his credenza, looking at the small electronic box that Tony's team installed yesterday, enabling him to monitor phones in the Visitor Center.

It *ding*ed, and the display blinked on, showing a call made to Karolyn's extension but didn't record a conversation. He wondered if it was Philip trying to connect with her.

He walked out of his office and saw Karolyn's desk with no Karolyn. He swore under his breath, then returned to his phone and dialed Teri's office. He got her voicemail and swore again. He pressed the hands-free button, dialed *050*, and heard a reassuring "Yes, boss?"

"Tony, I need to see my Karolyn and Teri Harlan, in my office immediately—It's critical. I don't know where they are, so I need you to locate them and bring them to me."

"Why don't you page them, boss?"

"Don't you think I thought of that?! Quit wasting time arguing and go find them!"

* * *

Will parked his rental in the tower garage, glanced at his watch, and said, "Shit." However, his tardiness did nothing to increase his pace as he trudged toward the lobby. Dreading his late entrance into the Board Room to join the TaiChin discussions in progress, his demeanor transformed instantly when the tower receptionist told him Arthur had changed today's agenda to a series of visitor briefings and tours.

Elated by the chance to put off facing O'Donnell and McNeil, he didn't want to waste his good fortune by joining the tours. He decided this was the perfect opportunity to personally inspect the 913 cargo door-lock installation.

The Tailia plane was now out on the flight ramp, and the walk resulted in annoying perspiration under the arms of Will's dress shirt by the time he reached Ship 913. He scowled at the lead-man as he showed his badge and climbed aboard. The mechanic ignored him.

Plebian. I have an executive badge. He should salute me.

He stepped past the crew working in the cockpit, who also paid no attention, and climbed down the ladder into the forward cargo compartment.

Looking around to be sure he was unobserved, Will took a small screwdriver from his pocket and removed a panel on the upper section of the cargo door to admire his work: the custom-designed fail-safe vent-door mechanism. The actuator appeared normal, unless examined closely. He gently lifted the wiring to reveal the small motor, reversing circuit, connectors, and pager hidden underneath.

Perfect. I'm a genius.

A tiny catalyst for a major catastrophe, Will ran his fingers over the small Skytel, unable to contain his grin. Exhilaration sprang from thoughts of retribution against an industry he abhorred, and a boss who treated him like a disease he was afraid of contracting.

He carefully repositioned the pager and circuit behind the motor, being sure it was out of sight, and reattached the door panel.

28

Grateful for a little extra sleep, Sheila yawned as she poured herself a cup of coffee and then picked up Lisa's empty cereal bowl from the kitchen table.

It's nice having Rich around today. Probably a lot safer too...I sure hope Teri and Karolyn will be okay.

She walked into the living room when she heard Rich open the front door.

"Hey. Teri left a message while you were taking Lisa to school. I was still asleep. Sorry I missed—"

The phone rang, interrupting her. "Maybe that's her calling back."

She answered with the *handsfree* button, and after quick hellos, Teri told them she and Karolyn were calling from a conference room on the second floor.

Karolyn quickly recapped Porter's visit to Dr. Vale, leading them to discover that phone taps were providing O'Donnell with his apparent all-powerful knowledge of everything they'd been doing.

Rich's predictable string of epithets, mixed with Sheila asking questions about Vale's admissions, lead to a moment of chaos.

Teri said, "We'll give you both more details later, but right now we're up against it. Sheila, we need to know if you've made any progress."

"Sorry, Ter...Yes I did, actually. I was able to activate a prototype version of Arthur's remote application that I found on a test server to access the backend of McNev's system. Then I extracted files of current data and compared them to the same data using the new program."

"Nice work—did it show something we can use?"

"Definitely—the program is some sort of 'Poison Pill.' The line rate was down, rejections were way up, and the cash flow was in the toilet."

Rich added, "Instead of McNev's actual data in the Due Diligence presentation, Arthur's software will show McNev's finances on the verge of insolvency...like someone committed fraud."

Karolyn said, "That actually makes perfect sense." She shared O'Donnell's half of the conversation with Zhou that she and Porter overheard, finishing with, "So, what you found confirms it, Sheila. Arthur, apparently with help from Zhou and Crandall, is hijacking the system and substituting detrimental performance data to derail the partnership."

This was followed by everyone talking, speculating on Arthur's motives, until Karolyn said, "Hold on, guys. These are good theories, but no matter what the reason, we've got real evidence now, thanks to Sheila. And McNeil needs to be told, ASAP."

After everyone agreed, Rich asked. "Were you able to contact Lin?"

Teri answered, "Not yet. Karolyn and I decided to check in with you two first, and then we're going to the Visitor Center and hopefully bring him with us to see McNeil."

Karolyn added, "Our big challenge is Arthur, who's stashed Hugh in that small office right next to his…"

Rich finished her thought. "Yeah, the dickhead obviously figured out not to let McNeil get anywhere near you."

Karolyn replied, "Exactly. So we'll have to out-figure Arthur and find a way to get Hugh alone long enough to tell him what we've found…Oh, I also have one more thing for Sheila."

Karolyn quickly summarized their discussion with Ames on EPM, and asked Sheila if she could find out who owned it.

Sheila chuckled, "Piece of cake, Karolyn. This prototype is a bit crude compared to the version Arthur is using, but I can still go anywhere in the system's databases with it."

Karolyn said, "So you can run essentially the same application Arthur has been using to create this whole mess and get us information that will help nail his ass?"

"Essentially, yes."

"I'd definitely call that poetic justice." The satisfaction in Karolyn's voice was impossible to miss.

With a pause in the discussion, Teri was about to tell Rich what she'd found out about J. C. William when her pager started beeping. It was an extension she didn't recognize, *601*, followed by *911*.

Teri spoke hurriedly to fill Rich in before answering the page.

"Rich, listen—I found out J. C. William is *Will Crandall*—his first name and initials, backwards—unbelievable. Anyway, Duke told me Crandall created this fake director, and set up full signature authority in the system at McNeil Aerospace. But Duke said it was years ago, and he put a stop to it. He had no idea Will was using it here."

Rich swore again, asking for details, but Teri cut him off.

"Sorry, we'll have to call you back. I just got a 911 page from an internal extension. It might be Philip."

Teri asked them to sit tight and clicked off the call. She dialed *601*.

When a very relieved Philip Lin answered, Teri asked, "Are you okay? Where are you?"

"Yes, I'm in the Visitor Center. I slipped away but I don't have much longer. I need to meet with you and Karolyn right away. I have critical information for Mr. McNeil."

She was about to discuss where they should meet when Karolyn's pager started beeping, displaying the number of the cellular phone she and Porter purchased last night. The number was followed by 911.

Karolyn said, "You and Philip figure out something, Ter. I'll go down the hall and call Porter back."

Teri shook her head *no*, told Philip to hang in there and they would call him back in two minutes, then pressed disconnect.

She looked at Karolyn. "We're safe in here. I don't think you should chance it. Call him from here."

* * *

Arthur saw his new toy light up again. It was a call to an extension he didn't recognize. The recorder caught only fragments of the conversation, but he recognized the voices of Teri and Philip and heard something about "critical."

Figures the damn thing doesn't work right. But I'll bet she's trying to get with Lin, then meet McNeil...and Karolyn's probably with her. Obvious move—amateurs.

He grabbed his phone and dialed del Balso. Tony didn't answer. He paged him with *901-911*.

* * *

Karolyn dialed Porter's cellular number on the Polycom. He answered on the first ring.

"Hey, where are you? Is Teri with you? Are you both okay?"

"Second-floor conference room, yes, and yes, I think so—why?"

Porter smiled at her from his end of the phone, hoping she knew how crazy he was about her.

"I need you both to listen carefully. I called my friend Mary in Security early this morning, told her about the shit storm, and gave her my cellular number. I asked her to keep an eye on del Balso and let me know if she saw anything weird. She just called to tell me del Balso has a team looking for you. Apparently ol' Art wants both of you in his office, like right now, so he's probably guessed you're trying to meet with Mr. McNeil."

He took a breath and kept going. "She also told me O'Donnell got some new monitoring device installed on the phones in the Visitor Center. She said Philip is in there. Did you talk to him?"

"Yeah, we just hung up. Sounds like he's also got info for McNeil. We were going there to pick him up and then try to figure out how to tag up with Hugh."

"Damn. If Art heard that, he's gonna detain him or get Philip brought up to his office. I don't know how far he'll go to keep you from meeting with Mr. McNeil, but I don't like this—you're all a threat to him now. Look, I'm gonna call Mary back and ask her to help. Does anyone else know where you two are?"

Karolyn said, "No, and no one scheduled this room—I checked."

"Good. Sit tight and don't call anyone till I call you back…and don't leave the room unless I page you with 911—then get the hell outta there."

* * *

As soon as Mary hung up from talking to Porter, she called Al Greer, explaining the situation and asking for his help. Al was still fuming about Mac and Rich getting suspended. He didn't hesitate.

"Just tell me what you need."

Mary gave Al some quick instructions and then walked next door to check on Philip. He was still sitting quietly in a guest office.

Good, we've been lucky so far.

* * *

Arthur stared at his phone, yanking up the receiver as soon as it rang. It showed extension *921*.

"Tony?"

"Yeah boss, I got your page. What can I do you for?"

"Where the hell are you?"

"We're right down the hall from you. Doing a floor-by-floor search for your two girls, from the ninth floor down."

God, I'm so not going to miss him.

"For chrissake, Tony. Do you think they're stupid enough to hide up here on the ninth floor?"

Arthur realized from Tony's silence that he shouldn't have used the word "hide." He spoke quickly before Tony had time to think about it.

"Look, I have the phone extension for the room they're in. It's 222."

"I think that room's on the second floor, boss, because the extension starts with a '2.'"

Arthur took a breath, gritting his teeth. "The second floor has lots of rooms. Call your office and have them look up the room number for extension 222 in the reverse directory. Then go get Karolyn and Teri and bring them to me!"

He was about to slam the phone down, but remembered what he'd heard on the monitor. "And Tony, have someone collect Philip Lin from the Visitors' Center and escort him directly to my office, as well—on the double."

"Sure, boss. I'll call Jimmy. He should be on the way to you in just a few minutes."

Arthur slammed the phone.

* * *

When Mary got a call from Tony asking her to look up an extension in the reverse directory, she figured he was closing in on Teri and Karolyn. She tried to buy them a little time.

"Sure, sweet pea, but my system's down. I'll give it to Gina. She'll get it for you and call you right back. Will you be on 921, where you are now?…Okay, stay put. It'll just be a minute."

Mary walked over to Gina at the front desk. There were two officers leaning over the counter, vying for her attention.

"Hey Gina, when you get tired of teasing those two, look up this extension in the reverse directory and call Tony at this number with the room location."

Guessing it would take Gina no more than five minutes, she called Porter to fill him in. Then she walked out the side door to check on Philip.

This time she saw del Balso's trusty sidekick escorting Philip out of the Visitor Center toward the executive tower. She muttered, "Damn," then turned and half-jogged around the building the opposite way, faking a slight stumble as she hurried toward them.

Jimmy was far from Mary's favorite person. But knowing he was as bright as a twenty-watt bulb and had a crush on her made this situation manageable. Jimmy came rushing over.

"Mary, are you okay?"

She took his hand and pretended to use it to steady herself. "Jimmy—I'm glad I caught you." She smiled at him, keeping hold of his hand as she continued breathlessly, "Tony just called. Mr. O'Donnell has an emergency and needs you on it immediately. He said there's big trouble out by salvage."

Jimmy looked confused. "But I have orders to get Mr. Lin up to Mr. O'Donnell right away."

Mary smiled again, moving her hand to Jimmy's shoulder. She felt him quiver. "I can handle that for you, Jimmy. The problem on the back lot is *way* more important. You go ahead."

* * *

Teri sat, watching Karolyn pace. "God—I hate this. Shouldn't we call Rich and Sheila back or something?"

"Porter told us not to call anyone," Teri answered. "Why don't we—"

Karolyn's pager interrupted her, followed almost immediately by Teri's. They looked at the *911* showing on their displays.

* * *

Arthur was so frustrated he actually started toward Karolyn's desk to ask her for help before he caught himself.

Too bad the one person who knows what the hell she's doing chose the wrong team.

He walked back to his desk, too jumpy to sit. He reversed course again to stand in his office doorway.

Julia, sitting at her desk next to Karolyn's, said, "Can I help you with anything, Mr. O'Donnell?"

He found Julia annoying. Winton hired her, and Arthur knew it was because she was younger than Karolyn and even more attractive. Today she was wearing a too-short and too sheer dress, combining to create a major distraction.

He tried to focus on what she'd asked him. "Hmm? No, thank you."

As Arthur answered, he heard Tony running down the hall, shouting.

"Got it! Conference Room 207, second floor. Let's roll!"

Two officers were trotting with del Balso to the elevator. Arthur heard it *ding* its arrival, and the noise as they piled in.

Finally. Now I'll get those two under control.

A second after the elevator closed, he heard the other elevator arrive. Mary from Security emerged from the hallway and walked toward him.

"Excuse me, Mr. O'Donnell. I just wanted to let you know that Jimmy was delayed, but he'll be here shortly with Mr. Lin."

At the same moment, Julia got up from her desk and swore as she snagged her dress, pulling it up to her waist. "Dammit!"

Arthur thanked Mary dismissively, and in a momentary lapse of discipline, turned to admire all of Julia's exceptional legs and part of her derriere. She smoothed her dress back down and approached Arthur as Mary walked away.

Julia said, "Excuse me, Mr. O'Donnell. Mr. Quon just called."

As Arthur looked at her blankly, still disengaging from appreciating her assets, Hugh McNeil walked out of the small office next to Arthur's, and said, "Be right back, Arthur." He disappeared down the hallway.

Julia repeated herself. "Mr. Quon...Zhou Quon?"

O'Donnell shook off his fog. "Mr. Zhou. Zhou is his surname."

Julia flipped her long, silky, dark hair.

"Whatever. Anyway, he sounded real mad. He thought you were coming down to the Visitor Center to meet them."

* * *

Teri and Karolyn looked at the 911 messages on their pagers, then at each other. They said, "Oh, shit," in unison.

"What do you think?" Teri asked.

"Porter said run—so let's start by seeing if we can get out of the building."

Karolyn opened the conference room door and looked both ways, seeing an empty hallway. She took Teri's hand.

"Come on. We'll head this way and take the stairs."

Teri tugged on her hand and whispered, "Wait. Take off your heels."

With shoes in hand, they stepped quietly into the aisle and walked quickly toward the stairs at the north end of the building. Fortunately, a wall hid them from the large office area of cubicles. Karolyn was in the lead, holding Teri's hand behind her as she rounded the corner leading to the outer hallway.

Wham! Karolyn ran smack into an exceptionally large man and bounced off, back into Teri, who caught her. They stumbled, attempting to stay upright, as Karolyn looked up, stifling a gasp.

Teri said in a loud whisper, "Al! Thank God! Are we glad to see you! KB, it's okay. This is Al, a friend of mine."

Al whispered, "Nice to meet ya. We gotta go."

They turned right, hurrying down the outer hall past the elevators, and through the stairwell door. Just as it shut behind them, they heard the elevator *ding*, and del Balso's loud voice as its doors opened.

"It's quicker to go this way!"

Tony and two officers turned and ran down the hall in the opposite direction.

Teri and Karolyn followed Al down the stairs to the ground floor. They stopped to slip their shoes on and emerged from the rear entrance of the executive tower.

The plant spread out in both directions. To their right, past two other buildings, was the Security complex and Visitor Center. They walked left into an alcove hidden by a patio wall and support columns underneath the tower. Al led them over to the Cushman utility cart he'd parked in the corner. Philip Lin was standing next to it.

Teri and Karolyn shook Philip's hand, telling him how glad they were to see him, and then Teri turned to Al.

"What are we waiting for? We need to go!"

Al held up a massive hand. "Shhh, just a minute..."

He looked back at the tower as the rear door opened again. Out came Mary with Hugh McNeil, hurrying toward them.

Mary wasted no time on pleasantries. "Okay, everyone into the cart!"

"Easier said than done," Karolyn muttered, as she looked at the two small bench seats, with Al taking up most of the front one.

Philip sat next to him and Hugh climbed into the back seat. Teri and Karolyn squeezed in side-by-side next to McNeil, trying to maintain some semblance of decorum.

Mary said, "I have to get back to the Security office. Call me on the walkie if you need me." She rapped her fist on the back fender and said, "Okay Al, hit it!"

* * *

Al stomped on the gas pedal and the Cushman shuddered, sounding like a Disneyland Autopia, and using all eleven of its horsepower to get moving. They drove a roundabout route past fabrication buildings and storage sheds. After riding in silence for a minute, McNeil spoke. "Well, this is certainly unexpected, but it is a rather exciting adventure."

His smile broke the tension as he continued, "Mary paged me. She said you all had critical information for me and there was a confidentiality issue involving Arthur. I've known Mary for years. I learned never to question her when she has that tone."

Philip turned sideways, facing the back seat. "Hugh, I'm glad to see you again, even under these circumstances. I was told you were...How do you say it? *Sequestered*, this morning. I've been trying to find an opportunity to tell you...I'm afraid the partnership is in jeopardy."

Karolyn and Teri looked at each other, surprised by Philip's familiar tone.

Hugh noticed their expressions. "I've known Philip a long time...before we started working on the partnership."

"Yes, we go back a ways," Philip added. "I would also like to say that Ms. Harlan and Ms. Babcock are two of the most exceptional people I have ever had the pleasure to work with."

Hugh acknowledged the compliment with a smile toward them, and then asked if this had anything to do with the conversation he'd had with Rich the other day when he mentioned "looking into things."

Karolyn answered, "Yes, sir, exactly right," with Teri nodding her concurrence. Hugh continued smiling at them as they clung to each other, trying not to fall out of the cart.

They arrived at a dusty Quonset hut in a far corner of the plant, past the flight ramp, that Teri remembered from years ago. It looked as though it hadn't been used for quite some time.

Al said, "Nothin' happenin' out here anymore since the merger, really. There's still a conference room but no phone and no heater—sorry. Oh, and there's a restroom...sort of."

29

Tuesday, 2:30 p.m.

Mac sat at the kitchen table in Sheila's house, admiring the 1930's-era mosaic counter tiles, their white porcelain bright in the afternoon sun, as he reflected on their strange circumstances. A strangeness that was magnified when Rich asked him if he wanted a beer.

Mac raised his eyebrows. "It's the middle of the afternoon,"

"And we're suspended. What are they gonna do—double suspend us?"

Mac chuckled. "No beer, but thanks for making me smile." He took the computer printout from his briefcase. "Here's the listing of everything approved by J. C William in the past thirty days. I stopped by the plant, and one of my guys brought it out to the gate…said Al had some work emergency."

They examined the report, correlating several attempted sabotage dates to William-approved work orders. Rich noticed a work order dated two days after the Herrera report.

"Look, Mac. Here's the work order for the Tailia custom cargo door-lock assembly."

"Yep, and we might be able to tell what they did if we could get a look at it. I wonder if your sister could…"

Appearing at the bottom of the stairs, Sheila said, "Could what? Find out who owns that EPM Company? I just did."

* * *

After confirming his work on the Tailia plane, Will wandered the plant and took a late lunch, reveling in his achievement while continuing to avoid Arthur and Hugh. Now it was time to assimilate into the TaiChin tour and cover his absence. He consulted the schedule and headed to Sub-Assembly to catch them at their final stop. As Will walked into the hangar looking for Zhou, he spotted Duke holding forth in the center of the group and waved.

Duke excused himself and made a beeline for him, catching Will off guard. Without a word, Duke pulled him away from the group and into his office, shut the door, and immediately got belligerent.

"What the fuck are you doing, using your 'J. C. William' bullshit again, here at this plant?"

Will stood his ground, smiling to himself; he no longer had to put up with Darren's bullying.

"I happen to be in charge of special projects—on direct orders from Arthur, by the way—highly confidential work that can't go through regular channels. I never got rid of J. C. William because I thought I might need to use him again, and it turns out, I did. Anyway, it's pure genius. No one here has a clue."

Darren defaulted to full intimidation mode, poking Will in the chest with his finger. "Wrong, Einstein! You know who came to see me last night? Teri Harlan."

This topic being much more intriguing, Will stepped back, grinning.

"Teri, huh? You've been telling me you had the hots for her. Did you finally get her clothes off? C'mon—Don't spare any details."

Duke sputtered, "What? No! She's a total ice queen."

"Maybe she just doesn't like you."

"Screw you—and quit changing the subject! She told me there were active work orders authorized with your brilliant *nom de plume,* and when I looked into it, sure enough, I found them! I told you years ago not to use that again—ever. Do you know the shit storm you've created?"

Will had to put up with him for the influence he needed to move up at McNeil Aerospace. Not anymore. As he realized his power was surpassing Duke's, his smile shifted to a sinister smirk, matching the disdain in his tone.

"Listen up, Darren, and listen good. You may think you're an all-powerful VP, but you're nothing to me. I don't work for you, and I run in circles that don't include you. Why the hell do you think I didn't tell you? You weren't even brought in on the partnership until two days ago. But I was, and I have Arthur's authority now, so you can go screw yourself."

"You listen to me, you little…"

Will turned his back and said, "No—I won't." He walked out, slamming Duke's office door, and making Marla jump.

* * *

"I don't care where you've looked or what you're doing or how you've got all the gates covered. I needed them two hours ago!"

Arthur listened and then shouted again. "They couldn't just disappear into thin air! You're a fucking moron!"

He slammed down the phone and spun around to see Hugh McNeil standing in his office doorway. His attempt at regaining his composure resulted in an awkward smile.

"Sorry about that Hugh…another crisis. Where did you go? I've been looking for you. I had to send the TaiChin people on the afternoon part of the tour without us, and no one can seem to find Philip Lin anywhere."

"I figured you or Duke could handle the tour. I went outside for some air and decided to walk around the plant and talk with people. I know you were trying to keep me from being harassed today, but employees feel I've been aloof. It was time I got out there with them and the planes. Haven't done that for a long time. I found it very…enlightening."

He sat down at O'Donnell's table. "Come sit with me, Arthur. We need to chat about a few things."

* * *

After Teri, Karolyn, and Philip briefed McNeil on everything they'd learned, Hugh worked with them on formulating a plan to reveal the truth by preempting tomorrow's presentation. Once the five of them finished their meeting, Al used a private channel to call Mary on the walkie-talkie and then drove them back to meet her outside the Sub-Assembly building. Philip got out and Mary discreetly escorted him to rejoin the TaiChin group.

They'd returned Hugh to the tower, and Teri moved to the front seat next to Al so Karolyn had the rear seat to herself. Teri finished the last bite of an Oreo granola bar Al had given her, and turned sideways to talk with Karolyn.

"That was quite the meeting, huh?"

As they drove through the tunnel to the east side of the plant, Karolyn leaned forward so Teri could hear her.

"Yeah, for sure. Hugh was stunned when Philip told him he'd discovered Arthur was behind Zhou's selection for the TaiChin position."

Teri nodded, adding, "Especially when he alluded to the mysterious circumstances surrounding the resignation of Zhou's predecessor."

Karolyn shook her head. "I guess, after all we've learned about Arthur, we shouldn't be surprised…And I totally agreed with Hugh's decision not to confide in Winton. Jackson may not be in on it, but more than likely he'd tip off Arthur, either intentionally or out of stupidity."

Teri asked, "So do you think Arthur, Crandall, and Zhou will really face the music tomorrow?"

"Hugh and Philip are certainly committed to exposing them but I'm not sure about their idea for the morning meeting…It all really hinges on Porter and his new Chinese pals."

Karolyn paused with a thoughtful look, and then added, "Hugh said he was looking forward to his chat with Arthur, but I'm worried he's underestimating how dangerous Arthur could become if he's cornered."

The cart putt-putted to a stop by the east gate and the lot where she and Teri parked this morning to avoid the scrutiny of the executive tower. Karolyn slid out of the back seat, putting a hand on Teri's shoulder.

"You sure you don't want to head out too?"

"Nah—it's after four. Arthur must've stopped looking for us. He's probably not even thinking about us now that Hugh is meeting with him.

I really need a walk to clear my head. I don't think anyone will bother me—I'll sic Al on 'em."

Al chuckled as Karolyn said, "Okay, just be careful...especially after the day we've had. Call me tonight after you've touched base with Rich and Sheila." She gave Teri's arm a squeeze, showing more encouragement than she felt, and said, "I'll see you in the Board Room tomorrow, and we can end this."

"Yeah, let's hope so...Do me a favor and stay close to Porter tonight, okay? Just in case."

Karolyn smiled. "Not a problem."

As she walked toward her car, Karolyn spoke over her shoulder. "Thanks for everything, Al. I'm glad to know you, even if our introduction was...unique. And watch her back, will ya?"

Al waved to Karolyn as the cart shuddered like usual, struggling to accelerate.

Teri said, "Bugged phones, chasing around the place like a bunch of spies...ever seen anything like this?"

Al shook his head. "Nope. This is definitely somethin' else." He stopped the cart. Then he turned toward her and met her eyes. "Teri, I'm so glad to have you back, girl. No way this old place would've had a chance without you."

Teri smiled. But on the inside she felt more like Marty in *Back to the Future II* when he came home to find his house and hometown in chaos.

"Thanks, Al. Getting McNeil on board was a good step, but we're not there yet."

Al nodded in agreement as he started the cart again. "I have to say I've changed my mind about him. From a distance, I thought he was just another clueless corporate bigwig, not giving a damn about anything except the bottom line. But the way he listened to you and Karolyn...and then when he was seriously pissed over Mac and Rich getting suspended, and gave Mary full authority to reinstate them—no screwing around. I guess I underestimated him."

Teri nodded. "Yep—first impressions can definitely be off base. A couple of weeks ago, I thought Arthur was this perfect, brilliant executive. And now here we are, struggling to keep the scumbag from destroying the company."

Al parked the cart next to his office complex in Final Assembly and Teri climbed out. "Thanks for the ride back. I'm just gonna walk the line for a few...being near the planes makes me feel better..."

* * *

Still flushed from his boss just witnessing his outburst at del Balso, Arthur walked the few steps from his desk to the table experiencing a rare twinge of panic. He sat stiffly as his mind skimmed through an inventory of plausible responses with no idea of what was behind Hugh's need for "chat."

"Arthur, I have a major concern...I think Crandall and Zhou might be conspiring to put the partnership in jeopardy."

Arthur nearly beamed with relief, but managed to maintain his serious expression as Hugh went on.

"Philip met with me in confidence to report the discomfort he'd encountered last week in Hong Kong, including some inappropriate behavior between them. We agreed that I would have a serious talk with you about Crandall and he would clear the air with Zhou."

Admitting a touch of good fortune, Arthur silently congratulated himself on the perfect set-up for his revised PEP finale. But Hugh's next concern wasn't nearly so helpful.

"There is a major bone I need to pick with *you*, though; suspending Rich and Mac was unacceptable."

Arthur knew precisely how to respond. "You're right, Hugh. I'm sorry. I overreacted because Darren was so upset. I'll take care of it."

"You don't need to. I already authorized their reinstatement—It's being processed."

Arthur swallowed his annoyance. Hugh was obviously angry, and it wasn't worth the risk of getting any more of it on him.

"Okay, good. That's the right decision, Hugh—thank you. And again, I apologize."

"Apology accepted. Now let's get back to Crandall. I want to hear your candid assessment of Will's recent performance...and be specific on any issues you've had."

Arthur embraced the opportunity to seal Will's new scenario, adopting a somber tone. "As a matter of fact, Will's increasing closeness to Quon has concerned me, also. I noticed it in my conversations with him, and more importantly, Karolyn shared her observations in Hong Kong with me. And of course, I trust her completely."

He paused for emphasis, adding the *pièce de résistance*.

"Unfortunately, I suspect Will could be involved in even more problematic actions. I just got wind of a scheme Will is apparently using to authorize some sort of covert work orders for Final Assembly. Worse still, I found out he may be involved in something illegal with the executive private accounts and the processing company, EPM. This morning, I personally assigned Vernon Ames to work with Teri and look into the situation."

Thinking he might gain some potentially useful information, Arthur added, "So, let me ask you, Hugh. Do you have a problem with Will, personally?"

"Frankly, I don't think my personal opinion of Crandall is relevant." From McNeil's expression, Arthur instantly recognized the dead-end and backed off.

Hugh moved on to a strong admonishment. "It's good that you've been keeping your eye on him and now I expect you to take care of it. If you think he should be gone, let's process Crandall's termination."

As evidence of his superior reactions, Arthur took Hugh's curve ball without flinching. "I think it might be best if we hold off for a few days. I need time to finish investigating, and we can use Will in the finalization meeting tomorrow, especially when we get to the contract legalese. But I assure you, Hugh, if Will's dirty, we'll nail his ass, and believe me, I *will* put the fear of God in him tonight."

Hugh thanked him and gathered his things to return to his hotel for the evening. Arthur waved as McNeil walked out of the executive suite to the elevators.

"Not to worry, Hugh! Consider Will Crandall handled. Everything will be fine."

30

"Hey, Charlie, hurry up, will ya?"

Steve stared at the gauges on the Dayton T. Brown portable hydraulic test stand with his attention on *Outlet 1*. As he waited for his coworker to connect the line, he absent-mindedly rubbed the bezel edge around the gauges. Then he scowled at his fingers, all of which were completely coated in hydraulic fluid, reminding him just how much he hated Skydrol.

He was about to open the valve when a hand with well-manicured nails suddenly appeared atop his.

"Stop—You don't want to do that." A nice-looking woman in heels stood next to him, adding, "That's a new pressure line he just connected."

Steve stopped and blinked at her, admiring her skirt with a diagonal zipper, something he'd never seen on the assembly floor. He searched his brain for an astute response but all he managed was, "So?"

"It's full of air. If you don't fill it with fluid first, you'll contaminate the whole hydraulics system with air bubbles."

Teri spent a few minutes showing the two mechanics how to run fluid in the line before pressurizing the system for the test.

When she finished, Steve said, "Thanks a lot. You just saved our asses…By the way, who are you?"

* * *

Teri was still shaking her head as she walked beneath the wing of LazerAir Ship 914. While her passion for hydraulics systems might exceed most mechanics', it was troubling that a testing disaster had been avoided solely because she'd decided to take a walk through Final Assembly.

How many more screw-ups happen around here on a daily basis?

Her thoughts drifted to having a serious conversation with Mac and Al about improving training. When her focus returned, Teri realized she was gazing up at the forward cargo door. Inset in a frame about two-thirds of the way toward the top was a small rectangular door reminiscent of a pet door.

Teri remembered asking what the "cute little pet doors" were for when she was a new hire. She smiled at the recollection of Mac's laughter when he'd explained.

"Those are vent-doors—part of a fail-safe mechanism. The cargo doors are secured by heavy steel cupped-shaped hooks that wrap around thick lock bars, like fingers, to keep the door sealed. If the lock isn't fully engaged, the little door won't seal, and it keeps the aircraft from being pressurized—keeps them on the ground till they fix the lock problem."

Looking at the vent-door triggered a vivid memory. She and Rich had been chosen for a special Everett redesign team, prompted by a tragic accident that occurred on one of the forerunners of the ME-420 Widebody. The cargo door had been improperly closed with a forklift, bending the hooks partially around the lock bar and "fooling" the fail-safe mechanism.

The improperly sealed door burst open at cruising attitude, causing a severe decompression that ripped out the passenger compartment floor. The control cables were destroyed, making the aircraft unflyable. The plane had crashed, leaving no survivors.

Everett top management put their best people on re-engineering the fail-safe mechanism to prevent any possibility of reoccurrence. Because Teri was recognized as an exceptional mechanic and Rich had been a rising star in quality assurance, senior management assigned them to the team that worked with engineering on the redesign. The new design solved the problem, resulting in several parts from the prior design becoming obsolete.

In a flash, Teri knew why Rich's mystery connector looked familiar. She spoke out loud. "Damn, that's where I've seen it!"

Someone grabbed her elbow. "Seen what?"

Teri whirled around. "God almighty, Al—You scared the pee outta me! I just remembered where I'd seen the electrical connector that Rich found in that report—It was obsoleted in the failsafe vent-door redesign!"

"Yeah, that's great, Teri, but I wish you'd pay more attention."

"What?"

"Look up—on your nine—the catwalk. One of del Balso's goons. Probably been searching all day…now he's found you."

Teri looked to her left and saw an officer glaring at them from the hangar balcony, and taking his radio from his belt.

Her pager vibrated. She pulled it from her pocket and saw Sheila's number.

"It's Rich—Damn, I totally forgot to call him back."

"Yeah, well, right now, you need to get outta here. Let's go."

They walked quickly to the main aisle and jumped into Al's Cushman.

* * *

Following his confrontation with Duke, Will chose to walk to the Visitor Center rather than rejoining the group. After telling the receptionist he was waiting for Zhou Quon, he paced the lobby, lost in a mental replay of the scene in Duke's office, and contemplating ways to screw with him.

"Mr. Crandall?"

He shook off his reverie, noticing that the receptionist remembered his name, and walked over to the counter. Her nameplate read: *Reception*. He looked at the young woman more closely, maintaining his well-practiced unassuming expression.

Doesn't even have a real nameplate. Not bad looking, though. Young, innocent, perhaps even tasty in a pinch.

The receptionist blushed as she looked up and said, "Sorry, I didn't mean to bother you…I'm Brenda. I thought you might be more comfortable in one of the guest offices. There's coffee on the table down the hall. I just made a fresh pot."

Will leaned on the counter, waiting for it. Yes! There it was—that barely noticeable widening of her eyes. He flashed his five-star smile and detected accommodation when she smiled back. "I can send Mr. Quon down to you as soon as he and the TaiChin group return."

Her tone was pleasant, and he sensed something more.

Is that ambition? Or hope?

"Mr. Zhou," he said, correcting her.

"Hmm?"

He noticed her eyes again; more pronounced this time. He hesitated for a second, enjoying the confirmation of his effect on her, then explained, "It's Mr. Zhou. His *given* name is Quon." His tone was the epitome of executive-disdain: condescending, patronizing, and totally dismissive.

"Oh."

He paused again to savor her crestfallen look.

That's right, twit. This powerful, great-looking executive, who's superior in every way, has absolutely zero interest in you.

"I'll take that first office, and I take my coffee black."

Shortly after he was seated in the tiny cubicle-office, Brenda quietly set a cup of coffee on the desk without looking at him. After she left, Will leaned back in the chair, pondering Arthur's rewrite of tomorrow's scenario in response to Winton's relocation fiasco.

The phone buzzed, interrupting him.

"Yes?"

"Mr. Crandall, the TaiChin Group has returned, and Mr. Zhou is coming to you now." Brenda clicked off, making Will smile.

She sounds pissed, but she got Quon's surname right—That's why I'm an executive.

Quon walked in and Will stood to hug him, saying, "I've got good news…something to celebrate."

Zhou pushed him back, and with an unpleasant expression, off-loaded his pent-up frustration.

"O'Donnell's new plan has McNeil with Winton presenting Due Diligence results...Now both of them will face disgrace when they show that data. He said—"

"Whoa, what? McNeil too?"

"Yes, he—"

Will interrupted again. "I knew Arthur had balls, but putting McNeil in the crosshairs of fraud allegations—that's impressive."

"Let me finish! He told me discrediting McNeil would make the takeover easier, then the arrogant ass demands more money! And what about the delivery flight? I'm supposed to be *on that plane* with Lin, and if I refuse, I'll lose face!"

"Don't worry, Quon. There'll be so much havoc created tomorrow you'll have the perfect excuse. Just explain that you need to stay and help sort things out."

"That would work only for a Westerner—You never understand my culture."

Will's nostrils flared. He took a calming breath. "Arthur or I could make a formal request for you to stay so it won't appear to be your decision, all right?"

Quon's scowl lightened slightly. "Yes...good, thank you. But here's another thing—Lin disappeared today and didn't come back to our tour until late afternoon, escorted by some security woman. He apologized, saying he had 'personal business,' but I don't trust him. You can't trust the Taiwanese."

Will looked thoughtful. "I'll tell Arthur. He'll know if it's important." He smiled and added, "But speaking of Lin, I checked on our surprise."

Quon's eyes brightened.

Will held his arms open, and said, "It's perfect!" They embraced again, and when they stepped apart, Will added, "And I have a gift for you."

He handed Quon a neatly folded piece of paper with a Skytel number and a mini-pager. "I want you to have this. It's my honor to give you the power and the privilege. You make the call when it's time."

Quon nodded solemnly, and then began a slow smile that grew to a rather sinister grin. "I thank you...and what is this?" he asked, holding up the miniature pager.

Will said, "It's a duplicate—When it goes off, it confirms the page has been delivered. I have one also." Will returned Quon's grin as he took an identical pager from his coat.

Quon pulled Will close, holding him tight until the phone buzzed, which made them jump. Will picked it up and heard Brenda's all-business coldness.

"Mr. Crandall—Mr. Zhou's limo is here, and Mr. O'Donnell called. I told him you were *privately engaged* with Mr. Zhou. He wants you to call him—immediately."

Will swore as Brenda disconnected.

* * *

Teri smiled at Al, who insisted on driving her out of the gate to her Jeep. She thanked him, gave him a quick hug, then left the plant, and drove to a nearby strip mall where she'd spotted a pay phone. She hurried into the booth, searching in her purse for quarters.

* * *

After Mac left, Rich had been sitting in the living room, stewing over possible reasons for Teri not calling him back, until the ringing phone interrupted him. When he answered and heard her voice, the relief in his own was unmistakable.

"Thank, God! I'm so glad to hear from you. Are you all right? I've been worried sick since we talked this morning."

Teri apologized for not calling back. She summed up their adventures, including Porter, Mary, and Al working together to help them, and then meet safely with McNeil and Lin. She described McNeil's astonishment as they filled him in on what they'd found, and also confessed that she and Karolyn had been spooked by Arthur dispatching del Balso's team to search for them.

"It was crazy. We were running around like Tom Cruise in *The Firm*...without the guns, of course—thank God."

Rich reacted by expressing a strong desire to dispose of O'Donnell physically, but Teri reassured him.

"Rich, it's okay. I'm fine, except for riding in that damn Cushman which pretty much ruined my skirt and destroyed another pair of nylons. Karolyn's fine too—nothing happened. We both left safely."

Teri shared the highlights of the McNeil-Lin plan for tomorrow.

"Hugh called their strategy a *double-check*. I'm not a chess player, but it made Philip smile...I just hope it works. I'll feel a lot better once Hugh turns the three of them in."

Rich said, "I'm really sorry I won't be there to see it. I'm also worried you could still be in danger."

"Then I have good news for you. Hugh was furious about your suspension. You should be getting a call from HR any time, reinstating you and Mac as of tomorrow."

"Sonofabitch—that's great! I don't know how you pulled it off, but I'm really glad I'll be there with you!"

Rich told her he also had good news, hardly taking a breath as he continued. "Mac and I got the number of the work order in the Herrera report and Sheila was able to access the details through the backend of the production system. The information wasn't formatted, but we pieced together the description of some strange mod to the lock and fail-safe mechanism for the forward cargo door on 913."

Teri jumped in. "I think you and Mac are totally on the right track! I was walking around Final Assembly earlier, and I remembered where I'd seen your connector. We obsoleted it during the redesign of the vent-door, remember?"

"Wow—You're right! I knew we'd seen that damn thing before! I wonder what the hell they're doing?"

He paused for a second before finishing his thought. "Well, now that Mac and I are reinstated, we'll be able to go to the flight ramp tomorrow and check it out. I guarantee that whatever it is, we're gonna nail Crandall for it...*and* Sheila discovered he's also using his bullshit 'J. C. William' as the owner for EPM!"

It was Teri's turn again. "No kidding—that's incredible! All the pieces are falling into place. We're really close to exposing both Arthur and Crandall!"

They reluctantly said good-bye with the promise to tag up first thing tomorrow.

* * *

When Julia buzzed Arthur's intercom and said Will was on the phone, he yanked up the handset and snarled, "What the hell were you and Quon doing in there?"

Will shot back, "Nothing, for chrissake! And don't start with me—I just spent twenty minutes calming him down, plus I got a whole truckload of shit from Duke earlier."

"Duke? What did he want?"

"He wanted to scream at me for using my J. C. William undercover approval strategy. Apparently, Teri—the know-it-all—somehow found out. She's unbelievable!"

Arthur heard this morning's tape of Richmond's call to Teri last night, asking her to speak with Duke. Apparently she'd been successful. Deciding to keep that tidbit to himself, he smiled, realizing her annoying knack for investigating was now working to his advantage.

Will continued, "Anyway, Duke really pissed me off." Arthur refocused, needing to make sure Will believed he had his back.

"Well, you did great work getting 913 completed, plus accomplishing what I needed with those other work orders. So don't worry about Darren—I'll set him straight for you."

"Thanks, Arthur, I appreciate it...So Quon told me about your plan for tomorrow's meeting. He's seriously pissed at you for demanding more money to set up McNeil, but I think it's brilliant. I assume you'll be sharing that extra with me?"

"I agree it was a stroke of genius...and yes, of course." Arthur no longer intended to pay him a dime, but played along because he needed Will to follow a specific scenario, facilitating his early exit.

And now was the time to begin the set up. Casually, Arthur said, "Oh, by the way, I have to take care of something right after the meeting tomorrow, so I'll need you to stay and manage the chaos with Quon."

Arthur smiled as Will replied, "Not a problem, it'll be fun to watch McNeil humiliated and speechless...FYI, I told Quon one of us would formally request that he remain here to help us pick up the pieces. He's afraid he'll lose face, refusing to board the Tailia delivery flight."

Arthur kept his tone smooth. "That sounds reasonable; why don't you take care of it?" *While I slip out unnoticed in the midst of the confusion.*

Satisfied with his excellent scenario staging, he changed subjects.

"Is everything in place for 913 once it's airborne?"

"Yes. I gave the Skytel number to Quon. He was incredibly pleased—and quite eager."

Arthur said, "I'm surprised at you, letting him have the pleasure."

"My pleasure will come from seeing McNeil crushed. And besides, if it ever gets discovered, Quon will be responsible. My hands will be clean."

"How very pragmatic, Will. I didn't realize the depth of your animus for McNeil."

"Mr. Perfect Chairman of the Board? Yeah, given the way he looks through me like I'm an aberration that should just disappear...I plan to revel in his agony when he learns he's lost a brand-new plane and killed most of TaiChin, on top of his precious company getting torn apart."

Arthur shivered, unexpectedly chilled by Will's tone. He was even more impressed when Will switched topics as casually as if he were discussing the weather.

"Oh, Quon said one more interesting thing...Lin disappeared today. I thought you'd want to know."

Arthur seized the chance to spin his conversation with McNeil and further cement Will's scenario. "Thanks—Yeah, I found out from Hugh that Lin met with him, but he's totally clueless. I assured Hugh you were vital to tomorrow's meeting, so don't worry about anything. Just keep your distance from Quon until it goes down."

"Got it. It's perfect—everything's in place. I'm going to see Quon tonight to celebrate."

"Sorry to change your plans, but I've got work for you."

"Come on, Arthur…Is it so important it can't wait till tomorrow?"

"Yes. It needs to be handled tonight. Teri's been digging into Private Accounts. If she discovers something, it could spell disaster."

"Not for me. I don't know anything about it."

"Listen to me. Certain things she might uncover could come back on both of us. We've worked too hard to let one loose end destroy everything. I had her office searched, but none of her research was there—it must be with her. Pay Teri a visit at the condo and retrieve it for me."

Will didn't reply.

Compliance was vital to his sacrifice-diversion scenario, so Arthur offered inducement.

"I can tell you're disappointed, having to forego your fun night with Quon. So why don't you stay and play with her, instead? I think it's time you showed Miss High-and-Mighty what it means to be inducted into the Will Crandall fan club…Still got your key?"

Arthur knew he'd acquiesce. Not only was there the lure of sexual pleasure, but a chance to even the score with another person Will held in contempt.

"Okay, Arthur. That does sound fun—Teri will be my pleasure this evening."

Arthur hung up, smiling.

If he can't see he's the sheep, he deserves to be fed to the wolf.

Arthur's phone rang again: *X050*. He hit the speaker button and said, "Yes, Tony?"

"Boss, sorry I let you down. I was calling to tell you Lin showed up earlier in B1 and one of my guys spotted Harlan out in Final Assembly talking to Greer. But he's pretty sure Greer drove her to the East lot and figured she's left for the day. No one spotted Karolyn. Really sorry, boss."

The crisis was over; Arthur was back in control. "You know what, Tony? Don't worry. Everything's going to be fine."

Arthur disconnected but didn't put down the phone. He had one more call—to the person he'd chosen to play the wolf.

* * *

Getting the call from HR confirming his reinstatement added to Rich's optimism. He and Mac would solve the mystery installation on 913 tomorrow, sinking Crandall and Arthur for good. His smile was genuine as he walked toward the kitchen, but he was stopped by the phone ringing again.

Jeez Louise, now who's calling?

He picked it up. "Richmond residence, Rich speaking."

It was O'Donnell. He felt his upbeat mood evaporate. After Rich listened for a moment, his knees nearly gave way as he replaced the receiver. He snatched it up again and made a frantic call, then slammed down the phone and strode into the kitchen. Lisa was stirring noodles while Sheila grated cheese.

Rich said, "Nice job, Ladybug. I need to speak to your aunt for a sec—be right back."

He took Sheila's arm and moved back into the living room out of Lisa's earshot, speaking in a panicked whisper.

"Can you wrap up something for Lisa to eat and see if she can stay with the Taylors? And then grab your car? We've got to get to the condo as fast as we can—Crandall's headed there, and Teri could be in danger! I called, but she didn't answer. I'm gonna call Porter's cellular to see if he or Karolyn is closer to the condo, while you take Lisa next door. I'll fill you in on the way—please, hurry!"

Moments later, Sheila was driving the Z toward Newport, zipping through traffic on PCH, as Rich explained.

"Art just called and apologized for my suspension, saying he'd overreacted and was glad I was returning tomorrow. I knew it was bullshit, but I didn't say anything. Then he tells me he'd just finished talking with Crandall, who was raging about Teri researching Private Accounts. Of course, I knew you'd discovered the J. C. William connection, but I stayed quiet. He said Will was talking crazy and was going to the condo to *make Teri pay*. He didn't know if Will would really harm her, but said he'd feel better if I could go check on her."

Rich looked at his sister with a grim expression.

Sheila said, "Oh my God, you think he was serious?"

"I have no idea. He sounded sincere, but we both know what a gifted liar he is."

They were quiet for a moment, and then Rich added, "I don't think we can take the chance he made it up just to screw with me."

As they sped along the coast, Rich fell into silent, ominous reflection. He'd known for more than two years that McNev had been infected by a plague of degenerate executives. That's why he'd talked Teri into coming back—to help him fight them. But now that they'd proven themselves to be malicious, he was kicking himself for putting her in the middle of it. Guilt weighed him down in the seat like an uninvited passenger.

My gut warned me, but I did it anyway. Is my fight against the "Evil Empire" that important? Or did I just risk the woman I love for the sake of my own ego?

At the core of Rich's commitment to help save the company was his abhorrence of injustice. Abusing power over others for personal gain had always enraged him.

Growing up in Southern California, Rich couldn't say that he or his sister had to fight against inequity on a daily basis. Their parents lived in an upscale Orange County coastal community, surrounding them with a wholesome environment and excellent schools. But for as long as he could remember, Rich's sense of fair play had been obsessive.

He'd inherited his passion for doing what was right from his father, who'd spent years infusing Rich with his work experiences as a senior manager at Everett. He talked to Rich for hours about the ethical standards involved in building airplanes, stating that his mission—to protect the integrity of aircraft production—was absolute. That belief system became a major part of Rich's identity.

As Rich stared out the window, his gnawing concern for Teri dredged up a troublesome recollection from his senior year in high school.

The class president, Sid, unfairly blessed with both Adonis looks and Mensa brains, was idolized by everyone. Sid and his friends were the innermost of the "in crowd," and ran the senior class hierarchy, manipulating everyone and anyone who could be advantageous to them. Rich had spent too many teenage hours in anguish, trying to decide if he loathed Sid for being an ethically bereft user of people, or if he was simply jealous.

The incident now flooding Rich's memory was of Barbara, the beautiful blonde he'd adored, who'd gone to Senior Prom with Sid because he was everyone's idol. The salt in the wound of Rich's broken heart was that Barbara had chosen to go with Sid after first accepting Rich's invitation.

Rich clenched his fists as he recalled the heartache of prom night: the girl he longed for, attending prom with a pretentious, devious egomaniac. He reflected on his grim premonition of Barbara being in danger that night, which had been tragically accurate; she became a victim of date rape following the dance. Although she'd reported it, Sid was never prosecuted, and what should have been the joy of graduation for Barbara became her nightmare.

Rich never got over his repugnance of those who commit deleterious acts against others for their own pleasure or personal gain, and do so with impunity.

He prayed that on this night, his feeling of foreboding was wrong.

31

Tuesday, 6:15 p.m.

Teri closed the door, turned the deadbolt, and hoisted her briefcase onto the enormous conference table. Navigating around it to the bedroom, the familiar feeling of disquiet was in her face immediately, like an annoying houseguest. As soon as she packed her things, Teri planned to head out for dinner and relocate to a hotel.

She began packing on autopilot, her mind still replaying the events of the day and her conversation with Rich.

Could Crandall and his alter ego really be behind EPM as well as the manufacturing subterfuge? Does he have that much influence...or even the brains? I never even saw him today—I wonder where he was.

Teri stopped suddenly, realizing she hadn't changed her clothes. She unbuttoned her blouse, stepped out of her skirt, and sighed as she stripped off another pair of ruined pantyhose. As she reached for her jeans hanging on the back of the bathroom door, her eyes lingered on the spa tub.

Maybe one last time before I go...there's still that bottle of St. Michele Pinot in the fridge.

Instead of the jeans, she grabbed her California Dynasty robe hanging next to them, slipped it on, and headed to the kitchen. She was turning the corkscrew into the cork when she heard a key click in the front door deadbolt. Startled, she dropped the corkscrew in the sink and tiptoed cautiously around the counter to the living room. She peered at the front door and froze, staring in disbelief as Will Crandall strolled in.

"Hello Teri...Catch you at a bad time?"

She retreated into the kitchen behind the bar counter, aware of the blood rushing to her face.

"What the hell are you doing here? How did you get in?"

He stopped next to the conference table. "I have a key to this place. Did Arthur neglect to mention that?"

Will hoisted himself backwards onto the table, sitting so he could jump down and block her way to the door, if need be. With a cocky smile, he eyed her appraisingly.

"Nice robe—or is it a kimono? Anyway, the white satin looks lovely with your hair...and I'll bet what's underneath is lovely as well."

Fighting her reaction to the surge of adrenaline, she redirected his focus. "You didn't say what you're doing here."

"No, I didn't—how rude. I'm here to collect your research on Private Accounts—Arthur needs it...He also suggested I stay and entertain you. I'm quite the game aficionado—the adult variety—I have a passionate fan club."

Teri's stomach lurched as she racked her brain for options. Could she make it past him to the front door? If she got out, where would she go, barefoot and in a robe? Will was next to one phone and the other was in the bedroom. If she ran for that one, Will could trap her. Her head spun. *Don't let him see how scared you are—stall.*

"Can I make you a drink?"

This caught Will completely off guard. He chuckled. "Now you're talking."

Teri forced her voice toward normalcy. "Pinot Grigio, or Maker's Mark?"

"Maker's over ice, thanks. And I have to say, I'm pleasantly surprised. Not only by your taste in bourbon, but also your congeniality. Keep this up, and I guarantee we'll have a delightful evening."

He slid off the table to stand at the bar counter opposite her. He spoke conversationally, as if they were in a work meeting.

"So, Duke told me you shut him down last night...called you an 'ice queen.' Not that I blame you, he's disgusting...Fortunately for you, I am not."

Teri made the drink deliberately, doing her best to control her racing pulse. She set it on the bar top in front of him, attempting to mirror his casual demeanor. "I thought you were into men."

He laughed, but it was mirthless. "I'm into whatever suits me." He raised his glass to her, adding, "And if *you* suit me, our time together will be so much more pleasant...for you as well as me."

Thinking she might talk her way out, she tried sounding business-like. "Will, I've had a really rough day. If you want my research, it's there in my briefcase. Why don't you just take it and be on your way?"

"Now, *that's* annoying. You sounded like a bitch just then, getting all superior. *I've had a rough day, why don't you be on your way?* Doesn't that sound rude?"

Teri didn't respond, maintaining a stony expression as Will took another sip. He set his glass down hard and shook his head. When he spoke, his tone turned bitter. "Is it so inconceivable to you that women find me irresistible? I'll bet as sure as I'm standing here, you've never even experienced a genuine orgasm."

She forced herself not to react, but he seemed to catch her tension.

"Ah, see? How do I know? Because you are a person who needs to control everything..." He leaned on the bar, widening his eyes as if sharing a secret she was dying to hear. "The key is surrender—the bliss of submission—letting yourself enjoy it."

Teri concentrated on looking unfazed, keeping her thoughts to herself. *What I'd enjoy is having Porter here to kick your ass. Or Karolyn…she probably could too.*

Will drained his glass in a last gulp and said, "I'll tell you what. Before we get to that boring research, let's have some fun for a change. I can teach you a great game for beginners…help you develop those submissive skills. It's called: Bondage Seduction."

He moved around the counter and approached her. Teri stepped back, reaching behind her for the corkscrew in the sink. But when she took hold of it, her shaking hands scraped it against the stainless steel and Will heard the grating noise. In a flash, he grabbed her wrist.

As if correcting a novice's mistake, Will said, "That's *not* in the rules, Sweetheart," and forced her hand down against the edge of the sink.

"Ow, dammit!" Teri winced, dropping the corkscrew. It bounced off the counter onto the floor and Will kicked it away.

Brandishing his patented smile, he said, "It's okay, you'll get the hang of it…Here, I'll help you get started." In one swift motion, he pulled her against him with his left arm around her waist, using his right hand to loosen the tie of her robe. But the silky fabric caused Will to lose his grip and she wriggled free. She slapped his left cheek with a loud *smack*.

Will reeled back in surprise and then leered at her. "Oh, okay. So, that's how you like to play? Fine by me!"

He started toward her once again as Teri withdrew. Her vison narrowed until her focus was consumed by his lustful expression as it escalated with sinister confidence. She folded her arms across her chest; a feeling of paralysis gripped her.

Suddenly she was fifteen, backing into the corner of her old bedroom, shaking uncontrollably. Her stepfather, looking as big and unstoppable as a school bus, stalked toward her. She'd experienced his anger before, but the look in his eyes that night was something she'd never seen. The terror of being trapped by brute force was visceral, his breath and touch, detestable.

Although she'd escaped being fully violated because of her mother coming home, the intensity of her fear and lack of control, created a simmering outrage at her core that stayed with her.

She'd put her anger to good use, fueling a singular determination to excel in school and in her career. And through years of diligence and increasing competence, Teri developed the confidence to maintain equal footing in a male-centric workplace. Sadly, her memory of the frightened teen being cornered was something she'd never fully conquered, and it came rushing back to her now.

The self-assurance that sustained her in business evaporated as Will closed on her. She retreated until she had nowhere to go, standing against the kitchen wall, petrified and unable to stem the flow of tears.

He took hold of her hands, and as she struggled, he said, "You're doing great, Teri—defiance spices up the game! But we should move to the bedroom…you'll be more comfortable."

He began pulling her from the kitchen while she tugged back, adrenaline fueling her resistance.

Wham! The front door banged open, and she nearly fell over backwards as Will suddenly released her. He whirled around, ending up face-to-face with Karolyn who'd raced into the kitchen.

"Karolyn! How nice of you to join us—I love three-ways."

Will spotted the corkscrew on the floor and made a threatening move toward Karolyn, apparently intending to grab it. She had other plans.

From two feet in front of him, Karolyn struck like lightning. Raising her knee for power, she whipped her right leg forward, rotated her hips, and buried the toe of her sneaker squarely in Will's genitals. A flawlessly executed front groin kick, worthy of an *A* in her taekwondo class.

Howling with pain, Will dropped to his knees, holding himself with both hands, while attempting to curse and moan simultaneously.

Karolyn snarled, "Shut up, you sleaze-wad." She stood over him, and taking Teri's hand, helped her step past Will. "Are you all right?"

Without answering, Teri embraced her, trembling.

"Hey, easy, kiddo. It's okay. My turn to come to your rescue."

They turned together at the sound of heavy footfalls coming through the open front door. Stepping out of the kitchen, they withdrew around the far end of the conference table, recognizing the two exceptionally large Chinese men as Zhou's bodyguards.

Will pulled himself to his feet with the aid of the bar counter, perking up as they walked in. "Gentlemen—good timing. Take these two into the bedroom and tie them up…and get the blonde out of her clothes. I want them both ready for lessons." He gave Karolyn a malevolent smirk. "Time for some payback." Teri squeezed Karolyn's hand, a fresh wave of adrenaline making her queasy.

But the two bodyguards did not comply. They remained motionless, staring at Will. Suddenly, Teri felt Karolyn's hand tighten on hers. Porter appeared in the doorway.

With a look of superiority, his voice full of contrived bravado, Will nodded toward Bordon and said, "Would you two *please* get rid of this asshole?"

The massive pair remained still, their expressions stoic.

Porter rested a hand on Li's enormous shoulder, grinning as he spoke. "Ladies, I think you remember my friends Li and Wang from Hong

Kong? Honey, why don't you take Teri in the bedroom and get her some clothes?"

Then he spoke quietly to Wang, who was even larger than Li.

The bodyguards turned in unison toward Will, whose attempted indignation transpired in a rather pathetic, shrill tone. "Hey, just a damn minute! You two report to Zhou Quon—You're supposed to protect me!"

Porter's grin widened. His words carried an exuberant sarcasm. "Oh sorry, Will. Did I forget to tell you? The three of us had some long talks in Hong Kong. It turns out we have things in common...including our agreement on what a piece of shit you are."

As Li and Wang stepped toward him, Will retreated into the kitchen until he had nowhere to go.

* * *

"Did he just call you *Honey*?" Teri asked, as she pulled on jeans and a sweater.

Karolyn leaned against the dresser, a tiny smile forming at the corners of her mouth. "We've gotten a bit closer. He's stepped into his role as my protector quite...enthusiastically."

"I see," Teri replied, returning her smile. "How did you two, and those two, know I needed help?"

"It was a good thing Porter bought that cellular phone. Rich called him on it, out of his mind with worry. He said Arthur had called to warn him that Will was after you for the Private Account research. Porter called me because he was with his 'boys.' I told him I could handle Will."

Teri laughed, letting go of some tension. "Well, you sure as hell did! Thanks again." Putting her arm around Karolyn as they opened the bedroom door, she added thoughtfully, "You know, I'm gonna get my own cellular phone. I think everybody could use one."

* * *

Will was bound to one of the chairs from the conference table with yellow nylon cord. Porter stood over him with a look of satisfaction. "I told the boys they could go...you okay, Teri?"

She nodded. "Thanks to 'Miss Kick-Ass,' here."

"She's got some moves, doesn't she?" Porter smiled at Karolyn, and Teri could see the warmth in the look he gave her.

Turning back to Will who was thrashing and most likely swearing, though his words were muted by duct tape, Porter added, "Didn't think we needed to hear anything he has to say until we're ready."

The front door flew open again, making Teri jump. Rich and Sheila ran in breathlessly, both yelling, "Teri, are you all right?" They reached her simultaneously, smothering her in a three-way bear hug.

After extracting herself, Teri took a seat in one of the chairs by the front door. With Rich, Sheila, Karolyn, and Porter standing around her, she summarized her encounter, downplaying her trauma. She finished by highlighting Karolyn's dramatic entrance and take-down of Will.

"I thought we were in trouble again, though, when Li and Wang showed up."

Seeing the question marks on Rich's and Sheila's faces, Karolyn explained they were TaiChin security, that Porter had made friends with them in Hong Kong, and that he'd been meeting with them when he'd heard from Rich. Gesturing toward Will, tied to the chair by the table, she added, "They also helped with Wonder Boy over there. I'm sure he's still shell-shocked by his sudden change in fortune."

Teri looked at her four friends gathered around her and suddenly found her words heavy with emotion. "Anyway, I...thank you—all of you."

Rich shook Porter's hand vigorously. "Thanks, man. I'm really glad you two got here so quick. By the way, it's nice to finally meet you."

"Likewise." Porter hesitated, then added, "And Rich, I'm really sorry about that night in the canyon—I didn't know. I'm just so thankful you're all right."

Rich stepped back. His eyes were as wide as if Jimi Hendrix had suddenly appeared in front of him. "It was *you*?"

Teri dropped her head in unspoken agony. *Damn. Why now, after everything that's happened? I knew I should've told him—shit.*

Rich stood motionless, silently processing the entirety of the situation.

Porter said, "Oh my Lord, no one told you." He walked over to Will, thumping the side of Will's head for emphasis. "It was actually this asshole right here who claimed you were a corrupt union official trying to ruin the company. But I'm the bigger asshole for believing him. I shoulda done my homework, and I didn't. I'm so sorry...And now I know you're one of the good guys with a daughter who sounded just magical on the phone...I've been thanking God every day that you're okay."

A long and very awkward silence followed, as Teri held her head in her hands, Karolyn stiffened, and Sheila looked dazed. It lasted until Rich finally relaxed and said, "You know what? Apology accepted. After what you and Karolyn did for Teri...Well, let's just say, we're gonna start fresh." He shook Porter's hand again.

While Teri's cheeks reddened from her excessively audible sigh of relief, Karolyn turned to Sheila, extended her hand, and said, "Hi, I'm Karolyn. Nice to meet you."

Her nonchalant manner could not have been more perfectly juxtaposed to the circumstance. It triggered a round of hearty laughter, chasing away the tension.

32

With Will stashed in the bedroom out of earshot, five members of the Harlan-McNev unofficial investigation team gathered to formulate a plan. Carefully setting her steaming mug of coffee on a coaster, Teri said, "Sitting around this damn table, I feel like I'm in a staff meeting."

Rich and Karolyn chuckled as Porter quipped, "Wouldn't know. Never been to one."

Although none of them had chosen to be in this situation and no one but Porter had experience applicable to what likely came next, Teri didn't need to give a motivational speech. Her natural leadership simply kicked off a discussion.

"Okay...Sheila, this morning you told us about the due diligence data being subverted...do you know how they plan to disrupt the meeting?"

"There's a start-button icon on the McNev System Home-Screen that launches the Due Diligence Review presentation. So whoever clicks on it will unknowingly redirect the system to the new databases containing the alternate data...those figures show McNev circling the drain."

Teri made notes on a pad. "Obviously intended to ambush Winton and McNeil, plus derail the partnership...but we have no idea why."

Rich and Karolyn nodded, as Karolyn said, "Exactly—that's what we need our new friend to tell us."

Porter added, "No problem. Once we're ready, I have the feeling Crandall will tell us everything."

As Karolyn smiled at him, Sheila touched her arm. "Karolyn, you asked me this morning to find out who owned that EPM company. The ownership record shows *J. C. William.*"

Karolyn shook her head, "Wow, Crandall again? The little prick is into everything."

Teri looked thoughtful. "You know, when Will showed up tonight, he said *Arthur* needed my Private Accounts research."

Rich interjected, "Wait a minute—Art told me on the phone that Crandall was raging about making you pay for discovering his scheme."

Teri shook her head. "Will wasn't raging—twisted and disgusting, yes, but he said Arthur sent him."

Rich's temper flared. "Sonofabitch!"

Karolyn said, "One of them is lying...but they're both so good at it."

Nodding toward Porter with a resolute expression, Teri said, "Well, we'll get to the truth tonight."

Rich downed the last of his coffee and raised his hand, getting a wry smile and a touch of tone from Teri. "Yes, Rich?"

"We should also ask 'Mr. J. C. William' about his alter-ego authorizing work orders with bogus work codes, orchestrating intentional damage."

Teri said, "Good," writing as Rich continued.

"And let's see what he says about that special-order cargo door-lock for Tailia's plane. Especially now that you remembered the obsolete connector I saw in the report—that's definitely suspicious."

Making another note, Teri said, "Right, ask Will about the 913 cargo door-lock—"

She stood abruptly, dropping her pencil. "Oh, my God! Is he rigging it to crash the plane?"

* * *

Rich and Porter dragged the chair from the bedroom with Will still bound to it, and shut off the clock radio they'd left blaring to prevent him from overhearing their discussion. Rich said, "Nice touch, Porter. I'm sure Will enjoyed the Spanish language station."

Will appeared to step up his protest, judging by the sudden increase in muzzled epithets. Porter just smiled.

They moved Will into the center of a small circle the five of them formed with their chairs. Rich remarked, "Hey, this looks like one of those 'kNOw Excuses' circles we've heard about."

His quip elicited a quick smile, then Teri's expression turned serious as she addressed Crandall. "We debated calling the police and having you arrested. But we decided to give you a chance to cooperate and help us set things right…Don't make us regret it. Be smart and answer our questions."

She nodded at Porter who ripped the duct tape from Will's mouth.

"Ow, for chrissake, that hurt!"

Teri watched Will expectantly as Porter hovered over him, looking like he'd appreciate it if Will needed persuading.

Will said, "So, Miss Harlan, you're the boss and this is your little posse? Pathetic."

With a slightly curious expression as he looked at Sheila sitting next to Karolyn, he added, "I don't even know who you all are. Not that I give a damn."

Teri ignored him and asked their first question. "Tell us about this new software program that's going to be used for the Due Diligence presentation in tomorrow's meeting."

"Go screw yourself—you weren't so tough a while ago, quivering in your little white robe."

Will cowered at Porter's raised fist, but then Porter suddenly stopped in mid-swing and turned to Teri. "Excuse me one second..."

He walked to the kitchen and rummaged through a couple of drawers. A moment later, Porter was back at Teri's side, holding a small cheese grater, a double-edged grapefruit knife, and the corkscrew. "Don't have my regular tools, but these'll do."

Teri said, "Porter, wait. What are you doing?"

"You need the truth and he needs to learn some manners." With a look of surgical concentration, Porter reached behind Will and raked the grater back and forth across the knuckles of Will's left hand.

Will yelled, "Goddammit—that hurts! I don't know anything!"

Porter grinned. "Glad to hear that. I'm just getting started."

The four of them stared, dumbfounded, as Porter pinched Will's left ear lobe with his fingers and held the corkscrew to it. Will's smug hostility quickly evaporated. "Wha—what are you doing? I'll talk! Just stop, you crazy bastard."

Porter's expression was almost serene as he started to break the skin with the tip of the corkscrew. "I think you'll look nice with pierced ears."

Will screamed, "Stop!"

Karolyn stood and pulled Porter's hands away with a gentle but firm grip. "I think you got his attention, PB. Put it down...for now." She moved in front of Will, getting in his face. "Ready to be polite and tell us the truth, you cocky little prick?"

Will nodded vigorously.

Teri started again. "We already know you and Zhou have a thing, and as you so eloquently put it, we don't give a damn. We want to know why you and he are sabotaging the partnership."

Will shook his head in contempt. "You think there's a partnership? You're as clueless as McNeil and Winton. There's no partnership—it's all a set-up!"

Continuing in a disdainful tone, he explained the plan to abort the negotiations at the eleventh hour, using Arthur's program to make it appear McNev was concealing fraud. He told them Zhou was to act outraged and accuse Winton, so Lin would pull out too.

Karolyn shook her head as she asked, "So Lin doesn't know, and the Hong Kong meetings were a sham?"

Will turned to her. "Duh—of course! That's where it was supposed to go down!"

Porter whacked the top of Will's head. "*Manners*, dipstick."

When Teri spoke again, her impatience equaled Will's derision. "*Okay*—Isolate everyone in Hong Kong, torpedo the partnership, and blame Winton—*got it*—we want to know *why*! And what do you mean, there's no partnership?"

He gave Teri a hard stare before replying with his predictable superior sarcasm. "You're supposed to be the smart one...Don't you get it?"

Porter said, "No—*you* don't get it," picking up the grater again and moving behind him.

"Jesus—all right, I'll lay out the end game for you. McNev's in financial ruin, overwhelmed by bad press from fraud allegations. McNeil becomes desperate...desperate enough to accept a bargain-basement rescue offer from Zhou's sponsors—some Chinese power faction with a truckload of cash. They're paying the tab for Arthur to mastermind the whole scheme."

Teri, Karolyn, and Rich all looked at each other, appearing to reach the same conclusion.

Teri said, "So Arthur is using the partnership as a façade to set up McNev for some nefarious hostile takeover, and Winton takes the fall?"

"You're finally catching on...Although Arthur's brilliant updated scenario for tomorrow has McNeil up there with him, so now he'll be implicated as well."

There was quiet while Will's disclosure sank in.

Karolyn broke the silence. "You said something about McNev being financially ruined—Do you mean there's actual fraud taking place?"

Will toned down the sarcasm to avoid losing more skin.

"Ahh, you're not just a pretty face...Arthur's also getting paid to collapse McNev from the inside. I'm not sure exactly what he's doing, but I do know it's called embezzlement.

"He's using some remote application to hide it all. He bragged to me about designing it—called it his *God Program*. He found some girl-genius to develop this magic software to change data in the financial system whenever he needs to, undetected. He's been falsifying journal entries every night for at least two years..."

Sheila put her face in her hands as Karolyn jumped up, interrupting him. "Holy hell! I was right there, and I never knew. I was such a fool to believe in him."

Will's expression revealed a slow, spiteful smile, looking as if he was enjoying their guilt or mocking their naiveté. Whatever it was, Porter and Rich did not appreciate it. They stood together, glaring down at Will.

Rich said, "You find this amusing?"

"No, what's amusing is you people thinking you can 'set things right.' But this here"—he tugged at his restraints—"I find this annoying and painful."

Porter said, "Obviously not painful enough." He retrieved the grater, pressing it to Will's nose, pausing just short of breaking the skin.

"No—not the face! Christ, what else do you *want* from me?"

Rich said, "Tell us about the phony work orders, Mr. 'J. C. William.'"

"Another scenario by Arthur to wreck the company...work orders for intentional damage to create chaos in Final Assembly. I used JCW to authorize them, and Arthur paid Herrera under the table to organize it."

Rich shook his head as Will continued.

"C'mon Richmond, you're not stupid...You really think O'Donnell brought in idiots like Winton and Duke because he thought they were effective? He used cost-cutting to mask his embezzlement and run his scenarios while the morons in the ExCon collected their bonuses, content to believe they were all-powerful executives."

Rich's anger boiled over again. "You chicken-shit weasel. You're destroying people's livelihoods! I should just..."

As Rich raised his hand, Teri stood and pulled it down. "Don't, Rich. He's not worth it."

Will sneered, "That's right, be a good boy—Obey your queen bee."

Whack! Without warning, Rich back-handed Will so hard it nearly knocked him over.

Porter nodded to Rich. "Nice one—that'll leave a mark for sure."

* * *

They took a short break, stowing Will back in the bedroom while they munched on the pizzas Karolyn ordered, and discussed what they'd learned. Porter used his cellular to call Wang and then McNeil to confirm a 10 p.m. meeting. Once they finished and took their seats around Will again for some final questions, the fight in him seemed diminished. His nose was red, as was his right cheek, in addition to being swollen.

He said, "Look, I've told you everything. Let me go, and I promise to disappear. I just want to get the hell away from Arthur—and all of you. Plus, I gotta take a leak."

Teri said, "Good. That'll motivate you to answer the question we haven't asked yet...How much is Arthur being paid for all this?"

"I don't know. He didn't tell me."

Porter handed Rich the grapefruit knife. "It goes under the fingernails. Would you like the pleasure, or shall I?"

Will still had enough energy to yell. "No! I'm telling you straight! It has to be over ten-million, though—he's giving me ten percent, and he said it'd make me a millionaire." Will's expression hardened. "And like that wasn't enough, Arthur asked Zhou for more because now he's putting McNeil in the crosshairs...he's got some major balls. And I need the restroom—bad."

Teri said, "One more answer, and we'll let you relieve yourself."

Will sighed irritably. "What?"

"Private Accounts—are they Arthur's scheme to hide the money he's taking out of the company?"

"I'd say it's a good guess, but I really don't know anything about Private Accounts. Arthur just said we'd both be in deep shit from your research...which is why he sent me here." Looking dejected, he added, "Jesus, he really screwed me."

Rich turned to Teri and Karolyn. "You two believe him?"

Before they answered, Sheila interjected, speaking for the first time. "If you really know nothing about Private Accounts, why does the EPM ownership record show *J. C. William?*"

Will looked at Sheila, hesitating. This time it only took Porter reaching for the grapefruit knife.

"I used J. C. William for the work orders, that's all—I don't own this EPM thing—I've never even heard of it...It's gotta be Arthur."

Sheila looked thoughtful. "If Arthur changed the ownership record using his remote program, it would show up in a transaction file...But it won't be in the McNev system. He'd keep it somewhere secure..."

Sheila sat up straight like the kid in class who's just figured out the answer. She asked Karolyn excitedly, "Where does Arthur keep his most-private information? I remember him using special Montblanc notebooks that locked—Has he switched to anything electronic?"

"Yes! He got an HP Palmtop a while ago. He uses it constantly."

"Is it a 100LX? And does he connect it to his PC?"

Karolyn nodded, "I think so, and yes, all the time—both at work and at home."

Will had been staring at Sheila, and interrupted impatiently. "I just got it—you're Arthur's girl-genius!" Sheila shot Will an icy glare and then looked away, completely ignoring him.

Will said, "Hey—I still gotta pee!"

Porter stepped directly in front of Will. "Either hold it, or piss your pants...your choice." He watched with an amused expression as Will squirmed while Teri, Rich, and Karolyn refocused on Sheila's brainstorm.

Sheila continued, "I still have his home computer IP address from working on his project. If he's connected tonight, I can access his PC and then get into the Palmtop."

Teri said, "Like, hacking?"

Sheila chuckled. "You sound like a TV crime drama. It's really just 'accessing'... unless you count having to finagle a couple of passwords."

Joining in Sheila's enthusiasm, Karolyn asked, "Are you saying you can get in and see everything Arthur's been doing?"

Sheila nodded slowly, still thinking, as Karolyn added, "And I'll bet a year's salary that's where he'd keep track of the all funds he's been embezzling."

Sheila met Karolyn's eyes and grinned.

33

Tuesday, 10:05 p.m.

Hugh McNeil sat alone in a booth by the window of a quiet coffee shop in Corona del Mar. He stared out at the night, unsettled by his equally dark thoughts, and wincing at the pain in his rocklike trapezius. When Philip Lin walked through the door, he sighed aloud in relief.

McNeil's optimistic world-view, including a long-held predilection for partnerships that build on corporate strengths, had motivated both his decision to acquire Everett and to enter into negotiations with TaiChin.

Despite a solid track record in commercial aviation, Everett had been losing market share which stunted the company's ability to develop new models. Hugh saw a win-win opportunity to use his corporation's resources to reenergize Everett, while enabling McNeil Aerospace to expand into commercial aircraft. After the merger, Hugh was introduced to Arthur by a business associate who'd endorsed O'Donnell as a boy-wonder specializing in corporate makeovers. Arthur's seemingly excellent resume along with the recommendation, had prompted Hugh to hire him with the goal of taking McNev to the next level.

That same year, he'd met Philip at a seminar and found himself impressed by both Philip and the emerging technology of the Far East. He'd considered it providence and decided to pursue a partnership with the newly formed TaiChin Consortium. But as he sat there tonight waiting for Philip, he struggled coming to grips with their current situation.

Philip shook Hugh's hand as he sat down across from him.

After the server delivered Philip's green tea, Hugh said, "I appreciate you stepping into this with me. I know it's beyond the call of duty."

Philip put the tea bag in the pot, shaking his head. "I must apologize for my part, not spotting Mr. Zhou's insidious alliance sooner."

Hugh stirred the cream in his coffee. "Please don't blame yourself. I'm honored to call you my friend as well my colleague."

Philip touched Hugh's forearm. He looked up into the sincerity on Philip's face. "I still believe in the partnership we envisioned…I could not live with myself if we let them get away with destroying it."

Nodding to each other, acknowledging their joint commitment, Hugh asked, "So, were you able to connect with your President's Council?"

"Yes. Obviously, they are dismayed over the situation, but they accept that Mr. Zhou will be…how do you say it—*cut loose*, and the disgrace will end there."

"That's good—not our situation, but your Council's consent. Then we'll proceed as planned once we've secured the last piece." Hugh looked up to see Porter and Karolyn walking in with Wang following several steps behind them. He added, "It may be coming now."

Philip stood, letting Karolyn and Porter slide into the booth, then switched sides and sat next to Hugh. Wang chose to stand against the back wall near the restroom in an unsuccessful attempt to be inconspicuous.

Hugh said, "Porter, I wanted to thank you for your support of Karolyn and Teri in Hong Kong...and your contract is *not* terminated. Mary will have your badge, along with Rich's and Mac's, when you return tomorrow."

Porter nodded. "Thank you, sir."

Karolyn said, "We have a lot more to tell you both since our meeting this afternoon..."

Porter gently tapped her shoulder. "KB, I think it'd be best to have Mr. Lin speak to Wang first, so he can get back to the hotel before he's missed."

They agreed, and Philip stepped out of the booth, Porter tilting his head at Wang as Philip walked over to him. The two men stood against the back wall, speaking quietly for a couple of minutes, after which Wang handed Philip a microcassette with a slight bow. They walked back to the booth and Porter stood to walk Wang out.

Philip took his seat next to Hugh. "Well, here it is," Philip said, setting the tiny cassette on the table and tapping it with his finger. "It makes me sad to use it. I have no love for Mr. Zhou, but I will still feel the pain of his dishonor in front of his staff and mine, as well as yours."

Hugh said, "That's what makes you the kind of man you are, Philip. It's why I appreciate doing business with you."

When Porter returned, Philip said, "I know Wang did this at great personal risk. We both appreciate you garnering his support to help us."

"You're welcome, Mr. Lin. Wang and Li are good guys. No disrespect, but they don't think much of Mr. Zhou...or of Crandall." Taking a sip of his coffee, Porter looked at Hugh and added, "Sorry, Mr. McNeil."

"Don't apologize, Porter. I regret not heeding my apparently accurate intuition...I shouldn't have let him return your call last week. In retrospect, that was a costly error in judgment."

"It's all right, sir...I'm glad to hear you agree on Crandall, especially because of what we're about to tell you."

Karolyn jumped on the segue. "Guess who stopped in at the condo tonight?" She recapped Will's uninvited visit with Teri, including herself, Porter, Wang, Li, Rich, and Sheila showing up, but choose to leave out her exemplary groin kick. When she finished, Hugh and Philip wore stunned looks.

"Is Teri all right? Did you call the police?"

After assuring them Teri was uninjured, Karolyn explained, "Teri figured—and we supported her—that it would be more useful to have a Q&A session with Will than turn him in. I hope that was okay with you."

Hugh replied, "I trust you all to do what you think is best. I can assure you that tomorrow will be Mr. Crandall's final day of employment at McNeil Everett…and likely his last day without a criminal record."

He paused, with a thoughtful look. "Earlier, when I met with Arthur to divert his attention as we discussed, he told me Will was involved in some scheme with Private Accounts, and that this morning he'd assigned Teri and Vern-somebody to investigate. Is that true?"

Karolyn started to lift her coffee cup, then set it down. "Uh—no, not even close! I was *in* the meeting with Teri and Vernon Ames. She's the one doing the investigating—of him!"

Hugh shook his head. "Arthur is so convincingly sincere…I've fallen victim to either his charm or my own naiveté." He stared at the table, struggling once more to accept the reality of his Executive VP, then looked up to see Karolyn's empathetic expression.

"Don't be too hard on yourself, sir. Will may be a snake, but Arthur is an exceptionally skilled snake charmer. His near-perfect orchestration of this whole subterfuge shows us that he's a true master in the art of lies and manipulation.

"What I've realized recently, though, is *why* Arthur's deceit is so extraordinarily effective—It's because he's never thought of himself as dishonest. He's just so obsessively committed to his plans that successful completion is the only thing that matters to him. The best way I can explain it is that caring about anything else—like ethics, truth, or even people—is simply an irrelevant weakness to him."

She paused as her expression turned apologetic. "I'm only sorry it took me so long to see behind the curtain."

Hugh glanced sideways at Philip, who looked as impressed as Hugh felt. He noted Porter's expression was closer to adoration. "Karolyn, your insight is remarkable—you never need to apologize for it." He smiled, adding, "And you might also be happy to hear that in our conversation, Arthur did say he trusts you completely."

Karolyn nearly choked.

"I thought you'd find that amusing."

Karolyn shook her head as Hugh shifted gears. "So tell us, did Will shed any light on things?"

Porter grinned. "He decided he should cooperate."

Karolyn shared what they'd learned from Crandall: the details behind the Due-Diligence set-up Arthur had planned for tomorrow, and the scheme to devastate McNev, including the likely embezzlement. As he listened to Karolyn laying it all out, it seemed to Hugh that either the booth was getting larger, or he'd been shrinking into it. When she finished, Karolyn slid another microcassette across the table to him.

"This is from Teri. She recorded our entire conversation with Crandall. You don't need to listen to it till you're ready, but Teri said, 'When you're doing business with someone untrustworthy, it's good to have their own words on tape, just in case.'"

Hugh stowed the cassette in his inner coat pocket and sat silently for a moment, touched by the concern he saw in Porter's and Karolyn's faces. When he spoke, his distress was tempered by humility and determination. "As abhorrent as this situation is, I first need to thank you both for everything you've done to support Philip and me, and our company…and please convey our grateful appreciation to Teri, Rich, and his sister."

He turned sideways to Philip. "My friend, it's now painfully clear that Arthur and his reprehensible disciples, Crandall and Zhou, have nearly succeeded in hijacking our partnership. It is time we took it back."

"Yes…it *is*," Philip said.

Hugh tapped his finger on the microcassette from Wang. "We must have all three of them in the meeting tomorrow for this…and we must also be very sure Jackson does not use that damn program."

After Porter and Karolyn affirmed their support, Karolyn held up a finger. "There's just one thing I need to tell you, sir; Will won't be at the meeting."

Hugh felt the blood leave his face. "You mean, he's…"

Porter jumped in. "No, no, he's fine—mostly."

The color began returning to Hugh's cheeks as Karolyn said, "We can't have Will contacting Arthur. Plus, Rich and Mac have plans for him tomorrow morning."

Karolyn summarized what they'd found with the cargo door-lock as best she could, qualifying it as she finished. "Sorry, I didn't explain it very well—Rich or Teri would've done better. Teri remembered some obsolete connector and figured out that Will might have done something to the vent-door thing—she's amazing. Anyway, Rich and Mac will bring him upstairs to us after they get Will to show them exactly what he did, so they can fix it. You can get the whole story from them."

Philip, who'd been hanging on Karolyn's every word, said, "Please convey my gratitude to them. Our Tailia ME-420 is a prized asset to both Taiwan and China."

"I will, sir." She turned to Porter, adding, "And now Porter can be there with Mac and Rich to make sure there's no trouble."

As they stood to leave, Hugh said, "So tomorrow we'll put an end to this, and sadly, we'll be dispatching three of our senior executives into police custody. I can't decide which one is worse."

Porter said, "You don't need to, sir. Our criminal justice system will take care of that. The way I see it, they deserve each other...and everything that's coming to them."

* * *

The fog rolling in on the evening breeze drifted over the coastline like a down comforter settling gently onto a bed. Rich watched the mist waft around Teri as she leaned back against the railing of the condo balcony, then opened the sliding door to join her, closing it behind him.

"Is Sheila okay in there?" Teri asked.

"Yep. Will's still tied up at the far end of the table, and she's busy on her laptop...Karolyn and Porter should be back soon."

He stepped closer, adding, "It's nice out here. The sound of the ocean is like Zen therapy."

Teri sighed. "Yeah, one summer my parents rented a trailer on the beach in Corona del Mar. Going to bed every night listening to the waves...not sure I've ever slept that well since..."

Rich said, "I love the way your hair does that," brushing a few strands away from her face. He leaned back against the balcony railing next to her, putting his arm around her shoulder. They stood for a moment in silence before Rich offered, "We did good tonight, huh?"

When Teri didn't respond, he continued. "You know, I spent the whole drive up here, terrified you'd get hurt. I had a flashback to high school and that girl I told you about—my prom date—Barbara, who ended up with that asshole, Sid, ruining her life. I couldn't handle something happening to you."

"But it didn't, I'm okay. And it worked out. We got what we needed from him."

"You're shaking. You sure you're all right?"

"I think it's the aftereffect...adrenaline wearing off, plus all this shit going on."

Teri moved away, facing him. She stiffened noticeably, appearing to Rich as if she were arguing with herself. He marveled at the intense green of her eyes, almost glowing, even in the dim balcony light.

When she finally spoke, her words were measured. "You know, I've spent several angry moments in the last three weeks, swearing at you for dragging me into the middle of all this."

He was crestfallen. "You're right. I got you into an awful mess. I can't tell you how sorry I am."

"I know it was my decision, but it would have been easier if you'd given me more warning."

Rich looked down. "I never intended for you to take it all on by yourself."

She crossed her arms, and her posture told Rich she was unlikely to say *I forgive you* and embrace him.

"I know you didn't *intend* any of it, Rich. But the truth is, I walked in blind—and naïve—about how sick your executive team really is."

She ran her fingers through her hair, twisting it, and Rich could see her winding up. Her tone sharpened. "Allow me to share what's really happened so far. Winton *did* try something on his boat. I think he actually believed I'd be open to him seducing me. It was more of a high school groping thing, but I almost had to knee him to get him off me."

He felt his face flush as her voice continued to rise.

"Then, in Hong Kong, when Karolyn decides she's had enough and says 'no,' Winton forces himself on her, tearing off her dress. Porter and I had to bust into their suite to stop him, and Winton's not even *half* the slimeball Duke is!"

Her eyes flashed like angry emeralds as she continued. "You know what happened the other night when you asked me to find out who J. C. William was? That filthy prick wanted me to strip for him and get on my knees...said it was his price for information! The only way I got what we needed without totally debasing myself was to nail the bastard with his own words. Thank God I thought to bring my tape recorder!"

She took a quick breath. "And then tonight, it gets even better! Will—pretty-boy pervert—Crandall has a key to the condo, catches me half-dressed, and wants to *play*! Are you *kidding* me? The only one who hasn't tried anything physical is O'Donnell, and he's most likely the psycho behind all of this!"

Rich stepped back, off-balance from the shock as he searched for the right thing to say. He wasn't quick enough.

"And don't say you didn't know!" Teri's words flew like little missiles launching at him. "Your subconscious sure as hell knew! Because during your so-called mental sabbatical, you told me almost exactly what would happen! And I thought you were talking crazy—stupid me. You want to know what I think?"

She didn't give him a chance to respond. "I think you're in denial. There's no way to save a company being led by a narcissistic Executive VP who's a compulsive liar; a moronic, misogynistic President; a vulgar, mafia-wannabe Manufacturing VP; and a sleazy, crooked deviant who nearly attacked me! The whole lot of you are fucking insane!"

Rich's head was spinning. Rage, guilt, and anguish engulfed his mind and his heart, jumbled with jealousy and a dark twinge of sexual excitement—which added more guilt. He felt sick. Heartbreak and remorse may have been foremost, but they were overridden, and his response burst out in angry frustration.

"Don't you dare lump me in with those assholes! I'm nothing like them—I've been fighting them with every ounce of my being for months—years, even!"

Teri's shoulders slumped; her expression defiant but pained. Rich saw her tearing up and tried to soften his tone.

"Look, for more than a year, I've known things were off, but I couldn't put the pieces together. I called you because you happen to be the sharpest, most competent manager I know. I knew you loved building airplanes and solving problems as much as I do—and I also knew you were pretty damn tough!"

He caught his breath and used her tactic, pressing on before she responded. "And I was right too! Because you jumped in and started connecting dots, then got us all working together, forming an 'investigation team.' And now we're about to blow this thing wide open. Maybe it took my brain a while to catch up to my gut, but honest to God, Ter, I care about you. I never wanted you in harm's way. I had no idea I'd end up in a ditch or that this shit would get so deep!"

Teri slouched against the railing, and Rich could sense her exhaustion, like the emotional equivalent of a spent firework. He had to fight the urge to take her in his arms, kiss her passionately, and tell her he loved her. But he knew her well enough to know that it wasn't the right moment.

They fell silent, the angry electricity in the air between them, slowly beginning to dissipate.

Rich's thoughts shifted from frustration to quiet desperation. *How do I make her see I'm the antithesis of those assholes?*

He noticed Sheila had looked up from her laptop and was regarding them with a concerned expression. When he looked back at Teri, she appeared to be on the edge of dissolving.

Maybe I could just hold her...tell her everything will be all right.

But as he took a step toward her, the front door opened. Porter and Karolyn had returned.

* * *

Porter walked across the living room and opened the slider while Karolyn stopped to speak with Sheila. Rich and Teri waited with Porter on the balcony in uneasy silence, watching the two women in a whispered discussion. Three minutes later, which seemed more like twenty to Teri, Sheila stood and walked with Karolyn to join them.

Teri bristled at their apparent secretive closeness. "What was that about?" she snapped, realizing too late that her tone was harsher than warranted.

Sheila answered, "Jeez, Ter, take it easy. KB was just giving me a clue of what to look for on Arthur's Palmtop...accounts where he may have stashed his embezzled funds."

When Karolyn asked Teri if she was okay, all she could manage was a curt nod. She noticed the concern in Karolyn's expression, as she proceeded to recap their meeting with McNeil and Lin. Quietly assimilating everything Karolyn shared made Teri feel even more drained as she envisioned the challenge facing them tomorrow. She shook her head, trying to regain her focus. "Did you tell them about 913?"

"Not as well as you two could have, but we explained that Rich and Crandall won't be at the meeting."

Teri nodded slowly. "Okay...good, thanks."

Rich rested his hand on Teri's shoulder, and with a gentle squeeze, said, "That was a smart move, not confronting Crandall about 913 tonight. Now we can see his reaction tomorrow when it's time for him to show us his handiwork."

Teri's mood lifted a little, reminded of the confidence she'd always had working with him. She turned toward Rich, and their eyes met; she felt their connection. A touch of warmth, followed directly by regret for her earlier outburst washing it away. She wanted so much to talk to him—really talk. But she knew the moment wasn't right.

Wondering if it ever would be, she reached for his hand, and attempted a smile. "Just be careful."

After Porter opened the slider and they filed back inside, Karolyn gave him a hug and said, "You sure you're up for this?"

"Yeah. Wang offered to watch him, but it's too risky—Zhou would notice him missing." He walked toward the table, adding, "Besides, Will and I are in for a great night, right buddy? I'll make sure our Mr. Crandall is in an extremely helpful mood tomorrow."

After using Porter's cellular to call Mac about the plan for tomorrow morning, Rich helped Porter re-secure Will's hands and get him into the rental car. Will resisted, dragging his feet, and protesting beneath his duct tape, until Porter did something to his elbow that made him scream and become very compliant. Teri finished packing her things as she'd accepted Karolyn's invitation to stay at her condo.

Rich came back inside as Sheila was stowing her laptop in its case. She said, "You need to get Lisa, and I've got a full night's work going through Arthur's PC and Palmtop while he's sleeping."

"Yep, just one last thing." He grinned. "Porter and I thought of a way to use Arthur's secret weapon against him."

Rich put his finger to his lips. Then he picked up the condo phone, dialed Porter's cellular number, and waited for his voicemail.

"Hey Porter, its Rich. Listen, Teri's fine—no sign of Crandall. But we really need you to track the little prick down by tomorrow morning and bring him to meet Mac and me at the plant. We'll be at the east gate, past Final Assembly, around seven-fifteen. Thanks."

34

Arthur stood at his bedroom office desk, packing his Montblanc executive valise for his escape flight. In addition to a fresh shirt, underwear, toiletries, and a shaving kit, he added unique necessities, including a bottle of Valium, a length of MarlowBraid Classic rope, and a Ruger .357 revolver.

As he carefully stowed the handgun in a special zippered section, O'Donnell recalled the words of a former associate, a gun enthusiast, who'd given him the Ruger. "Arthur, this is the perfect weapon for you. It's lightweight and easy to handle, with a comfy black rubber mono-grip and manageable recoil. For its size, the accuracy is exceptional—and most important—it's sexy as hell."

His associate had insisted on lessons, and Arthur found he enjoyed shooting the Ruger at targets, but figured he'd never use it anywhere else. Now as he held it, he began to appreciate its power.

My exit tomorrow should be quiet and smooth, but it's good to be prepared...and I like holding it.

His pager buzzed. The display showed del Balso's home number. He'd told Tony to inform him immediately of any calls from the condo, rather than recording them for the next morning.

He dialed the number and Tony answered on the first ring.

"Boss?"

"You heard something from the condo?"

"Yes, boss. I put Jimmy on OT tonight, so he could stay and listen for anything coming from there."

"And was it Teri or Will Crandall?"

"Will Crandall? Why would he be there, boss?"

"Never mind." Arthur sighed, reminded again of how much he was going to enjoy not missing Tony. "Who was it?"

"It was Richmond. No idea what he was doing there. Maybe he's getting it on with Harlan."

Arthur was not in the mood, letting his tone make that clear. "What did he say?"

Tony read the transcript of Rich's call asking Porter to find Will and bring him to the east gate. He added, "Jimmy said it sounded like a regular message."

Arthur considered this, reflecting on his brilliance in getting Teri into the condo. They had no clue how he'd stayed two steps ahead of them.

He chuckled. *Teri and Karolyn are probably still puzzling over my omniscience.*

The call told him that Porter hadn't left town and was still helping them. Secondly, he could infer that either Richmond beat Will to the condo, causing Crandall to abandon his visit, or he'd scared Will off.

Damn—did I misjudge how fast Richmond could get there?

Although Arthur typically found Crandall's licentious inclinations to be off-putting, he'd designed this scenario specifically with a sexual element to instigate mayhem when Richmond arrived to find Teri in a compromising position with Crandall.

Apparently, she's now managed to elude Will. Maybe Crandall's right. If I had more time, I'd teach Ms. Harlan some humility, personally.

Arthur also surmised that the report of Richmond's *regular tone* indicated there'd been no altercation. If there had been, the stress in Richmond's voice would have been noticeable, and he wouldn't have asked for Crandall to be located.

Arthur exhaled loudly and cut to the chase.

"Tony, you need to stop those two from meeting with Crandall. I'll call Herrera and have him get his crew. Meet them at the east gate tomorrow at 6:30, so you'll be ready…Bordon does *not* get through the gate—watch for his piece-of-shit beige Lumina, and shoot him for trespassing if you have to. Then you personally escort Will to my office, and be sure he does *not* talk to Richmond, McKinley, or anyone else. Got it? No mistakes this time—get it done or get a new job!"

"I'm on it, boss."

Arthur hung up before del Balso could say good-night, then dialed Will's pager. After thirty minutes with no return call followed by a second page, '911,' his pacing increased. *Where the hell is he?*

He jumped at the *whir* of the fax machine, yanking the paper out as it emerged. In the next instant, his scowl was replaced by an expansive grin. *Ahhh, Zhou came through early.*

Opening his Palmtop, Arthur accessed the hidden file and his password-protected accounts spreadsheet. He entered the amount of Zhou's wire transfer and the confirmation numbers to the numbered account in Barbados he'd designated "Magnum." Then he tapped the icon to summarize his new total: $102,004,060. *Finally—nine figures!*

He walked downstairs and poured a glass of Glenmorangie. He took the scotch outside to bid adieu to his impeccable patio while taking advantage of his miniature firepit to dispose of several potentially compromising documents.

* * *

Karolyn's two-bedroom condo featured an open-plan living-dining room and a Thermador professional kitchen. The style was modern, highlighted by chrome and glass, on top of Canadian maple floors with tasteful area rugs. Upon her arrival, Teri was instantly aware of the welcoming vibe, in marked contrast to the disquiet of the McNev condo.

Via an extended stay under a cascade of fiercely hot water from dual showerheads, Teri managed to scrub off some of the layers of her distasteful evening. She sat on the bed in the guest bedroom, brushing her hair, and looked up when Karolyn came in to check on her.

"Thanks for letting me bunk with you, KB. I really wasn't up to finding a hotel."

Karolyn sat down on the bed next to her, using a wide-tooth comb on her own hair. "No problem—glad you're here." With furrowed brows, she added, "So, are you *really* all right? That was a helluva thing with Will…and you were like a big raw nerve when Porter and I got back."

"Sorry. I think everything that's happened is catching up to me. I have no idea how you stayed sane in the middle of it all."

Karolyn stopped combing, looking pensive. "I never really thought about it. When I started working for Arthur, using sex was what I did. And then it got to be…"

Teri held her hand up. "You don't need to go there, thanks. I got it."

Karolyn shook her head. "But there was a side to it that I hadn't recognized. Without really being aware, I'd created my own balance of power, because I knew how much he wanted what I could give him."

Teri mirrored Karolyn's head shaking. "I thought you said you loved him."

"Right, and that's how I lost my balance. I wanted to be his partner…I deluded myself into believing he could actually care for me."

"And what you did with Winton?"

"Ter, I did what I thought I had to. I'm not proud of it, but I survived. I can't go back and undo it."

Karolyn got quiet, looking solemn. After a long sigh, she continued haltingly, "I don't talk about this…as a matter of fact, I've never really told anyone…I'm from Idyllwild—small community in the San Jacinto mountains—grew up in a nice little cabin on a half-acre. Happy kid, good life. But when I was thirteen, one sunny morning in April, my dad was just gone—left my mom and me for the love-in scene in San Francisco. Mom didn't have much education—she worked in town as a cocktail waitress at the *Far-Out Club*."

Teri cocked her eyebrow.

"What can I say? It was the sixties in Idyllwild…you know, hippies—Timothy Leary even stopped in up there. Anyway, with my dad gone, mom would get 'extra friendly' with tourists, and we'd start having better groceries and going out to eat. Sometimes her latest 'friend' as she called them, would stay for a few days, but they never stuck around…pretty soon we'd be back to ramen noodles. I asked her why she let guys do that—you know, take advantage of her. She told me, 'Honey, it's time you learned this. Men aren't in control, they just think they are. *We* have the advantage, and we can use it to get what we need.'"

Karolyn paused, steadying herself.

"A couple years later, the boyfriends started looking at me more than her...I learned her lesson well. For twenty years, I've relied on keeping my wits and using this body to give me the advantage I needed to get by. So Winton wasn't that big of a deal to me...until *you* showed up.

"I know it sounds corny, but on the boat—the way you carried yourself—as an executive, equal to them, really struck a chord with me. Even though using sex was something I was used to, all a of sudden I realized how much I was underestimating myself...that afternoon, when Arthur sent me downstairs for Jackson...I *hated* the way that felt. And once it hit me that I was playing right into their bullshit, believing they're entitled because of their so-called *power*, it really pissed me off."

She paused again, then added, "I haven't had the chance to say it, but *thank you*. Really. Thanks for helping me step up to be who I *can* be. I like this me a lot better."

Teri just looked at her.

After a moment quiet enough to hear the air whispering through the heater vent, Karolyn asked, "Hey—are you in there? Please don't say you think I'm still just a whore or something."

Teri blinked rapidly several times. "What? No, of course not. It's just...I think that's probably the nicest thing anyone's ever said to me...and I don't deserve it."

"Come again?" Karolyn looked at her quizzically, and then noticed Teri's expression. She grabbed the box of tissues from the dresser and set it on the bed. "You look like you might need these."

Teri took one. "Thanks. You're not the only one who's been forced to take a hard look at herself. I realized that after my blow-out with Rich."

"Ahh, that explains your mood when we got back. You two argued while we were gone?"

"Yeah, out on the balcony. And it wasn't so much an argument. It was mostly me blaming him for everything. I got so angry from dealing with all this...Winton, and Duke—what a disgusting fungus he is...the other night, he told me I had to strip, and maybe even blow him, to get information about J. C. William."

"What? No way! You'd never..."

"No, I didn't, and I was smart enough to hide my little Olympus recorder in my purse. Amazing how his attitude changed, once he realized I could use his own words to nail his ass."

Karolyn smiled. "You and your recorder...nice one."

"Yeah, I guess. But I know what they all think of me." Teri shook her head with an ironic half-laugh. "Will told me tonight that Duke called me the *ice queen*. I've always just aimed to be the stand-up woman executive, trying to do what's right, you know?"

"Yeah, for sure—It's one of the things I admire most about you."

Teri took Karolyn's hand. "Thanks, but you shouldn't. And please don't take offense at this, KB. I think you're so awesome…but all I've ever really wanted is to do my job as a regular coworker alongside men, without them acting like I'm supposed to jump into their fantasy as a co-star in some damn porno flick!"

Karolyn pulled her hand away and looked down. Teri reached for it again, and this time held both her hands.

"No, wait—that wasn't a judgment of you, or what you just told me."

She looked into Karolyn's eyes, letting her see the sincerity and the pain. "What you've shared with me…I feel like I can tell you. During my outburst at Rich, tonight, I realized all my self-righteous anger is just a smoke screen. Underneath is something way more basic…it's *fear*."

She squeezed Karolyn's hands as she forced herself to go on. "All of this—me acting tough and losing my temper—It's just a facade. I never put it together until tonight, but it all goes back to my total dick of a stepfather. My dad died when I was ten—killed in a work accident. He ran a sheet-metal fabrication company. A year after he was gone, my mom married his business partner.

"One night, when my mom was out, I was studying in my room. My stepfather walked in—he'd been drinking. I wasn't much older than you were…fifteen…and I was so naïve…he had this strange look in his eye, something I'd never seen…"

Teri recounted the ugly memory of that horrible night: her crushing terror of being cornered, not being able to stop the stalking hulk of her stepdad. She poured it all out.

There were tears now, but she continued, holding tight to Karolyn's hands. "You did what you had to do because you were strong. I buried my fear because I couldn't face it, and tonight with Will in the kitchen…It took me back there again…there in my old bedroom; trapped—I couldn't move, couldn't breathe."

Her voice broke and she dropped her head, staring at the bed, her silence emphasizing the depth of her torment. Teri released one of her hands, reaching for another tissue, and as she wiped her eyes, Karolyn gently lifted Teri's chin.

"Hey, look at me. Getting all that out—that took a lot of guts. I should know, right? But now it's out and you can cut it lose. You were a teenager…For God's sake, give yourself a break!"

"But you still had to rescue me tonight."

"And what—you think that makes you weak? Don't be crazy. You'd be stupid if you weren't scared when some creep is backing you into a corner, forcing himself on you!"

Karolyn caught herself and softened her tone. "It's okay to be scared. Arthur scared the living shit outta me. I dissolved into tears with Porter the other night."

"That's different, KB. Arthur's a borderline sociopath, threating to kill you. Will didn't scare you in the least; you just kicked the little perv in the balls."

"Are you trying to tell me you're scared of men—sexually?"

Teri didn't answer but leaned against Karolyn and continued crying. As Teri's tears began to subside, they held each other for several moments in close-knit silence.

Karolyn broke it, speaking gently but earnestly. "Hey kiddo, you went up against three of the biggest sleazebags I've ever had the misfortune to work with...and it's not you, it's *them*! So give yourself credit—You stayed true to yourself, and you got past all of it. In my eyes that's real strength."

Teri wiped her eyes and sniffled, settling into a calm-after-the-storm countenance. With a hint of a smile, and shared bond that didn't need explaining, she said, "Thanks...you're a good friend."

Karolyn rested her hand on Teri's shoulder and met her eyes. "Likewise." She stood up and added, "A couple things you might find helpful...Come with me to my taekwondo class—it's not only great a way to get in shape, it's also good for building self-confidence. As Karolyn turned to go, Teri said, "You said 'a *couple* of things...'"

"Oh, right—In spite of your experience, just remember that not all men are sexist pigs...There's this one guy I know who comes to mind. Nice looking, strong chin, a little executive gray at his temples...a real stand-up type." Smiling, she added, "Get some rest—you've earned it," and closed the bedroom door behind her.

Teri snuggled beneath the covers, surprised by how much better she felt. She considered Karolyn's last comment. *I know Rich is different...I feel secure and confident working alongside him, exactly like I said I wanted. So what's the problem?*

She turned on her side, suddenly engulfed by exhaustion. But as she pictured herself sitting with Rich, immersed in a raw, honest, intimate conversation like she and Karolyn just shared, sleep did not come quickly.

Somewhere north of four a.m., Teri sprang upright, shaking off a dream-soaked image of Arthur wielding a handgun. A dark, ironic premonition popped into her head.

Maybe all that anxiety about having a talk with Rich is moot.

35

Wednesday, 6:30 a.m.

The marine layer, backlit by early-morning sun, was thick enough to create a kind of glowing mist that drifted over Mac and Al as they waited inside the seldom-used west gate. Mary, now in uniform, stepped out of the guard kiosk to meet Rich and Porter as they drove up in Porter's Ford Focus rental. She handed Rich his badge and walked around to the driver's side, giving Porter his badge along with a hug.

Porter said, "Great idea, using this gate. Thanks for meeting us."

"Sure thing, hon. Hugh told me to hand-pick my crew and said he'll make the official announcement later today…after he has a chance to tell del Balso I'm his new boss."

Porter grinned. "I'd sure like to see Tony's face when he does."

"Yeah—should be priceless." Mary pointed to her right, directing them to park near the kiosk. She noticed Porter's expression when he saw the enormous officer standing inside. "Don't worry, my friend. That's Dennis. We call him 'Meat,' and he's on our side."

Rich and Porter hauled Will out of the back seat, steadying him as he moved stiffly, the result of spending the night bound to a chair in Porter's motel room. Will had never been on Mary's good list, and she regarded him with a cynical smile. "Wow, Sweet Pea, you look like you had a rough night." Crandall would've cursed at her, only he knew the penalty would involve pain.

The five men climbed into Al's Cushman, with Will sandwiched uncomfortably in the rear seat between Rich and Porter, his hands still bound but hidden from view behind his back. Mac rode up front with Al.

They entered the flight ramp from the west end, driving past two other planes being readied for delivery: American Airlines Ship 916, and Ship 914, LazerAir, a South American airline. The planes had crews working frenetically, with 914 doing engine run-ups, making it nearly impossible to hear anything. There was so much activity on the ramp that no one paid them any attention.

When they reached the Tailia plane, it was bustling as well. Two mechanics climbed the airstairs carrying electrical components and disappeared through the passenger door. Toward the nose, a mechanic holding a toolbox was standing on a Marklift platform raised about eight feet, level with the forward cargo compartment. The cargo door was open. Al stepped out of the cart and whistled to the mechanic to come down.

Will started to squirm. "What are we doing here? I already told you what I know." Attempting to stand, he raised his voice. "You can't do this to me—I'm an executive, goddamnit!"

Porter cuffed the back of Will's head. "Sit down and shut it, pretty boy, or I'll quit being nice."

The mechanic stepped off the lift, setting down his toolbox.

"Hi, Al. I'm all finished…Hey, did he just smack that guy? Are his hands tied behind him?"

Al didn't miss a beat, speaking in a serious, hush-hush tone. "The guy with the Marine buzz-cut? He's McNeil's special security auditor from Corporate HQ."

Porter nodded.

"And on the right is Mr. Richmond—VP of Quality."

The mechanic waved tentatively at Rich.

"We're doing a security training exercise with that guy in the middle…It's confidential. Direct orders from Mr. McNeil."

"Oh, I gotcha. You need the lift?"

"Yeah, just for a few minutes."

"No problem." He looked at Rich. "Mr. Richmond, want me to tell the guys to stay outta the cargo compartment till you're done?"

Rich put his thumb up, saying, "Greatly appreciated!"

As the mechanic walked away, Rich turned to Al, slapping his shoulder. "Nice save. I'll take Will up on the lift. Mac, why don't you take the stairs and go through the main cabin? We'll meet in the cargo bay."

Al added, "Good idea. Don't want to overload this piece of junk. After you go up, I'll bring it back down with the base controls, and pray the hydraulics don't crap out."

Porter said, "Rich, I'll go up with Mac and wait inside the passenger door, just in case del Balso or Herrera shows up and tries to start shit."

"Good thinking, thanks."

As Rich and Al moved Crandall onto the Marklift, Will's expression was reminiscent of a condemned man being escorted to the gallows.

Al grinned. "Don't worry, Crandall. It's just like Disneyland."

* * *

The three men stood next to del Balso's Explorer, staked out behind the north side of a storage shed just inside the east gate. At the far corner, LJ Vale stared through the chain links of the east perimeter fence, searching anxiously past the endless rows of vehicles in the stadium-sized parking lot. Herrera stood at the opposite corner, watching for McKinley or Richmond coming from Final Assembly. Tony shifted from one foot to the other, annoying Herrera.

"Damn it, del Balso, can't you stand still?"

Tony said nothing, but LJ whined, "Where are Reiss and Davis? I heard Bordon is one mean mutherf—"

Herrera cut him off. "Don't be such a wimp, Vale. Three of us can take him."

This prompted a response from del Balso. "Hold on, Felix. I ain't getting involved in no fight. I got my guys on the look-out for his Lumina, but that's all I can do."

"Listen up, Tony, you weak-ass turd, we do whatever's needed to keep Richmond and McKinley away from Crandall. And that includes kicking Bordon's ass when he shows."

Before Tony could reply, a grimy Camaro came roaring through the lot and skidded to a stop, illegally parking on the end of an aisle. Reiss and Davis got out, grinning.

Vale waved to them with a relieved expression as Tony came out from behind the shed and jogged over to the guard in the gate kiosk. Del Balso took two "Special Visitor" badges from the counter, handing them to Reiss and Davis, while giving the officer his "I'm in charge" look. They walked back to join Herrera and Vale.

Reiss asked, "You really paying us a grand to beat someone up?"

Herrera nodded, and Davis high-fived Reiss. "Fuckin'-A!"

Playing with his badge, Reiss asked, "So, where are they?"

Herrera answered. "They aren't here yet, moron. We got here first so we can jump 'em when they show."

As Reiss gave Herrera a dirty look, Tony added, "Richmond's message said seven-fifteen, and it ain't even seven yet."

Herrera explained the plan to deal with Bordon and Crandall or Richmond and McKinley, depending on who showed up first.

Del Balso was trying to think of a good excuse to leave when he heard the squawk of the radio on the front seat of his Explorer.

"Control Center to Chief. What's your '20'?"

Tony stepped to the Explorer and picked up the walkie-talkie. "Chief, here. Final Assembly, east gate," his tone full of self-importance.

"Chief, possible 10-66...flight ramp. Request 10-21—code 2."

"10-4, Control."

Herrera asked, "What's up?"

"Suspicious person on the ramp. I have to call in to control—priority."

Tony started to jog back to the gate kiosk and Herrera said, "I'm coming with you!"

At the kiosk, Tony grabbed the phone and dialed the Control Center. *Now I can get the hell away from these idiots.*

Herrera elbowed Tony, turning the handset sideways so he could listen, and said, "Not that I don't trust you, but Arthur put me in charge."

They heard the Control Center officer. "Chief, you know anything about some security exercise on 913? Ramp camera picked up three guys who don't look like they belong there. I called the ramp foreman and he said a mechanic working 913 told him there was a security thing being run by Richmond, the VP...thought we should check with you."

As soon as Herrera heard *913* and *Richmond*, he put two and two together. "Shit! We've been set up!"

Del Balso gave him a blank look. "What?"

Herrera yanked Tony out of the kiosk, shoving him roughly, and shouted, "Let's go!"

As they jogged back to the shed and del Balso's Explorer, Herrera screamed at Reiss, Davis, and Vale, "Nobody's coming here—Those bastards tricked us! They're on 913, and we gotta stop 'em! Everybody in!"

* * *

They sped past Final Assembly and into the tunnel under the boulevard. Tony switched on the light bar and toggled the siren, screaming at the office employees to get out of the road. "Move, you useless cube-rats!"

The Explorer shot out the west end of the tunnel and onto the main access road. They accelerated toward the flight ramp, nearly colliding with Darren Duke's black Cadillac, as it came barreling toward them from the right. They drove side by side, with Duke bouncing in his seat, gesticulating wildly.

Both vehicles screeched to a halt next to 913 just in time to see Will Crandall, eight feet in the air, being pulled from the Marklift platform through the cargo door.

Several things happened at once.

Duke extracted himself from his Cadillac with surprising speed, blustering, and shouting, "Crandall! Sonofabitch, I was right! My guys saw you in a cart heading over here! What the fuck are you doing on my plane? Get down here, you pencil-dick!"

Duke pushed past Al, who was at the base controls lowering the lift, and clambered onto the platform. It bounced emphatically before coming to rest at the bottom position. Darren stomped the foot pedal and jammed the control lever all the way forward.

Al said, "Hey, go slow, you're too heavy!"

"Fuck that!"

Al watched with an amused smile as the lift shuddered and groaned.

Herrera, Davis, and Reiss piled out of the Explorer.

"They must be inside!" Herrera shouted, as he raced up the airstairs with Davis and Reiss right behind. Vale followed, in no particular hurry.

Herrera was first to the top, launching himself through the open passenger door. He rebounded like a racquetball slammed off the wall when Porter's fist rammed his chest. A loud *ugh* escaped Herrera's mouth as he staggered backward across the top platform, attempting to recover his balance.

Unsuccessful, Herrera gasped and slipped down the top stair, knocking Davis into Reiss, and the three of them slid and stumbled down all seventeen metal stairs, ending up on the ground in a heap at Vale's feet. Hearing the commotion, Mac and Rich joined Porter at the passenger door, glaring down at the three men lying on the concrete, moaning.

Mac said, "Nice move, Porter. Herrera looks good like that."

Porter turned to them with a questioning expression, and Mac answered with a grin, "Don't worry about Crandall. Tied him to a cargo rail—He's not going anywhere."

An ear-splitting *shriek*-grinding-*hiss* snapped everyone's attention to the nose of the plane, where the Marklift shook violently, plunged six-feet, and flung Duke over the platform railing, like a dog shaking off water. Once again commanding an audience, Duke shouted, "Aww, shit!" looking rather like a pig attempting a high-jump, and ending with a butt-plant on the concrete.

Mary arrived in another Explorer, lights flashing, just in time to see Duke stick his landing. She and her crew, including Meat, got out and approached Herrera and company.

Tony, still sitting in his Explorer, gunned the engine, made a U-turn, and left the scene, tires squealing. Rich, Porter, and Mac descended the stairs as some crew members who'd been working inside, gathered at the passenger door to gawk.

Meat and two other officers untangled Herrera, Reiss, and Davis, lifting them to their feet.

Pointing at Bordon, Herrera whined, "He broke my leg! And he's trespassing—arrest his ass!"

Meat yanked Herrera's hands behind him and used a zip-tie to bind his wrists as Mary said, "Shut up, Felix. You can see the nurse while we're writing up your termination papers."

Herrera snarled, "Termination—what? Who died and put you in charge, bitch?"

"That would be Hugh McNeil. I assume you've heard of him—and he isn't dead—He appointed me Acting Security Chief this morning." She turned to Rich, Mac, and Al. "And these gentlemen were nice enough to provide copies of work orders with falsified codes, for *sabotage*, that have you and your crew's names all over them!"

LJ Vale was sobbing as his hands were tied behind him. "I didn't do nothin'! I wasn't part of this."

Mary turned to him. "Nice try, Sweet Pea, but your name's on them too." She turned back to Meat. "Call the OC Sheriffs, and ask them to come get these morons."

Davis spat, "Hey, I got a Special Visitor badge, so why don't you blow me?" Meat smacked the side of his head, and yanked Davis's hands behind his back. Reiss chose to remain silent.

Mary addressed the pair. "Did either of you two boneheads bother to look at your discharge packet? No? Well, there was a copy of a letter notifying the Sheriff's office that you're banned from the premises…which means you two just committed criminal trespass, and *that* is a violation of the probation you received for property damage. So I'll redeem your visitor badges for two special 'go to jail' cards!"

As Meat called the Control Center, they heard groaning epithets from underneath the plane. Attempting to stand up, Duke wobbled and fell to his knees, then back on his butt, where he now sat, cursing and whining.

"For chrissake, somebody help me! Can't you see I'm hurt here? I think my leg is broke! What's wrong with you idiots? I'm a VP!"

Mary looked at the four of them, grinning from ear to ear. "Whaddya think, fellas? Paramedics or just the Marklift repair guy?"

* * *

Tony slammed to a stop at the ramp foreman's office and jumped out. After two minutes of pacing in circles mumbling to himself, he grabbed the phone on the desk.

"Boss, you ain't gonna believe this!" In a panicked voice, del Balso told Arthur how he'd discovered they'd been duped and rushed everyone to 913 to find Crandall being taken into the plane. He recapped the ensuing chaos, adding, "I knew it was a set-up, boss, but Felix don't never listen."

Tony turned and squinted back at 913, describing what he could see of Herrera, Reiss, Davis, and Vale being restrained. He'd just finished sharing his surprise at Mary being in uniform and apparently in charge, when a paramedic ambulance rushed by, which he figured was called for Duke.

When del Balso hung up the phone, shaking, the foreman at the desk said, "Man, I feel sorry for you. Your boss sounds *seriously* pissed."

Tony got back in his Explorer and drove toward the executive tower to wait at the pick-up point Arthur had just screamed at him. Even if he had to wait all day, he wasn't going to leave his Explorer until Arthur showed. *No more mistakes.*

* * *

Arthur bashed the handset into the base so hard it bounced out. This couldn't be happening. Not now, when it could upend his ideal escape scenario. Frantic, he recomputed how he could have been so wrong in his assessment of last night. He quickly deduced that the phone call Rich made must have been deliberate.

I can't believe Richmond would think of that. How could this group of amateurs turn the game on me?

Suddenly jumpy from a jolt of adrenaline, Arthur sensed he might be panicking for a second time. This did not happen to him. He stood, proclaiming out loud to his empty office, "I am in control. My contingency plan is perfect."

But his thoughts were scattered, and he noticed his hands shaking again. He forced himself to breathe and assess the scenario deviations since yesterday. Reconstructing the most likely turn of events, he was pleasantly surprised to hear a whispering voice helping him work things out.

If that phone call was a set-up, they must know about the phone tap. But how did they *know about 913?*

Arthur paused, thinking of something he must have missed, and responded audibly to his new whispering partner.

"Did Richmond get the report? No, wait—it's Will! They weren't looking for him...He was *with* them! That's why he didn't return my page! The little chicken-shit must've turned traitor—Damn him! So, how much did he tell them? And was Hugh playing me yesterday afternoon? Did Crandall talk to him too, or was it the double-trouble twins?"

He heard his partner reply with timely insight.

The eight a.m. meeting...It could be a trap!

Arthur replied, "Yes, it could be...That's why Karolyn told Julia she had to go early to set up! Well, I'm sure as hell not going in there to find out. I need to stay out of sight until my escape flight is ready."

He cursed. Then his usual flash of brilliance came to him to use the 913 debacle to his advantage.

Arthur realized how much he liked this new partner when he heard, *You are a genius.* Smiling, he said, "Thank you, I know," and then hit the intercom button. "Julia, get in here and bring your pad."

Arthur dictated what she should say, adding, "Repeat that to them, verbatim."

She tilted her head. "Sorry?"

"At exactly seven fifty-nine, march into the Board Room, get everyone's attention, and read what you just took down—word for word! Now go!"

Arthur shook his head, resuming his analysis.

He admitted that things were indeed deteriorating rapidly, but facing the collapse of a PEP so painstakingly orchestrated was beyond his experience. He began considering alternatives, but quickly brought himself up short; revising scenarios was no longer viable.

All that mattered was effecting a clean exit. Julia delivering his cover story would buy him time, but if they knew enough to sidestep the Due Diligence deceit, the chaos and diversion it was designed to create would disappear along with it. If that happened, there could be more trouble. Time to engage Plan B.

He opened his case, unzipped the secure pouch, and removed the Ruger. As he placed it deliberately on his desk, the voice whispered, *Ahhh...*

36

To say the McNev Board Room was once again defined by tension would be worthy of an award for Understatement of the Year. Teri and Karolyn sat opposite McNeil, with Winton to their left at the head of the massive conference table. Philip sat at the far end to avoid any appearance of collaboration. Zhou Quon sat next to him, giving Winton the evil eye.

McNev VPs, corporate counsel, and key staff from both teams of TaiChin filled in the sides. Conspicuously absent were Rich Richmond, Darren Duke, Will Crandall, and Arthur O'Donnell.

At 7:59 a.m., a knock on the door provided a welcome interruption to the mood that matched the dreary gray outside the wall of windows. Julia entered and approached the head of the table in a manner that compelled attention, then turned to address the room.

"Please excuse the interruption. Mr. O'Donnell asked me to inform you that a serious accident occurred a short while ago on the flight ramp. Mr. Duke will not be able to join you, as he had to be transported to the hospital."

A couple of attendees gasped. Karolyn and Teri glanced sideways at each other. Winton stood, speaking melodramatically. "How is he? Will he be all right?"

It was obvious to Teri that his reaction was driven more by a desire for attention from Julia than concern for Duke.

Julia continued. "Mr. O'Donnell was informed that Mr. Duke fell from a lift, but as yet has no further details." This was followed by whispering, and Jackson moving close enough to Julia to peer over her shoulder as if he could read shorthand.

"Mr. Crandall was also involved, and although his status is unclear, he will not be available until later. Mr. O'Donnell sends his regrets and asks that you proceed without him while he attends to the situation. He will join you as soon as he is able."

A McNev Operations exec asked, "How about Rich Richmond?"

Looking confused, Julia stammered, "I...I don't know."

Jackson quickly put his arm around her and said, "It's alright Julia, I'm sure he's fine." He walked her to the door, keeping her close.

McNeil stood and made his way around the head of the table to Teri and Karolyn. Jackson, who'd been wearing a sullen look since Hugh informed him of the agenda change without giving him any details, stalked back to join them.

Hugh said, "Jackson, remember, do not touch that Due Diligence Presentation icon. You're not to start anything until we finish our special briefing—"

Winton cut him off. "I'm damn uncomfortable with this whole thing, Hugh. I'm supposed to be in charge. What is it you're doing, anyway? I don't care about Richmond, but we definitely need Arthur so we can get rolling here."

He turned to Karolyn. "So why the hell are you just sitting there? Go get Arthur and bring him in—Tell him Hugh and I said to join us, immediately."

Hugh, Teri, and Karolyn looked at each other. Teri said, "I don't think…"

Karolyn stopped her. "No, it's okay. We do need him, and I'm the logical choice to go fetch him." She smiled at Teri. "I'll be fine."

Karolyn stood, addressing Winton. "Certainly, Jackson, I'll bring him right back."

Jackson nodded dismissively, and turned to Hugh. "Okay, I got this." He addressed the room in his command baritone. "Before we begin today's session, I decided to wait for Karolyn to return with Arthur, and Hugh concurs."

* * *

They waited, with the few forced conversations continuing to dwindle.

After fifteen excruciating minutes of near silence, Zhou stood and spoke in an accusatory tone that carried the length of the table. "Mr. Winton, do you have some sort of *problem* with the Due Diligence presentation you don't want us to know about? Are you in charge or not?"

Jackson hit his boiling point. Zhou had been rude to him yesterday, and seemed to be blaming him for relocating the final sessions here. He wanted to jump on the conference table, march the length of it, and kick the snide look off Zhou's face. However, he'd agreed to accommodate Hugh's so-called special briefing.

He looked to Hugh, who was gesturing by lowering his hands. He looked to his right; Teri was mouthing the words "Just wait."

That pissed him off. *She's obviously in the loop with McNeil…the pushy suck-up. How can she be apprised of the plan and I'm not, when I'm in charge?*

Time to bring forth his true executive leadership. *Screw this. I'm not letting a pissant like Zhou question my position.*

He stood, and without hesitating, addressed Zhou, intentionally transposing his surname. "All right, Mr. *Quon*, we'll get started. I'm sure Arthur will be right here. So, before we get to the main presentation, we have a special briefing requested by our Chairman, Hugh McNeil."

* * *

Before Hugh or Teri could stop him, Winton snapped his fingers at the AV technician in the corner. The curtains drew closed over the windows automatically, as the screen lowered to show side-by-side projected images. On the left was a photo that Porter had taken of Arthur standing on his balcony, talking on his phone. On the right was a TaiChin badge photo of Zhou Quon.

Over the murmurs in the room, an audio tape played through the ceiling speakers: a recorded phone conversation between O'Donnell and Zhou, courtesy of a bug planted in Zhou's hotel phone by his own security staff, in the persons of Wang and Li.

"I got your page. You'd better have good news to report."

"I'll get straight to the point. I need all my money up front."

"Screw you—no way. You get it after the take-down."

"Listen Mr. Zhou, if you want this completed, the total will be wired to my numbered account, no later than eight o'clock Wednesday morning. When Winton torpedoed the Hong Kong scenario, I had to completely re-orchestrate..."

As the recording reached, "...yes, it was that imperious bitch, Teri Harlan, joining forces with my slut assistant, who apparently thinks she's grown balls...," there were more gasps, and all eyes turned to Teri, sitting next to Karolyn's empty chair.

Her decision was instantaneous. She stood and excused herself, appearing upset by Arthur's words. But as soon as she shut the conference room door behind her, she ran toward Arthur's office to help her friend, spurred on by the fear of what she might find.

The recording continued in the Board Room, which looked like the setting of a surreal tennis match. Heads turned back to Zhou as Arthur's voice described the set-up to implicate McNeil and Winton in embezzlement. When the recording ended after Arthur spoke of Quon's "surprise" and charging ten percent extra, every eye was focused on Zhou.

Philip stood. "I feel your disgrace on behalf of all of us in TaiChin, but the shame must fall on you, Mr. Zhou."

Zhou sat rigid with an aloof expression while no one, including himself, said a word. Winton stood, and as his temper overrode his utter confusion, he broke the silence from the head of the table. "*Well*, Mr. Zhou? Nothing to say?"

Zhou snapped out of his stupor, as though his power switch had reset. He sprang to his feet, shouting, "Lies! All lies! O'Donnell is setting me up! I will not sit here and listen to this slander!"

Zhou bolted for the door, threw it open, and ran directly into a brick wall—otherwise known as Wang—who'd been waiting quietly in the hallway.

* * *

Rich, Mac, and Porter reentered the Tailia plane, leaving Al outside to keep an eye on things. They climbed through the access door in the main cabin floor, down the ladder into the cargo compartment. Will remained secured to a tie-down rail, struggling in vain against his restraints.

"What happened out there? Why did you leave me tied up? You guys are such jerk-offs."

Porter simply held up his hand, stifling Will's protest.

Rich said, "Look, Will, we know you authorized a special installation on the cargo door-lock. We have the work order and parts list, so now it's time you showed us your handiwork."

Mac added, "Including how you used the obsolete E-1101 plug."

Will took a lot of pride in his design, adapting an old connector in a modified circuit to add a reversing motor to the vent-door, hijacking the failsafe design. He imagined the Skytel receiving a page during flight, engaging the motor to open the vent at cruising altitude and depressurize the cargo compartment. By his calculations, within minutes the collapse of the cabin floor would execute a perfect re-creation of the Everett Tri-jet disaster.

Will managed to suppress his inherent smirk reflex, and stood silently, bracing himself. *I'm sure as hell not giving them the satisfaction of confessing.*

Mac took an electric screwdriver from his kit, and after removing four screws, lifted off the twelve-inch square door panel. He pulled the mechanism forward, exposing the entire circuit. It was the standard installation for the door-lock and failsafe vent-door, completely untouched.

Will stared in disbelief. *What the hell? Where did it go? My guardian angel must've taken it.* It took every ounce of his self-control to stifle a grin.

Rich said, "I don't see anything out of the ordinary here."

Mac pointed the screwdriver at Will's chin. "What are you playing at, Crandall?"

Porter grabbed the back of Will's neck.

* * *

"Julia, is Karolyn in there?" Teri spoke midstride as she passed her desk and reached Arthur's door.

Julia looked up and shrugged. As Teri grabbed the doorknob, Julia blurted, "Wait—"

Teri ignored her. She rapped her knuckles on the door, and without waiting for a response, opened it.

She stopped abruptly and stood motionless, focused on the glint from the barrel of the revolver in Arthur's hand. It was pointed at her midsection.

"Ah, Teri, we've been waiting for you. Come in, won't you?"

He gestured, waving the weapon toward the table. "Have a seat and lock the door…please."

Teri complied, but her shock at the handgun was dwarfed by the sight of Karolyn. She stood against Arthur with her hand resting intimately on his shoulder while his arm encircled her waist. He gave Teri a Cheshire-cat grin that made him look unhinged.

"I think little Miss Teri is at a loss."

Karolyn said, "Sorry, kiddo."

Teri stared at Karolyn with her mouth agape and her mind racing, sidetracked by sudden fury.

Arthur regarded Karolyn with the expression of a master who's pleased with his apprentice. "Karolyn came to her senses and realized which side she belongs on. She's just told me everything, including your little soiree with Will last night, and the ambush waiting for me in the Board Room. I'm almost sorry I missed it. I think I might have enjoyed seeing the expression on Quon's face. Did it go well?"

Teri didn't answer.

He shook his head with a small smile. "I'll assume it did. Hugh deserves credit for the misdirection. He nearly got me, but you and the rest of your little crew were running on pure luck…and it's run out."

Teri continued staring at Karolyn, furious at herself for the tear leaking down her cheek. "Karolyn, how could you? After everything we've been through."

Karolyn answered with detached coolness. "I understand things better now that Arthur explained it. It's really *your* fault we're in this mess. If you'd left well enough alone, everything would've been fine. Arthur never intended to harm anyone, and this company needs to be put out of its misery. He was going to share everything with me—enough money to do whatever I wanted—until you messed it up…He just gave me a second chance, and I took it."

A wave of nausea rendered Teri speechless.

Arthur nodded at Karolyn. "KB, grab that cord in my case and tie Teri's hands behind her back. We don't want her trying to be heroic."

Teri didn't resist as Karolyn tied her hands behind her back. She focused on trying to keep her wrists slightly apart like she'd seen in the movies, silently hoping it might actually work.

Thinking there was a chance to reach some bit of decency left in Arthur, she said, "Arthur, please stop this. I know you don't want people to get hurt."

Disdain flooded his tone. "That's right, I don't. But as Karolyn pointed out, it's your fault it has to be this way."

"I just wanted to help, that's all."

Arthur's reaction was one part sarcastic smile and two parts twisted sneer. "You just wanted to *help?* You think you're so damn smart, so superior. I understand rejecting Winton, but when Karolyn told me she had to *rescue* you from Will? Please! Save you from what—a good time? You're the epitome of self-righteousness."

He continued with escalating timbre. "And to think at one point I actually considered you to be special enough for me. But no, you chose Richmond! Another pathetic…"

Color filled Teri's cheeks, as anger overtook her dismay.

Her voice grew strong. "Rich, pathetic? You're the pathetic one! Totally convinced your every action is justified while you manipulate everyone with your deceptive schemes—I don't know how you fooled Karolyn, but you, Zhou, and your deviant little minion, Crandall, are all criminals, any way you slice it! And the fact you don't see it makes you fucking insane in my book!"

Arthur pushed out of his chair aggressively, raising the Ruger above his head and coming around his desk toward her. Rage turned his eyes to coal, and his words were menacing.

"Okay—now you're making me…"

In a flash, Karolyn darted around the other side of his desk and caught Arthur's arm. "No, Arthur—wait!"

She smiled alluringly at him. "I want her…and she wants me. Let's bring her with…the three of us on your island. Doesn't that sound good?"

He stopped, then lowered the Ruger and studied Karolyn.

Teri sat unmoving and silent, stunned for what seemed like the tenth time in as many minutes by what Karolyn said. She contemplated the trade-offs of getting pistol-whipped, shot, or going wherever they were headed, doing God knows what.

Arthur looked back and forth between Teri and Karolyn for several seconds. Slowly, a knowing smile turned up the corners of his mouth. He said, "Oh, I see. Well, *that* certainly explains a lot."

Still smirking, he addressed Karolyn. "All right, KB, we'll take her. But she's on a short leash, and I expect you to train her."

He looked at Teri again. She watched his smirk turning to a demented grin. "You're lucky she decided you'd make a good pet…but you won't be so smug after we housebreak you."

Arthur sat down next to her, grabbing a sheet of paper. "I just need to leave a note for Hugh."

Leave a note? He's totally lost it. Teri forced herself not to surrender to the insanity of the moment, concentrating on the cord around her wrists.

He finished writing and stood.

"Time to go, girls. And Teri, don't think just because Karolyn seems to be fond of you that we're gonna untie you."

The three of them walked across the executive suite to the elevators. Arthur carried his valise in his left hand, following Teri close enough to conceal her bound wrists, while his right hand pressed the Ruger's barrel against the small of her back.

For a moment, Teri wondered what might be happening in the Board Room, but quickly refocused on how she might get away from Arthur, whose behavior appeared to be fast approaching the border into the realm of the deranged.

He spoke casually over his shoulder. "We're leaving, Julia."

Julia answered without looking up. "Okay, bye."

They emerged from the tower rear exit to find del Balso waiting for them with his Explorer idling. Arthur opened the front passenger door, roughly shoving Teri in and pushing her skirt askew. As Arthur and Karolyn climbed in the back, Teri sat in escalating misery with her hands behind her, unable to even straighten her skirt. Tony gawked at her, seemingly hypnotized, until Arthur leaned forward over the seat next to del Balso's ear, and snapped, "Damn it, Tony, stop ogling her—She's a lesbian. Get us to the flight ramp!"

* * *

Although Rich enjoyed driving the Cushman carts, he wasn't smiling as he sat next to Porter, who was keeping his eye on Will in the back seat. Rich was lost in thought, trying to work out what could've happened to Crandall's "special" cargo door-lock assembly.

Inside the cargo compartment of 913, Porter had grabbed Will's neck hard enough to make him scream, but Will continued to plead innocence, swearing on his mother's grave that the entire plan was between Arthur and Zhou and he'd only signed the work order. No one believed him, and although Porter volunteered to take Will somewhere quiet and find some "tools of persuasion," they decided that doing their own investigating was the better alternative.

Mac and Al examined 913's ship's record in the foreman's office which showed the work order for Will's custom door-lock assembly as a completed installation. Yet the standard door-lock and failsafe mechanism they'd just seen had been successfully tested last night.

Rich knew the frenetic nature of work on the flight ramp often meant fixes authorized verbally, with a paper trail that could take days after delivery to catch up. Their hope was that someone on second or third shift last night identified Crandall's modification as problematic and ordered the mechanism replaced, discarding the Frankensteinian creation.

Rich turned right on the main road toward the executive tower where he and Porter were to meet their four allies in Winton's conference room. His thoughts drifted to the outcome of the morning meeting, picturing Teri, Karolyn, Hugh, and Philip, all smiles, as O'Donnell and Zhou were escorted from the front entrance into police custody.

That satisfying image was just starting to make him feel better when he looked to his left and saw a security Explorer speeding in the opposite direction toward the flight ramp. He recognized Teri in the front seat as soon as he saw the flash of chestnut hair.

Rich turned the cart around so fast it lifted the two wheels on the passenger side off the ground. Will rolled in the back seat, shouting, "Hey! What the—" and tumbled out onto the pavement. Porter grabbed the frame to hold himself in.

"Whoa, Rich, whaddaya doin'? We just lost Crandall!"

"Screw him! I saw Teri in that Explorer, and there were two people in the rear seat. I think one of them could be Karolyn and the other was O'Donnell!"

"Holy shit! Put your foot in it, man!"

They got to the far end of the ramp in time to see Arthur, Teri, and Karolyn climbing the airstairs of LazerAir 914, halfway to the passenger door.

Teri was in the lead, with Arthur pressing up against her, while Karolyn brought up the rear. Porter jumped out before Rich stopped the cart, and ran for the stairs, shouting, "O'Donnell, you no good sonofabitch—stop!"

Porter reached the bottom of the stairs, cursing at himself for leaving his Glock locked in the rental car's trunk. He shouted again. "I said stop—let them go!"

As all three turned toward Porter, Karolyn yelled, "Now, Teri!"—yanking Arthur's arm, and slapping the Ruger from his hand.

Teri had worked the cord lose enough to slip one hand free, and didn't hesitate. She shoved past Arthur as he whirled around, screaming, "You bitch!" back-handing Karolyn, and knocking her against the railing. Teri took two stairs at a time, thanks to her low heels, and jumped to the ground. She sprinted to Rich who was running toward her from the cart, and he pulled Teri into his arms.

"Gotcha."

He took her hand, shouted, "Let's go!" and shielded her as they ran for cover behind the Cushman. They knelt down and Teri leaned close, squeezing his hand. Breathing hard, she whispered, "Thank you."

Karolyn recovered quickly and following Teri's lead, bolted down the stairs. Porter caught her arm, swinging her to the concrete.

He shouted, "Go—run!"

Porter started climbing again but Arthur had already spotted his Ruger two stairs below and bent down to retrieve it. Porter knew instantly that the odds were against him scaling the ten stairs between them before O'Donnell could get a shot off. He could either sprint up, trying to take Arthur down, or change direction and attempt to shield Karolyn. His choice was easy.

He turned, jumped three stairs, and vaulted. He landed a few yards behind her and ran.

* * *

Arthur grasped the stair rail and pulled himself upright.

I can't believe I let myself get conned again.

He concentrated on slowing his breathing as he raised the revolver. A thrill rushed through him, like a superhero donning a cape, suddenly aware that he'd ascended to a new level of power and control.

In practice sessions, he'd never mastered the skill of leading his target, but now he was seeing the world in slow-motion, and Karolyn was running directly away from him. His lips curled into a triumphant sneer as he used both hands to align the Ruger's front and rear sights on the bounding waves of opulent blonde hair. He concentrated on the smooth steady pressure of his trigger finger.

* * *

Porter chanced a quick glance behind him, able to see the deranged expression on Arthur's face as clearly as if he'd had telephoto vision. He sprinted, grateful for the Doc Martens he'd been wearing since retiring his boots for the Hong Kong trip, and quickly closed the remaining distance between himself and Karolyn.

The Ruger fired with an air-splitting *crack!*

Porter leapt, silently praying his timing was right.

The round that was aimed true for the back of Karolyn's head, instead found its mark a quarter-inch inside Porter's right shoulder blade. They fell together onto the concrete next to the cart.

Teri screamed, "No!" and jumped up to help them. Karolyn pulled herself into a sitting position and held Porter's head. She spoke softly. "Breathe...good...keep breathing..."

As Teri knelt beside them, taking off her jacket to elevate Porter's head, Rich raced to the Explorer where del Balso sat behind the wheel in a daze. He threw open the driver's door and yanked Tony out, shouting in his face.

"Do your job, asshole! For once in your miserable career, do some good—Get that sonofabitch!"

Rich grabbed the radio off the front seat. He squeezed the Push-To-Talk key and yelled, "Control Center! We need paramedics on the west end of the flight ramp, right now! A man's been shot—Get Mary, and hurry!"

Del Balso came to life, as if Rich's words shook him from a years-long stupor. He ran to the airstairs, drawing the .38 Special from his holster, and shouted, "Arthur! Get out here! I'm takin' in your sorry ass!"

Tony climbed surprisingly fast, passing the halfway point of the stairs when Arthur appeared in the passenger doorway. Again Arthur assumed a flawless shooting stance, aiming his Ruger with both hands.

His twisted smirk became a maniacal grin as he said, "You're fired," but his words were lost in the earsplitting *cracks* of his revolver discharging two rounds.

Either from misplaced trust that Arthur wouldn't actually shoot him, or lack of competence in a life-or-death dilemma, Tony neither fired his weapon nor attempted evasion. He simply absorbed the deadly wounds to his chest and abdomen with a bewildered expression, staggered backward and fell over the stair railing. He landed like a discarded rag doll on the cold concrete.

Arthur nonchalantly reentered the plane and sealed the door.

37

12:05 p.m.

Sitting at the table in O'Donnell's office, Hugh McNeil stared at the intricate geometric design, rubbing his finger over the tiny gold plate with *Bernhardt* engraved in fancy script.

Hate to think what we paid for this…But he does have good taste…for a psychopath.

He returned his attention to the handwritten page in front of him, reading it for the fifth time.

> *Hugh:*
>
> *Please accept this rather crude note as my official resignation, effective immediately. Misses Babcock and Harlan will also be leaving, having chosen to join me in experiencing the pleasures of independent wealth.*
>
> *I commend you on your "Legal Trap" and near-success in baiting me to capture your Queen. I applaud any punishment dispensed for Zhou. He's certainly deserving.*
>
> *I have left you with quite a mess, so I offer Crandall in my stead, on whom you may exact whatever measure of retribution you see fit.*
>
> *Regards,*
> *Arthur P. O'Donnell*
> *PS: No need to process my final paycheck.*

Hugh wadded up the note and threw it at the office wall as he noticed Mary and man in a tweed coat standing in the doorway.

Mary cleared her throat. "Hugh, sorry to bother you. This is Detective Ed Cassidy from the Orange County Criminal Investigations Bureau, here for the investigation. He was assigned earlier with Zhou's arrest, and we just finished the walk-through of the flight ramp incident, so he's got the names of everyone involved. I need to get back out there, and he needs to get a statement from you, if that's okay."

"Yes, thanks, Mary." Hugh stood, and then addressed the detective. "I think I'd feel more comfortable in the small conference room down the hall." He stooped to retrieve the paper ball on the way out.

Walking to Winton's conference room, Hugh glanced sideways at Cassidy, guessing he was fortyish, and noting his wiry build was accompanied by uncommonly long legs. He watched Cassidy step into the room and sit down in one continuous movement without the slightest waste of motion, reminiscent of a very tall cat.

Cassidy said, "Mr. McNeil, I realize this has been a tough day, but I'd like to get a rundown of the situation and your statement on the shooting incident. Would it be all right if I record it?"

Hugh nodded, thankful for the detective's easy-going manner.

Cassidy switched on his Sony micro-recorder. "Let's start with the flight ramp. Mr. O'Donnell has been identified as the shooter, but you didn't actually witness the shooting. Is that right?"

"That's correct. Mary sent an officer to find me as soon as the call came into security control. He got me out there within minutes."

"What happened at that point?"

"I saw Teri Harlan and Karolyn Babcock tending to Porter Bordon, who'd just been shot."

Cassidy said, "Right, Bordon—He's your driver and personal security. But he wasn't with you?"

"Porter has actually been working with Karolyn, Teri, Rich Richmond, and others to help uncover a fraud scheme being inflicted on us by O'Donnell and Will Crandall, along with Mr. Zhou from TaiChin…until things got out of hand."

"So why didn't you involve the police earlier?" Cassidy asked. "Especially with one of the foreign nationals involved."

"We felt we had a solid plan to expose all three in a very clear way for everyone to witness…we intended to turn them in right after…But as you know, we were only successful in delivering Mr. Zhou."

Cassidy made notes on his pad, not belaboring the obvious, as Hugh sighed and rubbed his forehead, continuing without prompting. "In retrospect, had I known Arthur would resort to violence, I would have asked the Sheriff's Department to intervene sooner. I realize I probably caused this…I…" He started to falter.

"Mr. McNeil, I'm sure you didn't intend any of it…Why don't we finish up with the events on the ramp."

"Well, the paramedics arrived and checked Chief del Balso, but sadly it was too late. They turned their attention to Porter who was having difficulty breathing, and loaded him into the ambulance, doing something to his chest…Karolyn rode with him.

"Mary and two of her officers approached the plane—LazerAir Ship 914—but the engines were already spinning up, and before they reached the airstairs, the plane taxied off the far end of the ramp to the runway. Mary contacted the tower through security control, patching me through.

"The tower ordered the takeoff aborted, but apparently O'Donnell had control of the pilots because they never responded…Fortunately, there was no other air traffic at the time. I immediately called the President of

LazerAir. The delivery flight destination is the Simón Bolívar International Airport in Venezuela, and they agreed to attempt apprehending him on arrival…but that could be problematic."

Cassidy replied with an understanding nod. "I did some training sessions with the INM in Venezuela in '89. Their law enforcement is…different down there." Consulting his notes, he added, "I'd like to get some background on Mr. O'Donnell—Anything more you can tell me?"

Hugh pulled the wad of paper from his pocket, smoothing it out on the table in front of Cassidy. "Here—this might give you an inkling."

* * *

Teri stood in the restroom, taking stock of the disarray looking back at her. Only a few hours prior she'd been putting on her make-up in the bathroom of Karolyn's condo. That optimistic visage in the mirror this morning, now seemed a distant memory.

Her top was a mess. Her skirt was stained and torn. In an attempt to take the edge off, a voice in her head spontaneously resorted to gallows humor. *Damn, this place is murder on my clothes. I should ask Hugh for a clothing allowance.*

She managed to get the dirt off of her face and brush her hair, but other than lipstick, she didn't bother with makeup repair. She walked into the executive suite, looking for Hugh, but when she glanced in O'Donnell's office it was empty. Julia, still sitting at her desk doing whatever it was she did, made the surreal situation even more so. Teri stood in O'Donnell's office doorway for a moment as the scene from this morning spun in her head, making her slightly dizzy.

As she steadied herself with her hand on the doorjamb, she heard the elevator ding. Rich emerged from the hallway and walked over to her. The three looked at each other without speaking, the only real choice for too many inexpressible emotions. To her credit, Julia was at least perceptive enough to break the strained silence.

Pointing to her left, she said, "Mr. McNeil is in Jackson's Conference Room. I think there's a policeman in there with him."

Teri and Rich walked down the hall, continuing to keep their thoughts to themselves. As they opened the door, Hugh said, "Teri and Rich, please come in. This is Detective Cassidy."

Teri shook the detective's hand. "I'd like to say nice to meet you…but under the circumstances, I'll stick with pardon my appearance."

Cassidy smiled and nodded.

Rich shook his hand and added, "I assume you've been assigned to investigate the shootings?"

Cassidy replied, "Yes, I…" His pager buzzed. He added, "Excuse me a moment," and then stood. He was out the door in a single step.

* * *

Rich and Teri walked around the table. As they sat down side by side, Rich empathetically touched her arm, which she acknowledged with a subdued smile.

Hugh said, "Thank God you two are okay. And Porter…well, that was just heroic, protecting Karolyn."

Rich and Teri nodded in unison as Hugh continued. "When I walked through the ordeal with Detective Cassidy, I found myself struggling to believe what I was saying. Fraud is one thing, but this…"

Teri said quietly, "Arthur's gone completely off the rails—I could tell as soon as I saw him…I guess none of us really had any way of knowing. But Karolyn was amazing."

The door opened, and Detective Cassidy stuck his head in. "Sorry, I've got to meet with Mary. But Ms. Harlan and Mr. Richmond, I do need to speak with you both. I'll be back as soon as I can." He shut the door.

"He's not only tall, he's also a quick study," Teri quipped.

Hugh smiled. "He was assigned to the case earlier…I guess he interviewed Zhou. Anyway, Mary briefed him on the flight ramp shootings, so I think that's how he knows your names." With a sympathetic smile toward Teri, he added, "So you were saying about Karolyn—are you up to telling us what happened in Arthur's office?"

Teri gave them an executive summary of the events leading up to the flight ramp, omitting Karolyn's words she couldn't let go of: *It's your fault we're in this mess.*

When Teri indicated she was finished by looking down at the table and not speaking, Rich gave her hand a quick squeeze and perceptively changed the subject. He engaged Hugh with the likely disposition of Will's cargo door-lock mechanism.

"I'm almost positive someone realized it wasn't normal and had it replaced, so Mac and Al just need to track it down."

"Any idea what Will's modification was supposed to do?"

Rich shifted uncomfortably. "Possibly sabotage of some kind…but fortunately, it can't do any harm sitting in a bin somewhere. Mary had an officer escort Will to Medical Services, so he can be questioned again as soon as he's done."

Hugh nodded. "Ah, yes. I'm quite sure he's busy building a major case of feeling sorry for himself." Then looking up at the clock, he asked, "Are you two hungry? The rest of the partnership team is having lunch in the Board Room with Philip. I could have Julia get us a couple of plates."

Teri had tuned out of their conversation, her thoughts remaining on Karolyn and the scene in O'Donnell's office. *I'm sure she was playing along with Arthur to give us a chance, but…God, I wish could talk to her.*

When she heard Rich say, "Ter, are you okay?" she shook her head.

"Sorry—what?"

"Hugh asked if we were hungry."

"Ugh. No, thanks. I don't think I can eat anything."

Hugh said, "I'm not really hungry, either. How about we call Sheila to see if she has a status update?"

* * *

Sheila yawned and stretched, battling the familiar sleep-deficit hangover. She'd worked through the night to complete the task she'd volunteered for in their session with Will. Using his IP address from her original project, she'd remotely accessed Arthur's PC, and then his Palmtop through the serial cable.

Fortunately, Arthur left his AOL application open, preventing his Palmtop from going to sleep, thus eliminating having to break his passcode. She copied everything from his Palmtop, plus the relevant files on his PC, to her own server, then disconnected to avoid alerting him.

After taking Lisa to the Taylor's this morning, she began examining the files to find the trail of Arthur's financial machinations, including Executive Payment Management. Sheila's love for this kind of research—part computer wizardry, part detective work, and part enigmatology—caused her to lose herself, along with all track of time.

When the ringing phone interrupted her, she was surprised to look up and find she'd been at it for nearly four hours.

"Hey, do you have a minute? I've got you on speaker. Hugh and Teri are with me."

"Hey, Rich…Yes, I've made some progress. I can share what I've found so far."

Mirroring the grim expression on Teri's face, Rich said, "Thanks, but before you get to that, I need to give you an update. It's been a rough morning here."

He recapped the mayhem, including Porter taking the bullet meant for Karolyn, Arthur's escape after shooting del Balso, and the investigation now underway.

"Oh my God, I'm so sorry—Teri, are you all right?"

"I'm hanging in there. I'm mostly worried about Porter and Karolyn."

"I sure hope he pulls through. It's good that Karolyn went with him to the hospital."

Sheila fell quiet, digesting the news until Hugh broke the silence.

"So, Sheila, you said you'd made progress. Did you find anything that might help?"

"Well, Mr. McNeil, I've uncovered a lot, but I'm afraid it's not great news. I began with Teri's theory that McNev's consistent gross profit numbers might be inflated by improperly accounting for expenses. It took time to dig through the transaction log of Arthur's remote access program—the one Beth developed for him—but eventually I found a mountain of journal entries. When I traced those entries back through the GL, sure enough, they all lined up with expense postings that were significantly less than their corresponding Journal Vouchers…they were all fraudulent journal entries he'd made to the GL to lower expenses.

"They correlate consistently to inflated operating performance on the quarterlies, which is likely how he reported decent financial results while covering his embezzlement. But I'm afraid it's going to take an accounting team with more knowledge than I have to sort out everything he did."

The frustration on Hugh's face was palpable, but he kept himself together and asked, "Were you able to find anything on EPM?"

"Amazingly, Crandall was telling the truth about EPM. I found the log entry where Arthur used his program yesterday to change the EPM ownership record in the McNev system—probably his lame attempt to implicate Crandall. But EPM is definitely his baby. EPM's accounts are on his home computer and show a balance of cash-on-hand over four-hundred thousand dollars! I'd say Teri was right on about EPM—Arthur's got quite the little sideline business."

Hugh nodded a "thank you" at Teri, as Sheila continued.

"And thanks to Karolyn, who tipped me off to search Arthur's Palmtop for the codes, *Epsilon Pro Magnum*, I found his hidden file."

Hugh's brow furrowed. "Codes? Hidden Files?"

Sheila explained, "I'm sure it doesn't come as a shock that Arthur is more than a bit obsessive…which includes a major infatuation with puzzles and ciphers. I can picture him being delighted with himself when he turned EPM into 'Epsilon Pro Magnum'…loosely translated, it means: 'nearly nothing becomes something really big.'"

"Why would he do that?" Rich asked.

Teri answered before Sheila could. "I'd guess he gets off every time he opens a file, knowing he's the only one who can break the secret code."

Rich shook his head as Sheila said, "Good guess, Ter…self-affirmation of his intellectual superiority."

Hugh interjected, "Sheila, you said these coded files were hidden?"

"Right, Mr. McNeil. For extra security, he hid the file so it wouldn't show in the directory. But knowing what to search for and changing a control setting, I found it…those codes are in an Excel workbook of his bank accounts."

This piqued everyone's interest, adding energy to Hugh's voice. "Were you able to see the accounts and balances?"

"Unfortunately, no. He secured the workbook file with a five-character password—and that's where I'm stuck at the moment, Mr. McNeil."

"Please call me Hugh. After listening to your brother, Teri, and Karolyn talk about your work, I feel like you're part of our team...and I owe you a debt of gratitude for what you've done to help."

Sheila said, "You're welcome, sir. I'm sorry I wasn't strong enough to stop Arthur three years ago, before he started all this."

Hugh said, "No apology necessary. As I told Karolyn last night, I could say the same thing about myself...but maybe we *can* put a stop to it now. Is there any chance to crack this password?"

They heard Sheila sigh. "Possibly...Like his secret-code file names, Arthur prided himself on elegantly symbolic passwords...he'd most likely use numbers for an Excel password, so we should focus on a five-digit set that's significant to him..."

Teri spoke up. "During our Hong Kong flight, Karolyn shared a few of his obsessions. I don't recall her mentioning the Epsilon Pro Magnum codes, but I do remember her describing Arthur's preoccupation with the best places to live—that he knew the most affluent zip-codes by heart...five-digit numbers: part of a set?"

"Good call, Ter! Let's try it."

They heard Sheila typing as she added, "The zip-code for Balboa Island is 92662...nope."

She went through several beachfront zips, and then pulled up a zip-code directory on her computer, entering several and continuing to say *no*. She added, "So far, the only good news is that there's no password attempt limit—thank goodness for small favors."

Rich said, "How about Emerald Bay in Laguna?"

Sheila entered 92651, but no luck.

Rich tried again. "Maybe we're thinking too local. Can you look up the wealthiest zip in the U.S.?"

"Um, yeah, just a sec..."

They listened to the clicking of Sheila's keyboard.

"Okay, here we go. It's Manhattan—go figure. Trying 10012...nope, but that was a really good guess, Rich...Hmm, let me try something. It would be just like him to use this zip but rearrange the digits...10021, nope that's the Upper East Side, 10120...nope. Let's try a palindrome—10201...Holy shit—it worked! I can see the accounts."

While Sheila took a moment to scan the spreadsheet, she could almost feel Hugh, Teri, and Rich holding their collective breath.

The first thing she spotted was Arthur's personal account. Exactly as Karolyn had said, it was labeled: *Epsilon,* and the balance made her whistle to herself: *$1,420,757.*

Next to it was his PIN hint: *Pal 1+2=6.* Sheila quickly scribbled *Epsilon, 1221 or 2112* on a sticky note. *I've spent entirely too much time inside Arthur's head.*

Per her conversation with Karolyn last night, she kept this information to herself and moved down the list to the other accounts, which she began reading aloud.

"Okay, I found several business accounts labeled, *Pro* in a numbered series...each one has a string of regular deposits. Several hundred thousand...and it looks like all those funds were recently consolidated into a numbered international offshore account in Barbados...bingo! That account name is *Magnum*! Oh my gosh, there's a *huge* wire transfer from a Chinese bank last night."

Teri exclaimed, "Zhou!"

Rich added, "And now we know where he's headed—Barbados!"

Sheila's voice jumped an octave, rattling the speaker.

"Jesus, Mary, and Joseph! The total balance is over a hundred million dollars!"

* * *

Arthur forced himself to breathe, summoning all his willpower to resist reaching for a fourth Valium. He consulted his watch again, hoping they were approaching the halfway mark, but saw they'd been in the air less than three hours.

"Dammit! Six more hours!"

From his seat in the second row, Arthur had been checking on the pilots every two minutes, having told them to leave the door to the flight deck open. However, watching them at the controls, flying the plane without issue, was absolutely no comfort to him.

The two LazerAir employees catching a ride on their company's ME-420 delivery flight had boarded earlier and ensconced themselves in coach. Shortly after takeoff, Arthur decided a walk to the rear of the plane might distract him.

When he'd pulled back the curtain separating first class, he discovered why they'd chosen to sit aft. The Sales VP was *in flagrante* with a woman Arthur guessed was his coworker, judging by the LazerAir blazer that lay among her articles of clothing and underwear strewn about aisle twenty-four. He yanked the drape closed, that being the furthest thing from his mind.

He made several attempts to occupy himself by focusing on the triumphant freedom of landing in Caracas, visualizing the relaxing luxury of the cruise to Barbados and reveling in the power of one-hundred million dollars. But his reverie was constantly breached by waves of panic-driven nausea, making it impossible to concentrate on anything.

Fortunately, the cabin noise masked the now-constant conversations he was carrying on with his whispering companion, as they were the only thing he'd found to help him fend off hysteria.

"It was unfortunate that del Balso chose such an inopportune manner to finally show some balls."

Yes, but the look on his face was amusing. And you said you were going to enjoy not missing him. At any rate, it wasn't your fault—He forced you into it. You only did what was necessary.

"True. I still can't believe I fell for Karolyn's ploy. That's so unlike me. I hope she learned her lesson...she deserved to be shot."

But you already miss her.

"Don't be ridiculous. She betrayed me...or do I?"

Don't look back. Look forward...It's what you do.

"Yes, yes, I do. And because I was smart enough to consolidate my funds into offshore accounts, I can afford the best of everything right from the start...but I'll have to get comfortable in Barbados. I'm eager to meet my new assistant. She looked stunning in her picture..."

There you go. She's picking us up at the airport in Caracas and rooming with us on our cruise. I've heard South American women are very amorous...and highly skilled.

Arthur leaned back, finally drifting off into a blissful respite, but alas, it was not to be. The instant his head rested against the seat back, his hair-trigger panic reflex delivered another savage jolt of adrenaline.

"Goddammit!"

He sat bolt upright, unnerved, dismayed, and perspiring again.

Willing himself with every fiber of his being to avoid a meltdown, he returned to staring at his Rolex Sea Dweller, counting the seconds, and considering another Valium.

38

Cassidy reentered the conference room, and Teri could tell he sensed increased energy when he asked Hugh, "Did I miss something? You seem a little more upbeat."

Hugh said, "We just received news from our computer expert who's making progress on the financial front."

The detective nodded with an expression indicating he'd like more information, but was choosing not to pursue it at the moment. "All right, I'd like to get Miss Harlan's account of what happened when she entered Mr. O'Donnell's office through the events on the flight ramp."

Teri looked down without speaking, trying to decide how to answer truthfully when it meant discussing details she had no desire to disclose, especially in front of Hugh and Rich.

Cassidy said, "Ms. Harlan, would you like to talk in here or should we use another office?"

Before she could respond, Winton threw open the door, his booming baritone at max volume. "Hugh, what the fuck is happening around here? I need a word with you, right now! You left Philip and me babysitting the TaiChin weenies in the Board Room, arguing about ramifications and formulating a plan. I'm not supposed to deal with that drivel…I'm still the President of this place, goddammit—"

Teri interjected. "Jackson, what do you think *we've* been dealing with? Arthur shot two people! One's dead, and—"

Winton turned to her with a contemptuous look, reinforced by his tone. "Don't interrupt me, Miss 'High and Mighty.' This is a leadership issue way above your paygrade!"

Rich jumped up, looking like he was about to take a swing at Winton, but Hugh stood with him, holding up his hand to Rich as he turned toward Jackson.

"Jack, I believe I *would* like that word with you in private." Looking back at the three of them he added, "Please excuse us," and followed Winton out.

Rich spoke to the door as it shut. "What a complete asshat." He turned to Teri, adding, "Porter needs to take him and Crandall to a nice quiet room and spend a few quality minutes with his friends, Wang and Li."

Cassidy shook his head. "Wow, you two certainly have some interesting coworkers."

"You have no idea," Teri replied. Rich smiled at her, and with an understanding expression, said, "Ter, go ahead with your statement. I'll go see how Mac and Al are doing."

Cassidy nodded as the door shut behind Rich. "It looks like he knows you pretty well. I'm sure talking through what happened isn't easy for you…Take your time. Start whenever you're ready."

"Well, I opened O'Donnell's office door to find a gun pointed at me, and Karolyn—You know who she is?"

Cassidy said, "Karolyn Babcock…She's Mr. O'Donnell's Executive Administrator?"

"Yes, but more importantly, she's the person responsible for me being here in one piece, rather than O'Donnell's captive on a plane to Caracas."

Teri did her best to recount the morning, unabridged. She finished with her awe of Karolyn's move to knock the gun away, the panic as she ran to Rich, and the horror when she saw Porter fall. She was proud of herself for getting through it without so much as a mascara run.

Cassidy said, "Very thorough, Ms. Harlan, thank you. You said you've been working here only a few weeks?"

Teri nodded, and asked, "Now that we're finished, would it be possible for me to join Karolyn at the hospital?"

Rather than answer her question, Cassidy consulted his notes. "I'd just like to go back over a couple things…when you entered O'Donnell's office, Ms. Babcock was standing with her hand on O'Donnell's shoulder, and his arm was around her waist…but you don't think she could be his accomplice?"

Teri sighed. "No, like I said, I believe she was misleading him, trying to buy us time. Mr. O'Donnell was becoming unstable…"

"But didn't you also say she told Mr. O'Donnell she 'wanted to make you a pet?'"

"Something like that, but…"

Cassidy interrupted, but in a way that implied he was trying to help her consider things, rather than being accusatory. "I know you said she saved you on the flight ramp, and I can tell you think the world of her. But what she said about 'everything being your fault,' and her derogatory remarks…It seems a bit inconsistent."

Teri's head and stomach were reeling. She looked at Cassidy, aware but no longer caring that her cheeks were now becoming mascara-stained to the point of being cliché. "Why don't we go ask her?"

* * *

Karolyn sat in the uncomfortable waiting-room chair, struggling with the sensation she was still holding Porter's hand, as she'd been doing from the time they'd left the flight ramp. When the paramedics arrived she and

Teri had been frantic. Porter was gasping for air between coughs of red mist, slipping in and out of consciousness.

Seeing no exit wound in Porter's chest, the senior paramedic raised his shoulders to examine the entrance wound in his back. He listened to Porter's wheeze and immediately diagnosed his condition, telling his partner, "It's a tension pneumothorax—He's not compensating."

They lifted Porter into the ambulance and Karolyn shuddered, watching the EMT insert a large-bore needle and catheter straight down into the upper left side of Porter's chest.

She heard a soft hiss as the paramedic explained, "No exit wound means the bullet is still in there...musta tore things up some...air and blood leaking into the space around his lung...Outside air from the wound causes it to collapse. I'm equalizing the pressure so he can breathe while we transport him to the trauma center at O. C. Memorial."

Karolyn scrambled in and they took off. A couple of moments after leaving the plant, Porter regained consciousness, breathing a little easier. He squeezed her hand.

The awful wail of the siren still echoed in her head, recalling the fifteen-minute ride that seemed to last an hour. She'd leaned close to hear him.

"Thanks for holding my hand...makes me feel better." He paused for a breath. "Sorry I didn't get him...but I made the right choice...no way I was gonna let that asshole hurt you."

She smiled. "I know...you had to keep your promise." A tear rolled down her cheek. Porter reached up to wipe it away and winced, swearing, "Ow, dammit!"

The EMT gently pulled his hand down and said, "Sir, you need to keep your arms at your side."

Karolyn snapped, "Porter—His name is Porter."

"Thanks...Porter, I need you to keep still now. You just hold your lady's hand and rest easy. Try to stay awake."

Porter smiled up at Karolyn. "I like that...my lady."

He was quiet for another minute, catching his breath. "Hey, don't be sad. It's okay. Got a fairly decent story for the Big Guy now, thanks to you helping me get my act together."

"Stop talking like that. You're a tough guy, remember? You're not going anywhere. We still need your help to catch that sonofabitch."

"He'll get what's coming to him—his kind always do. Just remember you're somethin' special, Karolyn Babcock...Don't forget that, ever."

His eyes closed.

The EMT said, "Talk to him. It's better if he stays conscious."

Karolyn squeezed Porter's hand and told him about her dream of moving back to Idyllwild.

"It's only a couple of hours from here, but up on the mountain it's like a whole other world. There are cabins, surrounded by the smell of pine trees on a crystal-clean breeze...and after dinner, we can lie outside, staring up at endless stars. The night sky will be our own little corner of heaven."

Porter whispered, "Sounds perfect...count me in..."

He paused again, and then whispered, "You're my angel...my redemption."

When they arrived at the hospital, a trauma surgeon and nurse were waiting as they wheeled Porter in. The exam took only minutes before the surgeon said, "We need to get him to the OR—prep for an emergency thoracotomy."

Karolyn was escorted to the surgery waiting room on the third floor, where she'd been sitting down, standing up, and pacing for two hours. She'd replayed her conversation with Porter over and over, trying to shake the empty feeling that it had been *good-bye*.

* * *

As she and Cassidy exited the elevator on floor three of O. C. Memorial, Teri continued to speculate on the detective's mindset. On the drive to the hospital, she'd tried being conversational, telling him she appreciated his decision to let her accompany him to interview Karolyn.

She'd felt comfortable with Cassidy, getting the sense he approached his job the same way she did: honest and open, with a tenacity for facts. But he'd kept his thoughts about Karolyn's involvement to himself, while Teri spent the rest of the ride overanalyzing his lack of disclosure.

By the time they arrived, she'd managed to fill her head with anxiety about his judgement of Karolyn.

They found her alone in the small surgery waiting room, looking very much like Teri. Both had long abandoned their jackets, wearing torn skirts and disheveled blouses that could have been a matched set.

As they embraced, Karolyn said, "God, I'm glad to see you! Are you all right?"

Attempting a smile, Teri replied, "I'm okay I guess...given what's happened," noticing Karolyn's questioning look when she saw Cassidy.

Unaware of how wound up she was, Teri entered rapid-fire mode.

"KB, this is Detective Cassidy from CID of Orange County—He's in charge of the investigation. He's been interviewing all of us to get our statements—I told him..."

Cassidy stopped her, putting his hand on her shoulder. "Ms. Harlan, slow down. I know you're trying to help, but I need to get Ms. Babcock's account of events without any input from you." Cassidy softened his tone, adding, "Can I count on you to sit quietly while I take her statement?"

Noting Teri's stress level, Karolyn took her hand and walked her over to a chair. "Hey, kiddo, it's okay."

Teri nodded and sat down, her slightly pink cheeks amplifying her anxious expression.

Detective Cassidy turned a chair around next to Karolyn, then took out his recorder and a notepad. He held up the recorder. "Do you mind?"

Karolyn shot a quick grin toward Teri, who was too tense to return it. Turning back to Cassidy, she said, "Not at all."

Cassidy said, "Okay, Ms. Babcock..."

"Karolyn, please."

"All right, Karolyn, why don't you just start at the beginning?"

Karolyn nodded. "Well, to really understand what happened, you need some background. A good place to start would be with what you could call the key that opened Pandora's Box. When Rich Richmond—I assume you met him—got a look at a confidential report sitting on the credenza behind my desk..."

Over the next several minutes, Karolyn recapped their odyssey in an articulate, concise fashion, including giving Teri credit for starting the "McNev Investigation Team" that got everyone working together. Teri sat listening, captivated by Karolyn's courtroom-esque testimonial explanation.

"I went to collect Mr. O'Donnell for the eight o'clock meeting where Mr. McNeil, Mr. Lin, Ms. Harlan, and I planned to expose their scheme. But when I walked into his office, he pointed his damn revolver at my chest. It scared me, but frankly, it pissed me off even more.

"As I said, he'd been acting bizarre, sort of unraveling. I knew immediately that the best approach was to make him believe he was in control, so I played the part. I've been required to act like men are in charge and I can't keep my hands off them, countless times. I'm good at it, plus I'm sure Arthur *wanted* to believe me.

"Then Teri came in. I hoped she'd realize what I was doing, but I think she may have thought I'd actually turned on her. She's not an experienced actress and I said some harsh words to her..." She turned to Teri, and with a heartfelt tone, added, "You know I didn't mean it, don't you?"

Suddenly flushed, Teri nodded, as Karolyn turned back to Cassidy.

"I couldn't let her know without O'Donnell catching on, but I tried...by leaving the rope a little loose when I tied her hands."

She glanced at Teri again, who was now looking very relieved.

As Karolyn finished with a recap of breaking free on the airstairs and Porter getting shot by a bullet meant for her, Cassidy smiled at Karolyn's straight-talk reporting.

"Thank you, Ms. Babcock—Karolyn, excellent detail. I can't think of any follow-up questions at the moment. Ms. Harlan—"

He was interrupted in mid-sentence by the surgeon opening the waiting room door. He'd changed into clean scrubs, but looked exhausted.

Karolyn knew even before he said, "I'm sorry."

She stood listening, but quickly became too numb to absorb much of what he was saying.

"The bullet ricocheted off Mr. Bordon's scapula, cracking two ribs and lacerating his right lung. We had to perform a thoracotomy. The tissue cavitation and shattered bone fragments generated by the round caused severe damage to the blood vessels feeding his lungs. He fought hard, but in the end, we just couldn't stop the bleeding…Again, I'm sorry…"

Karolyn didn't notice Teri who'd gotten up and was standing next to her. She turned, teetering as she attempted to move, seemingly unsure of where to go. Teri caught her and Cassidy helped them back to a couple of chairs.

Cassidy watched them sit, sharing their pain. The bond between them was genuine and honest, worthy of respect.

He said, "I'll give you two a minute. I'll be outside."

39

3:10 p.m.

Rich walked past the B1 hangar on the way to the flight ramp, its four-story doors open wide like a yawning mouth showing the insides of some mammoth prehistoric creature. He'd made this walk many times, but this time was outside his experience.

He thought about his irritation over the years with executive decisions, arguing over schedules, priorities, and resources. Today it all felt like trivial bullshit.

How did things go from so right a few hours ago, to this godawful mess? This isn't how things were supposed to end up.

He found Hugh and Philip standing beside 913, watching the TaiChin team members climbing the airstairs. Although the day's events tempered any celebration, a quiet enthusiasm still surrounded them as they boarded Tailia's first plane. Mac and Al rolled up in Al's Cushman just after Rich arrived.

Philip shook everyone's hand. "I cannot tell you all how grateful I am for what you've done. In spite of the tragedy and chaos, you somehow managed to have our first ship ready for her maiden flight."

Mac said, "Mr. Lin, we went over every piece of paper and test result for 913. I think she's the most thoroughly inspected plane to ever leave this ramp."

Philip said, "Thank you, Mr. McKinley and Mr. Greer. We deeply appreciate all your work." He shook everyone's hands again, smiling as he addressed Hugh. "We'll talk soon, yes?"

"Definitely, Philip. With luck, we may be able to recover a significant portion of our lost funds. We're not giving up…and I apologize for having to forego your Delivery Ceremony."

"Your friendship and all that your team has done means more than any ceremony. And please give my sincerest thanks to Ms. Harlan and Ms. Babcock…I hope Porter pulls through."

They waved as Philip climbed the stairs. The door was sealed, and the stairs were removed. Rich watched as the starter motors on the engines' turbine shafts began to rotate the blades, slowly, then gradually increasing. He couldn't stop himself from enjoying the sights, sounds, and smells of a brand-new ME-420, including the rush he got from the loud *pop* when the engines lit.

His smile widened at the roar of the GE CF-6 engines spinning up to speed, generating thrust to move more than a quarter-million pounds of aircraft onto the taxiway. In spite of everything that had happened, he still felt like a kid rushing through the main gate at Disneyland.

Mac and Al climbed back into the cart, saying they had more paper to track down before admitting defeat on finding out what happened to the modified cargo door-lock mechanism.

Al asked, "Can we give you two a lift?"

Hugh glanced at Rich and said, "No thanks, we'll walk."

As they headed back to the tower, Rich said, "I didn't see Winton."

Hugh shook his head. "No...after his performance today and the disrespect he showed Teri, you won't be seeing him here again...ever."

* * *

Teri had her arm around Karolyn who leaned sideways from the adjacent uncomfortable chair, with her head pressed into Teri's shoulder.

As Karolyn's sobbing began to slow, Teri spoke softly. "Last night, I was the one crying on your shoulder...I know my pain doesn't compare, but for what it's worth, it was an amazing transformation. From my initial impression of Porter as a professional thug who did a terrible thing to Rich, to considering him a trusted friend and partner."

She paused, embracing the silence, and then added, "You know, I had a strong sense that he was somehow meant to protect you...I think he not only ended up saving you, I believe you did the same for him."

Karolyn lifted her head. "Damn it!"

Teri sat back, startled. "What?"

"All this crying...my contact slipped off."

Karolyn pulled a small bottle of saline solution from her purse, leaning back to put a few drops in her eye, realigning the lens with a well-practiced technique. The mundane act seemed to help restore her balance. "There, that's better."

She retrieved a tissue as well, and blew her nose. She said, "Thanks, Ter. Yeah, I felt it too...he said as much to me in the ambulance. It's just so unfair. He was decent...and so real...and carrying enough of his own shit not to judge me for mine. It just pisses me off that he died because of that soulless, narcissistic freak...Even knowing PB such a short time, it feels like I lost my best friend."

Teri took Karolyn's hands. "Hey, you still have me. I'm not going anywhere."

Karolyn sat for a minute, and Teri noticed she seemed to draw on an internal reserve that strengthened her resolve.

She smiled at Teri. "You're right...and to use your words, we're stronger together. Porter told me all he wanted was a chance to do some good. He gave his life to save mine and I'm not going to see our efforts wasted. Porter believed in justice…He deserves it now more than ever."

They stood together, side by side, composing themselves, and then left the waiting room to find Cassidy.

* * *

After meeting with the hospital administrator regarding Porter's information for the Medical Examiner, Karolyn and Teri exited the hospital through the double sliding doors.

Karolyn said, "I appreciate you staying with me."

Teri smiled supportively. "Of course." She spotted the Ford LTD—an unmarked but unmistakable police vehicle—waiting by the curb, and added, "There's Cassidy."

Walking toward the car, Karolyn touched Teri's shoulder. "Ter, what I said to Arthur about you wanting me, I didn't mean…"

"Forget it," Teri replied. With a grin, she added, "But you never know, I may jump your bones—better watch your back."

Calling her a smart-ass, Karolyn added a friendly nudge as they slid into the back seat together, and then changed the subject. "Did you hear anything from Sheila?"

Instead of answering, Teri pointed at the back of Cassidy's seat, giving Karolyn a *zip your lip* gesture. She wasn't quick enough.

Cassidy asked, "Who's Sheila?"

Teri replied, "A computer contractor, working for Mr. McNeil," which was mostly true.

"Is she the computer expert Mr. McNeil mentioned earlier?"

Looking at Karolyn, Teri mouthed silently, "He doesn't miss a thing", then gave Karolyn's hand a gentle squeeze while answering. "Yes, she did some account research, helping us look into O'Donnell's schemes."

Karolyn squeezed back, letting Teri know she understood, and made a mental note to follow up when they were out of Cassidy's earshot.

Cassidy continued. "Yeah, this is definitely a complex case. Embezzlement, fraud, both at the felony grand theft level…Which means our Economic Crimes Detail will be taking over the investigation. I'll be turning over my notes to ECD, and you all will work with them after that."

Karolyn suddenly clenched Teri's hand, and then abruptly let go with a wide-eyed look. She leaned forward, gripping the top of the seat next to Cassidy and getting a surprised look from Teri.

She said, "Detective Cassidy, I need to ask your advice…"

Cassidy nodded slowly, "Okay…"

Determination flooded Karolyn's tone. "Do we stand a better chance of getting O'Donnell's ass back here for fraud charges or *homicide*?"

Cassidy took a moment before replying. "Well, I'm no expert, but considering Venezuela's law enforcement procedures and no formal extradition treaty...I'd say, don't get your hopes up for any quick action, either way."

"Dammit! There's *got* to be a way to get that smug bastard!" She smacked the top of the seat with her hand.

"Believe me, Karolyn, I totally understand your frustration. But it appears Mr. O'Donnell wasn't one to leave anything to chance."

"Yes, the man had a plan for everything..." Her words trailed off as she shoved herself back against the rear seat. Karolyn's thoughts were a jumble of sadness and grief, countered by steadily building outrage. She looked at Teri who reached for her hand again, this time with a look of understanding.

Following several minutes of silence with the three of them deep in their own thoughts, Cassidy said, "Just to let you know, I called Mary while I was waiting for you two. I gave her the news about Porter, and she said she would inform Mr. McNeil and the others."

"Thanks," Karolyn replied.

Cassidy added, "I'm sorry I didn't have the chance to know him. But from what I've heard, and certainly from what he did, Mr. Bordon sounds like one of the good guys."

Karolyn said, softly, "Yes, in the end he was...And now he's gone because he tried to help stop someone who took everything from everyone—including their life—without giving a damn. Well, Porter did give a damn. He told me he 'wanted to set things right,' and somehow we've got to make that happen."

* * *

The sun was low in the windows of the executive suite by the time Teri and Karolyn returned with Cassidy. He made a stop in the restroom while the two of them proceeded to Winton's conference room. As they walked in, Hugh and Rich stood and hugged Karolyn, their sorrow and sympathy sincere in their words of condolence.

Karolyn and Teri sat down next to each other, across from Rich and Hugh. Hugh said, "Some positive news...Philip and the TaiChin team took off on Tailia's delivery flight a while ago. He was both amazed and grateful we were able to pull that off." When Teri and Karolyn exchanged looks, Hugh added, "He asked me to express his sincere thanks to you both."

Before either of them had a chance to voice their burning desire to refocus on tracking down O'Donnell, Cassidy opened the door, took two steps, and sat down next to Rich.

"So, Mr. Richmond, I've not had the chance to get your statement." Gesturing toward Hugh, Teri, and Karolyn, he added, "The accounts I've gotten from everyone described the events thoroughly and consistently. But if there's anything you'd like to add, we can find a room to talk."

Rich replied, "I'm sure they covered everything. I'm just thankful Teri and Karolyn are safe…And I hope Zhou, Crandall, and especially O'Donnell get what they deserve."

Cassidy nodded. "Mr. Zhou is already in custody. Mr. McNeil and Mr. Lin filed a very thorough complaint, and as I explained to Mss. Babcock and Harlan, our Economics Crime Detail will be continuing the investigation with all of you regarding the potential embezzlement by Mr. O'Donnell. And as I told Mr. McNeil, we'll also pursue his extradition on suspicion of murder, but that may not be a simple process…"

Karolyn bristled again at the inadequacy of this approach, looking at Teri for confirmation, but Cassidy continued. "We still need to deal with Mr. Crandall, who I'll describe at this point as a Person of Interest. Mary informed me he's being brought up here soon. But before I interview him, I was wondering if any of you have information or evidence to provide."

Hugh jumped in. "Well let's see…" He pulled out the microcassette of Teri's recording from their session with Will, and asked Cassidy for his recorder. Hugh fast-forwarded to Crandall's bottom-line summary.

"Jesus—all right, I'll lay out the end game for you. McNev's in financial ruin, overwhelmed by bad press from fraud allegations, making McNeil desperate…desperate enough to accept a bargain-basement rescue offer from Zhou's sponsors…"

Cassidy said, "Wow, you've got him on tape?"

Hugh nodded and fast-forwarded again. *"…Those work orders were for damage to create chaos in Final Assembly. I used JCW to authorize them, and Arthur paid Herrera under the table to organize it."*

Cassidy took the cassette, adding, "I'll log this into evidence," and slipped it into a plastic pouch.

Hugh nodded again as Karolyn gently squeezed Teri's arm. "Like you said, when you deal with someone untrustworthy…"

"Always get tape," Rich finished, as he slid a thick file folder across the table. "Here, Detective, these documents will support what's on the recording." He quickly explained the *J. C. William* ploy and the phony work orders Will used for intentional damage, including the work order for the sabotaged cargo door lock.

Cassidy said, "Thank you. I'll take these as well."

Rich said, "Absolutely… and he could also be charged with assault…" he looked to Teri and Karolyn, but before either said anything in response, the door opened, and an exceptionally large security officer pushed a wheelchair, occupied by Will Crandall, into the room.

Rich looked up, lifting his chin in a sort of reverse-nod. "Hey, Meat." Responding to a variety of expressions from the others, Rich added, "What? That's what everyone calls him," as if stating the obvious about the physically imposing officer.

Maneuvering the chair to the head of the table he said, "I'm officer Dennis Lonigan, but most everybody calls me Meat. Crandall here, was just released by Medical. Mary asked me to bring him up. I'll be right outside."

Will had significant abrasions on his forehead and cheeks, his left arm was in a sling, his right knee was wrapped with an ice pack, and his suit was a wreck. He scowled at Lonigan's back as he left the room, and then turned it on everyone else. "So here we are again. I see Hugh has joined your little posse, and who's the new guy?"

"I'm Detective Ed Cassidy from the Orange County Sheriff's Office, CIB."

Will didn't skip a beat. "Good. I'm glad you're here."

He pointed at Rich as he continued. "Let's start by pressing charges against Richmond, there, for assault. He threw me out of a moving cart...and I'd like to file charges against all three of them for holding me forcibly against my will. And wherever Porter Bordon is, he was in on it too."

40

"Porter's *dead*, asshole." Karolyn's voice was so full of rancor that her words stopped Will cold. Taken aback by both the news and Karolyn's ferocity, he mumbled, "Oh. I didn't know," and fell silent.

Cassidy maintained his smooth, in-charge manner. "Mr. Crandall, let's move to that small office, and you can give me your statement."

As Cassidy wheeled Crandall out, Hugh stood and said, "Please excuse me, also. I need to make some calls."

* * *

Although the holding cell wasn't crowded, Zhou Quon felt excruciatingly conspicuous in his two-thousand-dollar suit. He stood at the far end of the cell door, maximizing the distance from the four other occupants he considered to be reprehensible. Quon picked at the peeling green paint on the bars, trying to contend with his dire circumstance.

I do not belong in this repugnant place…I am superior in all ways to these pathetic dregs of Western society. But I will be strong. No matter what becomes of me, I must succeed.

A deputy appeared and entered the holding cell. Zhou had observed in the last several hours that a deputy would sometimes respond to a detainee's request. Having been informed earlier that he was allowed a phone call, Zhou had been calculating the right time to ask.

He slipped his hand into his jacket pocket. They'd confiscated the miniature pager that Will had given him, along with his personal belongings, but not the neatly folded paper he now held in his fingers. Although there was no clock in sight, Zhou had always prided himself on his innate chronometer. Even considering a margin of error for potential delays, he calculated the Tailia plane was now well out to sea heading toward the Aleutian Islands.

It is time, he thought, visualizing the explosive destruction of the ME-420 as it screamed into the sea at 500 knots, breaking into a million pieces sinking beneath the surface. *I will succeed—the world must be cleansed of Philip Lin.*

When the deputy was next to him, Zhou asked as politely as he could stomach, "Please—I would like to make my phone call."

The deputy turned to the other four and said, "Vale—up…let's go."

Zhou scowled at the miserable-looking skinny teen's stringy hair as the deputy grabbed Vale's arm and opened the cell door. Then the deputy turned back to Zhou. "All right—you too. I'll take you to the phones."

* * *

Teri and Karolyn sat facing Rich, their expressions glum. Karolyn drummed her fingers on the elegant table, while Teri clasped and unclasped her hands. Fully aligned with their obvious frustration, Rich said, "Yeah, I know. Here we sit—the three of us, while the Executive VP of Evil is on a plane to Barbados…"

Teri interjected, "And his insidious sycophant is in with Cassidy, spewing lies."

Rich leaned forward and stretched his arms across the table, placing a hand on top of Teri's and the other on Karolyn's. His voice full of emotion, he said, "I'm so sorry about Porter. This whole damn mess is…"

"…not your fault," Karolyn said, finishing his sentence. "But now it's up to the three of us to bring down the two who *are* responsible…tell us what happened with Crandall this morning."

After a quick recap of their confrontation on the Tailia plane, Rich added, "So even though we're sure Crandall rigged a vent door, his sabotaged design is *not* on 913. And of course he totally denies it…Al and Mac still haven't discovered what happened to it."

Teri shook her head in frustration while Karolyn irritably sprung from her chair to pace around the table. "Shit. This isn't right. We don't stand a chance in hell of getting Arthur back, and Will's just gonna weasel his way out of…"

Rich stood and met Karolyn in mid-pace. "Maybe not, KB." He reached into his coat pocket and pulled out a microcassette. With a melancholy smile, he placed it in Karolyn's hand and gently closed her fingers around it. "Porter gave this to me for safe-keeping. He would've wanted you to have it."

* * *

Dennis was pushing Crandall across the empty executive suite toward the hallway with Cassidy walking alongside when Will began squirming violently in the wheelchair. Dennis stopped and Will started screeching, "This is bullshit! I was tortured…I made all that up to protect myself!"

Hugh emerged from Winton's office, followed by Rich, Teri, and Karolyn coming from the conference room. Acknowledging his audience, Will escalated his tirade. "And I never touched that stuck-up tight-ass!"

In a sudden blur, Teri dashed across the suite, stopping short in front of Will. She grabbed a fist-full of his hair and yanked it toward the back of his head, roughly tilting his face up to her. Her fiery tone caught everyone by surprise.

"Yes—you did, you twisted pervert. It took twenty minutes under scalding water to wash away your vileness." She let his head go and he shut up, seeming deflated—But only momentarily.

As Hugh, Karolyn, and Rich caught up, exhibiting various degrees of startled expressions, Will started up again. "And the whole cargo door thing…that's bullshit too." He looked at Rich. "Richmond will tell you, there was nothing there! You've got nothing to arrest me for!"

With the same intensity she had in the conference room, Karolyn interrupted with a single word, "Stop!"

There was silence as Karolyn handed Cassidy the microcassette.

"What's this?" Cassidy asked.

"Evidence. Please play it, detective. Everyone should hear it." Cassidy pulled the recorder from his satchel and slipped in the tape. The unmistakable, whiny rant of Will Crandall's message from Porter's answering machine filled the executive suite.

"Bordon, Goddammit! You fucked up! We gave you orders to kill Richmond…and he's still alive, you moron…"

Karolyn leaned down in Crandall's face, delivering each word with menacing fury. "Porter sends his regards, you low-life piece of shit!"

Will attempted to push himself up and grab her, but Dennis shoved him back down—hard. "Not a chance, dipstick—they don't call me Meat for nothin'."

Cassidy put the cassette in an evidence pouch and said, "I got this…I think we're done here."

Karolyn turned to Rich and hugged him, whispering, "Thank you."

Dennis resumed pushing the wheelchair with one hand, the other clamped implacably on Will's shoulder. Teri stepped next to Rich and slipped her hand into his, giving it a squeeze.

* * *

At the elevator, Will performed an encore, yelling, "There's no way you can arrest me—I demand to see a lawyer!" inducing Cassidy to raise his voice for the first time.

"Mr. Crandall, you've been read your rights, including the choice to remain silent—*I suggest you exercise that one—starting now!*"

Ding! The elevator doors shushed open before Cassidy touched the button, startling everyone.

Dennis wheeled Will back, letting Mac and Al step out. They looked at the group with confused expressions. "What's going on?" Mac asked. But rather than wait for an answer, Mac rushed ahead, his voice wound as tight as wire around a stator.

"We came to tell you we finally found it! My God, the paperwork out there is *so* screwed up! That damn door-lock mechanism actually got *used* last night!"

Rich's eyes widened as Mac continued.

"LazerAir had a problem with the forward cargo door. They had to replace the lock mechanism, and some idiot found the one that got removed from 913 lying on a workbench. Apparently, no one red-tagged it and the mechanic didn't notice Will's handiwork, so..."

Rich interjected, "Are you telling us that LazerAir's 420 is on its way to Venezuela with Will's sabotaged piece of shit installed on it?"

Mac spread his arms in a dramatic gesture. "Yes—exactly!"

Al nodded vigorously, as the color left Hugh's face.

Beep, beep, beep!

Hugh jumped. His voice rising at least two octaves, he asked, "What's *that*?"

Will pulled the miniature pager from his pocket and held it up.

Teri and Rich figured it out at the same time. Teri blurted, "Sweet Jesus," putting her hands to her mouth while Rich snarled, "I thought you said you had nothing to do with this!"

Will answered with a sneer. "Yeah...well, I lied—so sue me! It may not be the Tailia plane, but you geniuses couldn't stop Zhou from making the call, and now there's a vent-door that's *opening*, thanks to my genius design. The cargo compartment should be depressurizing as we're standing here, and soon the passenger cabin floor will give way."

He looked at Hugh with a malicious grin, speaking with bitterness that rivaled Karolyn's. "So guess what, Mr. Chairman? I may be going to jail, but the joke's on you. All those times you looked at me like you couldn't stomach being in the same room...well, *I win*—you still lost a brand-spanking new ME-420!"

Rich swore, "Holy shit—O'Donnell," as he and Teri looked at Hugh with horror on their faces. Karolyn turned away, staring at the darkening sky outside the huge windows with a far-away look in her eyes.

Good—fuck him.

Eight people stood in McNev's executive suite that Wednesday evening, gathered around Will Crandall's wheel chair in stunned silence...until the person sitting in it threw his head back and laughed maniacally.

* * *

The blinking red light on the co-pilot's control panel kept pace with the alarm's accelerating *beep...beep...beep* until it shifted to a steady beacon of bright crimson. The copilot's voice reinforced the urgency. "We've got a pressure alarm. No compensation—still dropping!"

Arthur's stomach reacted first, forcing up a wave of vileness that made him gag. Then the cold air stream from the overhead chilled the sweat on his neck and made him shiver. Regretting his choice to take a fourth valium, he felt like a drunk marathoner trying to summon strength for the final kick.

Arthur wasn't an engineer, but he'd studied Will's design and connected the dots as his mind spun up to speed. First, he contemplated how the device found its way here from the Tailia plane, seeking to blame whoever had plunged him into this nightmare. But in seconds, his extraordinary intellect refocused as the voice answered the call: *You know you have a plan...so go save yourself...*

He lurched out of his seat, stumbled two rows aft, and knelt in the center aisle. Willing his muscles into action, he yanked the pop-up pulls and slid the heavy metal-plate access door from its frame in the cabin floor.

The cabin's air volume boosted the suction, pulling Arthur's legs through the opening as he placed a hand on either side of the frame. He dropped the five feet into the empty compartment, landing heavily on the cargo rollers, slipping, then struggling to regain his balance.

The co-pilot left the cockpit and rushed to the aisle, attempting to slide the plate back into the frame while bracing himself to avoid being sucked into the compartment behind Arthur.

Fueled by the cabin volume, the air escaping through the open vent increased to hurricane force. The screaming wind pulled tie-down straps and debris past him as Arthur seesawed to the cargo door.

The vent opening, two-thirds of the way up the main cargo door, was about level with his face. Arthur strained against the gale to keep from being engulfed, and reached up, attempting to pull the vent door back down into place.

Focusing all of his remaining strength in one last tug, he snapped the door off the actuator arm. "Goddamnit!" Arthur shouted, thinking luck had finally abandoned him. But as always, his good fortune prevailed. Instantly sucked into the opening, the door aligned perfectly and made a viable seal.

The wind noise stopped, and the voice congratulated him.

A one-in-a-million shot! You're amazing!

He needed only to wait for the plane to descend below ten-thousand feet, equalizing the external air pressure enough to allow the plane to make an emergency landing.

He laughed out loud at his uncanny ability to avert yet another crisis, answering the voice, "Yes, thank you...I know."

Suddenly overcome by dizziness from his considerable exertion, and compromised by a valium hangover, Arthur rested his weary head against the cold cargo door. An unexpected *Pop—Crack!* exploded in his ear.

The vent frame had deteriorated, generating a *whoosh* of rushing air accompanied by an aberrant sucking sound, as the opening enlarged just enough to set the vent door free.

The very thing that had been his salvation only seconds before, suddenly betrayed him. The door vanished in an instant, replaced by an overwhelming burst of suction, increasing exponentially.

Although Arthur wasn't holding his Ruger, he once again saw everything in slow motion. Only this time he did not feel powerful; he was not in control. His incredible mind had responded too late to assimilate the implication of the unyielding cyclone surging through the void, directly in front of his face.

It seemed fitting that Arthur have the last word. It was a simple one, as the ravenous vacuum swallowed him head first into his final brilliant move.

"Noooo!"

* * *

Karolyn and Teri sat at Karolyn's kitchen table sipping green tea. They'd brought home Chinese take-out, but only managed a few bites. As Teri began closing the containers of leftovers, Karolyn said, "Hey, you never got a chance to tell me...did Sheila find anything?"

"Yes, actually quite a bit. I'd say it's a 'bad news-good news' thing. She confirmed evidence of Arthur's significant fraud with McNev Finances, but she also found his offshore business account in Barbados...it's got more than $100 million in it!"

Karolyn whistled. "Holy shit! I hope Hugh has her snag it before Arthur finds out...if he's not already dead, that is." After a pause, she added, "Sheila is sure amazing...Did she happen to say anything about an *Epsilon* account?"

"No, but she found several Accounts labeled *Pro* and the big one he named *Magnum*. She said you were the one who told her to look for his *Epsilon Pro Magnum* codes...how did you know about those?"

Karolyn smiled. "And you thought I was just a pretty face...I watched Arthur—" Karolyn broke off, picking up the remote and unmuting the television which had been tuned to the 10:00 p.m. nightly news. "Look— it's about the LazerAir flight!"

"We go live now to Mateo Silva, our correspondent in Honduras. He's standing near a LazerAir passenger jet at Toncontín International Airport. Mateo?"

"Thanks, Gail. This is certainly an unusual incident. I'm at the end of the runway, where a LazerAir passenger plane made an emergency landing. The brand-new McNeil-Everett ME-420 Widebody, on its delivery flight, was scheduled to land at Simón Bolívar International Airport in Venezuela.

"A LazerAir team is here, but so far we don't know much. We've been told that the aircraft experienced severe depressurization at thirty-eight thousand feet due to a problem in the cargo compartment. There were only three passengers on the plane, which landed safely.

"But here's the bizarre part—only two passengers were in the cabin. The third one is being investigated by authorities here. We don't yet have a name, but he's thought to be an executive of McNeil Everett.

"We can't show it to you, but according to the emergency medical team, the lower half of a male torso was discovered wedged into some sort of rectangular opening in the forward cargo door."

"Oh, my Lord!" Teri covered her face with her hands. "What a way to die, even for Arthur...I'm not sure what I feel...He did save two passengers, the pilots, and the plane."

Karolyn hit the *off* button. She walked to Teri and faced her, resting her hands on Teri shoulders. Looking at her eye-to-eye, she said, "Ter, you know damn well, he wasn't trying to save anyone but himself." Her voice caught as she added, "And I know *exactly* how I feel." She lifted her eyes to the ceiling. "Justice, babe; rest in peace."

* * *

Friday, November 11, 11:30 a.m.
Ocean View Memorial Park, Corona Del Mar

Natural light from a window overlooking the Pacific Ocean filled the small chapel, adding a soft grace to the aura of simple sincerity. A short eulogy by Hugh and Karolyn included reading a note sent by Philip in which Wang had penned a Haiku (with possible assistance in translation).

> *Porter Man of Strong Heart*
> *Honor Protector*
> *Rest Forever Earned*

After the service, the small group walked to the gravesite where the minister offered a prayer, followed by quiet conversations of peace and justice that Porter deserved.

Sheila took Lisa to the crest of a small hill to look at the ocean. Karolyn spoke with Cassidy while Mac, Al, and Mary, accompanied by Dennis, gathered around Hugh.

Rich and Teri wandered away from the group, over by a large palm.

"So has everyone gotten past the shock of it all?" Teri asked.

"Slowly," Rich answered. "I just met with the team returning from Toncontín. The aircraft repairs were straight forward but dealing with the medical examiner...what was left of the body was... not that O'Donnell didn't deserve what he got..."

He let his words fade, shaking his head before adding, "Did you hear Crandall's facing multiple charges of fraud plus two counts of conspiracy to commit murder?"

"Yes, KB told me...I imagine he'll find those good-looks he's so proud of won't be such an asset where he's going..." They drifted into another silence as Teri felt the hint of an ironic smile cross her face.

They sat down on a bench set in the center of a lush miniature garden planted with Sea Lavender and Lily of the Nile. Rich turned toward her, his expression tempered by concern. "So more importantly, how are *you*?"

Teri sighed. "I pretty much lost it after last Wednesday...never been through anything like that...and never want to go through it again..."

Rich nodded. "I totally get that... I'm just thankful you're still in one piece."

Teri smiled faintly. "Sequestering myself at Karolyn's for the last few days really helped—lots of time to think."

She hesitated, pondering the serious-talk-with-Rich moment that she'd been avoiding, until he asked another question, interrupting her thoughts.

"So now that you've had a few days to think, have you decided?"

It took her several seconds to shift gears. "What? Oh, you mean McNeil's offer?"

His smile was full of anticipation. "You're absolutely at the top of Hugh's list for Exec VP. All you need to do is accept." Looking solemn, he added, "And I want you to know, it would be an honor for me to report to you."

She took his hand. "Thank you, that means a lot...But I don't think stepping into that position would be right for me, *or* the company...At this point, I'm not sure I'm even cut out for management. So for now, I think I'll try something different...thought I might talk with Mac. They could really use some better training on hydraulics systems."

He nodded. "Yeah, you're the only person I know who seems to *like* the smell of Skydrol."

Teri chuckled, "You've always been able to get a smile out of me." She fell silent again, staring at the edge of the flower bed, noticing where the brickwork wasn't aligned properly.

Rich rested a gentle hand on her shoulder. "Hey, something else is bothering you, isn't it?"

With a deeper sigh, Teri began, "Going through this whole mess...was like I got torn down and had to rebuild myself."

"Ter, I'm so sorry...I—"

She stopped him by reaching for his hand again. "I know, Rich. This is hard for me, so please just let me talk."

She continued, "The past few weeks forced me to see myself honestly—emotional pockmarks and all—maybe for the first time. I've spent my career trying to be this ideal tough, perfect manager...I mostly ended up being stubborn, bossy, and kind of arrogant."

Rich looked like he wanted to disagree but kept his mouth shut. She appreciated both.

"Anyway, dealing with Winton and Duke...and then my encounter with Crandall, ripped open an old emotional wound from when I was a teenager...I never told anyone—it finally spilled out that night with Karolyn, and in the end, I've come to accept the reality... my toughness had become a convenient mask...to hide my fear."

She took a breath, steeling herself.

"Since I left ten years ago, the only relationships I've even attempted were with men I met at work...Any feelings of attraction or desire for something to develop, got mixed up in my head with this obsessive notion to never let myself be vulnerable...I torpedoed every one, and afterwards, I'd rationalize it by telling myself it's my career—I'm a professional."

Teri stopped again, looking down at the bench, then looked up to see one of Rich's empathetic smiles, encouraging her to go on.

"I know how difficult I've been, while you've been nothing but good to me...What I'm trying to say is that whenever I start to get close, I...clearly I've still got issues to work through..."

Rich touched his finger lightly to her lips and made a soft shushing sound. "You know overanalyzing yourself can make you crazy, right?"

She blinked at him, and his expression softened. He continued with a self-effacing smile. "Hey—it's me. If anyone can relate to overanalyzing, I can...don't you remember? The nickname they gave us back when we worked together—the 'Never-tired Twins?'"

She thought back. "That's right...People used to ask us, 'Don't you two ever get tired of trying to fix everything...'"

Rich chimed in, "And we'd say, '*Never*'...sometimes we even said it in unison."

She recalled those days with him, totally focused, bordering on obsessive, and then somehow they'd find a way to solve the problems no one else could. In spite of herself, she felt a tiny smile emerge, along with a touch of pink creeping into her cheeks.

Rich regarded her with an understanding smile. Then his expression took on a deep sincerity. "Ter, I really need you to hear this—it's important. You are the most amazing, honest, insightful, beautiful, and bravest person I know. And you just fought your way through five weeks of hell—you need to give yourself some credit!" He paused, with a gaze that seemed almost reverent. She felt herself getting warmer.

Continuing to look into her eyes, as if ensuring his words would reach her heart, he said, "And in case I haven't been clear about this, I love you...So unless you tell me to get lost, I am here for you, no matter what."

She tried to smile, unable to stop the color now blossoming on her face or the tears welling up in her eyes.

He held both her hands. "Let's just take things one day at a time, okay? How about we start with dinner?"

"You mean like a date?"

"Well, since McNeil or I can't talk you into being the boss, then yeah, it could be a date."

She squeezed his hands. They felt strong, calming, safe. She smiled. "Yes, I'd like that."

~ The End ~

EPILOGUE

The next sixteen months brought considerable change for everyone involved in what came to be known as "The McNev Executive Incident."

Darren Duke was terminated, replaced by Norton (Mac) McKinley, who was promoted to VP of Manufacturing, with Al Greer as his Deputy.

Bradley (Rich) Richmond was promoted to fill the Executive VP position at the beginning of 1995.

Sheila Richmond was given a contract to redesign the company financial systems, working with McNev's accounting team—minus Vernon Ames. Although she was actively recruited by Hugh McNeil for McNev's new Director of Information Technology position, Sheila turned it down.

Karolyn Babcock was promoted to Director of Finance. Along with Rich, Hugh, and Philip Lin, she played an instrumental role in helping to rebuild McNev. Partnering with Sheila, Karolyn's effective collaboration efforts with banking executives in Barbados returned over one-hundred million dollars of embezzled funds to the company.

Teri accepted a consulting assignment with Mac McKinley to create a new training course for hydraulic systems testing. The project resulted in revamping the entire curriculum for assembly training. In May of 1995, Teri launched her own business in Irvine, developing and delivering technical and management training programs to aerospace companies across Southern California.

In June, Sheila deeded her house in Laguna to her brother, choosing to travel extensively in Europe. She ended up settling into a small villa in Saint-Raphaël, on the French Riviera.

Although Lisa missed her aunt, she loved spending time with Teri and Karolyn, especially evenings when her father worked late. Lisa also joined them each Wednesday afternoon, supporting the OC National Science Foundation on the development of a new program, SMET: Science-Mathematics-Engineering-Technology, forerunner of STEM. SMET was being created to educate and mentor junior high and high school girls who aspired to be aerospace engineers and rocket scientists.

That September, Karolyn surprised everyone by taking an early retirement, and relocating to Idyllwild. Then, in mid-November, Teri, Rich, and Lisa were invited up to her new estate.

The elegant invitation included photos highlighting the chef's kitchen, massive stone fireplace, and vaulted ceilings with skylights, enabling indoor star gazing after dark. Teri smiled broadly and shook her head as she looked at the last photo: The majestic gated entrance, graced by a unique artisan-crafted estate sign emblazoned with a single symbol:

'ε'

ACKNOWLEDGEMENTS:

Thanks to my two awesome co-workers of the 1990s, Susan Chuang and Paul Gowler, for helping me conceive the idea behind Executive Malice and inspiring me to write it.

Thanks to my best friend and eminently talented artist, Audrey Steffan, for her amazing cover.

Thanks to my editors, Jan Ackerson, and Robin Quinn, and my Proofreader, Rosalie Lander, for helping elevate Executive Malice's level of quality and professionalism.

Thanks to George Kenny and Theresa Santy, published authors who tolerated me as a newbie, providing encouragement and gentle feedback.

Thanks to George and Betty Shultz for their expertise and time invested in final editing.

Thanks to my Writing and Publishing Coach, A. G. Billig, for her counsel and encouragement, helping me cross the finish line.

Thanks to Tony Todaro and the Greater Los Angeles Writers Society for their invaluable seminars.

Special thanks to my multi-talented friend, Maraea Weinberg, for her expert finance consultation, storyline feedback, and additional editing.

Thanks to my artistic and talented web designer, Taylor Riethle for her creativity in the future development of thegoodmanageronline.com

Thanks to Village Books in Fairhaven, Washington for their publishing support and partnership.

And thanks to my children, Marryn, Robyn, and Jonathon, for their many hours of reading and candid feedback.

Thank you so much for taking the time to read Executive Malice!
I sincerely hope you enjoyed it.

I plan to continue writing about the startling workplace debacles discovered by Teri and Rich when they became management consultants in the early 2000's.

I'll be posting their adventures on my new website starting early in 2021

ABOUT THE AUTHOR:

R. L. (Rick) Hann retired after thirty-five years of working in management positions for three major aerospace corporations in Southern California, as well as the consumer electronics industry.

Over the course of a career divided equally between HRIT systems management, management development, and management training, he came to think of himself as an *expert in bad management*. He's currently spending his time creating material to help employees (and managers) survive the Corporate Jungle, planned for release through a new website: thegoodmanageronline.com.

Rick lives in Fairhaven, Washington, where he enjoys reading, research, and writing, while communing with the trees.

Lightning Source UK Ltd.
Milton Keynes UK
UKHW040648141020
371563UK00001B/19